P9-BZG-332

"Karen Chance will enthrall you with her world of vampires, mages, and a fair maiden tough enough to kick their butts." —*USA Today* bestselling author Rebecca York

Praise for *Claimed by Shadow*

"A nonstop thrill ride from beginning to end, a wildly entertaining romp with a strong, likeable heroine. The story is fast-paced and barely lets up from the word *go*, lightened with plenty of wry humor and more than a dash of romance." —Rambles

"Ms. Chance is a master. . . . A series well worth getting hooked on." —Fresh Fiction

"A great writer of supernatural fantasy that is on a par with the works of Kim Harrison, Charlaine Harris, and Kelley Armstrong." —*Midwest Book Review*

"A thoroughly engaging story that is as good as, if not better than, the first book, *Claimed by Shadow* should not be missed." —Romance Reviews Today

"Magic aplenty populates this fast-moving, rather dark tale of power, corruption, double dealings, and painful attractions, as Cassie comes to grip with her new role in this follow-up to *Touch the Dark*. It is nice to see a strong, capable heroine taking charge with a kick-butt attitude while attempting to balance right and wrong in the face of impossible odds." —Monsters and Critics

"If you liked *Touch the Dark*, you're going to like *Claimed by Shadow*." —SFRevu

continued . . .

Praise for *Touch the Dark*

"A grab-you-by-the-throat-and-suck-you-in sort of book, with a tough, smart heroine and sexy-scary vampires. I loved it—and I'm waiting anxiously for a sequel."
>—*New York Times* bestselling author Patricia Briggs

"Exciting and inventive." —*Booklist*

"Fast and heavy on the action, *Touch the Dark* packs a huge story. . . . A blend of fantasy and romance, it will satisfy readers of both genres." —Fresh Fiction

"A very promising start to a new series, and an exceptionally entertaining first novel." —*Locus*

"A really exciting book with great pacing and a huge cast of vivid characters. This is one of my favorite reads of the year."
>—Charlaine Harris, *New York Times*
>bestselling author of *Definitely Dead*

"A wonderfully entertaining romp with an engaging heroine. Here's hoping there's a sequel in the works!"
—Kelley Armstrong, *New York Times* bestselling author of *Broken*

"With *Touch the Dark*, Karen Chance takes her place along with Laurell K. Hamilton, Charlaine Harris, MaryJanice Davidson, and J. D. Robb to give us a strong woman who doesn't wait to be rescued. . . . The action never stops. . . . Engrossing."
>—SFRevu

ALSO BY KAREN CHANCE

Touch the Dark
Claimed by Shadow

Embrace the Night

Karen Chance

A ROC BOOK

ROC
Published by New American Library, a division of
Penguin Group (USA) Inc., 375 Hudson Street,
New York, New York 10014, USA
Penguin Group (Canada), 90 Eglinton Avenue East, Suite 700, Toronto,
Ontario M4P 2Y3, Canada (a division of Pearson Penguin Canada Inc.)
Penguin Books Ltd., 80 Strand, London WC2R 0RL, England
Penguin Ireland, 25 St. Stephen's Green, Dublin 2,
Ireland (a division of Penguin Books Ltd.)
Penguin Group (Australia), 250 Camberwell Road, Camberwell, Victoria 3124,
Australia (a division of Pearson Australia Group Pty. Ltd.)
Penguin Books India Pvt. Ltd., 11 Community Centre, Panchsheel Park,
New Delhi - 110 017, India
Penguin Group (NZ), 67 Apollo Drive, Rosedale, North Shore 0632,
New Zealand (a division of Pearson New Zealand Ltd.)
Penguin Books (South Africa) (Pty.) Ltd., 24 Sturdee Avenue,
Rosebank, Johannesburg 2196, South Africa

Penguin Books Ltd., Registered Offices:
80 Strand, London WC2R 0RL, England

First published by Roc, an imprint of New American Library,
a division of Penguin Group (USA) Inc.

First Printing, April 2008
10 9 8 7 6 5 4 3 2 1

 REGISTERED TRADEMARK—MARCA REGISTRADA

Printed in the United States of America

To Tracy Amber Lewis

Chapter 1

A weeping angel shattered in a crack of gray dust, sending its wings flying off in two directions. It took a second for me to realize I wasn't dead, and then I dove for the side of a nearby obelisk. I pressed flat against the ground, feeling the mud seeping into my already drenched clothes, while a barrage of shots struck sparks off the granite overhead. I was starting to suspect that this tomb raider thing might not be as much fun as I'd hoped.

Of course, that was pretty much the story of my life lately. A chain of events that might very charitably be classified as disasters had left me with the position of Pythia, the supernatural community's chief seer. The Silver Circle, a group of light magic users, had expected one of their tame acolytes to inherit the office since it had happened that way for a few thousand years now. They'd been less than thrilled when the power went to me instead: Cassie Palmer, untrained clairvoyant, protégée of a vampire crime boss and known cohort of a renegade war mage.

Some people have no sense of irony.

The mages had expressed their displeasure by trying to send me off to explore the great mystery of what lies in store for us after death. Since I wasn't that curious, I'd been attempting to stay under their radar. It didn't look like I was doing so hot.

I decided to try for better cover beside a crypt, and was halfway there when something that felt like a sledgehammer knocked me to the ground. A bolt of lightning exploded against a nearby tree, causing the air to tingle and writhe with electricity and sending blue-white, hissing snakes scurrying over a tangle of exposed roots. It left the tree split in half, blackened along the center like old firewood, the air flooded with ozone and my skull hammering from the near miss. Above me, thunder rolled ominously across the sky, an appropriate bit of sound effects that I would have appreciated a lot more during a movie.

Speaking of irony, it would be really amusing if Mother Nature managed to kill me before the Circle got the chance. I crawled in the general direction of the crypt, temporarily night-blind and helpless, blinking away afterimages. At least I discovered why gun grips are ribbed: so when your palm is sweating with abject terror, you can still manage to clutch the thing.

My new 9mm didn't fit my hand as well as my old one, but it was rapidly becoming a familiar weight. At first I'd decided it was okay to wear as long as I shot only at supernatural bad guys who were already shooting at me. Lately, I'd had to broaden that definition to anytime my life was in danger. I was currently leaning toward a slightly more comprehensive rule somewhere between proactive self-defense and the-bastards-had-it-coming, which, if I survived long enough, I intended to blame on my deranged partner rubbing off on me.

I found the crypt by running into it face-first, scraping a cheek on the pitted limestone exterior. I strained my ears, but there was no sign of my attackers. A hail of shots rattled against a nearby path, ricocheting off the cobblestones to fly away in all directions. Okay, no sign other than the fact that someone kept *shooting* at me.

I hugged the wall and told myself not to overreact and waste bullets. I'd already lobotomized a cupid after a gust of wind blew a few leaves across it, giving it a fleeting sense of movement—and that had been with the glow of an almost full moon to see by. It was worse now that the wind had blown dark clouds in, and the spatter of rain made it impossible to hear quiet footsteps.

The firing finally stopped, but my whole body continued to shake, to the point that I dropped the reserve clip I'd fumbled out of my pocket. The old one still had several rounds left, but I didn't want to run out at a crucial moment. Another shot hit the cupid I'd decapitated, shaving off one of its little butt cheeks. I flinched and my foot kicked something that splashed into a nearby puddle. I got to my knees, searching around in the grass for it and trying to curse quietly.

"A little to the left." I whirled, gun up, heart pounding. But the dark-haired man leaning against a moss-stained fountain didn't look concerned. Maybe because he no longer had a body to worry about.

I relaxed slightly. Ghosts I could deal with; I'd even been expecting them. Père Lachaise isn't Paris' oldest cemetery, but it's huge. I'd had to reinforce my shields to be able to see anything past the green glow of thousands of ghost trails, crisscrossing the landscape like a crazy spiderweb. It was the main reason I'd left my own ghostly helper behind. Billy Joe could be a pain, but I really didn't want him serving as a midnight snack for a bunch of hungry ghosts.

"Thanks."

"You're American."

"Uh, yeah." A bullet pinged against an iron railing nearby and I flinched. "How'd you know?"

"My *dear*." He looked pointedly at my mud-spattered jeans, once-white tennis shoes and soaked gray T-shirt. The last had been an impulse buy a few days ago, something to wear to target practice to remind my exacting coach that I was still a beginner at this. Its quip, "I don't have a license to kill. I have a learner's permit," was starting to look really ironic now.

Lara Croft would have worn something a lot less mud-covered, and she would have had her hair in a sexy style that still kept it out of her face. My own curly mop was at the stage where it was too long to stay out of the way and too short to keep in a ponytail. As a result, I had wet blond strands falling into my eyes and clinging to my cheeks, adding to the overall lack of cool.

"When good Americans die, they go to Paris," the ghost said, after taking a drag on a small cigarette. "But you're not dead. I suppose the question must be, are you good?"

My hand finally closed over the clip, and I slammed it into place. I surreptitiously looked him over, wondering what answer was likely to get me some help. I took in the long velvet jacket, the silk cravat and the lazy smile. "Depends who you ask."

"Prevarication, how divine! I always did get along better with sinners."

"Then maybe you can tell me how many people are out there?"

Another ghost drifted up, wearing only a pair of low-rise blue jeans. He looked vaguely familiar, with shoulder-length brown hair, classic features and a slightly petulant pout. "About a dozen. They just shot up my ugly-ass memorial."

The older ghost sniffed. "Your legions of fans will doubtless have you another inside a week—"

"Can I help it if I'm popular?"

"—and will then proceed to vandalize it and everything in the vicinity."

"Hey, be cool."

The older ghost bristled. "Don't talk to me about cool, you preposterous pretender! I *was* cool! I was the *epitome* of cool! For all intents and purposes, I *invented* cool!"

"Can you two keep it down?" I asked a little shrilly. Sweat trickled down one side of my temple and into my eye, burning. I blinked it away and watched a few shadows slink closer. They existed only at the edge of my vision, and seemed to disappear whenever I looked directly at them. Then a spell exploded overhead, lighting up the area like a flare and giving me a clear view. Unfortunately, it did the same for my attackers. The Gothic arch above my head immediately rang with shots, causing bits of stonework to crumble on top of me as I ducked inside.

"This is ridiculous! You people are worse than the madmen Kardec attracts." The ghosts had followed me in. Of course. "Mystic, ha! The man never even rose, yet there's always someone praying or chanting or draping him with flowers—"

"He believed in reincarnation, man. Maybe he came back."

I fought my way out of a large cobweb, and managed not

to slip on the stone tiles, which were slick with rain and decaying leaves. "Shut up!" I whispered viciously.

The older ghost sniffed. "At least the mystics aren't rude."

I squinted down at the vague squiggles that were supposed to be a map and tried to ignore him. It might have been easier if I wasn't soaking wet and filthy with a pounding headache. I really, really wanted to get out of here. But, thanks to a certain devious master vampire, that wasn't an option.

I was prowling around a cemetery in the middle of the night, dodging guard dogs, lightning bolts and crazed war mages, because of a spell known as a *geis*. The vamp in question, Mircea, had had it placed on me years ago, without bothering to get my permission or even remembering to mention that he'd done it. Master vamps are like that, but in this case, there might have been more than the usual arrogance behind his forgetfulness.

On the one hand, the spell provided me protection growing up—it marked me as his, meaning that no sane vampire would touch me with a ten-foot pole. On the other, it was designed to ensure loyalty to a single person: exclusive, complete and utter loyalty. Now that we were both adults, the spell wanted to bind Mircea and me together forever, and it didn't appreciate my noncooperation. That was a problem, since people have been known to go mad from this thing, even committing suicide rather than live with the constant, gnawing ache that was just one of the spell's tricks when thwarted. But sitting back and enjoying the ride wasn't an option, either.

If the bond ever fully formed, our lives would be run by the dominant partner—which I had no doubt would be Mircea— leaving me stuck as his eager little slave. And since he was a member in good standing of the Vampire Senate, the governing body of all North American vampires, I would doubtless end up running their errands, too. The thought of what some of those requests might be was enough to put me in a cold sweat. It was what the Circle feared—the Pythia under the control of the vamps. And while I wasn't in favor of their method of preventing it, I could grudgingly concede the point: it would be a disaster.

Becoming Pythia had made me a target for anybody in the

supernatural community who was attracted to power—in other words, pretty much everyone—but it had bought me some time as far as the spell was concerned. How much, I didn't know. Meaning that I *really* needed that counterspell. And rumor was, the only grimoire that contained a copy was buried somewhere around here.

Of course, it would help if I could read the damn map. I squinted at it, but the only illumination was moonlight filtered through the remains of once beautiful stained-glass windows. Half of a seated Madonna looked out onto a charcoal gray sky, with the occasional flash of lightning outlining layered clouds. I had a flashlight, but turning it on would only make me that much better of a—

Something lunged at me out of the night. "Don't shoot!" a man whispered.

He smelled of sweat, metal and dirt, plus a static crackle of nervous energy that was practically his signature. I turned on the flashlight and saw what I'd expected: a shock of pale hair, which as usual was making taunting gestures in the face of gravity, a square jaw, a slightly overlarge nose and furious green eyes. The Circle's most famous renegade and my reluctant partner, John Pritkin.

I breathed a sigh of relief and clicked my gun's safety on. To know Pritkin was to want to kill him, but so far I'd resisted temptation. "You shouldn't sneak up on me like that!" I whispered.

"Why didn't you shoot me?" he demanded.

"You told me not to."

"I—that's—" Pritkin seemed momentarily incoherent, so I shoved the gun's barrel lightly against his stomach. At least I'd thought it was his stomach. I'd only intended to show that I wasn't defenseless, but in a flash, I was slammed against the side of the crypt, my gun arm pinned to the wall, my body stuck between the hard surface and a very angry war mage. I reluctantly admitted that there may have been a fantasy or two that began with this scenario, but I doubted the evening was going to end the same way.

"I knew it was you," I told him before his ability to vocalize returned. "You smell like gunpowder and magic." That was truer than usual because his coat, a thick leather duster that hid his weapon collection, had a large spot where the leather was crisped and curled up. Like maybe a spell hadn't missed him by much.

"Those are mages out there!" he whispered savagely. "So do they! And what the hell are you still doing here?!"

"I have the map," I reminded him.

"Give it to me and go!"

"And leave you here alone? There's a dozen of them!"

"If you don't leave *right now* . . ."

I raised my chin, even though I'd turned off the flashlight so he probably couldn't see it. "What? You'll shoot me?"

His hand clenched my shoulder, almost painfully. *Don't tempt the crazy war mage*, I reminded myself, just as a bullet sliced through the open doorway. It ricocheted several times around the crypt's inner walls before crashing through what remained of the Madonna. "If you're here much longer, I won't have to!" he whispered furiously.

"Let's just get the damn thing and we can both leave," I said reasonably.

"In case it has somehow slipped your notice, this was a trap!"

"Damn it, you can't trust anybody anymore!" The elderly French mage we'd visited in his sweet little country cottage had seemed so reliable, with his Old World charm and his kind eyes—and his lousy map that had sent us on the treasure hunt from hell. It wasn't fair; the bad guys weren't supposed to look like someone's grandfather. "And Manassier seemed so—"

"If the next word out of your mouth is 'nice,' I will make your life hell when we get back. Pure hell."

I didn't bother to dignify that with a response. Pritkin was just . . . Pritkin. At some point I'd learned to mostly roll with it. I'd often wondered if he gave the Circle half as much trouble before he broke with them over his decision to support me. If so, you'd think they'd have thanked me for taking him off their hands. Maybe they planned to send a nice bouquet to the funeral.

"Look, all we know for sure is that some mages got here

ahead of us. Maybe we all decided to burgle the place on the same night." I didn't really believe it—they'd attacked us almost as soon as we'd arrived and we hadn't even found anything. But I hated to give up on our best lead yet. And leaving Pritkin to pursue it alone wasn't an option. He had all the self-preservation instincts of a bug near a shiny windshield.

A strong hand clenched my arm. "Ow!" I pointed out.

"Give me the damn map!" ·

"Not a chance."

"Hey!" I looked up to see the younger ghost staring at us. "In case you missed it, people are trying to kill you."

"People are always trying to kill me," I said irritably.

"The only way you're dying tonight is if *I* kill you," Pritkin informed me.

"I've been in relationships like that," the ghost sympathized.

"We're not in a relationship," I muttered.

"Sheer bloody-minded—what?" Pritkin broke off his rant, which I hadn't been listening to anyway, to look around wildly. "What's happening?"

"You mean you let him talk to you like that and you aren't even getting any? Man, what a rip-off."

"Nothing. Just a couple of spirits," I said, shooting ghost #2 a look.

"Hey, standing right here."

"And," his counterpart chimed in, "I resent that 'just' comment. We're the two most active spirits in this entire—"

"Active?" A hand moved down my arm, the touch both gentle and rough, calloused from holding guns and doing push-ups and snapping people's necks. "Don't even think about it," I told Pritkin, then turned my attention back to the ghost. "How active?"

The older ghost preened slightly. "We see everything that goes on around here. The things I could tell—"

"So, if there were hidden passageways, you'd know?" I asked, as Pritkin found my wrist. A moment later, the map was snatched out of my hand. "Still not leaving," I told him.

"Oh. You're after the thing, aren't you?" the younger ghost asked.

I decided not to wrestle Pritkin for the map, which wouldn't be dignified. It also wouldn't work. "What thing?"

"The thing with the thing." He waved a negligent hand. I was starting to suspect that if you died stoned, your ghost stayed that way.

"Could you be a little more specific?" Before he could answer, there was a strange sound from outside, a dim, high-pitched whine. I felt a hand on my back, viciously shoving me to the ground. Then Pritkin was on top of me, crushing me into a fetal position while things exploded and rained fire all around us.

Red and violet spots danced behind my tightly clenched lids for several long moments. There were minute tremors in the ground, like the aftershocks of an earthquake, and my skin prickled with leftover energy. When I cautiously opened my eyes, I saw starlight seeping in from a gaping hole in the roof and clouds of disintegrated stone in the air.

Pritkin was on his feet again, firing at the mages, who fired back, gunshots echoing off the high, close-packed monuments like firecrackers. Most of the time I thought he was a little too quick to opt for the shoot-it-and-hope-it-dies solution. Other times, like when someone was trying to make a colander out of my head, it seemed okay.

"Over there," the younger ghost offered, pointing to the right. "Come on." He slouched off, ignoring a nearby snaky pathway in favor of a shortcut across the tombstone-littered grounds.

"One of the ghosts knows where the passage is!" I told Pritkin. He looked surprised and I scowled. Just because I didn't know seven ways to kill a guy with my elbow didn't make me *completely* useless.

He looked like he was about to argue about the wisdom of trusting random spirits, or possibly my sanity. But the mages accidentally did me a favor by sending a spell that exploded with a massive crack against a nearby chestnut tree. The burning trunk fell over, taking half the crypt with it. Luckily, it wasn't our half.

"Come on, then!" Pritkin yelled, grabbing me by the hand and starting off, as if this had been his idea all along.

"This way!" I dragged him after the ghost as a fresh haze of bullets rattled off the rubble behind us.

I found it hard going: the soggy soil sucked at my shoes with every step and the rain made it almost impossible to keep the flickering, pale image of our guide in sight. But Pritkin, damn him, slipped through the granite obstacle course like he'd laid it out himself. "How are you doing that?" I demanded the fourth time I knocked a knee into a very hard tombstone.

"Doing what?"

"You can see!" I accused.

"Here." I felt a hand against my cheek for a split second, and Pritkin mumbled something. I blinked, and suddenly everything had a weird, flat, grainy look to it, like bad TV reception. Leaf shadows moved over his face as a gust of wind shook a tree, spattering drops of rain on us, and I could just make out the edges of that familiar scowl.

"Why didn't you do that before?" I demanded.

"I thought you were leaving before!"

"Do you two want this or not?" the ghost asked, hands on insubstantial hips. He'd stopped in front of the image of a bored-looking woman leaning on a tombstone. Enough moss had grown over her granite gown that it was practically green. Green and slimy, I discovered, after the ghost directed me to tap her knee three times. Nothing happened.

"Now what?"

"You have to say the magic word."

"Please!"

He laughed. "No, I mean a real magic word. To get the statue to move out of the way."

A spell exploded in the branches of an overhanging oak and a bunch of burning leaves dropped around me, threatening to set my hair alight. "What is it?!"

"Don't know." The ghost shrugged negligently. "It's not like I need it."

"What's the problem?" Pritkin demanded, sending his whole arsenal of animated weapons at the advancing line of dark shapes. His knives swooped and danced, striking sparks off their shields with every pass, but it didn't look like they were slowing our pursuers down much.

"The ghost doesn't know the password!"

Pritkin shot me his best edge-of-murder glare and muttered one of his weird British swear words. I don't think it was the open sesame, but the spell he cast with his next breath worked almost as well. The statue split straight down the middle to reveal a gaping cavern.

Inside was as dark as a well, just a black hole silhouetted against the electric sky. I pulled out my flashlight and clicked it on, but it barely dented the darkness. Even worse, there were no stairs, only an iron-rung ladder descending into a claustrophobic tunnel carved into solid rock.

"I've seen many treasure hunters go in," the older ghost commented, having floated up beside me, "but few come out again. And those who do are empty-handed."

"That won't happen to us."

"That's what they all say," he murmured, just as a spell burst overhead. I shoved the gun and flashlight in my belt, grabbed the first rusty rung and half climbed, half slid to the bottom. Pritkin followed practically on top of me, and as soon as we were both down, he sent a spell back up the tunnel that caused a cave-in.

It blocked our pursuers, but it also cut off what little light there was. Once the rumble from the falling rock stopped, we were in dead silence and utter darkness. Apparently even enhanced vision needs something to work with, because I couldn't see a thing.

I clicked the flashlight back on. It took a moment for my eyes to adjust, and when they did, I yelped and stumbled back a step. The thin beam didn't show much—it was like the dark down here was hungry, eating the light almost as soon as it left the bulb. But I wouldn't have minded seeing even less. Along every side of a long corridor were bones arranged in patterns all the way to the low ceiling. Water had seeped in from somewhere, and a lot of the skulls were crying green tears and growing fuzzy green beards. It didn't make them look less creepy.

"The catacombs," Pritkin said, before I could ask.

"The what?"

"The Parisians started using old limestone quarries as underground cemeteries a few hundred years ago." He took the flashlight and pointed it at the map, frowning. "I didn't think they extended out this far."

"How far?"

"If these tunnels connect to those in the city, then hundreds of kilometers." He started shining the light here and there. I wished he'd stop; it lit puddles of water in the empty eye sockets, making the faces seem to move. "There have been stories of catacombs under Père Lachaise for years, but I thought they were merely rumors."

I stared at a nearby skull. It was bodiless, sitting atop a stack of what looked like femurs, and was missing the jawbone. But somehow it still seemed to be grinning. "They look pretty real to me."

The flashlight picked out a glint of gold, half buried in the mortar keeping a line of bones in place. I scraped at the cement with my finger, and it was so old that pieces of it just flaked off. The golden circle I revealed wouldn't budge, but I did get a better look at it. It appeared to be formed out of a snake that was chowing down on its own tail. "The ouroboros," Pritkin said, coming up behind me.

"The what?"

"An ancient symbol for regeneration and eternity."

"Like a cross?"

"Older." He shone the light around some more. "The Paris coven must have created their own catacombs, possibly during the Inquisition. Witches and wizards were sometimes disinterred and their bodies mutilated or burnt. This would have been one way of preventing that."

"You mean this is a mages' graveyard?"

"Possibly. The limestone pits were dug by the Romans. They were there for centuries before the Parisian authorities decided to make use of them. Perhaps the magical community had the idea first." From up the ladder came a sudden rain of stone and rubble. It sounded like our pursuers weren't giving up. "Can you shift us here?" he asked, pointing to a vague squiggle on the map.

My new job had more downsides than I could count, but there were a few perks, too. Well, one, anyway. The power that came with the office of Pythia allowed me to move myself and one or two others around in space and time. It was a damn useful weapon, and so far my only one. But it had its limitations. "I can't shift unless I know where I'm going."

"You've time-shifted before to places you've never been!"

"That's different."

There was a sudden avalanche, and a spell crashed into the floor behind us, igniting a storm of violent white light. It hit the skulls, causing them to crack and splinter, then bounced off the opposite wall, slinging stone fragments everywhere like flying daggers. Pritkin shielded me from the worst of the blast, then grabbed my hand and towed me down the corridor.

Since I didn't go bouncing off any walls, I assumed he could still see something, but to me it was a headlong plunge into nothingness. He'd clicked off the flashlight, I suppose to make it harder for our pursuers to track us, but without it the tunnels were so dark I couldn't tell whether my eyes were open or closed. "How different?" he demanded.

"The power lets me see other times, past places. Not the present," I explained, flinching. Afterimages from the blast were making reddish shapes leap in front of my vision, and I kept thinking I was about to plow into something. "If I want to do spatial shifts in the here and now, I have to be able to visualize where I want to go." And a shaky line on a bad map wasn't even close to good enough.

The corridor abruptly narrowed, to the point that it was impossible to continue side by side. Pritkin went first, pulling me along at something approaching a run. It was hot, the air was close, and the ground underneath our feet wasn't anything like level. It was soon obvious why someone would put a treasury here; without clear directions, you could wander around for months and never find anything.

Pritkin stopped, so suddenly that I ran into him. He spread the map out on the wall and handed me the flashlight. I clicked it on and saw a much less organized scene than before: bones had tumbled out of the walls and littered the floor, and in some cases they were mounded up in piles with no

effort at arrangement at all. Unlike the ones in the main corridor, these looked like they'd just been thrown around any old
way. I'm not usually sentimental about the dead—I meet too
many of them—but it still seemed wrong. Friends and enemies, parents and children, all jumbled up, with nothing to
give a history, a date of death, even a name.

"It would help if you shone the torch on the map," Pritkin
commented caustically. I obliged, and the beam lit up his face,
too. Its expression wasn't reassuring. "Are your ghosts here?"
he demanded.

"No. They wouldn't follow us beyond the cemetery limits." And it felt like we'd left those behind a while ago.

"What about others?"

"Why do you want to know?"

"Because this map is less than adequate! Some directions
would be helpful."

I shook my head. "These bodies were disturbed. I think
they were brought here from their original resting places."

"Meaning?"

"That their ghosts would have stayed behind." Not to mention that if it was mages buried here, they wouldn't have left
ghosts anyway. Supernatural creatures just didn't, as far as I
knew.

"But their bones are here."

"Doesn't matter. Spirits can haunt a house, even when their
bodies aren't there. It's all about what was important to them
in life, the place where they felt a connection." I looked
around and repressed a shiver. "I don't think I'd feel real connected to this place, either."

Pritkin finally settled on a direction and we took off again,
sliding through gaps in the rock that, at times, were barely
big enough for me. I don't know how he got through, but
based on the muttered comments that drifted back, it wasn't
without the loss of some flesh. Finally we came to a slightly
wider corridor, meaning that we still had to go single file but
could pick up speed. For a minute, I thought we'd succeeded
in losing our pursuers, but as usual, Murphy's Law caught up
with us.

We came barreling around a corner only to run almost directly into a party of dark shapes. There were yells and bullets and spells, with one of the last exploding against Pritkin's shields, popping them like heat on a soap bubble. "Run!" he snarled in my face. I heard rumbling, like distant thunder, and then the ceiling came down with a roar that consumed the world.

Chapter 2

It took me a few seconds to realize that I still wasn't dead. I was in a crouch, my hands protecting my head, expecting an attack, but the corridor was as silent as the tomb it was. The only people besides us were cemented into the walls or buried under the pile of rubble that their own spell had brought down on their heads. I collapsed back against the floor, breathing raggedly, and tried not to scream.

After a minute, I felt around for the flashlight and my hand closed over a cool plastic cylinder. I clicked it on, relieved to find that it still worked, and saw Pritkin lying on his side. He wasn't moving, and he had blood smeared through the stubble on his chin, bright and frightening. *Murphy and his little law can go to hell,* I thought furiously, shaking him frantically.

"Would you kindly stop doing that?" he asked politely.

I stared. I wasn't entirely sure, but a polite John Pritkin might be a sign of the apocalypse. "Did you hit your head?" I tried to move closer to get a better look, and my knee accidentally knocked a shower of stone pebbles onto the oozing gash on his forehead.

"If I tell you I'm all right, will you stop trying to help me?" Every muscle in my body relaxed at the familiar tone, all ruffled feathers and crisp impatience. That was better; that was solid ground.

"So, still alive?" I croaked.

"Damn right."

He just lay there, though, so I shone the beam around, giving him a minute. It took a few seconds to realize exactly what I was seeing. Pritkin had apparently gotten his shields back up, because they glowed blue and waterlike, rippling slowly in the yellow beam. But the cave ceiling wasn't above them anymore. Or, to be more accurate, it was there—it was just no longer attached to anything.

Huge, half-quarried blocks, some still bearing ancient chisel marks, lay on top of the suddenly very thin-looking shields. Every time they flexed, small showers of rubble and grit slid along the top and trickled down the sides, making soft shushing sounds in the quiet. The larger pieces had nowhere to go, but they moved enough to make it obvious that they weren't anchored to anything. Even the smaller, cobblestone-sized chunks would hurt like hell if they fell on us, and I didn't have to wonder what the larger ones would do. Two mages were giving gory proof of that barely a yard away.

I could have reached out and touched them, where they lay caught between the shield and the cave-in. Their bodies were oddly contorted, trapped in the stone and rubble like ancient fossils, their open eyes shining in the reflected light. Except that fossils don't usually come complete with evidence of how they got that way, at least not in Technicolor brilliance.

The red-streaked white of newly shattered bone stood out starkly against the mellow gold of the older specimens. One hand rested against the blue of the shield, caught in a gesture of defense, as if human strength could stand against the weight of a mountain. It made me wonder for an insane moment if it would leave a red outline, if the next time Pritkin raised his shields, it would manifest, too.

The air suddenly felt a lot heavier in my lungs. Despite the large number of impossible things that had happened to me lately, my brain couldn't quite seem to deal. It was loudly insisting that *huge slabs of rock* that weighed maybe a *ton each* didn't just hover in the air and that we were both going to *die any second now*.

I made a small, choked sound, but managed to swallow the bubble of hysteria before it could tear loose. If Pritkin had been a second later getting his protection back up, there would be four new bodies entombed down here instead of two. But there weren't. We were safe. Sort of.

Pritkin had rolled onto his back and was staring at me, hard and intent. "This is exactly why I told you to go home."

"I have a devastating comeback for that," I informed him with dignity. "Just not right now."

"Do you want to give up?" I blinked. I could count on zero fingers the number of times he had asked my opinion. "Because there are almost certainly more of them back there."

I remembered the ghost saying that there were twelve mages all together. Which meant that behind the rockfall, ten more were still hanging around, unless they were caught somewhere I couldn't see. Or unless they'd left, assuming that the cave-in had killed us. But no, I wasn't that lucky.

"You know what's at stake," I reminded him.

"I thought you'd say that." Pritkin levered himself to his knees with a grunt. The rubble shifted along with him, enough to bring another large slab crashing down. The jagged underside landed only a few feet away from my face.

Pritkin's voice, laced with its usual impatience, cut through my panic. "Let's go."

"Go?" It came out as more of a squeak than I'd intended. "How? Because I can shift us back home but I can't shift us beyond this. I don't know what's on the other side or even where the other side is—"

"Just stay close." Before he'd even finished speaking, his shields had changed from fluid waves to hard crystal, reflecting the cave-in through a hundred sharp facets. A few more rocks fell off, allowing more to rain down from above, striking off the new, rigid surface with dull thuds. Pritkin started crawling forward, and his shields went with him, almost scooping me off my feet before I got with the program and moved up close behind him.

It wasn't until I saw the body of one of the mages slide down the side and roll behind us that I completely realized what was happening. Our small bubble was plowing through the rocks and dirt like a crystal mole intent on making a new burrow. We hit a wall once, looking for an entrance that wasn't there, but we found it a few feet to the left and burst through, the cave collapsing in on itself behind us.

Pritkin dropped his shields with an audible sigh, and the dust we'd dislodged in our escape flooded in, almost blinding me. We forged ahead to get away from the choking cloud, which had no way to disperse in an area without wind or open air. But before we'd gone ten yards, we ran into what felt like another cave-in.

Once I blinked the dirt out of my eyes, I realized what I was seeing. A narrow tunnel stretched out in front of us, filled halfway to the ceiling with what looked like a mile of bones. Pritkin climbed on top of the broken human mass, flashing the light around. "There's a hole in the wall up ahead. It probably leads to another tunnel."

I eyed the pile of bones uneasily. Anything kept in close proximity to a person's aura eventually imprints with a psychic skin. I'd experienced more horror stories from inadvertently brushing up against a strong trigger than I could count. And I couldn't think of a stronger trigger than an actual body part.

"Hurry, damn it!" Pritkin thrust a hand down to me as the sound of voices echoed dimly from the corridor behind us. Somebody had heard our exit.

I hefted myself up gingerly, before I could think about it too much. The bones were old and dry, and crunched sickeningly under my weight. Many splintered, sending little knives into my palms and tearing my jeans, but there were no psychic flashes. Moving them must have ruptured any imprints that had formed.

When Pritkin said a hole in the wall, he wasn't kidding. I could barely squeeze through the thing, and it sounded from his language like he'd scraped off more than a little skin himself. "Move!" he whispered, giving me a push in the small of my back. I scrambled inside the small rock-hewn cavern on the other side of the hole, and almost tumbled down a set of stairs that started after only a few feet.

The claustrophobically low stairwell was extremely uninviting; mostly I just saw the darkness that pooled in every niche and corner. I really didn't want to go down there. Then a spell hit the ceiling behind me with a crack like cannon fire and I reconsidered, scrambling down the stairs ahead of Pritkin.

A second spell hit while we were still on the steps. It went on and on, like a slow-motion bomb blast, causing gravel to pepper the back of my hands and neck like hail. It sent me sliding down the stairs, but the vibrations rode up through my legs, making it almost impossible to find a foothold. And then it didn't matter because there was no foothold to find. The rock disintegrated beneath my feet, and I tumbled through darkness and empty air before slamming into freezing water.

It took me a moment to realize I wasn't drowning. The water came only up to my waist, but it was like ice and the cold shot right up my spine. Worse was the by-now-familiar billowing cloud of dust, trapping me in a choking haze. Instinctively, I sloshed farther away from the rockfall, trying to breathe, and found myself treading water. I grabbed a moss-covered skull that jutted out from the wall, my fingers finding purchase in the eye sockets. I held on, too grateful to be repulsed, gasping in great lungfuls of air.

"Pritkin!" It was barely a croak, but a moment later the flashlight beam hit my eyes, blinding me.

"Still alive?"

I tried to answer, but my lungs decided this would be a good moment to expel all the foreign matter I'd breathed in, and I ended up heaving and choking. I lost my grip on the slimy bone and slid under the frigid water. For a long, terrifying moment, I was lost in an endless sea of black that immediately chilled me to the core. Then two broad hands were fumbling for a grip on my shoulders, pulling me back to the surface, reminding me where *up* and *down* were.

"Miss Palmer!"

I spat out a mouthful of limestone paste, the result of oily water mixed with dust, and gasped in some air. "Damn right."

Pritkin nodded and flashed the light around, giving glimpses of a corridor where the floor rippled oddly and everything was suddenly shades of gray and pale, unearthly green. It looked like the entire lower levels had flooded. I can swim, but I wasn't in love with the idea of navigating a dark underground stream with barely enough headroom to breathe.

"I'll deal with this," Pritkin said grimly. "Shift out of here."

"And if they keep coming?"

"I'll manage."

And he called me bloody-minded. I took another breath to inform my lungs that asphyxiation would have to wait, and pushed back off into the flood. "Just swim."

Pritkin didn't answer, unless you count a curse, although that could have been due to the spell that hit the water behind us, instantly raising the temperature from chilled to boiling. I screamed, and coherent thought fled. I didn't think, just grabbed his hand and *shifted*.

A second later, we landed in the same corridor, but with no dust cloud, no mages and no flood. I'd been treading water in the other time, so I was only a few feet off the ground. Pritkin, unfortunately, had been floating, and he fell from a little farther. Like about six feet.

He hit the rocky floor with a thud, a curse and a crack, the last from the demise of the flashlight. I tried to ask how he was, but a stitch was biting deep into my side and, for a long moment it was impossible to draw oxygen into my lungs. I slid down the wall to a seated position because my knees suddenly felt too rubbery to be reliable.

"What happened?" Pritkin gasped after a moment. With no flashlight and no deadly spells zipping around, it was pitch-dark, but from the direction of his voice, it sounded like he was still on the floor.

"I shifted us back in time," I managed to croak.

I decided that it probably wasn't good that I was still feeling shaky and nauseated despite being this close to the floor and completely motionless. I couldn't figure out what was wrong. I'd shifted only twice today, once to get us to Paris from Manassier's cottage and once just now, yet I was exhausted. It looked like bringing another person along for the ride took a lot out of me. Too bad no one had bothered to give me the manual.

"A little warning next time!"

"You're welcome."

"When are we?"

I spit out more chalky-tasting dust. Now I knew why Lara Croft always carried a canteen. My body was dripping, but my throat was parched. I swallowed dry, while running through the mental Rolodex my power gives me. "Seventeen ninety-three."

"What? Why?"

"Because I didn't feel like being boiled alive?"

"You could have shifted us back a day, a week! This is no bloody use at all!"

Of course, I thought sourly, Lara Croft would also have some nice convenient techie thing to get her out of this. And a partner who wasn't a complete ass. I cautiously stood up and found to my surprise that I was only faintly dizzy. I strained my ears, but all I heard was my own harsh breathing and a faint drip, drip of water from somewhere.

"Let's go," I said, fumbling around until I found Pritkin's hand. His skin was cold from the water, and his pulse was fast but not bad. Not, for example, like mine, which felt like it could burst a vein. I needed to make sure I didn't have to shift again anytime soon. Like for the rest of the week.

Pritkin stayed where he was. "Go? Where?"

"To find the Codex! I thought it might be nice to look for it without somebody shooting at us for a change."

"An excellent sentiment. Except for the small matter of the Paris coven being one of the oldest in Europe. They may have abandoned this facility in our time, but in this era there are doubtless mages all over the place. Not to mention snares and traps. If we haven't already tripped a protection ward, we soon will!"

"Do you have another suggestion?"

"Yes. Shift us out!" Even in complete darkness I was positive I could see his glare.

I sucked in a breath, more annoyed than I could remember—well, more annoyed than before John Pritkin, anyway. "Why didn't I think of that?"

"You have shifted multiple times in a day before—"

"And it wiped me out before."

"You never mentioned that."

"You never asked."

There was a brief pause. "Are you all right?"

"Yeah, peachy." I really hated his suggestion, but I couldn't think of a better one. "Let's at least clear the corridor first," I said in compromise. "Then I'll try to set us back a little early, before the fireworks start."

It took forever to get down that corridor, not because of the darkness but because Pritkin was certain someone or something was about to jump us. But the only problems were the usual—heat, bad air and the fun of trying not to fall on the uneven floor or scrape off a little more skin on the wall. We finally came to a branch in the path and Pritkin stopped. "Are you certain you're up to this?"

"What's your plan if I say no?"

"Wait here until you say yes."

"Then I guess I'm up to it." I don't suffer from claustrophobia, but I was getting really tired of those tunnels. I gripped his hand tighter, focused on our era and *shifted*.

This time the world melted around us slowly, like paint dissolving in water, bleeding away in slow drips. I normally don't feel the passing of years, just a weightless free fall that ends with me whenever I planned to be. I felt it this time. Reality rippled around us in a nauseating, frictionless, gravity-free waver. I was suddenly grateful I couldn't see, because what I could feel was terrifying: For a long moment, I was a tearing stream of dislocated atoms, consciousness ripped apart, with a body that was so elongated it neither began nor ended.

Then I snapped back into myself, only to have the whole process start again. There were snatches of conversation, a few notes of music and what sounded like another explosion or cave-in, all in quick succession, like someone flipping a radio too fast. And I finally realized what was happening. This trip wasn't one long jump, but a series of smaller hops, with us flashing in and out of other times as we slowly made our way back to our own.

I could feel time, and it was heavy, like swimming through molasses. Pushing through the centuries was like running a marathon. In the dark. With weights tied to my legs.

When we finally broke through, it felt like oxygen when drowning—shocking, unexpected, miraculous. I'd half expected to materialize underwater, but apparently we'd passed the flooded area, because I stumbled into a mostly dry wall. I sat down abruptly, tilting my head back, swallowing a relief so sharp it made me light-headed.

Pritkin crawled over to lean against the wall next to me. "Are you all right?"

"Stop asking me that," I said, then had to go very still to deal with the nausea. It felt like my stomach had been a couple seconds behind the rest of me, and when it caught up it wasn't happy to be there.

"I take it that's a yes."

I swallowed, still tasting dust, and told myself that throwing up would be very unprofessional. "Yeah. It's just . . . the learning curve can be a little rough."

After a few minutes of sitting quietly with my eyes closed, I managed to relax and start breathing evenly. "You don't have to do this," Pritkin said. "I could—"

"I couldn't shift out of here right now if my life depended on it," I said truthfully.

"Your power shouldn't fluctuate this greatly," he told me, and I could hear the puzzled frown in his voice.

"The power doesn't fluctuate. My ability to channel it does. The more tired I am, the harder it gets."

"But it shouldn't be this difficult," Pritkin repeated stubbornly. "My power doesn't—"

"Because it's yours!" Damn it, I didn't have the breath for one of our long, drawn-out arguments right now. "This isn't mine. I wasn't born with it. It's on loan, remember?"

The power hadn't originated with the Pythias, who had once been the priestesses of an ancient being calling himself Apollo. I'd met him exactly once, when he'd promised to train me. So far, he'd paid that promise the same amount of attention he had my objections over receiving the office in the first place: none. Unfortunately, I didn't have anywhere else to turn.

Unlike most Pythias, who had been trained for a decade or two on the ins and outs of their position, my intro to the office had lasted about thirty seconds—just long enough for the last incumbent to shove the power off on me before she died. And everyone else who might have given me a few pointers was under the control of the Circle.

We sat there for a while in silence. I eventually summoned the strength to pull off my shoes and toss my waterlogged socks against the far wall, where they landed with little splats. It didn't help much because I just had to put the wet shoes back on.

"Before you completed the ritual to become Pythia, your power controlled how and when it manifested," Pritkin said, as I dragged myself to my feet. I'd almost fallen asleep for the second time against his shoulder, wet clothes, hard floor and all. "Is that correct?"

"Yeah. I was only allowed in the driver's seat after I bought the car, so to speak." Which was better than getting thrown back to another century every time I turned around, to fix whatever was about to get messed up—usually without having a clue what it might be.

"Then you must start monitoring your endurance. Otherwise, you could become trapped in another time or overtax your system, possibly resulting in serious injury."

"You don't say?" I started down the corridor, my feet feeling like they were encased in cement. "I'd have never figured that out on my own."

"I am serious." Pritkin grabbed my arm, in his favorite spot, right over the bicep. I was probably going to have the permanent indentation of his fingers there someday. "You must begin experimentation, to discover your limits. How many times can you shift before you reach exhaustion? Does going farther back in time cause more of a drain than more recent shifts? What other powers over time do you possess?"

"If I'm not letting someone piggyback along, three or four, depending on how tired I am to start with; hell, yes; and I don't really want to know," I answered him, in order. "Now, can we deal with the current crisis, please, and leave the twenty questions for later?"

Pritkin shut up, but with a meaningful silence that said this wasn't over. I let him brood while I concentrated on not falling on my face. We felt our way down another dark, dusty corridor.

We finally found the storeroom by the simple method of running into it. Or, to be more accurate, into the rusty iron-work gate that blocked the entrance. I backed up a few steps while Pritkin scuffled around. I heard a match strike and suddenly I could see. Watery yellow light filtered outward from a small lantern set in a niche, allowing him to check the area for booby traps. He didn't find any, which seemed to worry him more than the reverse.

"What's wrong? Manassier said this place was abandoned."

Pritkin ran a hand over his hair, which despite the water and the sweat and the limestone dust was still acting like an independent entity. "Can you shift yet?"

"Maybe."

"If anything goes wrong, you are to shift away *immediately*. Do you understand?"

"Sure."

Pritkin shot me a suspicious look, and I gave him my best bland expression right back. He'd asked if I understood, and I'd said yes. I hadn't agreed to anything.

He smeared his finger across the door mechanism, cutting through an inch of dust and grime. Something clicked and he pulled back before cautiously nudging the door with his toe. It swung inward obligingly, but he hesitated on the threshold. "I don't like it. This is too easy."

I personally thought easy was just fine. In fact, it was about damn time easy showed up. "Maybe our luck is chang—"

Pritkin stepped into the room and disappeared with a strangled sort of sound. "Pritkin!" There was no answer. I knelt by the threshold, but there was nothing to see—only a small, empty cave, with no exit, and no mage.

I got a death grip on the iron bars of the door and reached out. My hand encountered nothing but dusty limestone for about two feet, then disappeared into the floor. I snatched my arm back, but there didn't appear to be any damage. An illusion, then.

I stretched out on the floor, closed my eyes and leaned

over, to the point that my forehead would have hit stone if there really had been a floor there. When it didn't, I opened my eyes in blackness. After a moment, my sight adjusted to show me dirty fingers, white with strain, clinging to a shard of limestone three or four yards down. They were human, and below them, almost out of sight, was a familiar, spiky head.

"Grab my hand and I'll shift us out," I called, hoping I could actually do it. The head snapped up.

"What did I just tell you?!" Pritkin demanded.

"Hi, I'm Cassie Palmer. Have we met?"

Steel entered the suddenly soft tones. "Miss Palmer. Move away from the edge. Now."

"I'm not going to fall in," I told him irritably.

"Neither did I! There's something down here." I couldn't see Pritkin's face very well, just a pale blur against the shadows, but he didn't sound happy. Some people thought he had only one mode—pissed off. In reality, he had plenty of them. Over the past few weeks, I'd learned to tell the difference between real pissed off, impatient pissed off and scared pissed off. I suspected that this was the last kind. If so, that made two of us.

That feeling amped up a few notches when he cursed and fired several rounds at something out in the darkness. The faint, acrid smell of gunpowder floated up to me as I wiggled forward, keeping my legs spread, hoping that if I distributed my weight over a larger surface I wouldn't cause a rock slide. I stretched until I heard something pop in my shoulder, but I wasn't even close. And if I couldn't touch him, I couldn't shift him.

I bit my lip and stared up at the floor that wasn't there. It was kind of odd seeing it from this angle, as if the ocean's surface had been smeared with dirt and pebbles. It didn't help my concentration, so I pulled back up to a sitting position and stared at the top of it instead.

Once upon a time, my reaction to scary things had been to run and hide. It was an effective strategy for staying alive in the good old days when all I had to worry about was a homicidal vampire. The difference between then and now was that once upon a time I'd had problems I really *could* outrun. Now

I had duties and responsibilities, the kind of things that are always with you. There were about a dozen nightmares vying for the top spot every day, each of them spectacularly horrible in its own way. And right at the top of the list was the fear that I'd have to stand by and watch another friend die trying to help me.

I was suddenly really glad I couldn't see the bottom.

The rock felt crumbly under my fingers as I slithered over the side. Or maybe that was my hands shaking. A cascade of small rocks disappeared beyond the illusion and some of them must have hit Pritkin, because I heard him swear again.

"What the *hell* are you—"

"Sheer bloody-mindedness, remember? And can you see my leg?"

I was holding on to the edge of the chasm by my arms and elbows, and still felt unbelievably unsteady. I carefully did *not* look down, but for a few seconds, I strained to hear the rocks hit bottom. I never did.

I tried to feel around with my toe without falling off, but met only air. Damn it, what if I needed to be touching bare skin? Why hadn't I thought to remove my shoes first? I tried toeing one off, but the water had made the sneaker shrink around my foot. "Grab my ankle."

A lot of less than genteel language echoed off the walls. "I can't grab anything without letting go!"

"You have two arms!"

"Listen to me." Pritkin's voice was low and controlled, the tone he used when he was pretending to be reasonable. "I can't let go of the gun. There's something down here. It pulled me in. It could get bored with me at any moment and come after you. You have to—" He broke off at the sound of shouts and explosions and booted feet echoing down the corridor. "Shift, *goddamn it!*"

"*Grab my leg!*"

I lowered myself down to the point that my head was barely over the top of the chasm, but still touched nothing. The damn rock was falling apart under my fingers and nervous sweat was making my palms slippery. My arms were sending sharp little pains up to my shoulders and there was no purchase on the side of the chasm for my feet. How the hell far down was he?

And then it didn't matter, because a pair of booted feet stopped right in front of my eyes. I craned my neck enough to see an older man with salt-and-pepper hair and pale gray eyes smiling down at me. Manassier. Well, didn't that just explain a lot.

"I didn't think you would get this far," he told me in his thick accent. And to think, only that afternoon, I'd found it attractive.

Somewhere along the line I'd bitten my tongue hard enough to taste copper. I swallowed blood. "Surprise."

He shrugged. "No matter. I still collect the bounty."

"There's a bounty?"

"Half a million euros." His smile grew. "You are about to make me rich."

"*Half* a million? Are you kidding me? I'm the Pythia. I'm worth way more than that."

He took out a gun, a Sig Sauer P210, which I recognized because of the shooting lessons Pritkin had been giving me. My aim wasn't any better, but I could identify all kinds of guns now. Even the one about to kill me.

"I'm a simple man," Manassier said, "with simple needs. Half a million will do nicely."

It figured that I'd get the nongreedy crook. I swallowed a crazy urge to laugh. "You don't have to shoot me," I gasped. "I can't hold on much longer anyway."

"Yes, but if you slip, the Circle may say you died of natural causes and not pay the bounty. And then all this was for nothing."

"Yeah. That'd be a shame."

He clicked the safety off. "Now hold still and this won't hurt."

"That would be a nice change." My body felt like it weighed a ton, my arms were liquid with fatigue, and my shoulders were aching in their sockets. It would be such a relief to just let go.

So I did.

I heard him yell something in French and felt a bullet whiz

by my head, but it was unimportant because I was falling, and there was nothing to hold on to, just sliding dirt and limestone rocks crumbling beneath my hands. My arms flailed wildly, grasping for the one thing I had to find, but for a long second I felt only air. Then my fingers collided with something warm and alive and I grabbed it and we were both falling. There was a dizzying rush of air and my power wouldn't come and all I could think was that I'd killed us both—then my brain whited out and my heart tried to stop and reality twisted and bent around us.

And we tumbled into a casino lobby half a world away.

I hadn't judged things perfectly because of the whole abject terror thing, and we fell from about four feet above the ground. Pritkin hit the floor first, with a pained grunt, with me clinging to his back. And then everything got incredibly still for a minute, as it always did whenever I survived something insanely dangerous and really stupid. The fact that I recognized the phenomenon probably meant it had happened a few too many times. I lay there quivering, hearing an upsurge in the polite babble of the guests and not caring. All I could think was, oh, thank God, I didn't kill us.

After a stunned moment, I coughed hard and rolled off. My face was dusty, my palms were scraped raw and I was panting and limp. Various muscle groups were twitching at random, seizing up with tight bursts of pain and then releasing. I felt like bursting into tears and screaming in triumph all at the same time.

Pritkin finally groaned and sat up. He was pale and sweating profusely, with damp hair plastered to his forehead. He had cuts on his face and hands and burns on his forearm.

I wanted to touch him, to reassure myself that we'd both actually survived, but I didn't dare. A gal could lose a hand that way. So I just stared at him instead, so glad to be alive that my aching back and trembling arms and ferocious headache hardly registered at all. "That was fun," I croaked. "Only, not."

Pritkin hauled me into a sitting position, one dirty, scarred hand cupping the back of my neck. "Are you all right?" His voice was sharp and biting, with a slightly panicked edge.

"I told you to stop asking—"

He shook me, and despite it being one-handed, it made my teeth rattle. "If anything like that *ever* happens again. You. Leave. Me. Behind. Do you understand?"

I would have argued, but I was feeling a little shocky for some reason. "I'm not good at abandoning people," I finally said.

A front-desk person scurried over, first-aid kit in hand, but Pritkin snarled at the poor guy and he quickly backed up a step. "Then *get* good at it!"

He stomped off, limping, one shoulder hanging at an odd angle. "You're welcome," I murmured.

Chapter 3

Pritkin and I had landed at Dante's, Vegas' cross between a haunted house and a casino. It was currently what he referred to as our base of operations and I called our hideout. And, as hiding places went, it ranked pretty high. Not only was it a well-warded, vampire-run property, but we'd recently helped to trash a large piece of it. It seemed unlikely that many of our enemies would think to look for us there. At least, that was the plan.

I was sitting in Purgatory, the lobby bar, the next afternoon, trying to scalp a shrunken head, when a vampire walked in. He was swathed in a dark cloak and hood that would have looked theatrical anywhere else, but the prickle at the base of my spine told me what he was. It looked like the plan pretty much sucked.

I watched him out of the corner of my eye while I finished dissecting the head. The clump of matted black hair finally came off more or less intact. I put down the piece of molded plastic I'd been working on and picked up the real deal, which was perched on an overturned ashtray nearby. It glared at me balefully out of one shriveled, raisinlike eye. "I can't believe it's come to this," it complained. "Somebody kill me now."

"Somebody already did."

"That's cold, blondie."

I put the long ponytail onto its wrinkled skin and adjusted it. The head, rumored to have belonged to a gambler who had welshed on the wrong bet, usually took orders at the zombie bar upstairs. It was currently unemployed, courtesy of a fire that had raged out of control for almost an hour. The head had somehow survived, except for its hair.

I felt kind of responsible—the Circle's war mages had set the blaze while attempting to barbecue me—so I had been trying to replace its singed locks with some taken from one of the fakes sold as souvenirs at the gift shop. Dante's isn't known for the high quality of its merchandise, ensuring that I'd spent an hour sorting through about a hundred heads, trying to find a good match. Not that my help seemed to be appreciated.

"I can't go around looking like this!" it said sourly as I reached for the superglue. "I'm the main attraction here. I'm the star!"

"It's either this or I scalp Barbie," I threatened. "They don't make wigs in your size."

"Sweetheart, they don't make anything in my size. And it's never stopped me before."

"I don't even want to know what that means," I said honestly.

The vampire was now scanning the crowded tables. Maybe he was here for a drink or a quick game of craps, but I doubted it. I'd recently turned down an offer of employment from the Vampire Senate, something that isn't generally considered healthy. The surprise wasn't that they'd sent someone to restate their offer in more emphatic terms, but that it had taken them this long.

I watched a harried-looking waitress, dressed in a few black straps and thigh-high boots, move forward to greet the new arrival. She walked like her arches hurt, which was probably the case. Bondage chic was Purgatory's shtick, chosen to match the name, but it wasn't made for eight-hour shifts on your feet. I could testify to that personally, having spent several days literally in her shoes.

The idea was to hide in plain sight. At least that's what Casanova, the casino's manager, had claimed. I suspected he just wanted the free help.

Casanova's master was Antonio, a Philadelphia crime boss better known as Tony, although his name these days was mud for crossing his own master—who happened to be Mircea.

Among other things, Tony'd tried to have me killed, which would have seriously interfered in Mircea's plans. Not being the forgiving type, Mircea had confiscated everything Tony owned, including the casino and its manager. Before being sidelined by the *geis*, he'd ordered Casanova to assist me, but hadn't given specifics. As a result, Casanova's "assistance" had taken the form of a lot of fill-in jobs for which I'd yet to see a paycheck.

But until Pritkin found us an actual, honest-to-God lead, I didn't have much else to do. Except to stare obsessively at the clock, wondering how many seconds of freedom I had left. Staying busy helped with that. A little. And Casanova had a point about the outfit. My shiny PVC shorts and bustier combo didn't hide much, but with elaborate eye makeup and a long black wig, I barely recognized my strawberry-blond, blue-eyed self. I fiddled with the head and tried to look nonchalant, hoping the disguise would hold up.

The man sitting beside me started complaining. "A thumbscrew?" He slapped the drinks list down on the bar. "What the hell is that?"

"You're not in Hell," the bartender corrected him. "And no souls eat or drink in Purgatory."

"Then what do they do?" the guy asked sarcastically.

"They suffer." I thought the bartender's dungeon master garb, consisting of a bare chest, hangman's hood and studded cuffs, should have already made that clear. If not, the couple dozen torture devices serving as wall art might have clued the guy in.

"I *am* suffering—from thirst!" the tourist insisted.

"A thumbscrew is a screwdriver," I explained helpfully.

"Gee, thanks, Elvira. So what I gotta do? Solve a riddle before I can order a drink?"

"It's not that hard," the bartender said patiently, placing a flaming cocktail in front of another guest. "A Lynching is a Lynchburg lemonade, an Iron Maiden is an old-fashioned, a—"

"All I want is a Bloody Mary! You got one of them?"

"Yes."

"What's it called?"

"A Bloody Mary."

The vampire had paused beside me. "It won't work," I told him. No way was I changing my mind. Vampires in general aren't to be trusted, but the Senate makes the average vamp look like a paragon of virtue.

"That's what I've been trying to tell you," the head spat. "This is an outrage!"

I set the ungrateful thing back on its ashtray and swiveled to face my unwanted visitor. "And why bother with a disguise? It's not like I wouldn't know what you are."

"It wasn't meant for you," the vampire said, throwing back the hood.

A pair of rich brown eyes met mine, the color as soft and familiar as well-worn suede. Only their agonized expression was new. I started in shock. "Rafe?"

He collapsed against the bar, holding his stomach as if he'd been punched. I slid off my stool and helped him onto it, feeling him shiver despite the thick, fuzzy wool cloak he clutched around himself. The streets outside were shimmering in the late June heat, yet he was bundled up like we were scheduled for a blizzard. I'd known him all my life, and I'd never seen him look this bad.

We'd met at the court of the vampire who turned him, the aforementioned Tony, who had ordered Rafe to paint my bedroom when I was a child. I doubt that Tony had done it to please his resident clairvoyant. It just fit his warped sense of humor to give the greatest artist of the Renaissance the most menial jobs he could find. But Raphael had actually enjoyed it, and in the months it took to litter my ceiling with angels, stars and clouds, we'd become fast friends. He'd been one of the few things that had made growing up at Tony's bearable.

Rafe's lips were cold when he kissed me briefly, and his hands were like ice. I warmed them in mine, worry gnawing at my insides. He wasn't supposed to be cold. Vampires are as warm as humans unless they're famished, but that couldn't be it. Like all masters, Rafe could feed from blood molecules drawn at a distance. If he felt like it, he could drain half the bar without anyone noticing until the bodies started hitting the floor.

"I'm all right, Cassie." Rafe squeezed my hands and I immediately felt more centered. He always had that effect on me, maybe because he comforted me so often as a child. I'd grown up believing that, if he said something was okay, it must be true, and old habits die hard.

"Then what is it? Something's wrong." He swallowed, but instead of answering, he just looked at me pleadingly, his face dancing with neon shadows from the glass "flames" that surrounded the bar. My short-lived calm fled right out the window. "Rafe! You're scaring me!"

"That wasn't my intention, *mia stella*." His voice, usually a lightly accented tenor, was a harsh croak. He swallowed, but when he tried to speak again, he only strangled. He let go of my hands to claw at his throat, his face contorted in a rictus, and I stumbled back a step, colliding with the cool column of mist that was Billy Joe.

Some people have spirit guides, wise, serene types who give them help from the great beyond. I have a smart-aleck ex–card shark who spends more time rigging the casino games than he does advising me. Of course, considering that his mortal existence ended with him taking a header into the Mississippi, courtesy of a couple of cowboys he'd been cheating, that might not be such a bad thing.

"He's fighting a command," Billy said unnecessarily.

I shot him an impatient glance. Billy's status as the life-challenged segment of our partnership often means he knows more about the supernatural world than I do, but of the two of us, I know more about vamps. Growing up at Tony's had seen to that.

Even vampires who become masters are still bound by their own master's control—unless they reach first-level status, which most never do. But older vamps have more flexibility in interpreting commands than a newborn. A lot more, if they're smart and willing to risk punishment. And Rafe had stretched a point for me before, informing Mircea of Tony's plan to kill me even at great risk to himself. If he hadn't helped me, I'd have never lived long enough to become the Pythia.

"Tony isn't around to give any orders," I said slowly, and

some of the terrible tension left Rafe's face. The bane of both our existences was literally out of this world, hiding somewhere in Faerie. "He couldn't have forbidden you to see me—unless it's an old command."

For a long moment Rafe held himself unnaturally still, the flickering lights of the bar the only movement on his face. Then, slowly, almost imperceptibly, his head moved side to side. I glanced at Billy Joe, who had drifted off a few feet. The flames filtered through him eerily, gold and red and translucent umber. He pushed his Stetson up with an insubstantial finger. "Well, that sorta narrows it down."

I nodded. With Tony gone, there was only one person left whose commands could make Rafe choke at the mere thought of contradicting them: Tony's master.

The bar was hot and humid with too many bodies, but chills shivered down my arms anyway. Unfulfilled longing swept through me, blood and bone and skin stretched paper thin as part of me *yearned*, reaching out for someone who wasn't there. I glanced up at the sign over the bar: LEAD ME NOT INTO TEMPTATION; THAT WOULD MEAN BACKING UP. No freaking kidding.

Rafe was looking at me with big, concerned eyes. I could only think of one reason for him to be here: to ask me to see Mircea. And wasn't that just all I needed. I bit back the urge to scream. My nerves had a perpetually scraped-raw feeling these days, but it wasn't Rafe's fault. "You may as well go back," I told him unsteadily. "There's nothing I can do."

Rafe shook his head in a wild, negative motion, causing his dark curls to dance madly about his face. He looked around the room, eyes shifting in sudden darts as if he thought someone might be sneaking up on him. His nerves were showing, something he'd never been able to completely control, even at court. It had cost him more than once.

His gaze returned to my face, and there was desperation in it, but also determination. "I am not well," he said, and paused, as if waiting for something.

I blinked, fairly sure I was missing the point. Vampires don't get sick. Shot, burned, staked, yeah; the flu, not so much.

"I can summon a healer," I offered. Dante's was more than familiar with little accidents. A couple of hungry gargoyles had decided to snack on some of the animal acts the night before, only to discover that the trained wolves weren't wolves at all. The result had been a near apocalyptic battle in the lower levels that had given the on-site medical staff something to do for the rest of the night. And that sort of thing wasn't exactly unusual.

"I do not think a healer would be able to help," Rafe said slowly, his eyes brightening as no visible retribution was taken. I realized what he was up to as he looked at me eagerly. If he pretended he was talking about himself instead of Mircea, he could get around the prohibition. The thought drifted through my mind that Mircea must not be up to his usual standard, to have left such an obvious loophole.

"It doesn't matter," I said, hoping to forestall a painful explanation. "If I could do anything, don't you think I would have?" The *geis* that was putting me through hell was doing even worse things to Mircea. It strengthened depending on how long it had been in place, and due to a little accident with the timeline, he'd been dealing with it longer than I had. By about a century.

My former rival for the position of Pythia, a lunatic named Myra, had decided to remove the competition by a little creative homicide. She couldn't kill me, because there was a rule prohibiting the murderer of the Pythia or her designated heir from inheriting. But being savvy about all things time-related, Myra had worked out an alternative. If Mircea died before Tony and I had our little blowup, it would remove his protection from me, allowing Tony to do the dirty work for her.

The only problem with her plan was that it required fiddling with the time line, and my power didn't like that. It kept sending me back in time to prevent the assassination attempts. And during one of those trips, I met Mircea in a period before the *geis* was placed. The spell immediately recognized him as the other component needed to complete itself and jumped from me to him. That not only gave him the *geis* a century early, but it ensured that when he had the original spell cast on us, he ended up with two strands of it, not one. And, as I could attest, one was bad enough.

"But . . . there is no one else!" Rafe looked almost frantic at my refusal. He also looked surprised. I had a sudden rush of guilt, which was monumentally unfair. Mircea had started this, not me.

"If I knew the counterspell, I'd have cast it already," I repeated, with a little more bite to my tone than I usually used with Rafe. What did he think I'd been doing for the past week, anyway?

The book containing the only known counterspell was the Codex Merlini, a compilation of ancient magical lore that had been lost long ago—assuming it had ever existed. Most of the people Pritkin and I had contacted had been of the opinion that the Codex was nothing more than a myth. It was like the rest of the Arthurian legend, we'd been assured by one supercilious mage after another. There'd never been a Camelot, except in the imagination of a medieval French poet. And there was no Codex.

The only exception was Manassier, who'd had his own reasons for sending us on a wild-goose chase. So far, everyone else had refused to talk, didn't know anything, or was looking to get rich quick off a couple of desperate suckers. I'd been battling rising panic already, and Rafe's distress wasn't helping.

"Please, Cassie!" His voice cracked around the edges, and my stomach clenched at the almost heartbroken look on his face. If it had been anyone else—any vampire, anyway—that look would have had my paranoid instincts muttering furiously. But Rafe didn't have that kind of deception in him. At least, he never had before. And I suspected his basic character was pretty set after more than four hundred years.

"I told you, I don't have the spell," I said, more gently. "Maybe in a few weeks—"

"But I'll be dead in a few weeks!" he blurted out.

For a moment, the world tilted. There was a hollow roaring in my ears and the bar seemed to be closing in, with not enough air, not enough light. It felt like the heavy bass of

Purgatory's continuous pulse was suddenly pounding inside my skull.

Rafe stared at me soberly. "I am sorry, Cassie. I didn't intend to tell you that way."

For a moment, I just stared back, understanding whipping through my mind with a white-hot sizzle. I'd known the spell was vicious—my own reactions had been more than enough for that—but that it could go so far I'd never even considered. Mircea was a first-level master. There were only a handful of them in the world, and they were almost impossible to kill. The idea of his dying because of a spell, any spell, was crazy, but especially one that hadn't even been designed as a weapon.

"There has to be some mistake," I finally said. "I know you're suffering, but—"

"Not suffering, *mia stella*," he whispered. *"Dying."*

"But if I go to him, it'll only make things worse!"

Rafe flinched when I dropped the wrong pronoun, but it didn't stop him. "The Consul has called in experts from around the world. And you know they would not lie to her." No, I didn't suppose so. The Consul headed up the Vampire Senate, and was easily its scariest member. "I heard one tell her that if you complete the spell, perhaps it will free . . . me. But he knew of nothing else that would."

"I'll find another way," I promised, feeling sick.

Rafe looked genuinely puzzled at my refusal. Like asking me to risk a lifetime of slavery was no big deal. "I do not see what is wrong with this one. Mircea would never hurt you—"

"That's not the point! How much have you enjoyed being Tony's eternal errand boy?"

"Mircea is nothing like that *bastardo* Antonio," Rafe said, appalled.

I shook my head in frustration. No, Mircea wasn't Tony; despite the *geis*, despite everything, I knew that. But he *was* a vampire. And the one thing no vamp could resist was power. If the *geis* gave Mircea control over mine, he *would* use it. And, just like with Tony, I'd have no say about what he did with it.

Tony wanted me dead mainly because I'd set him up for the Feds. I'd had a number of reasons for helping them out, but top of the list was that he'd used my visions to point him to wherever disaster was about to strike—and therefore where an opportunity for profit was to be found. Young and naive, I'd believed him when he assured me that he wanted the information to warn the people who were soon to be in distress. When I found out what he'd really been doing with it, I'd sworn never to be used like that again. Not by him, not by anyone.

I swallowed, knowing this wasn't going to go over well. But I had to ask. "Tell me the truth, Rafe. Did Mircea send you?"

If he really was dying, it would make sense for him to send Rafe to tell me so. Mircea had saved my life by refusing Tony his revenge. I owed him one, and I would have expected him to try to cash it in.

What didn't make sense was why he would order Rafe to put on an elaborate pretense, to make me think he'd actually told him to stay away. But although Mircea looked to be in his early thirties, he was five hundred years old. And, like most of the older vamps, to call his thought processes Byzantine was a serious understatement. I'd discovered long ago that the easiest way to figure out what a vampire really wanted was to look for whatever would benefit him the most, and ignore everything else. And what would benefit Mircea was completing the *geis*.

Rafe blinked at me, and for a moment there was something lost and wide open in his expression, almost bruised. "You think I would lie to you?"

"If Mircea ordered you to, yes. You wouldn't have a choice!"

"There are always choices," Rafe said, offended. "Had I been ordered to tell you a lie—" He gave a small shrug. "I cannot help it if I am not so good an actor at times."

"But you're fond of Mircea. It might be an order you'd agree with."

He sighed in exasperation. "Mircea has many fine qualities, Cassie. I know them well. But he has flaws, too—one in particular that I hope will not prove fatal. He is stubborn. Too stubborn to listen to the Consul's experts when they tell him he cannot defeat this. Too stubborn to believe that even his power can fail. And too proud to admit it, even if he did believe!"

That did sound like Mircea. And I'd never really stopped to wonder how he would react to the *geis'* malfunctioning. If anything, I'd assumed his only thought would be to use it to get me under his power. But while I'd almost become used to my life spinning out of control, it definitely wasn't the norm for him. Mircea manipulated other people, used them to get what he or the Senate wanted. He wasn't accustomed to having anyone, or anything, do the same to him.

"And consider this," Rafe said urgently, "when you think on deception. Mage Pritkin has no reason to save Mircea. If he dies, the spell is broken. All he has to do is stall long enough for that to happen, and you are free."

An automatic denial rose to my lips, but died before I could utter it. The Codex contained some mysterious spell that Pritkin didn't want found. We'd agreed that once the book was located, I'd let him remove it before I searched it for the counterspell to the *geis*. But what if he didn't trust me? I didn't know enough about the magical community to know whom to ask for information. So all the experts we'd spoken with had been Pritkin's. Had all that "you go, I'll stay" stuff in Paris been about my welfare or an attempt to make sure I didn't find anything? What if the real reason we kept striking out was because that was what he wanted?

"I almost forgot. I have something for you." Rafe fumbled under the cloak for a moment, then brought out a small package wrapped in a piece of black felt. "The Fey returned them to Mircea. As your master, they assumed he could get them to you."

I parted the felt and into my hands dropped a ratty old pack of tarot cards. They were dirty and creased, and more than a few were missing the corners. I was a little surprised to see them, since I'd lost them while on a disastrous trip to Faerie in search of Myra. I'd been happy to get out of there alive, and hadn't worried too much about what I left behind.

A card suddenly poked up from the deck with no help from

me. "The Magician Reversed," a resonant voice began, before I shoved it back inside and slipped the pack into the pocket of my shorts. It did not add to my peace of mind.

My old governess had had the deck spelled to report on the overall spiritual climate of a situation. It was supposed to be a joke, but over the years I'd noticed that its predictions were depressingly accurate. That was a problem because, no matter how I tried to twist it, the Magician Ill-Dignified was never a good thing.

You know the guys with the three beans under the shells at carnivals? The ones with the stuffed animals that are going all moldy because they never actually give any away? The Magician Ill-Dignified is a lot like that: a salesman or con man who can make you believe almost anything. You can avoid him, but you have to be on your toes, because he will not seem like a deceiver.

The card was safely tucked away, but an image of the tiny magician's face still seemed to hover in front of me. And my imagination was giving him Pritkin's bright green eyes. I didn't know how far he was willing to go to ensure that the mystery spell stayed lost. And if Mircea died, my biggest reason for finding the Codex died with him. Maybe Pritkin didn't view a single death as too high a price to pay to keep the secret.

Especially if that life was a vampire's.

Chapter 4

R afe watched me in silence for a moment, then cleared his
throat. "There may be an alternative."

I waited, but he just sat there, his jaw working but no sound
coming out. "I'm listening."

"I can't tell you," he finally said, sounding defeated. Apparently Mircea's command hadn't been so flawed after all.

I glanced at Billy, who sighed and shrugged. He doesn't
like possessions, but they do allow him to tiptoe through
someone's thoughts, gathering stray information here and
there. And I doubted Mircea had prohibited Rafe from even
thinking about whatever it was he didn't want known.

"Drop your shields," I told him, "and hold that thought."

Rafe looked a little nervous, but since Billy slipped inside
his skin a few seconds later, he must have done as I asked. I
glanced around, wondering what the tourists would say if they
knew that a ghost was currently possessing a vampire a few
feet away. It made Dante's staged shows look a little tepid by
comparison. Then Billy stepped out of Rafe's other side,
looking freaked. "Oh, *hell*, no."

"What did you see?"

"Nothing. Not a damn thing."

"You're lying." I couldn't believe it. Billy has a lot of
flaws, but he doesn't lie. Not to me.

His jaw set and his hazel eyes looked as implacable as I'd
ever seen them. "If I am, it's for your own good!"

There are, so tradition says, four main reasons for a ghost
to appear to mortals: to reproach, to warn, to recall and to ad-

vise. I could add a few more: to annoy, to obstruct or, in Billy Joe's case, to seriously piss off. "I'll be the judge of that!" I told him angrily.

"And your judgment's been so great so far?"

"I beg your pardon?"

"Every time you get involved with the vamps, it's a bad thing." Billy held up three translucent fingers. "Tomas. 'Oh, Billy, he's just a sweet street kid who needs a home.' A sweet street kid who happened to be a master vampire in disguise, who betrayed you and almost got you killed!" A finger went down. "Mircea. 'Oh, Billy, I've known him forever, he's nothing to worry about.' Until he placed that damn *geis* on you and maneuvered you into the Pythia thing, that is." Another finger folded under, leaving me staring at a rude gesture. "See why I'm a little worried here?"

"I'm involved anyway!" I reminded him tightly.

"You won't like it."

"I already don't like it. Just tell me!" The bartender was looking at me a little funny. Probably wondering why I was yelling at the bar.

"Your buddy has been doing some investigating," Billy said, with obvious reluctance, "and heard a rumor. But it's probably no more than that. People have been speculating about the Codex for centuries—"

Rafe shook his head, then grabbed his throat again. The bartender began slowly edging away. I sent him a smile, but the expression in his eyes said clearly that he thought we were nuts. It would have bothered me less if I didn't halfway agree with him.

"Billy!"

He sighed. "The word is that the Codex was never lost, that the mages have had it all along but circulated the rumor because they didn't want anyone looking for it."

"Wonderful," I said morosely. "All I need is another run-in with the Circle."

"Cass," Billy said, almost gently, "there's more than one."

It took me a moment to understand what he meant; then my eyes automatically slid over to Rafe. "The Black has it?" I whispered in a savage undertone.

The Black Circle was a group of dark magic users, people with no scruples about how they obtained power or what they did with it. They had recently allied with some rogue vampires against the Silver Circle and the Vampire Senate, in a war that threatened to engulf the entire supernatural world. So far, I'd mostly managed to stay out of it. I really wanted to keep it that way.

At least Rafe had the grace to look slightly abashed. "I'm trying to avoid making any more enemies," I said tightly.

"And if Mircea wants to raid a dark stronghold, he has the people to do it," Billy pointed out. "He sure as hell doesn't need us."

I nodded emphatically. For once, Billy was making a lot of sense. Rafe looked lost, unable to hear Billy when he wasn't in residence, so to speak. "Mircea has a capable stable—" I began, only to have Rafe cut me off with an agitated gesture.

"None of them will do anything," he croaked, sounding half-choked. I went around the bar to get him some water.

"Why? Do they *want* him to die?"

"No!" He looked around agitatedly, but his almost yell had been lost in the thrum of music and the hum of conversation. He leaned over the bar and dropped his voice to a whisper anyway, so much so that I practically had to lip-read. "There might be a few who resent their positions, who think they could do better elsewhere, but most are wise enough to see . . ." He trailed off.

"See what?"

Rafe took the glass I handed him, but didn't drink. He put it down and started rubbing both hands across the bar top in an unconscious, distressed motion. "That with Tony gone and Mircea dead, there will be no one to protect us. The family will be ripped apart, each of us taken by other masters to add to their power base. And they won't know us, Cassie; they won't care. We'll be commodities to them, nothing more. Things to be used and discarded when we fail to please."

I mentally cursed myself for not thinking that far ahead. Of course Mircea's death would be more than a personal tragedy—his position as family patriarch ensured that. And it would be devastating for people like Rafe.

He'd never had much respect at Tony's, where a steady trigger finger counted for more than artistic genius. But at least he'd known the rules of the household and where he fit into the hierarchy. In a new family there would be a constant struggle for position—maybe for decades. And Rafe was no warrior. He might not last long enough to carve a new place for himself.

"Then why won't the family help him?" I demanded. "It's their butts on the line as much as his!"

"Because the Consul has forbidden it!" Rafe whispered. "I am risking her wrath by even being here!"

Well, that explained the nervousness. "Why would she do that? She needs Mircea alive!" As scary as the Consul was, she couldn't hope to win the war alone. The Senate was ultimately only as strong as its members, and it had already lost more than a quarter of them to combat or treachery. She couldn't afford to lose Mircea, too.

"She says that everything that can be done is being done, and that we'll only make matters worse by interfering. But I think there is more to it than that. You're the obvious person for us to seek out, and she doesn't want us to aid you."

"But I'm trying to help!" Lifting the *geis* would benefit me as much as Mircea, and if there was one thing I'd have thought the Consul understood, it was self-interest.

"I know that, Cassie. But she doesn't. She believes that you are still angry with him for placing the *geis*, and may attempt some form of revenge. She knows you don't have to help him; that once he dies, the *geis* is broken—"

"She actually believes I'd do that? Stand by and watch him die?"

Rafe's hands clenched on the bar top. "I don't know what she might think under normal circumstances. But these are not normal! We are at war, and she is afraid of losing him. Even more, she's afraid of your power. Fear is not an emotion she feels often, and when she does . . . she tends to overreact. Perhaps, if you spoke with her . . ."

I shot him a look, but didn't bother to reply. I had a suspicion that the Consul's plan to rid Mircea of the spell might involve killing the one who had placed it on him. Which, thanks to the aforementioned timeline snafu, was me.

"Mircea isn't going to die," I said, trying to convince myself as much as Rafe. "He's a Senate member, not a newborn!"

Rafe didn't answer. Instead, he held out his hand, opening the palm to reveal a slim platinum hair clip. I recognized it immediately. Unlike a lot of ancient vampires, Mircea didn't usually dress in the clothes of his youth. I'd only ever seen him in them once, and that had been to make a political statement. He preferred understated, modern attire, with the only outward sign of his origin the length of his hair. He once told me that in his day only serfs and slaves had short hair and that he'd never been able to overcome his prejudice against it. But even there he conformed to modern conventions by keeping it confined at the base of his neck in a clip. That one.

I stayed a good two feet away, desperate not to trigger a vision. Just thinking about Mircea was hard enough; I couldn't risk seeing him. But this time, my caution did no good. A wave of images crashed into me, sweeping me away.

I blinked a new scene into focus, my ears ringing from the sudden silence. Low-burning candles cast a puddle of watery gold light around a large bed, raised up several steps from the rest of the room. I had an impression of comfortable surroundings—dark wood, soft carpets and a lot of heavy antiques—but I couldn't focus on them. All my attention was taken up with the body lying on the crumpled sheets, skin china-pale next to the chocolate-colored fabric. Dark blue shadows softened the clean, strong lines, draping them with a subtle beauty completely unlike electricity. Watching the flames run orange-gold fingers along Mircea's muscles, I finally understood the allure of candlelight.

He'd unbuttoned his shirt but kept it on, and it was all he was wearing. It was plastered to him, the thin white fabric gone nearly translucent from the sweat that soaked it. I took in a swift succession of images, none of which did anything for my equilibrium: nipples drawn to tight points, stomach muscles quivering, hips slick and straining, eyes liquid amber.

His body, already taut with pain, suddenly shuddered and

twisted violently. His back arched, throwing out his chest, flexing every muscle until it looked as though his spine would break. His fingers splayed across the damp sheets helplessly, his thighs trembling as if he'd just finished a marathon. His head craned back against the mattress, teeth clenched, the tendons in his neck standing out starkly. I stared at him with a heart-squeezing ache that made me want to grab him and cling, as if that would somehow keep him safe. Instead of damning us both.

His limbs finally went slack and he sprawled on his back, still breathing hard, shivers racking him for long minutes. A few locks of glossy dark hair had stuck to his throat. Other than his eyes and the pale blue veins visible just under the skin, they were his only color.

His face was free for once of its usual pleasant mask and he looked desperately hungry, almost feral. His eyes were wide open, focused intently on the ceiling, and he was muttering something in a hoarse, indistinct voice. Then he paused, hands fisting in the damp sheets beneath him. There was a smear of blood on his lips from where he had bitten them in the seizure. He licked it away as that sharp gaze flicked about the room. Although I wasn't actually there, although he couldn't possibly see me, I was suddenly speared by a pair of feverish, fire-lit eyes.

"Cassie." My name was half caress, half groan.

I found myself at the top of the steps, as if his voice had summoned me. I didn't panic—visions are not exactly unusual for me—but this one communicated something more than mere images. I could feel everything: the slick wood of the bedpost, fragrant with beeswax; the heavy brown velvet bed curtains, trapped by a soft satin cord, and the silken fringe that edged them, sliding softly over my knuckles. I'd never had that happen in a vision.

It slowly dawned on me that I might have accidentally shifted, although that seemed impossible. Since becoming Pythia, I'd had the power under my control, not vice versa. I decided where I went, and when. I started to move back when a shaking hand lifted and slid up my thigh, feverishly warm against my skin. Of course, I could be wrong.

Mircea's hair hung limp and snarled and his cheekbones stood out sharply under bruised-looking flesh. Despite the solidity of his body, he looked worn. But the eyes were the same—burning, glittering, dangerous. The intensity in them caused me to decide that maybe I should panic a little after all, especially when my skin started prickling, and not with fear.

With no warning, my legs went out from under me. I fell into a depression already warm from his body, his scent clinging to everything like a drugging haze. The musk of it was almost a taste, surrounding me with something dark and sweet and wild. It jumbled my thoughts, my brain trying to catalog too much at once: the sheets, crisp old-fashioned linen, so finely made that they might have been silk; dust specks glittering in the candlelight like gold dust; a few drops of sweat falling from Mircea's hair and landing on my cheeks like tears; and the weight of his body over me, his thigh pressing between my legs, firm and blood warm.

He took my mouth hard, teeth and lips almost savage. He bit my lower lip until it stung, then licked the marks with quick motions that soothed only enough to leave me even more sensitive for the next bite. He growled against me, the words meaningless but the thought clear as crystal: *Mine.*

Just when I decided that there was nothing in the world but that skillful mouth, he started shaping my body with his hands, sliding over my hips and stomach, up to my breasts and shoulders, then to my throat and down again. The thin PVC conducted warmth almost as well as bare skin; every touch burned, every possessive sweep of his hands said *mine* without the need for words.

I'd been living with the hunger the *geis* caused for so long that I'd almost become used to it, almost forgotten how satisfaction felt, until the heat of his touch reminded me. His fingers tightened with bruising strength, but I barely noticed. Another teasing bite was followed by a slow, caressing kiss. My eyes slipped dreamily closed as I was marked with lips and teeth and the addictive slide of his hands.

His feelings resonated through the bond as loudly as if he'd spoken, and I could feel him hard above me. It hurt that we were still apart, still separate beings when the *geis* wanted us one. It was a deep, hollow ache, like hunger that has gone beyond starvation, past where the need is a pang to become a long, gnawing nothingness. I'd never known hunger like that for food, but I recognized it anyway. Hunger can have so many forms.

I'd spent my whole adult life starting over. I'd been constantly on the run from someone, Tony or the Senate or the Circle, never staying too long in the same place, never getting to know people because I'd soon be moving on again, leaving them behind. I'd learned not to want things, not to try to hold on to anything, because if I got used to it being there, it would be that much harder when I had to let it go. I'd watched person after person with paranoid eyes, keeping them all—potential friends, enemies, lovers—at a safe, painful distance. And all the while, the hunger grew, for someone who would stay, someone permanent, someone *mine*.

And now the *geis* was whispering, so seductively, that I could have it all: Mircea, a family, a whole world that I understood and that understood me. I might be human, but I didn't think like one. I hadn't realized how much I didn't until these last few weeks, when I'd been lost in a sea of human magic that made no sense, in human reasoning I couldn't follow and in human quarrels that might end up destroying me. I had a sudden, intense longing for cool skin, calm voices, and ancient eyes. For *home*.

Only I didn't have one of those anymore. It was just so me, I thought bitterly, stroking the sharp lines of his cheekbones with my thumbs. The only place I truly felt at home was the last place I could ever go.

My hands buried themselves in his hair, even while my brain tried to treat this like all the things I'd ever wanted and not been allowed to have. But my usual compartmentalizing and compromising weren't working. Nothing about me wanted to hear "later" or "wait" or "too dangerous," not with dark strands running through my fingers, wrapping like a silken restraint around my wrist, just as soft as they looked, and beautiful, so incredibly beautiful.

I explored his body while hunger and a deep possessiveness battled it out with a lifetime's caution. I *wanted* this, so badly. My hands shook as they rode the curve of his legs to the hollow of his knees, the crest of his thighs. It wasn't enough and it was too much. I badly needed to get out of there, but I'd never wanted to stay so much in my life.

I caught his shirt, shoved it down his arms. His shoulders were broad enough to make me stretch to bare them, the muscles knotted with tension as my hands slid over them, sweat slicking my palms. *I could have this*, I argued with myself, *just for a minute*, a few stolen seconds before I did the smart thing and got out of there.

I stroked up his biceps to the hard wings of his collarbones and the strong column of his neck. Mircea was all long, sleek lines, the angles softened by lean muscle, the classic body of a runner, a swimmer, a fencer. I reached his cheek and followed the line of his jaw, where a muscle quivered helplessly, to lips that opened beneath my touch.

His tongue slid across my fingers the way his voice had shivered across my skin as I traced the curve of that full lower lip. Our eyes met, and I felt like I could fall into that amber gaze for weeks if I let myself. I expected him to kiss me, but his lips found my collarbone instead, mouthing it lightly, his tongue sliding along the bone before moving back up to explore the vulnerable skin of my throat.

Teeth brushed against me, a small sensation precisely where a vampire would bite, but I felt no fear. Unstuck, unmoored, floating almost gravity-free, but not afraid. He withdrew slightly, his tongue making a slow, possessive glide, right over my pulse, and I once again felt teeth. They weren't the dull blade of a human's, but a razor-sharp reminder of what, exactly, was in bed with me. But I still wasn't worried. Because Mircea never bit me.

Only he'd gripped the flesh over the jugular, just hard enough for me to feel it, and he wasn't letting go. It was a light sensation, no pain, but my pulse was beating hard against the pressure of his lips and there was a claustrophobic ache when I swallowed. "Mircea," I began, and felt fangs slide into my flesh.

For a frozen moment, my heart stuttered in my chest, torn between pounding its way through my rib cage and stopping altogether. But I couldn't concentrate on what his lapse in control might mean because the pain was immediately followed by a weightless swell of pure need. He was grinding our hips together as his teeth sank deeper, bright agony broken by strobing flashes of intense pleasure, everything bleeding into a surreal wave of sensation that rose and fell with each sinuous move of his body.

I started making these *sounds*—high, strangled whimpers and faint little gasps that didn't sound like me at all. I arched as Mircea began to feed, the sensation rippling through me with an almost audible sizzle. It seemed to free some part of me that had been stretched too tight for too long, like an elastic band pulled beyond its limits. It finally broke with a snap I felt all the way to the bone, as if a dislocated joint had suddenly popped back into place. The sheer *rightness* of it caught my breath, hummed through my veins, telling me that I belonged here, right here, only here. I gasped in wonder, indescribable tension flowing out of me as I relaxed into Mircea's embrace.

I could feel my blood surging into him, warm and alive and pulsing hotly. I tried to push him away, but my hands found his shoulders instead, pulling him closer. Mircea locked one hand in my hair, bringing the other behind my hips, melding us together . . .

And then I was sitting seaside, the green-blue water lapping at my toes, half buried in the sand.

I looked around wildly, disoriented, expecting an attack from someone, somewhere. I rolled over and clutched the beach, trying to present a smaller target, and was momentarily blinded by the sun in my eyes. I froze, sure that someone would use the advantage to sneak up on me, but nothing happened. I blinked for a few seconds until I could get a clear view, but all I saw was sun and sky and sand—and, on the crest of a rocky hill, a small temple slowly crumbling to pieces.

Nothing continued to happen. After a moment, my heart stopped trying to thud its way out of my chest, and my breathing returned to something like normal. I lay there and watched a flock of little brown birds dive in and out of the temple's roof, where it looked like they had a nest. Other than the waves lapping around my ankles, they were the only things moving on the whole beach.

I finally sat up and, when nothing attacked me, got to my knees. Enough adrenaline had left my brain that I could think again, so I knew who it was that I should be seeing. The being who had once owned my power had shown himself to me before in a similar situation. He seemed to find it funny to pay his visits at the most awkward moments possible.

One of the small brown birds hopped along the sand, its feet making vague indentations that the water quickly filled in again. It ran out to the wet sand when the waves retreated, looking for whatever edible morsel they might have left behind, then raced them for the beach whenever they started back in. It finally tired of the game and hopped over to me, looking for a handout. I blinked and when I looked again, a handsome blond in a too short tunic rested on the sand beside me. For a second I thought he'd crushed the little bird, but then I realized the truth.

"It's all me, Herophile," he said, gesturing about. "The waves and the sand and, of course, the sun, although it is easier to converse in this form."

"My name is Cassandra!" I snapped.

He'd given me the name of the second Pythia at Delphi, his ancient shrine, at our first meeting. It was supposedly some kind of reign title, but I didn't feel comfortable using it when I didn't know how to do the job it represented. Not to mention that, as names go, it pretty much sucked.

"Where have you been?" I demanded. "You promised to train me. That doesn't translate into hanging me out to dry for a week! Do you know how close I just came to screwing everything up?"

"Yes. That's why I pulled you out of there." He glanced up from toying with a piece of seaweed. Unlike the last time I'd seen him, he didn't look like he'd been covered in gold dust. But I still couldn't see his face, which was merely an oval of light. It wasn't so much majestic as odd, like talking to an oversized lamp. "You can't continue this way. Something must be done about the *geis*—it's a distraction."

"A distraction?!" I could think of a lot of ways to describe it, and that wouldn't have been on the list. "Mircea is dying and I'll probably be next!"

"Not if you retrieve the Codex. The answer you seek is there."

"I know that! What I don't know is where it is or how to find it. Every lead we've had has led to a dead end—almost literally with the last one! Or weren't you paying attention yesterday?"

He finished braiding the seaweed and fastened it around my wrist, bracelet style. "If it was easy, it wouldn't be a test."

"I don't need any more tests; I need help!"

"The help you need, you already have."

"Then I guess I must have missed it!"

"You will find what you need when you need it. It is perhaps your greatest gift, Herophile. To draw people to you."

"Yeah, only they all seem to want me dead."

He laughed, as if my impending demise was the funniest thing he'd heard all day. "I promised to train you. Very well, here is your first task. Find the Codex and lift the *geis* before it causes more complications."

"And if I can't?"

"I have every faith in you."

"That makes one of us."

"You'll succeed; I'm sure of it. And if not"—he shrugged casually—"you don't deserve your position."

And then I was back, clinging to strong, bare shoulders, fingers slipping on sweat-slicked skin. Even to someone used to the abrupt way visions came and went, it was a bit of a jolt. Especially since Mircea was still feeding, and it was still amazing.

I'd never felt this connected, this anchored, this close to anyone, and I wanted it to go on forever. Only that's what it seemed to be doing, I realized after a moment. Despite the fact that my heart was thundering in my ears and little spots were swimming in front of my eyes and my breath was coming in strangled gasps, he wasn't stopping.

"Let go, Mircea," I said as clearly as I could, considering the fangs in my throat. Nothing happened, unless you counted the tightening of his hand on my hip, fever-hot even through the material. "Mircea! Unless you plan to kill me, let go!"

I pushed as hard as I could, not caring at that moment if the movement tore my neck, just wanting him off. My hands were at an awkward angle on his shoulders and my strength was no match for his, but something about the action seemed to get through. He stopped.

I could feel the hesitation in him, need warring with whatever reason he had left, and for a long moment I really didn't know which would win. Then slowly, as if he were moving underwater, he pulled back, his teeth sliding out of me cleanly.

"Cassie . . ." He looked dazed, and his voice was rough and cracked a bit at the edges. "I thought you were a dream."

I stared at him dizzily. "I think maybe I am."

He stared at me, swallowing harshly, the feverish glitter of his eyes even brighter, like an addict who has had a fix. "Then my dreams are improving."

I kissed him, a quick tangling of tongues, heat and softness. "We're working on a solution."

"I know." He paused and looked around the room, as if he was expecting to see someone or something. When he didn't, he fell back, a shudder shivering through him as he pulled away.

"You know? How?" The only answer was the tightening of his muscles under my hands.

He closed his eyes, blocking out my face. "You must go, Cassie."

It was good advice, but it made no sense that Mircea was giving it to me. I knew why I was doing my best to avoid completing the *geis*, but he had no reason to do so. It would get him out of his current torment and gain him a valuable servant. There was no downside.

"You don't want to complete the *geis*?" I asked slowly, sure I was missing something.

"No." His fists clenched in the sheets, hard enough that the knuckles showed white. "I want you to leave!"

"I don't understand—" I touched his shoulder, not thinking, my own mind still muddied from the spell, and he flinched like I'd slapped him. He jerked away from me, all the way to the other side of the bed, and sat there facing the wall. "Go, Cassie! Please."

"Yes, all right." Something weird was definitely going on, but I didn't have time to figure it out. There was a crack like a gunshot, and I jumped, then realized that no one was shooting at me. The hand Mircea had curled around the huge bedpost had snapped it in two like a twig.

In the next heartbeat, I was flying, the room swallowed by darkness behind me. I blinked hard, trying to clear my vision, and when I looked again I was back in the bar. The bartender gave a sudden start at the sight of me and fled to the back room.

I stared blankly after him, then caught a glimpse of myself in the mirror behind the bottled liquors. It reflected wide eyes, flushed cheeks and a kiss-swollen mouth. I put a hand to my neck, and it came back red. I stared at the blood on my palm, and tried to say something. I failed.

Rafe handed me a napkin and I pressed it to my throat, Mircea's kiss still throbbing on my lips. Already, the lack of his touch was a fierce ache behind my ribs, as if he'd left fingerprints on something deeper than skin. "Now do you understand?" Rafe asked softly.

I slowly nodded. That had been no vision. I'd unconsciously shifted, straight to Mircea's side. And if I'd lost that much control, how much worse must it be for him? The *geis* wouldn't kill him, I realized; it would drive him mad. And to stop hunger like that, sooner or later a person would pay any price.

Even take his own life.

Chapter 5

Crystal Gazing is not the supernatural community's most respected journalistic voice. Its tagline, "All the news that's not fit to print," pretty much says it all. But, once in a while, its scandal-hunting reporters turn up a story that the more respectable papers reject as mere rumor. And even more rarely, that rumor turns out to be true.

But so far, although there was a lot of speculation about the identity of the new Pythia, no one had managed to come up with my name. It was only a matter of time, but I was grateful for any reprieve. And the lack of new information had allowed juicier stories to bump that one to the back pages. Today's screaming headline concerned an unknown woman who'd been raiding the Circle's facilities, although as usual, the article was short on facts and long on terms like "vixen vigilante" and "fetching fanatic." I silently wished her luck. Her activities might account for why no one had yet managed to track me down.

My break was over, so I stuck the rag in my locker, getting ready to go back to work. My current time-killing activity involved Casanova's never-ending search for new ways to make a buck. He'd somehow conned an up-and-coming fashion designer into renting one of the overpriced shops in the gallery. Part of the deal had been space for a fashion show at the beginning of each new season, along with the services of the showgirls as models and enough casino grunts to handle the heavy lifting. I, of course, was one of the grunts.

A pretty brunette was at the locker next to mine, and we

paused to size up each other's outfit. Hers consisted of a lot of corpse-like paint, a necklace of skulls and a skirt composed of withered arms. They'd been cut off at the elbow, so they formed a miniskirt effect, and were moving around just enough to be creepy.

"Zombie," she told me, fixing her lipstick in the mirror on the inside of her locker.

"I beg your pardon?"

"You know, the ones that used to work upstairs?"

"I thought they'd been shredded." They'd gotten in the way of the Circle's hunt for me. And although zombies are pretty resilient as a rule, they hadn't done so well when facing a cadre of war mages.

"Well, yeah. But you know the boss. He didn't want to waste a resource."

"What are you saying?"

"He said zombies smart enough to wait tables but docile enough not to snack on the clientele are hard to come by. He's using a human waitstaff while he locates some more, but he wanted something to remind everyone that it's supposed to be a *zombie* bar, so . . ."

"He harvested their body parts for your costumes?"

"It's not so bad," she said, seeing my expression. "Except for getting felt up every time I sit down."

"What?"

She frowned down at her skirt. "One of these guys keeps goosing me. But when I complained, the bokors said they couldn't replace them all, so I'd have to figure out which one. But they all look the same."

We regarded the shriveled gray things around her waist for a moment. I managed not to shudder every time a bony finger brushed against her bare skin, but my dress wasn't so coy. As with much of the collection, it was spelled to respond to mood, with a repertoire that would make a chameleon envious. It had been showing tranquil nature scenes all morning, but now it switched to a dirty yellow-brown haze, the color of sunlight filtered through smog.

"I haven't seen that costume before," the brunette said, her eyes narrowing.

"I'm helping with the show."

"You're modeling? But they told me they didn't need any more girls."

"I'm just doing backstage stuff. But the designer wanted us to dress up, too."

"Oh. That's all right, then," she said, mollified. "I thought something was wrong. I mean, you're okay and all, just not exactly—"

"Model material?" I smiled, but my dress took on the sulfurous yellow-gray of the San Francisco skyline. Great.

"Yeah, exactly." She scrunched up her nose at the new hue. "Ugh. How do you get it back to a prettier color?"

"I'm not sure." And the designer, a pouty blond named Augustine, was not likely to approve of the change.

"Cheer up," she told me breezily. "If you're backstage, probably nobody will see you anyway." She bumped the locker closed with her hip and gave a sudden yelp when one of the waving arms goosed her. And just like that, my dress returned to the color of a nice, sunny day.

Well, that had been easier than I'd thought.

One good thing about my latest assignment had been the chance to get a friend a job. Since she didn't have a passport, a Social Security card or a strong command of the English language, I'd been wondering how she was going to earn a living. Especially since her references were about four hundred years out of date.

I found Françoise backstage and helped her into her designated dress, a solid white sheath with a long skirt and cap sleeves. It was cute, but I couldn't understand what it was doing in a collection that made even wealthy witches twitch before placing an order. Then a small dot detached itself from one shoulder, unfolded eight tiny black legs and went to work.

A row of other dots that I'd mistaken for buttons peeled away from her shoulder and followed. By the time the dress was buttoned up, the spiders had covered half the bodice with a tracery of black embroidery, as delicate and intricate as the cobwebs they mimicked. The designs were constantly being woven and unwoven, so quickly that it looked like silken fireworks were exploding all over the fabric, each blooming in a unique design before morphing into another even more elaborate.

I gazed at the dress in covetous admiration while Françoise drew on her gloves. All of the models were wearing them as a way to tie the collection together. In her case, they were long and black and did double duty, hiding the scars where, four hundred years ago, a torturer who knew his craft had left her permanently disfigured.

She'd started life in seventeenth-century France, where she'd run into the Inquisition, which hadn't approved of witches so much. She'd eluded them, only to get dragged into Faerie against her will, by slavers trying to make a fast franc selling young witches to the Fey. The scars had occurred right before the kidnapping, and her purchaser, a Fey nobleman with a jealous wife, had not dared to heal them. She'd eventually escaped to the Dark Fey, who decided that she would be more useful as a slave than as a meal. They, of course, hadn't even noticed the scars.

The whole adventure lasted only a few years from Françoise's perspective, but the Fey timeline isn't in sync with ours. By the time she managed to escape, the world she knew was long gone, making her the only person I knew that fate liked to mess with even more than me. Luckily, she was tall, dark and exotic, characteristics that hadn't been prized in her own century, which preferred women petite, fair and traditional. But in our time it had been enough to persuade Augustine to overlook her lack of credentials. It seemed that yesterday's unfashionable Amazon was today's supermodel.

Once Françoise was set, waiting for makeup she didn't need, I turned my attention to trying to corral a rogue handbag. I finally cornered it between a rack of dresses and the wall. I pounced, grabbing the scaly handle as it thrashed and wriggled and did its damnedest to claw me in the face.

Augustine appeared at my shoulder, but didn't bother to help. He watched the fight for a moment over the top of wild purple spectacles that were about to fall off his long nose. They looked like something Elton John might have worn to sing "Rocket Man," with wide frames shot through with glitter. They didn't go well with his pale blue eyes or artfully arranged curls. Of course, it was kind of hard to think of anything they would have complemented.

"There are some . . . people . . . who are demanding to see you," he informed me. "They don't have tickets, and frankly—"

"What people?" I asked, dreading the answer. I could number the ones who might consider me a friend on one hand. And except for Rafe, none of them knew where I was.

"Well, I don't know, do I?" Augustine's eyes flashed. "Why don't I stop everything I'm doing *seconds before the show* to take care of your scruffy friends, who aren't even on the guest list?"

I didn't immediately answer, because the bag was currently winning. It had already sprouted four stubby legs and a tooth-lined snout. Now a tail covered with hard jade scales protruded suddenly from the rear, giving it enough leverage to thrash out of my grasp. It dropped to the floor and hurried off after a snakeskin belt. The belt tried slithering away, but the bag caught it by the tail, swallowing the writhing thing in a couple of gulps.

I wrestled the truant fashion accessory to the floor with Françoise's help and wrapped a scarf around the snout. "What do they look like?"

"That's my point," Augustine snapped, tossing his curls. "They look like rejects from a low-budget production of *Rent*. Not to mention the *smell*. Get rid of them. Now." He flounced off in a huff.

I peered out from behind the curtain separating backstage from the catwalk, trying to spot my visitors, but it wasn't easy. The ballroom was packed with witches dressed to impress. It looked like big hats were in for summer, because at first all I could see was a field of brightly colored circles, bobbing and swaying like flowers in a breeze. There was no one in sight who looked like they smelled of anything that cost less than a hundred dollars an ounce. Then a couple of witches who had been partly blocking the view settled into their seats and I saw them.

Augustine was wrong; they weren't friends.

The music started up and the first model elbowed me out of the way, gliding onto the catwalk, her leopard-skin bag slinking along beside her. I hardly noticed, my eyes on the two figures who had squeezed in the back door. I didn't recognize them, but I knew what they were. The bulky coats they had on were a dead giveaway: war mages. And despite their scruffy appearance, I doubted they'd come to upgrade their wardrobe.

They were nonchalantly scanning the crowd, and I'd seen those casual glances on Pritkin's face often enough to know how much they took in. I moved farther into the shadow of the curtain, wondering if I could shift out unseen, when one of them nudged his companion and nodded at a group of dirty, poorly dressed children huddled against one wall. The mages started forward, faces grim, and the kids broke into a run. Most people had found their seats, so there was nothing between the kids and their pursuers except the two vamps acting as greeters.

There was a temporary alliance between the Circle and the Senate because of the war, but that didn't erase centuries of dislike and mistrust. Especially when war mages had been responsible for an attack on the premises a little over a week ago. The vamps blocked the way with insolent smiles on their faces, and the mages skidded to a halt.

The kids had run down the aisle flanking the wall and were now climbing onstage. Most people were watching the catwalk, which had been designed to extend out into the middle of the room, so they didn't garner more than a few puzzled glances. They headed straight backstage, but stopped on the edge of the frenetic activity.

They looked back and forth between me and several blonde models who were struggling into their outfits. Then a black boy of maybe fourteen nudged a small girl. "Which one?"

The girl had dishwater blond hair and big brown eyes that focused on me unerringly. "That one." She pointed with the hand not clutching a beat-up teddy bear.

The bag in my arms made a sudden lunge, causing me to almost lose my grip. Françoise said something that didn't sound French and it froze, a shiny black claw all of an inch from my face. "You want for me to take the crocodile?" she asked.

"Sounds like a plan." I passed the wicked thing over gratefully.

The boy looked at the girl with a dubious expression. "You sure?"

She nodded and went back to chewing off the bear's head. The boy walked over and held out a hand. The T-shirt he was wearing was thin and shot with pinholes, and his jeans were out at one knee. One of his tennis shoes had lost its lace and was being held together with a safety pin, and a ratty old sweatshirt was knotted around his waist. But the handshake was firm and he met my eyes. I had a weird sense of déjà vu, even before he spoke.

"I'm Jesse. Tami sent us."

"Tami?"

"Tamika Hodges."

I stared at him, feeling like someone had just kicked me in the gut. He stared back, dark eyes defiant, expecting to be ignored, rejected, thrown to the wolves. I recognized the look. A decade ago, I'd been about his age, and just as scared, just as defiant, just as sure I couldn't trust anyone. For the most part, I'd been right.

Years before I decided to destroy Tony, my ambition had been just to get away from him. I'd ended up in Chicago, because that was where the bus I'd caught happened to stop. As someone who had rarely been allowed to leave Tony's compound outside Philly, and then only with half a dozen bodyguards, I found my new freedom to be a very scary thing. I had money, thanks to a generous friend, but I was afraid to stay somewhere decent, sure that I would wake up to find a couple of Tony's goons looming over me. Not to mention that it's a little hard for a fourteen-year-old to check into a hotel on her own. So shelters it had been.

I soon discovered that there were a few problems associated with shelter life. Besides the drunks and the druggies and the knife fights, there were also limits on the length of your stay. The more long-term variety had a staff who might report a teenager on her own to the authorities, so I tended to gravitate to the two-week versions. That was long enough to get comfortable but not long enough for anyone to get to know me.

Most of this type kept records, though, and once your time was up, you weren't allowed to return for six months. The time limit was necessary to keep people from taking up permanent residence, but it also ensured that I went through all of the nicer shelters in a matter of months. I finally ended up in one that was so overcrowded, a third of us were living in a dirt-floored courtyard with a fence around it. Everyone was issued a sleeping bag at night and told to find a spot outside. The bigger and tougher crowd laid claim to the straggly grass and soft patches of dirt, leaving the hard concrete patio to the newbies and the junkies and the crazy old lady who made bird noises all night.

I'd woken up one morning to the feel of a cold arm next to mine, belonging to a young guy who'd OD'd in his sleep. It was the same day Tami showed up, on one of her regular sweeps looking for kids who had slipped through the cracks of the magical world. When a pretty African American woman with kind brown eyes and a voice that seemed much too big for her small frame offered me a place to stay, she hadn't had to do much talking. Only a couple of minutes after meeting her, I was dragging my backpack across the dirt to her beat-up Chevy.

Luckily, Tami had been legit, taking me to join a motley crew of other strays who jokingly called themselves the Misfit Mafia. The name made me do a double take the first time I heard it, but after a while it seemed oddly fitting. I'd run from one mafia to another, but with a definite difference: the new one tried to keep people alive instead of the reverse.

I eventually left the group to return to Tony, in order to try to take him down, and by the time I finally had all my plans in place, three years had passed. And then there was the blowup and the missing don and the bounty on my head, not to be confused with the shiny new one the Circle had recently laid. With one thing and another, it had been more than three years before I returned to the abandoned office building we'd called home. And all I found was echoing space, dirty windows and dust-covered floors.

I don't know why it was such a surprise. The magical underground changes fast, with three years being more like three decades. I'd stayed in Chicago a few days anyway, feeling restless and strangely anchorless. I hadn't dared to contact Tami after returning to Tony's, for fear he'd find out and take revenge on her for helping me. But subconsciously I'd always assumed that I would return one day and that nothing would have changed. And now that it had, I wasn't sure what to do about it.

Growing up in a place where any sign of weakness was quickly exploited, I'd learned how to bury inconvenient emotions, not how to release them. When even the youngest vamp was better than a lie detector at sensing physiological changes—a slightly elevated heart rate, the tiniest catch in breath, the too rapid blink of an eye—you learned self-control or you didn't last long. I discovered in Chicago that a lifetime of practice is hard to reverse, even when you don't need that skill anymore.

I'd roamed aimlessly around a few old haunts, including the bakery where she'd worked, but nothing had looked the same and I didn't recognize any of the people. After a few days, I realized that Chicago hadn't been home; Tami had, and she was gone. So I left some flowers in a corner of the old building, even knowing I was just feeding the rats, and moved on.

"How did you know where to find me?" I asked Jesse.

"Jeannie knew. She sees stuff sometimes. She said you'd help us."

"Jeannie's a clairvoyant?"

"Yeah. She not very good. She don't see much and mostly it's stupid stuff. She's only five," he said disparagingly. "But Tami thought it was a good idea. She said we was to go to you, if something happened to her. After it all went down, we got on the bus."

"After what went down?"

"The mages came. They took her." Black eyes bored into mine, already anticipating the answer to a question he hadn't yet asked. I knew that look, too. I understood a thing or two about betrayal.

"I'll take care of you," I heard myself say, and wondered if I was crazy. So far, it had been a chore just looking after myself. Tami must have been desperate to send them to me, when I had the biggest target on my back of anyone. I wanted to ask a thousand questions, but there wasn't time. I'd get some answers, but first we had to lose their pursuers.

I peered around the side of the curtains again to see that Casanova had joined the vamps holding off the mages. He was wearing a vest that jumped and crackled with animated flames—part of the menswear line, I assumed. It set off his dark hair and olive complexion nicely, but didn't do much for his expression. War mages weren't his favorite people. But while he could give them a hard time, he couldn't throw them out without cause, and they were between us and the exits.

I did a swift count of the gang, which numbered eight in total. Nine, I corrected, as the baby a girl was clutching a little too hard started to sniffle. Way too many to shift.

I glanced at Françoise. "I could use a diversion."

" 'Ow beeg?" she asked casually.

"Beeg."

"D'accord."

She moved to the other side of the stage and started chanting something under her breath. Within seconds, a bank of dark clouds rolled in, settling over the catwalk with complete disregard of the fact that we were indoors. Chairs were knocked over as people scrambled to their feet, and the background murmur almost instantly became a roar. The witches apparently knew a bad sign when they saw one.

The mages suddenly stopped playing nice, shoved identification in Casanova's face and started up the aisle at a run. That was about the same time that something slimy and green hit the catwalk. I didn't even have a chance to identify it before a lot of other somethings followed, bursting out of the rumbling black mass of clouds like popcorn. The current model's pretty chiffon dress went from a pleased peach to an angry dark green, a hue that almost matched the skin of the toad that had slammed into her shoulder.

She screamed as part of it started oozing down her chest, and she stumbled back down the catwalk. But as it was fast being littered with little broken bodies, most smashed and split open, it was pretty much inevitable that she'd slip and go sliding on her butt. Things sort of went downhill after that.

Protective spells were being fired off on all sides, which, when they impacted the kamikaze amphibians, caused fleshy fireworks in midair. This made the witches in the middle of the room, who were being liberally splattered with frog guts, even less happy, causing them to turn on their sisters with abandon. That slowed down the mages, but I could still see them, grim and determined, wading through the fracas toward us.

"Are there any more of you?" I asked Jesse.

He said something, but I couldn't hear him over the sound of the audience's chairs smashing into the battered mages. Of course, they were slamming into a lot of other things, too, blown here and there by the wind and the spells and the mayhem. But I didn't notice anyone else disappearing under a mountain of expensive painted wood. It looked like the mages had stepped on one too many witches' toes.

"What?"

"No!" Jesse screamed in my ear. "We were the only ones who got away!"

"Okay. Let's get away again."

Chapter 6

Miranda took one look at my dress, which had shifted to an agitated swirl of autumn leaves, and her ears went back. It was convenient to have such an obvious hint to her mood, since I'd never learned to read her very well. The fur on her catlike face might have had something to do with that, or possibly gargoyle expressions were too different from human ones for me to decipher.

The current group of Misfits crowded in behind me, leaving dirty footprints on her pristine white tile floor. I'd brought them to the room-service kitchens since I wasn't sure where Miranda lived. She was the leader of the group of Dark Fey that Tony had been using for cheap labor, but I only ever saw them at work, chopping and dicing with preternatural speed or pushing laden carts through Dante's halls.

They rarely paused except to pose for photographs with guests, who assumed they were midgets in suits. I wondered if anyone ever noticed that their film always came out slightly blurry, the same way their eyes never quite managed to focus on the small servers. Tony had spent a fortune to ward the casino, although considering the amount of alcohol that the majority of the guests put away, he probably hadn't needed to bother. I doubted he'd been so generous in accommodations for his workers, so what I wanted from Miranda was likely to hurt.

One of the kids, a girl who looked about twelve but who I later learned was sixteen, was holding a baby. It was maybe four months old and a little rumpled around the edges, wearing a pink T-shirt with a diaper and only one sock, its cheek flushed from being pressed against the girl's chest. I was about to launch into my carefully prepared speech when Miranda smiled, showing sharp fangs in her long, grave face. She was no longer looking at me.

I turned to see that several gargoyles had edged to within arm's length of the girl, close enough that she sent me a pleading look while clutching her infant tighter. "They won't hurt you," I assured her. "The Fey . . . well, they're really fond of babies."

It was a ridiculous understatement, as was becoming obvious. One of the larger gargoyles, with a dog's head above her spotless chef's whites, almost ran into a wall because she was waving at the infant while making a cutesy little face. Miranda's eyes were also fixed on the child, with enough longing in them that I started to worry. "Right?" I gave her a poke, and she swatted a paw at me. The claws weren't extended, thankfully.

"My people would defend a crèche with their lives," she told the mother with quiet dignity.

The girl looked relieved, but kept an eye on the closest gargoyle. He was one of the smaller variety, with floppy donkey ears under a tall chef's hat. He tentatively stretched out a hand mangled even more than Françoise's, with all but one finger missing. But the remaining digit ended in a long, curled claw of dense grayish black.

His hand was shaking, causing an iridescent shimmer to slide up and down the surface of the claw like an oil slick. The baby noticed the pretty colors and gurgled, reaching for it. The creature snatched it away in a blur of motion, letting out a bleat and falling backwards over its own squat tail. This, of course, further intrigued the baby, who fussed until her mother put her down, then crawled toward Donkey Ears with the intent of a hunter after prey, her one sock trailing and her chubby hand extended. The gargoyles retreated in a mad scramble.

Donkey Ears found himself trapped between the ferocious baby and a bank of ovens, which were filling the room with the scent of cinnamon and butter. Maybe that was what attracted the kid, or possibly she was just curious; either way, she crawled fearlessly up to the cowering creature and held up her hands demandingly. He stared at her with big eyes until Miranda cleared her throat. Then he snatched up the child, who made a contented sound and fisted her hands in his tunic before stuffing most of his scarf into her mouth.

My job wasn't too difficult after that.

Ten minutes later, we were gathered around the prep counter, wolfing down cinnamon rolls and milk. The kitchen staff had been feeding me up for a week. It had taken me most of that time to realize that they weren't being kind: I was their resident guinea pig, someone to let them know what recipes worked and what didn't. Apparently gargoyles don't have the same taste buds as humans. And now they had a whole slew of new taste testers on whom to experiment.

Despite the disruption caused by nine hungry kids descending on a sugar feast, I did try to explain. "Miranda, I appreciate this, but before you agree to babysit, there are a few things you should know."

Miranda didn't comment. She had appropriated the baby from her terrified underling and was spooning applesauce into the child's face at an alarming rate. She let out a small purr of approval when the little girl failed to spit up.

"See, the thing is . . ." Jesse, who was already on his third cinnamon roll, shot me a sharp look. It clearly said, "Do not screw this up for us." I swallowed, but plowed on nonetheless. "The kids who end up as runaways in our world usually have . . . well, there are reasons."

"Like with us," she murmured, clearly not listening to me.

"Yes . . . sort of." The gargoyles had fled Faerie because of prejudice and escalating violence, both of which were certainly familiar to Tami's kids. But out of their usual element, the Fey were likely far less powerful than the Misfits. "Look, if you're going to help me shelter these kids, at least until I can figure something else out, you need to understand—"

I stopped because a sharp toe connected with my shin. I shot Jesse a look, but he was already out of his chair. "I gotta talk to you," he said pointedly.

I rubbed my leg and scowled. "Fine."

We ended up outside, sitting beside the loading ramp used to bring larger items into the kitchen's storerooms. A couple of gargoyles were down below, scattering bread crumbs on the asphalt, peering upward hopefully. "What're they doing?" Jesse asked.

I'd wondered about that, too, until I'd spent a little time in the kitchens. "Let's just say that baked goods are usually okay around here, but eating meat requires a certain sense of adventure."

He nodded, then remembered that he was supposed to be pissed at me. "What's the big deal? Are you *trying* to ruin this for us?"

It looked like Jesse was a proud graduate of Tami's course on the Best Defense. Unfortunately for him, so was I. "I am *trying* to be honest with Miranda about what she's letting herself in for. I think that's only fair, don't you?"

He jerked a thumb at the nearest gargoyle, which had a feline head that contrasted oddly with a lumpy, reptilian body. "You think we could hurt *them*?"

"I think the bunch I used to run with could."

One day in particular came to mind. A couple of drug dealers, who had set up shop in the bottom floor of our building, had decided they could do without additional squatters. They burst in one morning after Tami went to work. I'd been babysitting Lucy, an eleven-year-old empath, and Paolo, a twelve-year-old Were who had been abandoned by his pack. I never knew why, because he hardly spoke the whole time he was with us, which wasn't long. We found his mangled body a couple of weeks later, after he fled our protection in advance of the full moon. The Weres had been smart enough not to come in after him, and waited until he left. The dealers weren't so wise.

Not that they had a chance to find out what even a young Were can do. Lucy had been home with me for a reason. Most of the kids who ended up at Tami's magical halfway house held things together pretty well for a while. They tried to fit in and avoid calling attention to themselves while they figured out how things worked, so they wouldn't screw up and be sent away yet again. But something always set them off sooner or later, usually after they'd been there long enough to start to relax.

When they finally lowered their defenses, it all spilled out: rage at the condition that made them a pariah from birth, pain that the people they loved had turned on them, terror that any minute they'd be caught and dragged back to the special schools that were more like jails. They were supposed to stay there until they were certified safe, as no threat to the magical or non-magical communities. Most would never leave.

Tami had thought that the breakdowns were positive, letting the kids get it out of their systems and start to heal. Only none of them had previously involved an empath. Especially one who could not only read emotions, but could project and magnify them.

The other kids had fled, off to find somewhere, anywhere, else to be until it wore off. Tami had been frantic, needing to go to work as she was virtually our only income, but not daring to leave Lucy alone in that state. I'd volunteered to stay with her because she seemed to find being around me soothing. After a childhood monitoring my emotions at Tony's, I didn't project as much as most people. But that day, it hadn't made a difference.

I'd been watching the door with steadily mounting panic as wave after wave of emotion crashed into me, most of it too close to what I dealt with every day to be easily shrugged off. Paolo, who had stayed behind because he was trying to avoid leaving scent trails for his pack, had been almost literally climbing the walls. And we both had shields.

When they burst in, the dealers ran straight into the wall of pain Lucy had been building all afternoon. The feelings she'd suppressed since her family had dropped her off at her new "school," then driven away and never come back, had all spilled over. And her talent had magnified them a few hundred times. Instead of frightening us or whatever the men had planned, they ended up shooting each other to death in a fit of someone else's rage.

Jesse was watching me narrowly. "You think *we're* the monsters, don't you?"

I blinked at him. I'd almost forgotten he was there. I didn't let myself think about Tami's too often, and it felt odd to do it now. "I have a broader definition of normal than most people," I finally said. "But you know as well as I do that having you here could cause . . . some issues."

Jesse stuck his chin out. "Astrid's a null," he said sullenly.

"Astrid?"

"The girl with the kid."

"Ah." So that was why Françoise had gone to the far side of the stage to work her spell. Nulls exerted a dampening field on magic for a space around them. For the stronger, it could be up to a city block in size; for the weaker, it was much smaller. But even a low-level null would have interfered if she was close.

"That's how she got away, after she found out about the kid. They couldn't track her."

I nodded. Nulls weren't automatically incarcerated like some mages with malfunctioning magic, because they weren't considered a threat. But if Astrid had been discovered pregnant, a lot of pressure would have been put on her to terminate it, so as not to pass malfunctioning genes along. No wonder she'd run. And nulls were damn hard to find when they didn't want to be.

Tami was a low-level null herself, which had helped her to keep the Misfits safe and the chaos to a minimum, at least when she was at home. And her abilities ensured that any runaways she took in didn't have to worry about registering on a magical tracking spell. Which made it strange that, after so many years, the mages had caught up with her now.

"Okay. I'm relieved to hear that." And I was. Astrid's presence might help tone things down, but she couldn't be everywhere, and there were seven kids to watch besides the baby. I needed to know what I was taking on. "But we both know that not everyone here is a null."

Jesse kicked concrete with his heel and said nothing. "Jesse."

"I'm a fluke, okay?" he blurted, in the same tone someone might once have used to say "leper."

"That doesn't tell me much." "Fluke" is a catchall term for

magical oddities dealing with what humans call luck. Not good luck, not bad luck, just . . . luck.

A famous example, even among norms, is the odd experience of the French writer Émile Deschamps. In 1805, he was treated to some plum pudding by a stranger, Monsieur de Fortgibu, at a Paris restaurant. Ten years later, he saw plum pudding on the menu of another establishment and tried to order some, only to have the waiter tell him that the last dish had just been served, to a customer who turned out to be de Fortgibu. Much later, in 1832, Deschamps was once again offered plum pudding at a restaurant. He laughingly told his friends that only de Fortgibu was missing to make the cycle complete—and a moment later de Fortgibu showed up.

Of course, what the history books don't say is that de Fortigbu was a fluke. His magic associated certain things with particular people, places or events. Every time he saw one of his cousins, for instance, she was wearing blue; the scent of oranges accompanied every visit to his favorite bookseller; and if he got within a few yards of Deschamps, pudding invariably appeared.

Most humans claimed that events like these were mere coincidence. Magical healers, on the other hand, speculated that they were somehow linked to memory. Images of people or places are stored in everyone's brain in connection with some type of sensory data. A flower a man's grandmother liked, for example, might make him think of her whenever he saw one. Being a mage, de Fortgibu had simply carried that to a new level: his malfunctioning magic insured that when one cue appeared, the other also did.

But not all flukes had magic that manifested itself in the slightly batty but mostly nonthreatening way of de Fortgibu's. One young man caused massive undertows whenever he got within five miles of the shore and had to be banned from any access to the beach. Another caused seismic activity and was restricted from going anywhere near an active fault line. That particular group of flukes was memorable enough to deserve their own name: jinx.

A jinx was basically a walking Murphy's Law, with "accidents" caused by out-of-control power cropping up on a regular basis. And unlike the random stuff that most flukes caused, a jinx's actions were invariably harmful. There was a time, a few hundred years back, when they'd been killed on sight. I really, really hoped that wasn't what I was dealing with here. Not that Jesse was likely to admit it, if it was.

"How strong are you?" A jinx of any type was dangerous, but a strong one would be a walking disaster. Literally.

"Not strong," he assured me fervently. "Not strong at all! And I'm the only one. The others are . . . pretty harmless."

"Uh-huh." None of the kids, most of whom appeared to be around seven or eight, had looked like a threat. But, then, neither had Lucy. "Define 'pretty harmless.'"

"If you're gonna throw me out, just do it!" Jesse said furiously. "But the others are okay. I'll clear out if you'll let them—"

"I didn't say I wanted you to leave! I just want to know what I'm dealing with here."

Magical children didn't fall through the cracks for no reason. It was almost a certainty that the kids all had some kind of talent that made them persona non grata in the magical community. Yet Jesse would admit only to a null, a fluke and a seer, swearing that the other five were just scrims, the current PC term for mages with little ability. I had my doubts. Scrims formed the largest population of magical runaways, but Tami hadn't concentrated on them when I knew her because they didn't have handicaps that could benefit from a null's calming influence. They could also pass for norms, avoiding the magical community and its laws altogether if they chose. That was not an option for people like Lucy.

But doubts or no, I couldn't force him to tell me the truth. And with Astrid around, hopefully it wouldn't matter anyway. Her power should negate the kids' abilities, whatever they were, as long as they stayed close. Giving me time to find out what had happened to Tami.

I decided to change the subject. "How did the mages find you?"

Jesse shook his head. "I don't know. They just busted in one morning and Tami screamed at us to run. Astrid tried to drain them, but there were too many and they had guns. She didn't stand a chance."

"But she got away."

"'Cause they didn't want her. They were all about Tami. They hardly even looked at the rest of us until they caught her."

"Why?"

Jesse fidgeted with the sleeves on his god-awful pea green sweatshirt. "Uh, I don't know?"

"That sentence would work a lot better without the question mark at the end," I said dryly.

When he stubbornly stayed silent, I sighed and gave in— for the moment. If and when he learned to trust me, his memory might improve. Any lies now would only make it that much harder for him to admit the truth later.

"I'll see if I can find out what happened to Tami," I told him. "I know a few people who may be able to tell me if the Circle has her." Jesse's expression clearly said that he didn't give much for my chances. Knowing the Circle, neither did I.

We got up to rejoin the others, but were stopped at the door by a small parade. A line of little bird bodies was climbing out of a large trash can and slowly lurching inside. They'd obviously been in the trash for good reason: no feathers, skin or even flesh was in evidence, just brittle bones held together by cartilage and, apparently, thin air.

Jesse said a word I'd have preferred he didn't know at his age, and looked at me fearfully. "He doesn't do it all the time, only when the baby's fussy or . . . or something."

I followed the trail of pigeon corpses inside, where they joined a bunch of others, who were doing an odd shuffling motion on the floor around Miranda. I finally realized it was supposed to be a dance. The baby was happily waving a sauce-covered spoon at them, while a maybe eight-year-old Asian boy grinned proudly.

"Necromancer?" I asked softly.

Jesse scuffed a shoe over the now quite filthy tile. "I forgot about him."

"Uh-huh." I wondered what else he'd "forgotten."

I explained the situation as well as I could to Miranda.

"Yesss, okay," she hissed, wiping a lump of sauce off the baby's chin. "Yum, yum, yum." The little girl burbled at her and Miranda bared her fangs in the closest she could get to a smile. I gave up.

I cautioned Jesse to see that everyone stayed out of sight and close enough to Astrid to decrease the likelihood of any accidents. Then I went looking for my partner. I needed to clear a few things off my to-do list before I had to start keeping it in volumes.

Chapter 7

Finding Pritkin wasn't difficult. He and one of his buddies were where they'd been most of the week—holed up a storeroom in the lower levels of Dante's, poring over ancient tomes. When I opened the door, he looked up from a giant volume with the trapped expression of a hunted animal. His hair, which usually defied the laws of physics, was hanging in dispirited clumps and a smear of red decorated his forehead and one cheek, courtesy of the book's disintegrating leather binding. I'd gotten the impression that research wasn't his favorite thing. Maybe because he couldn't beat up the books.

"What are you doing here?" he demanded.

"Show was canceled."

Nick looked up from the middle of a ring of books, scrolls and, incongruously, a modern laptop. He appeared harmless, a bespectacled redhead with so many freckles that he almost had a tan, his hands and feet too big for the rest of him, like a Great Dane puppy. But the gangly young man was actually a mage, and since he was a friend of Pritkin's, he was probably a lot more dangerous than he looked.

He took in my ensemble, which had settled on a watery gray afternoon. A few random orange blossoms scattered across the silk intermittently, as if blown by gusts of wind. It looked a little tired. "Any particular reason?"

"It's raining."

Nick's eyebrows drew together. "I thought you were showing in the ballroom."

"Frogs," I clarified.

The small doll-like creature perched on a stack of books at Nick's elbow finally bothered to acknowledge my presence. "Did you say *frogs*?"

"Kinda put a damper on things."

Nick glanced at Pritkin, who sighed. "Go." Nick didn't need to be told twice. Maybe he was tired of research, too.

His diminutive companion rolled her eyes and went back to ostentatiously ignoring me. The pixie, named Radella, was a liaison from the Dark Fey king. By "pixie" I mean a tiny, foul-tempered creature who made even Pritkin look diplomatic, and by "liaison" I mean spy. She was here to do two things: drag Françoise back into slavery and make sure I didn't cheat on the deal I'd cut with her king. He wanted the Codex, too, and figured I was the gal to get it for him. The pixie looked like she was starting to have her doubts.

She wasn't the only one. I'd agreed to the king's proposal for a number of reasons. I'd been in his territory and under his control, so saying no might have been very unhealthy. I'd needed room and board for a friend, a vampire named Tomas, in the one place where even the Senate's long arms couldn't reach. And the king had promised me help in solving the biggest riddle of my life.

Tony had always avoided telling me anything about my parents. My guess was that he'd assumed I might be a little upset if I learned about the car bomb he'd used to kill them, thereby allowing him to keep my talents all to himself. Or maybe he'd just felt like being a bastard. He always had liked combining business with pleasure.

It was the same vindictiveness that had led him to decide that merely killing my father wasn't good enough. He'd been an employee of Tony's, one of the humans kept around to manage things in daylight, but he'd refused to hand me over when ordered. And no one ever told the boss no and got away with it. So Tony paid a mage to construct a magical trap for my father's spirit, allowing him to continue the torment from beyond the grave.

I hoped to pry Tony's trophy from his cold dead fingers someday, but that required finding him first. And my last trip into Faerie had proven that I was no match for the Fey.

Without the dark king's help, I would never get anywhere near the bolt-hole Tony had found for himself. And for some reason, the king wanted the Codex as much as I did. A fact that worried me more than a little whenever I let myself think about it.

"What happened to your neck?" Pritkin demanded.

My hand went to the scarf I'd tied over the puncture marks. One edge of the gauze pad I'd put over the wound was sticking out above the chiffon. Trust Pritkin to notice, and to comment. "Cut myself shaving."

"Very funny. What happened?"

I hesitated, trying to think up a good lie, and Pritkin snorted. I sighed. "Mircea happened."

"Where is he?" Pritkin was halfway to his feet before I shook my head.

"Relax. I went to him, not vice versa."

"You went to him? Why?!"

My fingers made patterns in the dust on a nearby book's cover. The skin below was old and flaking, and looked vaguely reptilian. I pulled my hand away and resisted an impulse to wipe it on my skirts. "I accidentally shifted."

"How do you *accidentally*—"

"Because it's getting worse!" I tried to read his scribbled notes, but they were in some language I didn't know. "Any luck?"

"No." He saw my expression. "I told you this could take some time."

"And what am I supposed to do in the meantime? I'm sick of waiting tables and doing fill-in work for Casanova. Some days I feel like I'm going out of my mind!"

"Going?" the pixie muttered.

Pritkin was staring at the stacks of books as if they'd just insulted his mother. He finally pulled out a huge blue one from the bottom of a pile. "You aren't in any immediate danger, as long as you don't have any more 'accidents' involving Mircea."

"And what about him?" I demanded. "It's getting worse."

"He's a master vampire. He can take it."

Instead of replying, I reached across the table to remove

the top from the small white pot by Pritkin's elbow and looked pointedly inside. The inch of liquid it held was faintly green, with a pleasing floral scent. Chrysanthemum, as a guess. I glanced up to see him giving me the evil eye.

"Don't think I don't know it was you."

I'd had Miranda start replacing the black syrup he called coffee with something more organic two days ago, after the last time he got tanked on caffeine and bit my head off. I was pretty sure he was cheating, but I didn't call him on it. I honestly didn't think he could survive without his daily fix—or, to be more accurate, that nobody could survive *him* without it.

"You're the best argument for decaf I've ever seen," I said. "And, honestly, you don't find anything weird about eating bean sprouts and tofu and drinking twelve pots of coffee a day—?"

"My record is six."

"And I thought you Brits liked tea. But maybe water would be—"

He snatched the pot away. "I need that!"

I got a better look at him and decided he might be right. He might have had a chat with a shower recently, but not a long one. His eyes were red, and when he moved his head just right, the light showed a fine coating of reddish-blond stubble on his cheeks and chin. Add that to a T-shirt and jeans that he appeared to have slept in, and he was looking rough, even for him.

"You need to get some sleep," I heard myself say. "You look like crap."

"And who will handle things then?"

"Nick and me." Pritkin shot me a look and I bristled. "I'm not a trained researcher, but there has to be *something* I can do."

"Yes, you can get me some damn coffee!"

I told myself that throwing something at his head, however richly deserved, wouldn't help matters. He'd probably dodge anyway. "The vampires heard a rumor that the dark mages might have the Codex."

"How helpful. Did Mircea tell you that before or after he almost drained you?"

"*Rafe* told me."

"Good to know you're keeping up with the family."

"What is your problem?"

Pritkin ignored me. "I don't suppose 'Rafe' also had an address?"

"No. But you must have *some* idea—"

"Dark mages never stay in one place for long. If finding them was easy, we'd have destroyed them by now!"

"There must be rumors."

"There always are. And by the time the Corps hears them and sends a team in, the dark have long since decamped—and often left us a nasty surprise."

The "Corps" was the official term for the war mages, the enforcement arm of the Silver Circle, who tended to be a lot more fanatical about their jobs than human police. They really did have a license to kill, and they believed in exercising it. I didn't want to deal with any group that regularly made the Corps look bad. But if they had the Codex, I didn't have much choice.

"You're not going to find them in dusty old books," I pointed out. "What are you doing down here?"

The pixie flipped over a page in one of the larger volumes. She had to plant her feet and use both hands to manage it. "We'd explain," she panted, "but it requires words of more than one syllable."

"Trying to find another solution to that *geis* of yours," Pritkin replied.

"By doing what?"

"By attempting to create a spell that can break it." He wasn't even looking at me as he said it, but had already gone back to scanning another arcane passage.

I reminded myself sternly that Pritkin was a friend. It was easier to think of him that way than to be constantly frustrated by the fact that I wasn't allowed to murder him. "We already know where the counterspell is. It's in the Codex!"

"The *geis* was doubled, if you recall," Pritkin said curtly.

"Then we'll cast it twice!"

"Magic doesn't work like that. Do you recall what happened when you went back in time and met a Mircea who did not yet have the *geis*?"

"It jumped from me to him," I said impatiently. Pritkin hardly needed to ask, considering that he'd been there at the time.

"Doubling the spell and setting up the feedback loop you now have."

"Yes, but with the counterspell—"

"You act as if there are still two distinct spells, when that is by no means certain!" he snapped.

"I don't understand." I kept my temper because it was rare that I could get him to talk about this at all, and I wanted answers.

"The *geis* was designed to be adaptable. That was its chief strength, but the adaptability also made it too unstable for most uses. Often, it changed from the original spell to something new over time, adapting to meet the needs, or what it perceived as the needs, of the caster."

"You sound like it can think."

"No more than a computer program can. But like a sophisticated program, it does adapt to new input."

"Like what?"

Pritkin's green eyes met mine coolly. "The spell itself is logical. What its designer failed to take into consideration is that most people are not. They are often confused about what, exactly, they really want, and the spell does not differentiate between hidden thoughts, subconscious desires, and acknowledged ones."

"What are you saying? That I'm trapped in this because I want to be?!"

"Not now, perhaps, but—"

"I don't want Mircea to die!"

"Yes, but that was not the point of the spell, was it? It was designed to bind two people together."

I stared at him, horrified. Was that why the spell had jumped from me to Mircea in the past, because I'd secretly wanted it to? If I'd been less attracted to him, or more in control of myself, could all this have been avoided?

"And it has been unsupervised for more than a century, doubtless growing and changing all the while." Pritkin went on relentlessly. "It is very likely that you are seeking the counter to a spell that no longer exists."

I stared at him, feeling panic well up in my throat, dark and bitter. Being under Tony's thumb most of my life had taught me not to try to control my surroundings; instead, I'd controlled the only thing I could: myself. The idea of having that last small freedom removed frightened me on more levels than I'd known I had.

"You're saying the counterspell won't work."

"You changed the parameters of the *geis* when you doubled it," Pritkin repeated. "It may well have become something with which the counterspell was not designed to deal. And if so, finding the Codex will do you no good at all."

I didn't reply for a long moment, just stared into clear green eyes that met mine unflinchingly. What he was saying sounded scarily plausible, but how did I know he was telling the truth? How could I be certain that this wasn't an attempt to persuade me to stop searching for something he didn't want me to find in the first place? It was hard to believe him when I had another authority telling me the exact opposite, assuring me that the Codex would fix everything and making finding it my first official duty.

"No good?" The pixie fluttered in front me, her little face gone livid. "It will keep my king from killing you!"

An image of the Dormouse from *Alice in Wonderland* suddenly flashed across my vision. I looked at the teapot longingly, wondering if she'd fit. Maybe if I pushed.

"I haven't forgotten our deal," I told her tersely. "And I don't respond well to threats."

"And I don't make them! You made a deal with him, human. You do not want to find out what he'll do if you break it!"

I glanced at Pritkin, who was being oddly silent, only to see that he'd gone back to his research. Apparently, thoughts of my possible death at Fey hands weren't enough to hold his attention. I slammed a hand down on the tabletop just to see him jump. "The Consul already has every magical authority in the book working to try to find a way around this thing! Why do you think you'll have more luck?"

"Because I must."

"That's not an answer!" He just looked at me. "Damn it, Pritkin, I'm Pythia now! I can't do my job if you keep deciding what I do and do not need to know!"

"If you're Pythia, then act like it!"

"I'm trying to. And I don't think that involves waiting around for fate to kick me in the butt yet again! I want to *do* something!"

The massive volume he'd been working on suddenly leapt up and slammed against the door, leaving a powdery blue stain where it hit. Before I could comment on exactly how useless childish gestures were, the door opened and a gingery head poked in. Nick looked like he thought he might be safer with the free-for-all upstairs.

He cautiously edged in, pushing a room-service cart and skirting the upended book. "It's stopped. But there has to be a couple thousand of them." His voice was almost admiring.

"What caused it?" Pritkin demanded.

"Augustine's best guess is that one of his competitors is trying to rain on his parade."

I winced at the pun, but Pritkin only looked even more severe. "There's going to be more of this kind of thing, with the Corps preoccupied with the war."

"What kind of thing?" I asked.

"Mages with vendettas deciding to take matters into their own hands," Nick explained.

"The Corps can't fight the war and police every mage with a grievance, and they know it," Pritkin finished grimly. "And what's all this?"

"Lunch. I met a waiter on the way back with the cart." Nick started sorting through the sandwiches, fruit and cookies. "Would you like something, Cassie? There's plenty here."

"Not really hungry."

"She'll eat." Pritkin said curtly.

"I *said*—"

"If you starve to death it would damage my professional reputation."

"I eat plenty."

"The same does not apply should I strangle you in understandable irritation, however."

"I'll have a sandwich," I told Nick. "No meat."

He came up with a benign-looking egg salad, which he handed over along with a box of apple juice. I eyed him thoughtfully. Unlike his friend, he was still a member in good standing of the Circle. He might be able to find out about Tami for me, assuming it was the Silver who had her. On the other hand, I didn't know his opinion on the whole magical handicapped debate. He might view them with the same vague embarrassment/lack of interest everyone else seemed to show and not think she was worth asking a few questions. But nothing ventured . . .

"Since she sheltered you seven years ago, I'm assuming she's not a teenager, right?" he asked after I'd sketched the problem.

"She was in her late twenties when I knew her, which would make her mid-thirties now. Why?"

"Then she's way too old for the harvesters," Nick said, around a mouthful of what I hoped was chicken. "They wouldn't waste their time, especially not if she was weak to begin with."

Pritkin caught my expression. "He's talking about the people who make null bombs."

Nick nodded. "That's when—"

"I know what they are," I said numbly. The bombs were highly prized, as they concentrated a null's usual effect, stopping all magic in an area for a period of time—including mine. I'd found out about them only recently, as Tami had never brought the subject up. Not too surprisingly, considering that the process required to make a bomb drains nulls of their life force, thereby killing them.

"Don't worry," Nick said, slathering mustard on another roll. "Like most mages, nulls come into their full power when they hit puberty, making them as strong then as they're ever going to get. Harvesters like to get them as soon thereafter as possible, to maximize the amount of life force they have to give. Your friend wouldn't interest them."

"Why would the Circle want her, then?"

He shrugged. "Beats me. Unless she was privy to important information of some kind."

I shook my head. "Tami doesn't know anything like that."

"But she knows someone," Pritkin pointed out. At my bewildered look, he sighed. "The Circle doesn't know where you are—the fact that they were willing to put a steep bounty on your head says as much. Perhaps they are attempting to lure you into coming to them."

"You think they took her because of me?" The sandwich, which hadn't been great to begin with, was suddenly tasteless.

"It's possible," Nick agreed, warming to his buddy's suggestion. "Half the Council was in attendance when you flashed in, told off the Consul, seduced Mircea and stole Tomas out from under her nose."

"It didn't happen like that!" I said, appalled. And it hadn't. The Consul had been in the middle of torturing a friend of mine to death when I made a desperate attempt to rescue him. It had worked, a fact that still amazed me, but for a while there, I'd been in serious jeopardy—not to mention scared out of my mind.

Nick shrugged. "Well, that's the story that's been going around."

"If they are trying to persuade you to try another foolhardy rescue, they would need to find someone you would consider worth the effort," Pritkin pointed out. "But Tomas remains in Faerie, and is therefore unreachable. Your parents, as I understand it, are deceased, and your childhood friends are vampires protected by the Senate." He thought for a moment. "Or ghosts. But even the Circle can't harm the dead."

For a minute, I just stood there, blinking stupidly. What did it say about my life, when even my enemies had trouble finding anyone close to me? I hadn't seen Tami in seven years. Had it really been that long since I'd had a friend vulnerable enough to act as hostage to fate? I guess it had. Except for Tomas, and that was anything but a reassuring thought. I vividly remembered the sickening twist in my stomach when I'd realized why he had been scheduled for such a horrible and demeaning death, maybe because I was suddenly experiencing it all over again.

The Senate had had a lot of reasons for wanting Tomas dead, but the execution had been made a public spectacle mainly in the hope that I would come after him. And I had, right into the middle of a room half filled with their allies from the Silver Circle. Who had apparently been paying attention to the lesson. Had they immediately started looking for a replacement for Tomas? Had I doomed Tami the moment I freed him?

"If the Circle has her, can you find out?" I asked Nick.

"I can try," he said slowly, apparently just realizing that this might be a sensitive subject. "But if they want you to come after her, surely they'll publicize the fact that they have her."

"Not necessarily."

"But—"

"Whatever memo they sent out about Tomas, I didn't get. I only stumbled over him by chance, after the execution had already begun." He'd still been alive because he was a vampire, and not easy to kill. Tami didn't have that advantage.

"Be that as it may," Nick said seriously, "the Council was given an up-close view of the kind of power the Pythia wields. They aren't likely to forget it. If they are setting you up, they'll take precautions. Which would make any attempt to rescue her extremely—"

"You aren't going to rescue her." That, of course, was Pritkin.

"Not without some idea where she is," I agreed. When I'd gone after Tomas, the Senate had exploded a null bomb so I couldn't just shift in, grab him, and shift out. It was a good guess that the Circle had their own stash of the nasty things, waiting to ensure that any rescue attempt I made ended with me being the one needing rescuing. If I was going to do this, I needed a plan. And forming one required knowing where she was.

"I'll do what I can," Nick promised. "But about the Codex, I still say we ought to check with Saleh."

"Who's Saleh?" I asked, trying to keep the desperation out of my voice.

"It's too risky!" The glare Pritkin sent Nick would've melted glass.

"I'm Pythia," I reminded him. "Breathing is risky."

"Saleh deals in information. Esoteric, hard-to-get, valuable information," Nick informed me, despite Pritkin's steadily reddening face. "The problem is his price."

"I can come up with the money," I said, thinking about Billy and roulette wheels and big payoffs.

"He doesn't deal in money," Pritkin snapped, cutting off whatever Nick had been about to say. "Only in favors. And you *don't* want to risk owing him one!"

"I'll decide that!"

"We could at least talk to him," Nick offered mildly. I kept hoping his low-key attitude would rub off on his buddy, but so far no luck.

"If he knows something, I'll get it," the pixie said, fingering her tiny sword. It would have sounded comical, except that I'd seen what the thing could do.

Nick shook his head. "If we make him angry, we'll never get anything out of him."

"The fewer who go, the better," I added. "Most people don't like to talk in front of a crowd." Especially if one of them is waving a sword in his face.

Pritkin looked like he was about to explode. "Did you hear nothing I said? The Codex is likely useless for your purposes. And I am not taking you near that piece of scum!"

"You don't have to take me anywhere," I told him impatiently. "I'll take myself."

"You're not going." It sounded final.

"I already know his name," I pointed out. "How hard do you think it would be for Billy to locate him?"

"Do you have any idea what he could demand? He'll try to trick you—"

"Then it's a good thing we'll be along to make sure he

doesn't," Nick said smoothly. He cocked a sandy eyebrow at me. "If you'll permit the escort?"

I glanced at Pritkin's face, which was bordering on purple, and sighed. Until I got some training in defense, a bodyguard or two was pretty much a necessity. Besides, I wasn't sure how to get rid of him. I said okay, even knowing I'd probably regret it.

Of course I was right.

Chapter 8

The room would have been elegant if it hadn't been for all the blood. The apartment's tasteful gold and cream interior clashed with the panorama of the Vegas Strip outside, but the view was less of a decor problem than the brown rivulets that had run down the embossed wallpaper and coagulated on the nice buff carpet. There was no body in sight, but there didn't need to be. No one could have lost that much blood and lived. Not even something not entirely human.

My dress had turned to eerie twilight, with twisted black branches clasping a harvest moon like bony fingers. It was creepy as hell, and fit my mood perfectly. I glanced longingly back at the foyer, but I couldn't cut and run when this had been my idea. The only good thing was that I'd managed to leave the pixie behind. I wondered if she'd figured a way out of the file drawer yet.

I reluctantly followed Pritkin through the wrecked living room while Nick stayed behind to check things out. We moved gingerly down a hallway, trying to dodge the worst of the blood. It wasn't easy. By the time I managed it, I'd decided that the victim must have taken at least a few of his attackers with him. No single body could have possibly bled that much.

Sure enough, the door at the end of the hall was ajar due to the corpse lying half out of it. Or, to be more precise, part of a corpse. The top half was several feet away from the remainder, and I didn't see a right arm at all. Of course, I wasn't looking too hard.

I carefully stepped over what was left of the body and immediately spotted the missing arm. It was affixed to the wall
inside the door, courtesy of a large axe that had severed it at
the shoulder. The arm hung by the remains of a sleeve that
may once have been blue but was now a stiff purple mess.

Swallowing hard, I stared around, sweat already forming
on my upper lip. The air-conditioning wasn't on, and despite
an occasional breeze through a shattered window, it had to be
ninety degrees in the apartment. But that wasn't the reason I
was perspiring.

The rays of midafternoon sunlight seemed thicker than
usual, clouded with dust and what I realized after a moment
were a couple hundred flies. They were hovering over what at
first appeared to be a random mass of body parts atop a king-
sized bed, but which I finally identified as the corpse of a
man. To put it nicely, it wasn't fresh. I'm no expert, but I seriously doubted that the newly dead would look like a fleshy
balloon about to erupt with fetid gases and decay. The sight
was gruesome enough that it took me a minute to notice that
he had skin the color of an after-dinner mint, a chalky blue
green.

"Djinn," Pritkin said curtly, before I could ask. "Do you
see him?"

I looked at him incredulously. "He's a little hard to miss."

"The spirit!"

I shook my head. If there was a ghost on the premises, he
was keeping real quiet. Or maybe he'd passed out from the
stink of whatever was seeping out of a gash in the djinn's side.
At least the flies seemed to like it; about a hundred had con-
gregated there in a working black mound. I gagged hoarsely
and tried to breathe through my mouth. It didn't help.

"Careful, Cass—you look about as green as he does,"
Billy commented. "Tell the mage that the only ghost around
here is me, and let's get outta here. This place is giving me
the creeps."

I swallowed hard. "Do you sense anything?" If anybody
could round up a freaked-out ghost, it was Billy.

"No, but I'll check around, just to be sure. Sometimes the

new ones hide." He doesn't get generous very often, so I must
have really looked bad.

"Thanks." I started edging toward the door, intending to
catch a breath of comparatively sweet-smelling smog, assuming I could get a living room window open. But Nick was in
the way.

I hadn't seen him come in, and he startled me. I gave a yelp
and pulled back so hard that I would have fallen if Pritkin
hadn't caught me. "I doubt he's here," he said curtly, setting
me back on my feet, "even if part of him survived. He'd be
after the murderer."

"What could a ghost do to anyone?" Nick scoffed.

Pritkin and I exchanged a glance. He'd seen firsthand the
damage a couple of pissed-off ghosts could do. But he didn't
mention it. "I'm going to check the rest of the apartment," he
said instead, and left.

"He may be the Corps' best demon hunter," Nick said,
scowling after his friend, "but I'll bet you know more about
ghosts. Saleh could have left one, right?" He looked from me
to the body, but it didn't answer. That wasn't too surprising,
as it no longer had a head.

"I don't know." I'd never met a djinn before, but I assumed that the same laws governed them as ruled other non-
human magical creatures, none of whom left ghosts. Of
course, neither do most people. It's actually a pretty rare condition all the way around, so whatever information this one
had carried into the great beyond was likely to stay there. But
I didn't feel up to giving a long explanation at the moment.
"Billy's gone to take a look around. If there's anything left of
him, he'll find it."

"Anything left? He's either a ghost or he isn't!" Nick
seemed a little stressed, with a vein throbbing insistently beside his right eye. He looked like the office type to me; maybe
fieldwork didn't agree with him, either.

"It's not that simple," I explained. "Not all ghosts are permanent. Some spirits linger around their bodies for a while
before accepting things and moving on."

"How long?"

"A few hours, maybe a few days. No more than a week, unless they're planning to stick around for the long haul."

"Based on the condition of the body, he couldn't have died more than four days ago. By your calculations, his spirit could still be here."

"Maybe. But I don't sense anything."

"Try harder," Nick urged. "He's no longer in a position to make demands. If you can contact him, he may be willing to tell us something."

"If he's here, Billy will find him. If he isn't—" I shrugged. "I don't do anything to attract ghosts, so I can't 'try harder.' They just tend to show up when I'm around."

"We can't afford to stay much longer." Nick spoke quietly, but there was a warning note in his voice that I didn't like. It suddenly occurred to me to wonder why the place wasn't overrun with war mages. It was their job to investigate murders in the supernatural community, and there looked to be enough bodies here to occupy them for a while. I'd just spied a foot—of a much more human golden brown—sticking out from behind the bed. I didn't look to see if it was still attached to anything.

"How long before anyone else shows up?" I asked uneasily. Pritkin and his fellow mages weren't exactly on good terms, and I would just as soon miss the reunion.

"There's no way to know. But Saleh was under interdict by the Council." Nick saw my expression. "It's like parole," he explained. "And when he doesn't show up for his weekly meeting, someone will be sent to check on him."

"Crap." I started for the door, but Nick grabbed me.

"What if you were to touch the corpse itself? Would that make for a stronger connection?"

I stared at him in horror. "I'm not touching that thing!" The very idea made my skin crawl.

"What about something he owned, then?" Before I could stop him, Nick crossed the room to tug at the dead man's shirt. I think he intended to rip a piece of fabric off for me, but the dead flesh peeled away with the cloth, flaking off the bone like a well-done fish. The shirt gaped open where he'd grasped it, giving me a glimpse of a belly that moved on its own. When I realized I was seeing maggots teeming beneath the skin, I gagged and almost lost it.

"That's it. I'm done." I staggered through the door and bumped into Pritkin coming up the hallway. "Is there a bathroom?"

"Two doors down to your left. There's no one in there."

For a second, I didn't know what he meant. There were only three of us along on this crazy errand to interrogate a dead man—unless you counted Billy, and he hadn't needed to use the facilities in quite a while. Then I realized that he was implying that the bathroom was free of corpses. I got a mental image of the bloated body behind me, choked and fled.

The dress seemed to like the bathroom better than the bedroom-turned-morgue. The mirror reflected back to me a hesitant pale rose, like the sky just before dawn. But although I stood over the sink for a long minute, trying not to heave up lunch, the sun didn't rise. I didn't blame it.

I'd just finished washing my face and hands, trying to get what felt like a greasy film off them, when a fine mist floated up from the drain on a cold silver glow. It resolved itself into a face, wavering in front of the mirror like a mirage made out of steam. It was vague and indistinct, not almost solid the way I usually see ghosts. I blinked at it, but it didn't go away. "Is it safe?" a tremulous voice demanded.

"Uh," I said stupidly. There really was no good answer. On a few memorable occasions in the past, I'd encountered spirits who weren't yet aware that they were dead. And no one ever appreciated being brought up to speed.

The misty eyes started moving around the bathroom. They detached from the rest of the head to float off, poking into things. One slipped under the door, and I winced, only too aware of what was coming. A few seconds later, the mouth opened in shock, but no words came out

"I know it's bad," I babbled, "but you're going to a better place."

The sightless head turned in my direction. "I'm a demon," it snarled. "I don't think so."

Okay, he had a point. The other eye returned from looking out the window and settled in the middle of his forehead. It gave him a weird Cyclops vibe, but under the circumstances, I didn't think that worth pointing out. "Who did this?"

"Don't you know?" I asked, surprised.

"I was asleep!" he said, sounding outraged. "I heard someone break in, got halfway out of bed, and then the lights went out." *Permanently*, I thought but didn't say. The eye focused on my face, really seeing me, for the first time. "And who the hell are you?"

"Just visiting," I said, edging toward the door.

"Not so fast." The face reappeared in my path. The wandering eye caught up with the other one and there was some jostling around while they fought each other for forehead space. When they finally settled, he looked at me accusingly. "You can see me!"

"I'm clairvoyant."

"Good. Then tell me who did this. Someone is gonna pay!"

I had a sudden idea. "Maybe we can work something out," I offered.

"Whaddya mean?"

"I need to know about the Codex," I said tenuously.

"Which one?" he demanded, suddenly businesslike.

"There's more than one?"

"A codex is a compilation of knowledge, babe. Which one are we talking about here?"

I swallowed. "The Codex Merlini. The lost volume."

His gaze sharpened. "What did you say your name was?"

"I didn't. Do you know anything?"

"Possibly."

I sighed. "I'm Cassie Palmer," I admitted, and the ghostly eyes visibly brightened.

"Okay, then." Saleh's voice turned brisk. "The Codex was lost centuries ago, but that isn't the main problem. Even if you find it, you won't be able to read it."

"It's in code?"

"Better. Codes can be deciphered, sooner or later, no matter how good. He was a little more creative than that."

"He? You mean, there really was a Merlin?"

"No, they called it the Codex Merlini because it was written by a guy named Ralph," Saleh said impatiently.

"You know that old story about Merlin getting younger every year, instead of older?" I nodded. "Well, the story-tellers got it mixed up."

"Meaning what?"

"Meaning that it wasn't the mage who aged backwards. He spelled the Codex so that, if it ever left his possession, it would start aging in reverse."

"Why would he do that?"

Saleh gave me a look that said he was starting to suspect that my IQ equaled my bust size. "So it would begin unwriting itself, of course! In our time it's just a bundle of blank parchment."

"But if someone was to go into the past . . ."

Saleh slid me an evil smile. "Then that someone could possibly retrieve it."

I felt my stomach sink. My new position meant that, among other things, I had the fun job of policing the timeline. But without some of those lessons I was missing, every time I went back, I risked messing up something I wouldn't know how to fix.

"Where is it?" I asked, knowing I wasn't going to like the answer.

"Wrong question," he murmured. "You should be asking where *was* it. Because you need to go back to a time when the text was still mostly intact, yet after it left Merlin's hands."

Someone rapped smartly on the door, and I jumped. "We need to go." Pritkin's voice carried clearly through the thin wood.

"Then where *was* it?" I hissed quietly. The only person who hated my jaunts into the past more than I did was Pritkin. I wanted to make the deal before he interfered and possibly screwed it up.

Billy suddenly zoomed through the wall like a firecracker on speed. "The mage is right, Cass. We gotta get gone. Now." He pulled up at the sight of the djinn's spectral face. "Who's that?"

"Saleh. I found him."

"Great. So let's go. There's a cadre of war mages coming up the elevator."

"Give me a minute."

"You don't have a minute."

"Billy! I may have found something!"

Pritkin started beating on the door. "What's going on? What's wrong?" Too late I recalled being told once that his hearing was super sharp.

I looked at Saleh. "What do you want?"

He gave me an eye roll. "What do you think? You're clairvoyant. I want to know who did this."

"I don't control my gift," I told him desperately, as Pritkin started throwing himself against the bathroom door.

"Then I guess I'll hang around with you until it decides to manifest," Saleh said pleasantly.

"Oh, I don't *think* so," Billy said, glaring daggers at the djinn.

I stared at Saleh, who gazed peacefully back. I sighed and gave in. "When did you die, exactly?"

"Monday morning, sometime around ten."

I glanced at Billy. No way was I going back to an apartment full of murderers in a vulnerable human body. "Some help here," I said urgently.

My body needs a spirit in residence to maintain life, but nobody ever said it had to be mine. I'd been told by someone who ought to know that I didn't need Billy to babysit my physical self whenever my spirit took a little jaunt. *Just shift back to the same time you left*, she'd said nonchalantly, as if timing a shift that closely was so damn easy. Needless to say, I preferred my solution.

"I do not believe this," Billy muttered, as one of the hinges gave way with a crack. I gave him frantic eyes and he said something profane before slipping inside my skin. "Don't be long. He'll figure out it's me when I can't get us out of here."

"What's going on?" Saleh demanded.

"I can't tell you what you want to know. But I can show you." I waved my hand through what was left of him and shifted.

The bathroom reformed around us, four days earlier. There was no sound coming from outside the door, so I cautiously stuck my insubstantial head through the wood and looked around. The absence of blood on the walls was enough to tell me that I'd made it ahead of the murderers.

Saleh streamed through the wall, looking determined. I followed, keeping an eye out for anything unusual. Like someone with a really big axe.

Saleh floated through the wall of his bedroom as easily as if he did it every day. On the bed was the sleeping djinn. In life he'd been pretty normal-looking except for the skin color. No turban, gold earrings or Middle Eastern garb in sight. Instead, he had a mop of curly brown hair, a well-trimmed goatee and a Lakers tracksuit. He also had a head.

The alarm clock on the bedside table said 9:34. Saleh and I glanced at each other, then settled down to watch. It didn't take long.

At 9:52, I heard the sound of running feet and the clash of weapons as, presumably, Saleh's bodyguards faced off with the assassins. A moment later, one of them stumbled through the door, before a magically levitating axe took off his arm. A sword wielded by human hands bisected him a moment later, while the figure on the bed woke up, blinked his eyes blearily, and started to look around. Before he could focus, the second bodyguard was dead and Saleh's head was playing basketball with the clothes hamper on the far side of the room.

I barely noticed the gruesome denouement, because my eyes had fixed with disbelief on the sword-wielding figure standing over the scene. I would have gasped, but my lungs didn't seem to work, my body suddenly empty of anything resembling air. A sickening disorientation hit me, and for a moment I couldn't move, couldn't think. Time seemed to stop as I stared in hollow shock at the face, splattered by his victim's blood.

He looked different, some part of my brain noticed. Instead of a ratty T-shirt and a brown coat that looked like it had been through one too many battles, his lean form was poured into close-fitting black jeans, a matching button-up shirt and a rich black leather jacket. It was his usual look, but upgraded, as if he'd suddenly developed a sense of style. His hair also appeared to have been brushed recently, and the stubble on his cheeks looked more like a fashion statement than someone who had forgotten to shave.

It was his expression that was the most radical alteration, though. I'd seen him angry more times than I could count, but that particular arrangement of features, like a hunting bird about to snap the neck of its prey, was new. I looked into a pair of familiar green eyes in utter denial. All I could think was, *No wonder he didn't want to bring me to see Saleh.*

"I don't believe this!" Saleh complained. "I don't even know him!" We watched Pritkin wipe the bloody sword on a corner of Saleh's sheets before sheathing it in a long scabbard slung across his back. He walked out with an easy, unhurried stride, frightening and graceful. He didn't look back.

"Some guy *saunters* in here, hacks me to *pieces* and I don't even *know* him?"

"Calm down," I said, feeling light-headed and faintly ill. "Keep your head."

"I don't *have* a head!" he snapped, and started for the door.

"We had a deal," I reminded him.

"Your book's in Paris," Saleh threw over what would have been his shoulder if he'd still had one. "Try 1793."

I stared at him. "What?" Damn it—I should have known that wasn't coincidence.

"Yeah. A couple dumb-ass dark mages stole it from Merlin that year and—"

"Wait." I glared at the djinn, wondering if I was being had. "Merlin lived in . . . well, I don't know exactly, but he couldn't have still been alive in the eighteenth century!"

"He was part incubus—everyone knows that," I was informed testily. "And demons are immortal. Now hush up if you want this, 'cause otherwise I'm gone."

I hushed up.

"So, yeah, he was alive in 1793, when he lost the Codex to the mages, who put it up for auction at a little get-together on October third. Right before they bugged the hell out of the city to get away from the public executions and the fires and the mobs and the pissed-off half demon who was after their butts. Anyway, dress to impress and maybe you can get a look at it before they sell it off."

"But, if they're planning to sell it, it'll be guarded! There has to be a better time—"

"Merlin was guarding the Codex until the mages got their greedy paws on it and, trust me, Pythia or no, you *don't* want to go through him."

"Then what about later? Who bought it?"

"Even if I had all day, I couldn't cover all the rumors of where it went after that night. You don't care anyway, since if you want it before the spells unravel, you have to get at it early. And that's Paris, 1793," he said flatly. "Try not to get beheaded. Trust me, it sucks." He started for the corridor again.

"Wait a minute! Where are you going?"

"Where you think? I got a job to do."

"Saleh!"

He paused beside the door. "This is none of your business, babe. Thanks to mystery man, I'm incorporeal again. Ten centuries of accumulated power down the drain, like that." He tried to snap his fingers, but the lack of actual hands frustrated him. He grimaced. "Whatever revenge I can come up with is well within the rules. And believe me, I can be *real* inventive."

He streamed out, leaving me staring witlessly after him. Well, at least that explained how he'd managed to leave a ghost: he hadn't. The spirit was Saleh's natural state. He'd just saved up enough power to form himself a body, the better to wheel and deal with mortals, I assumed. The question was, did I go after him?

I doubted if, in his current condition, he could do Pritkin any real harm. Ghosts, even new ones, have a limited power supply, one that is eroded very quickly by attacks on the living. Saleh wasn't a ghost, but since he'd just lost most of his power along with his head, I doubted he was likely to do any better. Add to that Pritkin's formidable shields, and he was probably pretty safe. Too bad the same couldn't be said for me.

If Saleh found a way to communicate with the mage, to accuse him or berate him for the crime, he might let slip how he'd acquired his information. And that would be very bad. If

Saleh didn't even know him, it seemed unlikely that Pritkin had a personal grievance against the djinn. Which meant that his reason for killing him was probably to keep him from telling me about the Codex. And if Pritkin hadn't balked at killing Saleh to keep it safe, why would I be any different?

In the end, I decided that the whole Saleh debate was stupid since I didn't know how to round up a djinn that didn't want to go. I finally shifted back alone, only to have Billy scream inside my head, "Get in the tub!"

When I just stood there, trying to catch up, he stepped out of my skin and gave me a shove, right in the center of my chest. Billy usually has trouble moving even small things, but he'd found some extra energy somewhere, because I almost flew off my feet. I staggered backwards against the old-fashioned claw-footed tub, lost my balance and fell in. At the same moment the corridor wall blew inward in a burst of plaster, wood and expensive wallpaper.

I lay among the debris, head spinning, eyesight going dark, for several confused seconds. The tub had been a restored antique, with the original solid cast-iron body. It had saved my life, but with a pounding head and dust-caked lungs, I was having trouble feeling grateful.

"Miss Palmer!" Pritkin's voice came from the hole where the door used to be. "Are you all right?"

I didn't look at him. I couldn't look at him. "Sure." I spit out blood—I'd bitten my tongue—and plaster dust. "Never better."

I climbed out of the debris and started for the sink, only it didn't appear to be there anymore. There was a sink-sized hole in the window, though, so I picked a shaky path across the destroyed bathroom and looked out. The fresh breeze was so distracting that it took me a few seconds to spy the remains of the plumbing eight stories below, in the middle of Flamingo Road. A taxi driver was standing outside his cab, staring at the big dent in his hood and looking puzzled. He looked up and our eyes met. I quickly ducked back inside. This place was about to be way more popular than I liked.

I peered into the hall and saw three unfamiliar war mages sitting with their backs to the wall. They looked pissed, maybe because they were trussed up like chickens about to be put on a spit. Since there were only three, I assumed they hadn't been expecting us. They seemed to recognize me, though, or maybe they were glaring at everybody on principle.

"We can try a memory charm," Nick said, regarding them doubtfully.

"It won't hold," Pritkin argued. "Not with their training." He looked at Nick, his eyes shadowed with concern. "It seems you just joined the resistance openly."

I blinked, but it didn't help. The mask was absolutely perfect. I'd grown up around creatures whose emotions were often shown in the barest flicker of an eyelash, in an infinitesimal pause in conversation. I'd thought I knew how to read people, but even concentrating with everything I had, I couldn't find a flaw.

The sleek, deadly predator I'd just seen was simply gone. In his place was a pale, tired-looking man with plaster powdering his skin and clothes. Pritkin ran fingers through his hair, which, already wet with sweat thanks to the ovenlike temperature in the apartment, gummed into punk-rock spikes. *At least he'll have to wash it now*, I thought blankly.

Pritkin noticed me, and the touch of his eyes was enough to make my skin prickle. "Did you find him?"

I stumbled over to lean heavily against the wall. My heart was pumping against my rib cage, hard and fast enough that I could feel the pulse in my neck. "No." I closed my eyes as if in weariness, because Pritkin had proven able to read them all too easily in the past. But I was proud of my voice. It was the one I'd cultivated at court, the one designed to tell even vampires exactly nothing. I forced my heart rate to slow down, my breathing to even out. "It seems that djinn are like vamps; they don't leave ghosts."

"You said you found something." I opened my eyes to see Pritkin coming toward me. Okay, maybe there was a flaw, I decided. The walk was the same. He had the deadly fluidity of a fighter, all leashed strength and readiness. He stopped a little too close for comfort, those clever green eyes searching my face.

He's Tony in a mood, I told myself sternly, *looking for someone to bleed because he's having a bad day. You feel nothing, no fear, because that attracts his attention better than anything else. You are calm, dreamy, serene. You feel nothing.* "There was a ghost trail in the bathroom, but it wasn't from the djinn," I said casually. "Someone else died here, a while ago."

"Are you sure you're all right?" Nick came up alongside me. His eyes were on my dress, which had retreated from hopeful dawn into foggy night, with little tendrils of white creeping cautiously across a murky background.

"Fine," I said steadily. "The sink missed me on its way to destroy a cab."

Pritkin stared past my shoulder at the ruined bathroom and his scowl deepened. "We need to go. There's nothing for us here, and the human authorities will arrive soon."

I couldn't make myself touch his hand, so I twisted a fist in his coat, which was back to the old battered brown. I wondered where he kept the cool clothes. I held out my free hand to Nick and prepared to shift us all back to Dante's. "Yeah," I agreed, my eyes on Pritkin. "We're all done here."

Chapter 9

Casanova had pointed out that it would be unwise for me to occupy a suite, in case the Circle had spies on the lookout for long-term guests. Instead, he'd stuck me in what had once been a small storeroom in back of the tiki bar. I still had several cases of cocktail umbrellas in boxes under my bed, and barely enough room to turn around. Pritkin had it worse, being stuffed into the dressing room once reserved for the club's famous dead performers. It was larger, since it had once held their coffins, but he swore it still had a certain . . . odor. At the moment, that thought cheered me up considerably.

I finished pulling the oversized T-shirt I was using for a nightgown over my head as Billy drifted through the wall. I brought him up to speed on my conversation with Saleh while he sat on the edge of the bed and rolled a ghostly cigarette. "We need a team," I concluded.

"We *are* a team."

I was tired and I ached, in more ways than one. I hugged my pillow, which had all the comfort of one issued by an unusually stingy airline.

"The Cassie and Billy show might have worked for staying a step ahead of Tony," I said. "It isn't going to be enough to let us burgle a Black Circle stronghold."

"And we've had such great luck with partners."

"We can trust Rafe."

"Cass, I know you like the guy, but come on. A great warrior he ain't."

"We don't need a warrior," I said irritably. "I'm not planning to attack the Circle!"

"And your plans always work out perfectly, huh?"

"Are you *trying* to be a pain in the ass?"

"Nope, it pretty much comes naturally." He lit up and regarded me through a haze of ghostly smoke. "There's always Marlowe."

He meant Kit Marlowe, the onetime Elizabethan playwright. He was now the Consul's chief spy. "Yeah, that'd be healthy."

"You'd be saving Mircea as well as yourself. I'd think that would cancel a few debts," Billy argued.

"It might, if they didn't blame me for getting him into this mess in the first place."

"But he put the *geis* on you—"

"Which, as my master, he had every right to do. I'm the one who had no right to double it, even accidentally." I saw the objection trembling on Billy's lips. "And yes, I think their reasoning sucks. I'm just saying."

"I don't like them any better than you do." Billy sounded aggrieved. "But who else is there? We keep meeting these powerful types, but they're all freaking nuts."

"I'm not taking anyone back in time I can't trust. Or anyone incompetent. Or who has their own agenda."

Billy let out an exasperated sigh. "It's gonna be a little hard to assemble a team if you keep to those kind of standards. Someone loyal and strong who doesn't want anything? Come on."

I found myself getting furious all over again at Pritkin, who was supposed to be exactly that. I'd started to let down my guard with him, just because he was smart and brave and sometimes strangely funny. I should've kept in mind that none of that meant he was on my side. *When I give my word, I keep it*, he'd once told me. Yeah, right.

I toyed with the bedspread, blue and gold brocade with scratchy lace. Not for the first time, I wished for something less flashy and more comfortable. I'd had a soft cotton coverlet at Tony's that I'd used for years. It had faded in the wash, its bright, cheap flowers turning to soft pastels over time, like an English garden. It had gotten a little ragged around the edges, but I'd never let my fastidious governess change it for anything else. I'd liked it the way it was, flaws and all. But like the rest of my stuff, like Eugenie herself, it no longer existed.

"Cass?" Billy suddenly sounded awkward, something almost novel for him. "You know Pritkin was a jerk, right?" *A jerk who also happened to be a friend*, a tiny voice at the back of my mind whispered. Stop it, *stop it*. "Cass?"

The lump in my throat had grown enough to be almost painful, and my eyes had started prickling embarrassingly, and wow, was it time for a change of subject. "I know."

"Okay, then. We're better off. I never trusted him."

"I don't trust anybody," I said fervently. It was the only thing I was sure of these days.

"Anybody except me," Billy corrected. "So what's the plan?"

"I have to get the Codex," I said, starting with the one thing on which there was no argument. Pritkin had said it wouldn't help, but I guess I'd just seen how much I could believe him. "Only I can't bring it back here. It's been roaming around for over two hundred years; who knows what taking it out of the timeline would do?"

Billy looked confused for a moment, and then his eyes got wide. "You can't be thinking what I think you're thinking."

I scowled at him. "If the mountain won't go to Mohammed—"

"Mohammed wasn't an insane master vamp!"

"Mircea's not insane." Not yet, anyway. "He's . . . tormented."

"Uh-huh. You're going to drag a *tormented* master vampire along to burgle a dark mage stronghold?"

"You have a better idea?"

"*Anything* is a better idea!"

"Don't yell."

"Then start talking sense!" I threw the pillow at him, which did no good because it passed right on through. "That doesn't change the fact that you're crazy."

I flopped back on the bed and threw an arm over my eyes.

He was probably right, not that it made a difference. If I couldn't take the spell to Mircea, I had no choice but to take Mircea to the spell. And I'd been saying just that morning that I wanted something to *do*. As last words went, they pretty much sucked.

"You need to get some rest." Billy tried to take my hand, but he'd expended too much energy back at the apartment and didn't have the strength. His fingers passed right through me.

"And you need to feed," I said, finishing the thought. I wasn't looking forward to the energy drain, but I was only going to sleep anyway.

"I'll make do," he said, after a minute.

I looked up, confused. I couldn't remember the last time Billy had refused to take energy. It was the main tie binding us together, his payment for helping out with my various problems. "What?"

"No offense, Cass, but you look like hell."

"Thanks."

"I don't need much gas to spy on the manic mage, anyway." He tipped his hat back and gave me a cocky grin. "And if we're lucky, maybe some of his old buddies in the Corps will find him and take care of one problem for us."

I fell asleep wondering why that thought didn't make me feel any better.

Rafe met me in the kitchens before dawn the next morning. With Pritkin no longer in the picture, I'd had to look elsewhere for help, and there weren't a lot of choices. I'd left a message on the private number Rafe had given me, asking to see him. I just hoped he wasn't going to freak out too badly when I told him what I wanted.

Shortly after we snagged stools at an unused prep table, one of the staff wandered over and deposited a white clay coffee cup in front of me. It smelled like rich dark roast and freshly steamed milk, and had a dot in the middle of the foam from the espresso added right at the end. Pritkin would have loved it. I pushed it away, feeling queasy.

"*Cucciolina*, you are a mess," Rafe told his newest admirer, as fat little hands gleefully smeared berry mush all over his green silk shirt.

Some of the staff were making pies for Midsummer's Eve, which explained why the baby had a ring of purple all around her mouth and jam stuck in her wispy blond hair. Miranda, who had been trying to babysit and supervise at the same time, had handed her over almost as soon as I walked in the door. The baby had immediately made a peevish little huffing sound, and when I just stood there, holding her awkwardly, she broke into an angry shriek.

Rafe rescued me, taking her despite his elegant attire and jiggling her against his chest. She hammed it up for a few seconds, wailing like I'd been sticking her with pins, before finally subsiding into anxious snuffles and pressing her face to his shirt. Considering how fast she recovered, it was pretty clear she'd just wanted to flirt with the cute guy.

A white china plate joined my coffee cup. On it was a largish, nicely browned muffin. I looked at the muffin and, as far as I could tell, it didn't look back. Since it had passed the first test, I broke it open and sniffed it. Peanut butter and anchovy. A little chef was casually loitering nearby, waiting for a verdict. He was going to be waiting for a while.

"She reminds me of you at that age," Rafe said, vainly swiping the baby's lips with a napkin. It only made bad matters worse: now she had purple cheeks, too. "You could never eat anything without getting it everywhere."

Jesse stifled a smile at the other end of the long table, where he and a bunch of the kids were playing Monopoly. They should have been in bed—it was barely four a.m.—but nobody at Dante's kept a normal schedule. Having a staff partially composed of people who caught fire in sunlight probably had something to do with that.

Most of the older kids were intent on the game, but one of the younger ones was sitting on the floor, playing with an Elvis Pez dispenser someone had given her. She seemed totally intent on it, but the door behind her nonetheless stayed stubbornly open. It seemed that her parents had once hidden their embarrassing child in a small room with no windows, until she discovered that locks just loved to open for her and escaped. Now it had become a bit of a habit. It made getting around the casino something of a challenge, though: elevator doors simply refused to close as long as she was inside.

Watching her, I finally figured out what had been bugging me. These kids were just too young. The average age was eight, with several in the four-to-five-year-old range. Which made no sense.

At fourteen, I'd been one of the youngest in Tami's brood. Most had been mid- to late teens, old enough to have figured out what their lives were going to be like in one of those special schools and to have engineered an escape. Sure, there were occasionally younger kids who came through, but they usually arrived with an older sibling or friend. I'd never seen Tami with so many really small children. How had they gotten away? How had they survived on the streets until she found them? I'd barely managed it, and I'd had more years and more money than most of them.

"I didn't come to court until I was four," I reminded Rafe absently. A tiny car from the Monopoly game had decided to trundle down the table to us and bumped into my hand. I turned it around and sent it back, where it collided with a briskly hopping shoe. It looked like someone had enchanted the game board for the kids.

"To live, no, but your father brought you as a *bambina*," he replied, giving up on cleaning the sticky child. He held her against his chest with one arm, the palm of his hand curled protectively around her skull.

"What?"

"He loved to show you off. Of course, you were better behaved than some," he said with a sigh, as the baby began chewing on his tie.

"I never knew that." I knew so little about my parents that the tiny piece of trivia felt like a revelation. In my mind, "mother" meant a cool hand, soft hair, and a sweet smell. It was my strongest memory of her. Unless I thought very hard, it was my only memory of her. And I recalled even less about my father.

"*Piccolina mia*, please to stop," Rafe said in exasperation, pulling his tie away and substituting a pacifier before his squirming armful could protest. Luckily, the small tussle seemed to have worn her out, and she soon curled into his chest and went to sleep. "The visits ended when you were about two," he added.

"Do you know why?"

Rafe started to shrug, then realized it might wake up his new girlfriend. "My guess would be that you began showing signs of your gift. Your father must have realized that Tony would take you if he knew."

Which he had, only a couple of years later. "How did he find out?" I'd never known how Tony discovered that I might be worth acquiring. The idea that the tip-off could have been something I did was nauseating.

"Tony never trusted anyone, not even his longtime servants," Rafe reassured me. "There were people watching your father, who doubtless also had people watching them. The only ones Antonio did not monitor were those of us with blood bonds to him, which he knew we were not strong enough to break." The last was said with uncharacteristic bitterness.

"I don't suppose . . . Can you tell me anything about them? About my parents?" It wasn't the first time I'd asked him, but Rafe had never been able to answer. He'd been under orders to stay mute, and as the vampire who made him had given the order, the prohibition was even stronger than Mircea's.

Rafe regarded me with compassion. "I'm sorry, Cassie."

"I just thought, maybe, with Tony gone . . ."

"But he still lives," Rafe reminded me softly. "As does his hold over me."

"But maybe Billy could—"

"And Antonio's ban includes communication through the spirit world."

My ability to communicate with ghosts came from my father. It wasn't surprising that Tony would have thought to add that little caveat. I'd always hated him, but I'd never thought him stupid. Disappointment settled into its usual place behind my rib cage.

"Can't Mircea break the blood bond?" I asked after a moment.

"I haven't asked him. In his condition . . . I don't dare do anything to weaken him further."

"Which kind of brings me to why I wanted to see you." I glanced at the kids, but none of them was paying us any attention. Jesse was biting his lip and glaring at the board, where tiny foreclosure signs had just appeared on a bunch of his hotels. As quietly as possible, I brought Rafe up to speed.

"You want to storm a dark mage stronghold?" Rafe asked incredulously when I'd finished. "On your own?"

"Not on my own," I corrected. A night's rest had helped to clear my head and made me reevaluate my plan. I needed to get Mircea to the Codex, but trying to handle him by myself was foolhardy. Fortunately, there was another option.

Besides Rafe and a few other trophies, Tony had specialized in acquiring badasses, the kind with the skills and personalities to complement his network of highly illegal activities. And some of them had had several hundred years to hone their skills. I was going after the Codex, and I wasn't going alone.

"But if you already know where it is, can you not simply—" Rafe made an indeterminate hand gesture that was supposed to indicate shifting.

I respected him enough not to roll my eyes, but it took an effort. "If I could just run in and grab it, yeah. But I somehow doubt it's going to be that easy. I need Alphonse."

Rafe only sat there, looking horrified, but some of his tension must have communicated itself to the baby, who woke up and started sniffling. I watched her warily, knowing what that meant. But Miranda, having terrorized the staff to her satisfaction, came and took her away before the explosion came. And Rafe was still just looking at me.

The reaction wasn't exactly a surprise. Alphonse was Tony's right-hand man and chief thug. After the boss did his disappearing act, Alphonse had taken control of the family's East Coast operations as Casanova had in Vegas. And, no, on the surface, nothing about him was particularly reassuring.

For one thing, he looked like a boxer who'd lost one too many fights: his features were all slightly off-kilter, as if they'd been smashed too badly to ever fit together properly again. For another, he sounded scarily like Don Corleone. It was due to tracheal damage from a vicious elbow to the throat in his mortal days, but that didn't change the fact that every time *The Godfather* was shown at Tony's somebody lost it and ended up bleeding all over the floor. Which may account for why it was so often on the playlist.

Even more worrying was the stack of thick, well-thumbed photo albums in his room that were filled with neatly labeled black-and-white prints. Some showed people in coffins, staring sightlessly upwards, others were facedown in gutters or sprawled on cracked pavement, still bleeding out. Alphonse kept pictures of everyone he'd ever killed. There were a lot of albums.

The photos had originally been Tony's idea. In the human world, Alphonse had been a monster, the kind they made movies about with car chases and explosions and enough gore to prompt news reports on the societal effects of violence in the media. In the vampire world, he was just good at his job. A little too good sometimes. Tony hadn't wanted his chief enforcer to end up on the Senate's bad side for going overboard once too often, but talking to him didn't help much and there are no such things as therapists in the vampire world. Then someone joked one night at dinner that Alphonse needed a hobby, and Tony's eyes lit up.

The unfortunate joker had been saddled with the job of finding something that Alphonse liked to do that didn't concern killing—or provide the entertainment himself. Everyone had assumed he was a goner, including him. That had been especially true when the pets were hunted for sport, the piano was used for target practice and the golf clubs were wrapped around his neck. But then he bought a camera and set up a darkroom and nobody saw Alphonse for a week.

When Alphonse had no corpses to model for him, he'd photograph anyone hanging around court. He particularly loved surprising people, catching them doing something embarrassing or from the worst possible angle. Under Rafe's beautiful ceiling in my bedroom had been walls papered with hideous images: me with eyes rolled up so that only the whites showed; with my mouth full of pizza; and with my jaw swollen to chipmunk size from a tooth extraction.

I'd hated them at first, hated waking up every day to grotesque versions of myself that I'd started to see reflected in the mirror whenever I looked too long. But I hadn't dared to take down Alphonse's offerings, which soon circled the room and started on another row. And, slowly, as my collection grew, I began to change my mind.

Alphonse's favorite model was his girlfriend, a buxom blonde with arms as thickly muscled as a man's, known as One-Eyed Sal. Her appearance lived up to her nickname, with the scar that ran through her left eye slanting down her cheek to just lift the corner of her mouth. She'd lost the eye in the California gold rush to another saloon girl who knew how to wield a broken bottle better than she did. Shortly thereafter, Tony had decided to add her to his stable. Body parts lost before the change don't regenerate, so Sal was one-eyed permanently. Alphonse didn't seem to mind, though, and her lopsided smile and scarred face featured prominently in his collection.

I'd been staring at his most recent shot of me one day, my eyes passing from my acne-covered cheeks and chin, which Alphonse had enhanced with a red filter to resemble a landscape on Mars, to a photo of Tony sprawled on his throne, looking even more bloated than usual. I'd barely even noticed Sal's newest photo in the middle, despite the fact that the lens had lingered lovingly on her scars. Between the two of us, she'd looked perfectly normal. Through Alphonse's lens, I'd realized, everyone was ugly; or maybe, through his lens, everyone was beautiful.

I still found it confusing, but I'd never looked at my photos quite the same way again. I'd even started to think that, compared to the frilly, posed shots my governess preferred, some of them were actually kind of interesting. Alphonse might be a murdering bastard, but unlike a certain war mage I could name, he occasionally made sense. And I was really getting tired of dealing with people I didn't understand.

I'd spent the last few weeks wandering around Pritkin's world, where I was supposed to belong, feeling like someone visiting a foreign country who only halfway spoke the language. Most of the time, I had no freaking clue what was going on, and once or twice I'd reached a state of confusion so severe that it felt like it might be causing brain damage. I couldn't win the game—hell, I couldn't even play—when I didn't understand the rules. I needed to level the playing field. I needed the vamps.

"Alphonse might be a first-class badass, but he isn't a first-level master," I reminded Rafe. "If Mircea dies, he'll be in the same boat with you, forced to fight for position within whatever family absorbs him."

"He needn't worry. There are many who would gladly add his . . . special talents . . . to their arsenal."

"Yeah, but how many do you think would be willing to make him their second?" Alphonse might carve out a niche for himself sooner or later, but no way was he going to end up second in command again. Not for centuries, maybe not ever. And I didn't think that would sit too well with the vamp I'd known.

"The Consul has forbidden anyone to help you," Rafe reminded me.

"Alphonse isn't so great at following orders," I reminded him right back. "I think he'll risk it." If I'd been giving odds, I'd have put them at ten to one at least. I was his best chance to hold on to his current position, which made me his new best friend. No matter what the Consul said. "I need Alphonse and a team of his craziest thugs. Can you get him?"

"I can contact him," Rafe reluctantly admitted. "But even if he agrees, I don't know if any of this will be soon enough."

"Soon enough for what?" I asked impatiently. "I know where the Codex is, Rafe. I just need help to get to it!"

"Yes, but Mircea . . . he's getting worse. And if he loses his faculties, will the counterspell reverse the damage? Or will he be left that way permanently?" Despite our position, which was a little too close to the ovens for comfort, he shivered.

I sat back in my chair, feeling dizzy. I'd assumed that once I had the spell, everything would go back to normal. But what if it didn't? And with the Senate in the middle of a war, what if they decided a crazed master vamp was a liability they couldn't afford? No wonder Rafe was freaking out. If the *geis* didn't kill Mircea, the Consul might.

Ironically, what I needed was more time. I had the location of the Codex; sooner or later, I was going to get that spell. But it wouldn't do me a lot of good if Mircea went crazy while I was making plans. Somehow I had to mitigate the effects of the *geis* while I figured everything out. And there was only a single possibility for that: the one place where I knew from experience the *geis* did not operate at full force.

"What about Faerie?" I asked. "If we could get him there, it might buy enough time to—"

"The Consul thought of that," Rafe said. His tone was even, but his agitated fingers were reducing my linen napkin to shreds. "But the Fey do not want any more vampires in their world, especially one in Mircea's condition. They refused a visa."

"Who did? The Light or the Dark?"

He looked surprised. "The Senate doesn't deal with the Dark Fey. Their treaty with the Light prohibits it."

"But I do." The Dark Fey king expected me to find and deliver the Codex. Until that happened, he needed to keep me happy. That gave me a lever to extort a few small favors, such as room and board for an ailing vampire.

"But, even were the Fey willing to help, how would we get him there?"

"What about the portal at MAGIC?" The Metaphysical Alliance for Greater Interspecies Cooperation was the supernatural community's version of the United Nations. It wasn't my favorite place, but we'd have to go in to get Mircea anyway, so it made sense to simply take him through MAGIC's own link to Faerie.

But Rafe squashed that idea. "It has not yet been repaired. Your passage last time was not . . . conventional . . . and it shattered the spell. The Consul has appealed to the Fey to allow another, but they say if we cannot control who enters their lands better than that, they are not certain they wish us to have one. We are in negotiations, but there is no knowing how long they may take."

And the Fey weren't known for doing anything in a hurry.

Not to mention that the portal, when and if it did open back up, was almost certain to be very well guarded. No help there.

"Damn it!" I hit the table with my palm, hard enough to slosh my untouched coffee everywhere. I was mopping it up with the napkin shreds when one of the mental Post-its I'd been filing at the back of my brain began waving about. "Tony has an illegal portal around here somewhere," I said slowly. "He used it for smuggling. I just don't know where it is."

Rafe gripped my hands, and for the first time he looked hopeful. "How do we locate it?"

"I don't know. But I know who to ask."

"You don't need a portal until you have the book," the pixie said, fluffing her tiny shock of bright red hair. She'd found a compact somewhere, possibly in the trash because most of the powder it once held was gone. She was using it for a mirror on the dressing table she'd made out of a bunch of CD cases. "And you haven't made any progress on that at all."

"You need it to get back home," I pointed out. "Unless you want to stay here?"

I looked around her makeshift apartment. It was fairly spacious from her perspective, taking up several shelves in the closet of Pritkin's study room. She'd fixed up the top shelf as the dressing area, while the bottom was a bedroom, complete with an oven mitt for a sleeping bag and a small flashlight for a lamp. She shot me a dirty look nonetheless. "Yes, I've found your world to be so hospitable."

"When I visited yours, I was almost killed!"

"And I was locked in a file cabinet," she spat.

"It beats a dungeon!"

"Ever try it?"

I'd seen the file cabinet, which looked like a bomb had exploded from the inside. "It didn't look like you had any trouble getting out."

"Only because it was made of some inferior metal, instead of iron." She shuddered. "I could have died, my magic leached away, my body slowly freezing in the cruel grip of cold—"

"Yes, but you didn't. And if we could get back to the point?"

Furious lavender eyes met mine. "The point is that the slave must return to the king's service and you must find the book you have promised him." She smiled evilly. "You do not wish to return to Faerie without it. The king is not known for his forgiving nature."

"Françoise isn't going anywhere," I told her, for maybe the tenth time. "And if the king's wrath is so dreadful, why did you offer to help us escape from him? Weren't you afraid of the consequences?"

The pixie fluttered her wings agitatedly. "That was different."

"Different how?"

"The mage offered me something irresistible." Her frown faded and her eyes suddenly shone with a softer light. "No one would have blamed me for taking it, not even the king."

"Offered you what?"

"It doesn't matter! I can't find it!" She kicked the jewel cases, then sat on the oversized spool of thread she'd turned into a seat, surreptitiously rubbing a hurt foot.

A memory suddenly clicked into place. "The rune stone. Jera." One of the reasons I'd managed to survive—barely— my one and only foray into her world was because I'd acquired some battle runes from the Senate. The Consul no doubt wanted them back, because they'd be useful in the war and because I hadn't exactly asked before taking them. But I thought that at the moment she might want Mircea more. And I couldn't see what good a rune stone would do her when its only power was making people more fertile.

The pixie glanced up resentfully. "He said he had it. He even showed it to me. It *looked* real."

"It *is* real." Understanding dawned. "You were willing to risk the king's wrath merely for the chance to have a child?"

"Merely?" Her tiny voice rose to a squeak. "Yes, trust a human to see it like that! My people hover on the brink of extinction, while your foolish, weak, puerile race, whose only accomplishment is to breed and breed and—"

"Yes, thanks, I get the point." I looked at her narrowly. "What if I could get it for you?"

A whirlwind of glittering green wings was suddenly in my face. "Where is it? Do *you* have it? I thought one of the mages—"

I smiled. No wonder she'd been sucking up. "I can get it."

"I'll believe it when I see it."

"Then you'll believe it soon. But I want the location of the portal in exchange."

"I'll find it," she promised fervently. "Just don't think of double-crossing me, human. You'll discover that I'm even less forgiving than my king."

Chapter 10

That afternoon I was checking in the convention that the hotel staff had secretly labeled the Geek Squad, a couple hundred role-playing enthusiasts who had arrived with bag and baggage, and in a few cases swords and armor, when I caught Pritkin staring at me. He was across the lobby, leaning against one of the fake stalagmites that erupted from the floor, all beard stubble and mussed hair and strong, lean build. His body looked relaxed, but his face held the same hawkish expression I'd last seen when he was standing over Saleh's headless corpse.

I scowled and handed a name badge to a guy dressed in a long trailing robe and a pointy hat. He shifted his staff to his other hand so he could pin it on. I didn't think it likely to help with ID much; he was the seventh Gandalf I'd seen that morning.

"I still don't understand why we can't set up *now*," the guy at my side whined. His voice was muffled by the mask he was wearing, but unfortunately not enough that I couldn't understand him. It had taken me a moment to identify the mask since he'd added plastic tusks that made it sag weirdly in front. I guess he hadn't been able to find a good ogre's head, because he'd converted a Chewbacca.

"I told you, we're doing some last-minute cleanup," I explained for the fifth time.

"They can't be cleaning the whole room at once! We can work around them."

"It's not my call," I said curtly, watching a bunch of guys

in elf ears who were pointing at the large creatures perched near the cavernous ceiling of the lobby. Each was six feet tall, grayish-black, with huge reptilian wings that ended in sharp, delicate claws. They looked like a cross between a bat and a pterodactyl, and most people mistook them for gruesome decorations. But the "elves" had apparently decided to use them for target practice: all three had bows in their hands and one nocked an arrow as I watched.

Before I could battle a path through the crowd, one of the creatures soared gracefully to the top of a stalagmite. Its new perch glittered with crystals in the low light, almost as brightly as the creature's dark eyes as it surveyed the tourists with predatory anticipation. It caught sight of the bow-wielding gamer and gave a shriek like tortured metal that echoed around the vastness of the lobby, drawing every eye in the place.

"Hey, cool!" the guy with the arrow said. "A yrthak!"

"That can't be a yrthak," another gamer said in a superior tone. "It has eyes."

A shiver of dread crawled down my spine. Once before, the casino's built-in security forces had mistaken innocent bystanders for dangerous intruders—and dealt with them accordingly. That time, it had been me and Pritkin in the hot seat, and we'd almost ended up dead. I somehow didn't think the average tourist was likely to fare even that well.

I dove between a couple of hobbits—or jawas or possibly very short monks—and grabbed the bow out of the gamer's hand. I tossed it to one of the security guys, who had jogged up from the other side. Casanova's love affair with filthy lucre was going to be the death of us all. "This was not the time to book in a bunch of norms," I hissed, sotto voce.

The guard just shrugged, holding the bow too high for the flailing arms of the outraged gamer to grab it. "No discharging weapons inside the casino!" he bellowed.

The young man scowled. "Zero charisma, okay?"

I turned to find Chewbacca still foaming at the mouth. "Look, lady, I got vendors with no place to put their stuff! What am I supposed to tell them?"

Even if Casanova had been paying me, it wouldn't have

been enough for this. I threw an arm around his hairy shoulders. "See that guy over there?" I pointed at Pritkin. "He usually handles stuff like this. Only he doesn't like that to get around, so you might have to be a little persistent."

Tall, dark and fuzzy pointed at Pritkin and yelled something to the half dozen vendors hanging around the entrance. They converged on the mage in a pack and I went back to work. Five minutes later, I felt a warm hand descend on my shoulder. "That wasn't very nice."

My skin prickled like someone was breathing on it. "Since when do you care?" I snapped. "Nice" wasn't even in Pritkin's vocabulary.

"It isn't one of my usual requirements," he agreed, sounding amused.

I didn't answer, my eyes on the group of gamers who were now trying to entice the "yrthak" down from its perch by waving a sandwich at it. It really concerned me that it hadn't gone back to its proper place yet. Even more worrying was the fact that its eyes were fixed not on the proffered food but on the nearest gamer's jugular.

"You can control those things, right?" I asked a nearby guard nervously.

The man didn't answer, but he moved a few yards closer to the "elves," his face about as happy as mine. Letting someone get eaten wasn't likely to improve his next performance evaluation. He pulled out a radio, looking worried. "We may have a situation," he told someone.

"I saw you watching me." The words were spoken directly into my ear.

"Bully for you," I said, as my nice orderly line of elves, trolls and ancient wizards went scurrying off to where the action was. Damn. I'd really hoped to be out of here soon.

Pritkin was standing close enough that the heat from his body was causing a little trickle of sweat to run down my spine. "Entertaining as this conversation has been," I told him caustically, "I have actual work to do. Why don't you go point a gun at something?"

He didn't comment, maybe because he was too busy licking a slow, wet trail up my neck. For a frozen second, I just stood there. I'd always assumed that Pritkin had some kind of allergy to human contact. He rarely touched people, unless he was moving me around like a mannequin, and he *never* made passes. Especially not such . . . obvious . . . ones.

I spun to see his smile widening, his eyes gone vibrant green. It was not an expression I'd ever imagined on his face—an almost feral sexuality. And his clothes were back to black. It gave me a very bad feeling, and that was before he reached out and pulled me against him.

Whatever I might have said was silenced by lips sliding softly over mine. I wasn't prepared for him to kiss me, much less like that. His mouth was warm and surprisingly sweet, and the faint scrape of stubble shouldn't have been the least bit erotic, yet it was. His tongue traced a feathery caress over my bottom lip in a way that felt positively indecent. I pulled back, seriously confused. "What—"

"No," he said, tilted my head and kissed me. Heat radiated from the heavy hand resting on my neck, and a thumb stroked light patterns down my throat. A sudden rush of desire made me forget to keep my mouth closed, and a tongue twined expertly around my own. Pritkin took his time, exploring me, tasting me. A hand rested on my waist, in what should have been a neutral spot, but it burned.

I jerked away, angry and confused. "Are you crazy?" One of the fun facts about the *geis* was the jolt of pain it gave me whenever I got close to anyone but Mircea. It seemed to have a particular grudge against Pritkin, upping the usual warning where he was concerned to a level that had me certain my eyes were dripping down my cheekbones.

He didn't answer, just somehow backed me into the reservation desk without laying a hand on me. Something was going on in the casino: I could hear screams and see camera flashes, and a bunch of guards ran by with a huge net in their hands. "I know you talked to Saleh," he whispered against my lips. "What did he tell you?"

Another inhuman shriek rent the air, this time from above. The second creature did not appear to like the fact that the guards were trying to trap its companion. It took off the top of one of the stalactites on its way to join the fight, and fake rock rained down on us from all sides. I barely noticed, being far more concerned about the body suddenly pressing hard against me.

"Answer me." The hilt of a sword was gouging into my ribs, I realized vaguely, and something was . . . was wrong about that. Where was the holster lump on his thigh? Or the ratty leather belt studded with weapons and potions, like a homicidal mad scientist? And since when did Pritkin wear *cologne*?

I suddenly panicked. None of this made sense. I was absolutely not standing in the middle of the lobby making out with *Pritkin* while all hell broke loose. I pushed at him, with no more result than trying to move a boulder. "Let go!"

Power flooded the air, making the hairs on my arms stick up in alarm and sending a scorching tide rolling across my body. "I said let go," I murmured, suddenly lost in a pair of crystal-clear eyes. His mouth claimed mine again, fierce and possessive, not at all shy of anyone who might be watching, and something about it made the rest of the world fall away into pure hunger. The scent of him was maddening—something elegant and expensive and completely unexpected, with the musk of skin and need beneath the rest.

He pulled back and I looked into the face of a stranger, one wearing an expression of hawklike intensity. *"Answer me."* The command surged through me with the irresistible force of a tidal wave. I opened my mouth in unthinking response, just as a new shower of plaster from above dropped on top of us.

I sputtered and choked on a mouthful of gray dust, and Pritkin gave a frustrated sigh. "For a place filled with incubi," he said dryly, "managing a seduction here is surprisingly difficult." I stumbled back into another group of security men headed for the crisis of the hour, and by the time we got ourselves sorted out, Pritkin was gone.

"You know, I'm not so forgiving, either," I said, glaring at the pixie. As if I didn't have enough trouble with Pritkin going *insane*, Radella had come up with exactly zilch.

Françoise was still pawing through the alarming number of weapons Casanova had stockpiled in a storeroom on Dante's lowest level. I'd decided that, given the number of people who wanted me dead, maybe I should stock up. And with Radella still scheming against her, I figured Françoise might be able to use a few items herself.

She held up something. *"Q'est-ce que c'est?"*

I squinted at it. "It's a Taser. It shocks people."

"Quoi?"

"Like lightning." I danced about a little and understanding lit her eyes.

She looked at the pixie, who was hovering well out of reach near the ceiling, and smiled. "Shock me and I'll cut your heart out," Radella promised.

Françoise didn't comment, but she clipped the small device to the olive green, army-style tool belt she'd found in a weapons locker. It looked a little odd next to her outfit. She was still wearing the dress from the fashion show, although the spiders were starting to look a bit lackluster. Two had stopped moving altogether, and the one on her shoulder had been weaving the same web for the last twenty minutes. It looked like the charm was meant to last for one day only.

Other than the dress she'd had on when she escaped from Faerie, it was the only outfit I'd seen her wear. It suddenly occurred to me that she might not have any others. I made a mental note to take her shopping.

"What seems to be the holdup?" I asked Radella, while examining a 9 mm. It didn't look like the grip was any smaller than mine, so I put it back.

"I can't find it, all right?" She fluttered to the top of a gun cabinet and sat down, chin in hand. Her iridescent wings drooped around her shoulders dispiritedly. "I've looked everywhere!"

"Then look again!"

"If the portal was here, I'd have found it!"

"Well, obviously not," I pointed out. "Because it *is* here."

"Then it should have been easy to locate," Radella groused. "The power output alone—"

"Come again?"

She gave me a disgusted look. "Portals don't run on batteries! They're rare not only because they're regulated but because few people have a power source capable of handling one."

"What kind of power are we talking about?"

"A lot. A ley-line sink is usually required, although there are talismans capable of opening a short-term gateway. But they're rare. I doubt that vampire had one."

"A ley-line what?"

"Where two lines cross and pool their energy," Radella said impatiently. I blinked at her. "Ley. Lines," she said, very slowly and distinctly. "You do know what those are, right?"

I had heard of them, but the memory was vague. Just something about a lot of ancient monuments being constructed on parallel lines. "Assume I know nothing," I told her.

She smirked. "I always do." Françoise said something in a language I didn't know and Radella flushed bright red. She slapped her tiny hand down, making the whole cabinet shudder beneath her. "Quiet, slave! Remember to whom you're speaking!"

"I always do," Françoise told her sweetly.

"Ladies!" I looked back and forth between the two of them, but nobody was going for weapons, which made it a pretty congenial conversation for those two.

"To put it really, really simply," Radella said icily, her eyes still on Françoise, "ley lines are borders between worlds: yours, mine, the demon realms, whatever. When those borders collide, you get stress, like when two of your tectonic plates rub together. And stress creates energy."

"Like magical fault lines."

"That's what I said!" Radella snapped. "Only in this case, there's no land to move, only magical energy getting hurled about. Therefore, instead of earthquakes or tsunamis, you get power, which can be used for various applications by those who know how."

"Like running portals."

"Under certain circumstances. If two particularly strong ley lines cross, they might generate that kind of energy, but it doesn't happen often."

"Then all we have to do is look for this sink thing," I said excitedly. "If it's putting off that kind of power, it should be easy to find!"

Radella sighed and muttered something I was just as glad I couldn't understand. "There are ley lines all around Vegas," she finally said. "But none cross anywhere near here. The closest area where they do is the MAGIC enclave, which is why it was built where it is."

"So what was Tony using?" I asked impatiently.

"As a guess?" Radella pursed her little mouth. It made her look like professor Barbie. "Death magic. Quick, powerful, easily obtained."

"As long as you 'ave the stomach for eet," Françoise muttered darkly.

"Wait a minute." I was really hoping I'd heard wrong. "You're saying that, even if I find Tony's portal, I'd have to kill someone to use it?"

Radella shrugged. "Well, you know. Not anyone you like."

"I'm not committing murder!"

"I theenk I could power że portal," Françoise said, "for a short time. With some help."

She was looking at me, but I shook my head. "I was never trained. Tony was afraid of having a powerful witch at court."

"But . . . you know notheeng?" She looked horrified.

"Pretty much."

"But, you run 'ere and zere"—she made some flailing motions in the air—"doing theengs, all ze time!"

"As opposed to what? Waiting for someone to come kill me?"

"But, eef the dark mages catch you, they weel drain you of your power! Eet would be awful!"

I smiled grimly. "Yeah. Only they'd have to get in line."

"Quoi?"

"Nothing." I glanced at the pixie. "We can worry about how to power the damn thing once we find it. Any little ideas on that?"

She looked thoughtful. "It has to be a hidden portal. It's the only thing that makes sense."

"We know it's hidden!" I said, exasperated.

"No, *hidden* hidden. As in, not in this world until summoned."

"Did you hear me just say I know nothing about magic?"

Radella scowled. "Think of it like a door. A door that uses energy whenever it's open. So you keep it closed until needed."

"When you open it with a sacrifice."

"Right. But if that's how this portal works, there's probably a special incantation to summon it."

"Let me guess. You don't know the incantation." It figured.

"It's different for every portal, a password known only to the users."

"Who are now all in Faerie," I reminded her. "How am I supposed to get it?"

A sly look came over her tiny, doll-like face. "Perhaps I could figure something out, for the right price."

I narrowed my eyes at the scheming little thing. "Now what?"

She fidgeted, trying to look nonchalant. I thought it was just as well she was too small to do any gambling; with a poker face like that, she'd have been soaked in five minutes flat. "I want a second casting of the rune," she finally blurted out. "In case the first one doesn't result in a child."

I got busy checking out another gun for a moment. I'd been under the impression that we'd already agreed that I'd give her the rune, not just cast it. Maybe the thing was more valuable than I'd thought.

"All right," I said slowly, trying to sound reluctant. "Another casting."

"With no restrictions! Even if I get with child on the first, I still get the second!"

"Agreed."

Radella swallowed. "What kind of help do you want?"

"Whatever is needed." I wasn't about to let her impose conditions, either.

"I knew you'd find a way to talk me into this insanity," she sniped, but her heart clearly wasn't in it.

"Do we have a deal?"

"Oh, you damn well know we do!" I smiled, and she

grimaced back. "Don't be so smug, human. You haven't heard my idea yet."

Dante's front entrance is something out of a medieval nightmare, with writhing basalt statues, tortured topiaries and an honest-to-God moat. The front door handles are agonized faces that moan and groan and utter its famous catchphrase, telling all who enter to abandon hope—along with their wallets. But demented decor is expensive, which explains why the back looks more like a modern warehouse, with loading ramps, overripe Dumpsters and a plain chain-link fence surrounding a crowded employee parking lot.

Françoise, Radella, Billy Joe and I landed in Dante's parking lot two weeks in the past. It was still a few hours before the sun, or anyone with any sense, would think about rising. In other words, high noon for the types I needed to see.

Radella's big idea was to go back in time before everyone who knew how to summon the portal left, and get the incantation out of them by whatever means necessary. I had amended that to exclude beatings, knifings or anything likely to result in the total trashing of the timeline. Françoise had added a refinement by mentioning that she could probably erase the short-term memory of anyone except a powerful mage. So we had a plan—we just needed the right guy. And Casanova's predecessor, a slimy operator known as Jimmy the Rat, was my best guess for man in the know.

"Je suis désolée," Françoise said, apparently talking to the bottom of the chain-link fence.

I exchanged looks with the pixie, who merely shrugged. I bent over to get a better look and found myself handcuffed to the fence post. "What the hell?"

Françoise stood back and crossed her arms, regarding me with a fair imitation of Pritkin in a mood. "We weel go. Eet ees too dangerous for you."

"Excuse me?"

"You 'ave not the skill in *magique, n'est-ce pas?*"

"What's your point?"

"You 'ad to breeng us 'ere; zere was no choice. But you do

not 'ave to risk yourself now. We weel talk to thees gangster while you remain where it is safe."

"I can handle Jimmy!"

Françoise didn't answer, but she got this look on her face, like she was perfectly happy to stand in the parking lot for the rest of the night discussing it. I tugged on the cuff, but she must have liberated it from Casanova's storeroom, because it was good-quality steel. All my efforts did was rattle the fence and piss me off.

"Okay," I said. "You go, me stay. Have fun."

"You aren't serious," Billy said incredulously.

"You weel stay right 'ere?" Françoise looked doubtful. Maybe she'd expected me to argue more.

I jangled the fence again for effect. "Do I have a choice?"

"I don't trust her," the pixie said, eyeing me narrowly. "We should stick her in a closet."

"I have a gun," I pointed out.

Radella frowned. "She's right. She could shoot the lock."

"I was thinking of something a little more animated," I told her, not entirely sure I was kidding.

"Eet is for your own good," Françoise said, biting her lip. She suddenly looked uncertain.

Radella snapped her fingers. "We knock her out. *Then* we stuff her in the closet. A really small one," she added viciously.

Françoise didn't even bother to look at her. "We return soon," she promised, then turned on her heel and strode away.

"Yeah, I'll just wait here like a glorified taxi driver," I called after her. Her shoulders twitched slightly, but I didn't know if that was from shame or from not knowing what a taxi was.

"Okay, that was really—" Billy began.

I held up my free hand. Françoise paused by the back door and looked in my direction. Probably wondering why my hand was hovering in the air. I waved at her and after a minute she and Radella let themselves in through the employee entrance. As soon as the door closed, I shifted two feet ahead. Behind me, the now empty cuff banged against the fencing.

"I forget you can do that now," Billy said.

"So do I, half the time." I rubbed my wrist and looked around. There was no one in sight. It occurred to me that maybe I should have looked before doing my Houdini impression.

"Why didn't you just show them that they were wasting their time?" Billy demanded.

"I figured we might as well get the mutiny phase of our relationship out of the way early." Besides, I didn't think Radella had been kidding about the closet. "Let's go find Jimmy before he sells them the Brooklyn Bridge or some—"

"Speak of the devil," Billy said, as someone who looked an awful lot like Jimmy ran out the back door.

I started forward after a surprised pause, hardly believing my luck. If I could get to him before he reached his car, we could talk without encountering anyone else or possibly being overheard. But then the door slammed open and a blonde ran out, looking around wildly.

"Wait, there's some bimbo with him," Billy cautioned. The blonde caught sight of Jimmy and took off after him, hiking up her low-cut black top as she went. Billy whistled appreciatively. "She's gonna fall right out of that thing if she ain't—"

He stopped abruptly, squinting across the lot, and I did the same, a vague feeling of unease creeping up my spine. The energy-conscious halogen lights didn't help a lot with visibility, but I saw enough to make my stomach fall. "I think we have a problem," I said numbly.

"Hey," Billy said, eyes wide. "I think that bimbo is you! I can tell by the shape of your—"

"Do you realize what this means?" I managed to shriek in a whisper. I hadn't figured out until that moment that I'd brought us back to the night I first saw Dante's—not a time I was real interested in reliving.

"Yeah." He glared at me. "Of all the times to come back to, why in the *hell*—"

"I didn't do it on *purpose*," I hissed. "Casanova told me the last shipment of slaves left for Faerie on this night. If we can't get Jimmy to talk, I thought we might overhear the incantation being used!"

"If we were in the right place at the right time, yeah. But this ain't it."

"You think?" My first visit to Dante's hadn't gone well. In fact, it had gone about as spectacularly wrong as humanly possible. There had been too many near misses, too many times that I and a lot of other people could have died had things gone slightly differently. I needed to find the team and get out, fast, before any of us changed anything.

Jimmy and the other me disappeared into the lines of cars, and the back door slammed open yet again. Pritkin and a couple of vamps appeared, and I froze. My eyes might be having trouble making out the action, but theirs certainly wouldn't be. And if they glanced over here and saw me, it could distract them from the task at hand. Which, among other things, included saving the other me's life.

I didn't move, didn't breathe, didn't blink. The black tank top and jeans I'd decided would be appropriate for the night's activities would help make me harder to spot. But they could smell me from this distance, even in a parking lot filled with gas fumes and garbage. One of the vamps paused, lifting his head slightly as if scenting the air, and I swallowed thickly. It was Tomas, my onetime roommate, who had had six months to get my scent down cold. If he sensed me . . .

But he didn't. The three men ran into the rows of cars and a few moments later all hell broke loose, with gunshots, screams, and someone setting a car on fire. I took off for the back door at a dead run. And skidded to a halt a couple of seconds later when the very last person I wanted to see appeared in my path.

I managed to catch myself before careening into him, but it was a close thing. I hastily scrambled back a couple of steps just to be on the safe side. "You're not supposed to be here!" I said accusingly.

One perfect eyebrow formed itself into an equally perfect arch. "Then we have something in common, *dulceață.*"

Chapter 11

I stared at Mircea in shock. "You're supposed to be downtown!" The version of me who'd just chased Jimmy across the parking lot had escaped from MAGIC earlier that night. And although its wards had allowed me to be tracked into the city, no one had been sure exactly where I'd gone. While Tomas, Pritkin and a vampire named Louis-Cesare came here, Rafe and Mircea had gone to Tony's main offices. Or so I'd thought.

"I was. I left Raphael there, in case you made an appearance," Mircea said, his eyes narrowing slightly. "May I ask how you knew that?"

"Probably wouldn't be best," I said, wishing hysteria was a luxury I could afford.

Mircea just stood there, looking ridiculously model-pretty with his tousled hair and faintly amused mouth, his rich black suit perfectly showcasing his—objectively speaking—extremely attractive body. I didn't know if he did it deliberately, but his clothes always seemed to run just a little snug around the biceps and thighs, drawing my attention where it absolutely had no place being. Not to mention that Mircea in black looked like sin. The only saving grace was that at least it wasn't leather—and why was I even going there?

He held out a hand. It was a silent invitation, but it made my stomach flip. My stomach was an *idiot*.

I jumped back, almost stumbling over my own feet. "Don't touch me!" The last time I'd encountered Mircea in the past, the *geis* had leapt from me to him, starting this whole mess by doubling the spell. Would I triple it if he got close enough now? Because I didn't think either of us could survive that.

Somewhere nearby, people were yelling and Pritkin was swearing and a couple of terrified-looking wererats scurried past, dripping blood on the asphalt. "We must go, *dulceaţă*," Mircea said mildly.

The fact that he was still using the pet name he'd given me years ago, meaning "dear one," was probably a good sign, but I doubted it was going to last. I needed to get gone, but I really didn't want to shift in front of him—it would tell him a lot more than I wanted him to know. But I couldn't exactly outrun him, and I sure couldn't let him get close enough to touch me.

"Cassie." Mircea looked at me reproachfully when I continued to ignore his outstretched hand.

But, I thought, desperately backing away, the screwup had come in an era before the *geis* was cast. *That* Mircea hadn't had it, so the spell had leapt from me to him to complete itself. But *this* Mircea did have it, had both strands, in fact, so he should be immune. Right?

"Cassandra!"

"I'm trying to think here!" I told him as he started toward me.

"You can think at MAGIC, where it's safe."

"You know," I said savagely, "considering how often I hear that word, it's amazing how frequently I end up almost dead!"

"That will not happen tonight," he said firmly, and took my hand. I stared at him in horror, waiting for the electric sizzle that would tell me I'd just managed to kill us both. But other than the faint tingle the *geis* always gave off, there was nothing.

Nothing except a sweet, cloying odor, like flowers on the verge of rot. Where had I smelled that before? Mircea said what I suspected was a very bad word in Romanian and abruptly pulled me behind him.

"Cass, you know the last time we were here, how a couple of dark mages showed up for the party?" Billy asked, his voice quavering slightly.

"Why, what does that have to—" I looked around Mircea's

coat to see a group of dark shapes silhouetted against the street lights. "Oh."

"I'm thinking maybe I missed a few on the recon," Billy said, looking freaked.

I did a quick count. "A *few*?" I squeaked. "Eight is not a few!"

In the distance, a blue cloud started to spread over the parking lot. I remembered that—Pritkin had employed some kind of tear gas in combat and almost choked us all to death. It had been no fun inside, my lungs burning for hours afterwards; of course, it wasn't currently a thrill a minute on the outside, either.

"The seer goes with us, vampire," one of the mages said.

I expected Mircea to try to talk him around, to use some of the famous charm that had made him the Consul's chief negotiator. I guess the mages did, too. Because they looked really surprised when the speaker suddenly went flying through the air.

He landed in the power lines overhead, snapping one of the bigger ones on impact and getting caught on several of the smaller. A hiss of electricity stuttered wildly around his body for a moment, then he plunged toward the ground, only to be snatched back up again by a line that had gotten tangled around one foot. He bounced a couple of times before starting to swing slowly in space, dangling upside down by an ankle like the Hanged Man in my tarot deck.

"That was unwise," the nearest mage told Mircea calmly, right before a wall of scorching hot air slammed into us. It lifted me completely off my feet and threw both of us back against the fencing. I missed the spine-shattering post, but it felt like some of the links might have become permanent additions to my anatomy.

Mircea was back on his feet in a blink, and two mages spontaneously caught fire. They put it out almost as quickly, however, and by the time I had crawled out of the metal net, they'd responded with a blistering ball of electric blue and white. It drove Mircea to one knee, but he caught it, hands sizzling audibly, then lobbed it back at the sender. The mages' shields deflected it into the power lines above, causing a pulse of electricity to run along them like blue fire. The streetlights popped in a long line like firecrackers, and a pulse of energy exploded against the hanging mage, sending him spiraling the rest of the way to earth with a power line snapping and stuttering around him.

The electrocuted mage was twitching slightly against the ground, like he might still be alive. Then I got a good look at his face, which was slack-jawed, with open, glassy eyes and a blackened tongue, and decided no, probably not. One of his colleagues apparently reached the same conclusion, but instead of mourning his friend, he elected to use him. He animated the corpse with a gesture, raising it vertically until it looked like a scarecrow in a windstorm, all jumping limbs and dangling, jittering feet, hovering just above the ground.

I glanced from the dancing corpse to the widening blue cloud, but enough flashes, rumblings and muffled gunshots were coming from inside that I felt marginally safe from having our fight overheard. It was the only thing I felt safe about, especially when a metal trash can came flying at our heads. It stopped in midair, about a foot from my nose, then reversed course and flew apart, razor-sharp fragments peppering the line of mages like shrapnel. Shrapnel that did not, it appeared, make it through their shields.

The rusty tan Pinto that slammed into the mages a second later didn't, either, but it did take their combined effort to throw it off. It went flipping away across the night, rotating three times before exploding against the nearest line of cars. Most of the mages were fine, if seriously pissed. But one was either younger or less well trained than the others, because for a split second he lost his concentration—and with it, his shields. And a second is all it takes.

A master vampire does not need to touch a person to drain him, a fact that Mircea took this opportunity to demonstrate. I think he was trying to intimidate the others into running, because he did not go for a clean kill. He extended a hand and the mage jerked to a halt, bloody tears suddenly springing to his eyes. But instead of streaming down his cheeks, they flowed outward, flying across the distance between us to

Mircea's palm, where the tiny droplets were immediately absorbed.

And then it wasn't only his eyes bleeding; it looked like every pore on his face had ruptured, sending not a trickle but a flood twisting through the air, like a long red ribbon. In a few short seconds the mage crumpled, face now snow white, bloodless lips open in a silent *oh*. He was dead before he hit the asphalt.

If intimidation had been the object, it didn't work. The mages merely scattered and mounted separate attacks. They probably assumed that Mircea couldn't watch the remaining six at once, and while he was dealing with one, the others would take him out. I was desperately afraid they might be right. The animated corpse moved closer, and a cloud of glass fragments from the destroyed cars rose up from the ground behind it, glittering in the flames like deadly diamonds. As if that wasn't enough, a group of burning tires rotated off the asphalt, looking like a squadron of UFOs against the dark.

I lost track of exactly what happened after that, as everything came at us at once—most of it too fast to see. I blinked and the next time I looked, a segment of fencing had jumped in front of us, acting like a shield to catch the various flying objects. I realized why the corpse had continued to move even after death when it crashed into the fence and the whole thing lit up with sparks. Around its foot, the downed power line was still coiled like a long black snake, hissing and crackling, spitting fire as deadly to a vampire as to a human. But it couldn't touch us, and in a moment, the body went dancing back across the parking lot like a demented puppet.

Mircea sent the segment of fencing flying toward the nearest mage, and it hit his shields with an avalanche of sparks. They held, ensuring that the hot metal didn't touch his skin, but they couldn't stop the fence from wrapping around him like a blanket. The links almost immediately began to glow with a new, more-intense light, melting into his shielding the way hot water sinks into ice.

The other mages had paused for some reason, and I didn't wait to find out why. I dove for Mircea, intending to shift us out before they got their wind back, even if it blew my cover.

But a solid wall of energy met my outstretched hand, searing a stripe across my skin that felt like a bad sunburn.

"Get out of here, Cassie," Mircea said, as I snatched my hand back.

"Here's a thought," Billy said. "Shift both of you out of here."

I gave him my "no shit" face. "I have to touch him!"

"What's stopping you?"

Apparently, he couldn't see the barrier any better than I could. But it was there. Mircea didn't have shields—he wasn't a mage and vamp magic didn't work like that. It had to be pure power he was putting out, surrounding himself and the mages in an energy field that had them trapped as effectively as any cage. But in a way, he was as trapped as they were. He couldn't drop the barrier without setting them free, and I couldn't get any closer as long as he kept it up.

"Mircea is stopping me!" I snapped.

"Cassandra! I cannot hold them forever!" A single drop of sweat ran down Mircea's cheek to hang suspended on the edge of his jaw. "You must go!"

Before I could reply, one of the mages tore free, a young man with acne and mismatched eyes, one green and one blue. He stumbled away from the others, his clothes smoking, his limp brown hair on fire. But a few whispered words put out the flames and when he turned, his face furious, there was something in his hand. Something warm and pale pink, the color of the webbing between his fingers.

The little ball looked innocuous, but I'd been around mages long enough to know how likely that was. And Mircea couldn't move, couldn't defend himself, without freeing the others to do even more damage. Fear, stark and violent, flashed down my spine and my heart started throbbing in my ears, which made no sense because I could feel my skin prickling as the blood drained from my face.

The small ball dropped to the ground and rolled a few feet before coming to rest against a tuft of grass growing up through the concrete. The mage sank to his knees, staring at me with surprise on his face. And then he fell over sideways, still clutching the widening stain on his chest.

"You shot him." Billy looked almost as surprised as I felt.

"I guess he forgot to get his shields back up," I said numbly.

I wanted to sit down. My insides felt trembly and my hand was shaking, which considering that I had a mostly full clip in the gun was probably a safety violation. But then the mages did something that sent Mircea smashing back into what remained of the fence, causing him to momentarily lose his concentration. And as soon as he did, the animated corpse came flying across the parking lot and leapt straight at him.

I screamed, knowing what fire of any type did to an unprotected vampire. Then I was shooting at random, an ache blooming in my chest so sharp it felt like a knife. But the remaining mages all had shields up. My bullets just pinged off a couple as if they were made of transparent steel, and were absorbed by others, like rocks falling into water. They'd killed Mircea and I couldn't even hurt them.

"Cassie!" I turned at Billy's voice, and found him hovering in front of Mircea, hazy and indistinct, like a double negative.

I stared in disbelief as Mircea slowly raised his head. Then I did a double take, my mouth literally dropping open, because he was hanging in the middle of a fence jumping with blue-white energy and there was no way he'd survived that. Just no way.

"Get him out of there or he's a goner!"

"What?" I said stupidly, and then someone grabbed me from behind. The gun went flying out of my hand and a fist cracked against my cheekbone, slamming my head back, making my ears ring. I tried desperately to shift, but I was dizzy and the pain was unbelievable and nothing happened.

"I have her!" a man's voice yelled in my ear, and from the corner of my eye I saw another dark shape advancing on us. But the arms around my waist wouldn't budge no matter how I fought. Someone was screaming nearby, a horrible, hopeless sound that messed with my concentration as much as the hands that were forcing my wrists together.

I kicked out with my foot, as hard as I could, and felt the impact against something soft. Someone swore and a pale, gaunt man with hard gray eyes appeared in front of me. He pulled a wicked-looking knife from his coat and held it in front of my eyes until I was able to focus on it. As soon as I did, he stabbed it down into my right wrist.

I could feel small bones breaking, then he gave it a twist and it tore against tendons, blood dripping down my arm as he ripped it out and held it in front of my face again. "Still want to fight us?"

For a moment, I couldn't scream—there wasn't enough air in my lungs. Then something hard and slick tightened around my wrists, right over the wound. And I gave a shriek that didn't sound right, didn't sound like me, but the pain slammed into me all at once and then I couldn't stop screaming.

"Shut her up!" someone said, and an arm clamped over my windpipe, cutting off the noise and also my air. I desperately tried to shift again, and for a second I thought I had it. Just like in the caves, I could feel time as a syrupy, elastic mass, only it wasn't quite right, wasn't enfolding me like I wanted.

Suddenly I hit the ground, stunned and bleary-eyed, and when nobody grabbed me again, I started trying to crawl away. But my hands were bound with a hard plastic tie, I couldn't put any weight on my broken wrist and my directional sense was shot. I ended up rolling into a puddle of something warm and sticky.

I looked down to see a diamond pattern burnt into the asphalt. All around it were shreds of fabric, which I finally recognized as crisped blue jeans and the singed remains of a cotton shirt. There were hard white bits sticking up here and there, marring the pattern, and something that looked like hair. It finally hit me. The fencing. Mircea had wrapped it around the mage, and it had burnt through his shields and then it had—

I scrambled to my feet and staggered away, bile rising in my throat, my breath coming hard and fast enough to actually hurt my lungs. My head was reeling, and when I tried to steady myself, the space around me shook instead. I would have run straight into the fence if Billy hadn't shouted at me.

"Your shoes! They're rubber-soled, Cass!"

For a moment I didn't know what he was talking about, but then blue-white fire flashed in front of my eyes and I got it.

The power line had come loose from its human delivery device and attached itself directly to the fence, slithering back and forth over the asphalt like a huge electric eel. My head kept swimming and my eyesight was trying to black out and my fingers didn't seem to want to do what I told them, even on the hand that didn't feel like it was on fire. Getting the sneaker off was a nightmare, and even holding on to it was a challenge—how was I supposed to use it for anything? And why was nobody trying to stop me all of a sudden?

I didn't want to risk touching the line directly, rubber soles or no. I tried throwing the sneaker, but my aim was even worse than usual and I finally ended up kicking it instead. It took four tries, but I managed to jar the downed line until it lost contact with the fence.

As soon as it did, I had a vague sense of Mircea jumping away and attacking the remaining mages. I heard what sounded like a neck snap and a body hit the asphalt nearby, but I couldn't seem to concentrate on it. It was all I could do to fight the urge to relax and sink into the welcoming darkness that hovered at the edges of my vision.

I stumbled backwards, and my heel hit something that crunched under the light pressure. When I looked down, I saw two bodies on the ground. The nearest was a woman, so elderly as to be cadaverous, her skin papery and mottled with age spots, her hair wispy and bone white. The other was a man, at least I assumed so, based on his clothes. The slight breeze sent tiny pieces of a disintegrating mustard-colored shirt blowing away, like pollen on the air. The body underneath looked like a recently unwrapped mummy, all crinkled brown skin stretched over visible ribs. I stared at them, stunned and uncomprehending.

"Cass! Cass!" Billy was talking to me, and something pale rolled against my remaining sneaker. "Throw it!"

My eyes finally managed to focus on the small item, which I identified as the ball the mage had been holding earlier. Billy must have retrieved it, but I couldn't understand why until I looked up and saw five more mages rushing towards us from the far side of the building. It looked like the cavalry had arrived, but with my usual luck, they were for the other side.

I shook my head, trying to clear it, and that jolted my arm, and oh, God, that hadn't been a good idea. Luckily the mages weren't paying any attention to me, either because they hadn't seen me yet or because, compared to Mircea, I didn't look like much of a threat. He was providing a hell of a distraction, stepping on one mage's neck while wrenching another's head almost completely off his body. It looked impressive, but if he had resorted to old-fashioned hand-to-hand, he was pretty damn drained. I didn't know if he could survive another attack and I didn't intend to find out.

I tried to grab the sphere, but my hands were slick with blood and I couldn't seem to keep hold. Every time I thought I had it, it slipped away, my fingers just not able to hold on. I accidentally kicked it and held my breath, waiting for it to detonate and kill us all, but it only rolled off a few yards until stopped by a ridge in the concrete.

"Cass!"

I looked up to see that I was out of time. The mages had paused a cautious distance from Mircea, but that was only because any master vampire deserved a certain respect, even a wounded one. Maybe especially a wounded one. But the attack would come any second now. And I couldn't stop it.

Chapter 12

"Billy! I can't get it!" I looked at him desperately. "You have to do it."

He shook his head. "I'm too drained. It took everything I had just to roll it over to you!"

I made another grab and trapped the ball under my hands, but it was too slippery. I had the impression that its surface wouldn't provide much in the way of traction even if I wasn't bleeding all over it. "Damn it! If I had more time—"

Billy looked at me like I was crazy. "You're Pythia! You have all the time you want!"

"I can't shift! I've tried." It was probably the pain, but I couldn't see past it. Maybe that was one of the things training taught, how to concentrate when your brain was fuzzy from blood loss and your hand felt like it was going to fall off and you had absolutely no time to get it wrong. I would have really, really liked to have had that lesson.

But I hadn't, so I had to go with what I knew. I stopped plucking uselessly at the sphere and looked at Billy. "Take a draw."

"Now?!"

"Damn it, Billy. Yes, now! Get your strength back and throw this thing!"

Billy didn't waste any time. He slipped inside my skin before I'd finished talking, and I felt the energy drain immediately. Unlike normal, it hurt. Maybe because I didn't have much left to give, maybe because Billy had to speed up the process, maybe because everything already hurt anyway. But whatever the reason, within seconds my heart was hammering, my hands were shaking and I could actually sense my life flowing out of me. My brain was stuck on a hamster wheel, *bad idea bad idea bad idea bad idea*, but there was nothing I could do; I didn't have the strength to stop it. I heard someone sigh, a long whistling release of breath, and then I was falling a very long way.

I landed on the asphalt in time to see Billy scoop up the ball. He almost lost it once, it almost slipped right through his still mostly transparent hand, but he caught it at the last second. The throw looked a lot like something I'd have done, a wobbly underhand that didn't land even close to dead center. It exploded a yard or so in front of the mages with a barely audible poof and a small cloud of hazy pink, as if a powder-filled balloon had been dropped onto concrete. The air seemed to ripple slightly, but the mages showed no discernible effects.

"It's a damn dud!" Billy cursed just as the first of the newcomers reached Mircea. He turned, his elbow connecting with the mage's face, and I had time to wonder why the man's shields weren't up, why they hadn't stopped the attack. Then it was as if his head just exploded, like instead of a man, Mircea had hit a face made of nothing more than colored sand.

"Lot's Wife," Billy said, sounding impressed. "Bad stuff, dark magic." I wondered if I should worry that his tone was approving.

The other mages had stopped, frozen in various stages of movement. One had been running, caught with a single leg raised, and his own momentum toppled him over. He exploded against the asphalt and Mircea gave a purely vicious smile. He walked to the next human statue, a young man with sandy blond hair, and gave him the barest push with the flat of his hand. The mage toppled backwards into another, and they both hit the ground with a bang, dissolving into a cloud of multicolored dust. It so mixed them up that it was impossible to tell where one body started and the other ended.

Mircea went on to the last while I stared at the flesh-colored sand pouring out of a scuffed leather tennis shoe. A gust of wind blew across the lot, pushing little grains of the substance against the cheek I couldn't seem to lift off the asphalt. They didn't feel like sand; they didn't feel like much of anything at all.

I heard the thud as another body hit the ground, felt the billow of wind as it broke into crumbly pieces, but I couldn't focus on it. *Shock*, I thought vaguely. I knew what I technically should be feeling, but I wasn't sure I was actually feeling it. My whole body hurt, but the pain seemed to reach me only through a buzzing, staticky distance.

I stared at the pile of human remains and wondered what the spell did. Billy was saying something. Maybe he was trying to tell me, only I couldn't understand him. *Maybe it sucked all the water out*, I thought vaguely. Was that what was left of a person with the moisture mostly gone? A pile of crumbly, chemical-smelling stuff that looked like a human, but couldn't be because people didn't turn into powder when you touched them? That was just wrong, not possible.

Like me shooting a man through the heart.

Someone knelt beside me and cut off the plastic bracelet. I could see flashes of white through the bloody meat of my wrist, but it didn't look like a vein had been hit. It felt bad, though. I was hauled into someone's arms, my back against a warm chest that was breathing too quickly, or maybe that was me. I tried to slow it down but nothing happened, so I decided it wasn't me after all.

Strong hands stroked through my hair, gently separating the tangled strands for a moment. Then a whisper of breath was at my ear. "*Dulceaţă*, I can heal this, but it would be better if we went to MAGIC. There are healers there with more skill than I possess."

Mircea, I thought. He was the one smelling like smoke and blood and sweat. That seemed odd; I always associated him with expensive cologne. I looked down and there were black smears and fingerprints on my skin where he had touched me. That seemed odd, too, although I couldn't think why.

"Cass, we gotta get out of here. He can't take you back to MAGIC." Billy hovered in front of my face, and that was all right. Because he looked the same as always.

"I can't go back to MAGIC," I said, parroting Billy's words, and my voice sounded almost normal. Weird.

"It is a bad break, *dulceață*, and there are many bones in the wrist. I may not be able to repair all of them perfectly."

I looked up into his face. It was dirty and sweat-soaked, and there was a fading pattern of diamond shapes all over his left cheek. But new skin was already pushing the crisped away as I watched, leaving it to blow off like so much ash in the wind. And his eyes were the same, bright with intelligence, soft with concern, full of understanding, beautiful. He was okay. Mircea was going to be okay. Relief was so sharp that, for a second, it hurt more than my wrist.

I wanted to say something, but there was too much raw emotion burning too close to the surface. I didn't think you were supposed to say what I was thinking, anyway: that, even if my endgame was short, I liked the idea that his wasn't. It was sort of a future by proxy, and while it wasn't quite what I'd hoped for, it was good enough. It felt good enough. So I just looked at him instead, unblinking, until I couldn't see more than a blur of pallor and darkness, the colors all bleeding into each other for some reason.

"I will heal it here," Mircea said harshly, cradling my wrist in one large hand.

He looked strange, feral and too tightly controlled, with something brimming right under the surface, rage or frustration or both. The others could see it too, because the vamps were all trying to act submissive and the pixie was gazing at him with big worried eyes. Françoise was sitting on the ground next to us, but she looked hesitant, like she had no idea what to say. It occurred to me to wonder what they were all doing here, but then Mircea did something that made warmth spread up my arm, and the sudden lack of pain made me catch my breath in wonder.

I looked down to see my wound closing and odd little shiftings taking place under the skin. *Bones realigning*, I thought vaguely, and that part wasn't so pleasant, but it still didn't hurt and suddenly I could even think a little better. I could feel my blood shoving roughly through my veins, and my skin felt tight and flushed, but there was no lethargy, no pain.

Mircea was biting his lip as he followed the lines of tendon and muscle in my hand, reshaping them with his finger as if it were a scalpel. It was a light sensation. He barely brushed my hand, but I shuddered. A touch that simple shouldn't be so powerful.

Mircea didn't notice. His eyes were wide open and brighter than I'd ever seen them, the rush from combat still humming behind them like electricity. He was utterly concentrated and strangely young-looking, and when he finally raised his head to tell me he was through, I grabbed him by the shirt and kissed him, hard.

It wasn't a great effort. I got the angle a little off and our teeth clicked together and we both tasted like adrenaline. I didn't care. My fists clenched in his shirt, crushing the heavy silk, and I couldn't seem to make them let go. And I needed them to because I couldn't hit him until they did and I really, really wanted to hit him. I was furious suddenly, completely livid. Because he'd almost died, damn it, and I hadn't been able to do anything, and he'd almost *died*.

Mircea didn't object, didn't try to pull away; instead he drew me closer, close enough to hear his heart beat, close enough to feel him breathe. He took charge of the kiss, slowing it down, until it was all warmth and sweetness and inevitability. His hands glided up my back and into my hair, combing through my curls and making me shiver. I'd never known that anyone could kiss in English, kiss in apologies, but apparently he could. I wasn't sure what he was apologizing for, but it felt right. Like he should be sorry for scaring me like that.

He didn't kiss fair, and he didn't kiss all at once; he kept giving it up and taking it away until I thought I'd die of frustration. I felt like screaming, but didn't have the breath to waste, and when I thought I would go completely insane he finally made a quiet, hungry sound and met me in the middle. And it was suddenly all panting, groaning need rising between us like steam.

I could feel the *geis* react, faint tremors humming just beneath the skin, symptoms of an imminent explosion. And I didn't care. I had somehow never noticed the tensile strength of his body, of those hands, lean and strong and achingly gentle. A flash of what it would feel like, pressed down beneath his weight, sent heat spiraling through me. I wanted that. Wanted everything.

And then he broke away, looking shocked and a little wild, like he hadn't during the fight, when it would have made sense. I looked at him, with the rumpled hair and the dirty face, and wanted to kiss him again. Not because of a compulsion, but because he already tasted familiar, because I wanted more of the warmth that seemed to bubble up through my skin whenever we touched.

But I couldn't. This Mircea was two weeks behind the times, so to speak. For him, the *geis* had just woken up. But the more contact we had, the faster it was going to grow. Putting my Mircea through even more hell.

I jerked away, and he let me go. But his puzzled gaze shifted from me to Françoise and Radella. "Is there something you wish to tell me, *dulceață?*"

I glanced at Françoise, but she gave me one of those French shrugs that I've never been able to interpret. Great. I looked back at Mircea and swallowed. "I don't feel well," I told him honestly. "Can we talk a little later?"

After an almost imperceptible pause, Mircea nodded. He stood up, still staring at me while issuing orders, sending the vamps who had shown up far too late scurrying around like frightened ants. I sat on the ground and watched them, wondering what they were doing until I saw that one of them had some kind of industrial vacuum. He started sucking up the remains of the mages who'd been hit by the Lot's Wife spell. Another followed him, tossing shoes and other non-sand-like bits into a large-size garbage bag.

I no longer hurt anywhere, but I still felt exhausted and slightly removed from everything. Mircea must have hit me with a suggestion, the vamp equivalent of an all-night bender. I didn't think it would be a good idea to try to shift again just yet.

Another vamp had started breaking apart the two withered

corpses. They were so old that their bones snapped easily, brittle like dried sticks. They made a crunching sound as he shoved them into a garbage bag. I watched them, the shiny gloss of the suggestion dulling my reaction. I knew they must have been killed by a spell meant for me, but at the moment it didn't seem all that important. The vamp managed to get both of them into one bag. It looked like he'd brought the good kind, because it stretched but didn't break.

Another vamp suddenly ran screaming across the parking lot. He'd managed to set himself on fire trying to extinguish the Pinto. Mircea looked disgusted, but he moved off to help. He'd have probably done as much even if the guy hadn't belonged to him. He was a senator, and had to uphold the Senate's unofficial motto: always clean up your mess.

I felt a slight twitch of pain in my wrist, the kind that said the suggestion might be weakening and maybe I should think about finding some aspirin. But I didn't move. I slumped there watching the stuff that never makes it into movies because it's not exciting. It's just people doing a job. After the action comes the fire extinguishing and the street sweeping and the explaining to families that somebody isn't coming home. Only that last wouldn't happen here. No one knew who the dark mages were or where to find them. If the man I'd killed had a family, they wouldn't know anything was wrong until he just never came back.

The thought hit like a narrow, very sharp knife, slid right between the ribs. All the pieces of myself that I didn't talk about, didn't think about, came rushing back. And for a minute, I saw another scene.

Mac, a friend of Pritkin's and briefly mine, had followed me into Faerie and died there to protect me. I still had nightmares about it, my mind showing me surreal images of his hands pressed to the trunk of a tree, the bark growing liquid and pushing up between his fingers. It flowed over his wrists, paralyzing him as it surged up his body until skin, hair, everything, was covered with the same monotonous, uniform gray. Like a shroud. I usually woke up in a sweat, my heart pounding, when it covered his face.

When there was nothing human left.

It hadn't happened quite like that, but I couldn't complain about my brain's editing process; the reality had been worse. I was sick of being the person who got people killed. I'd sworn it wasn't going to happen anymore, and yet here I was, not just the reason for it but the actual instrument. A man was dead tonight, and I'd done it. I'd killed him.

My mind was horrified, sickened, disbelieving. But my emotions appeared to be taking a break. I wasn't trembling, wasn't ill, wasn't, seemingly, anything. The most I felt was kind of numb. Just numb. Despite the fact that the mage hadn't been my only casualty.

Billy might have thrown the Lot's Wife, but I'd donated the energy that made it possible. At the very least, that made part of the responsibility mine. But those deaths didn't seem as real, somehow. I'd seen magic all my life, but it wasn't the same. Vampires were magical creatures, but the ones at Tony's had mostly used speed, strength and a lot of human weapons to kill. Some of what they did could be pretty spectacular, not to mention gruesome, but at least it made sense. Unlike an innocuous little ball that could drain five people of life in a matter of seconds. The gunshot, though, was something else. I'd seen the expression on the man's face, watched the blood well up between his fingers from a wound I had caused. No. There was no denying that one.

And beyond the guilt and the pain and who knew what else I was going to feel when Mircea's comforting numbness faded, I'd also probably completely screwed up the timeline. A lot of people were dead who weren't supposed to be. Or were they?

It was really hard to think, and, ironically enough, time-travel paradoxes aren't my best thing. But there were a few oddities I was starting to notice. Like, if this wasn't how things were meant to play out, why hadn't I met Mircea the last time I was here? And why had I seen only two dark mages that night instead of the dozen or so who'd apparently been hanging around? If Mircea and I hadn't fought them off before, who had? Because I hadn't seen anyone else volunteering.

"Cassie. We should go," Françoise said gently.

I looked at her blearily. She appeared to be bouncing up and down without actually lifting off the ground, and all her edges were blurry. I decided that was probably me. "How did it go?"

She grimaced. "Don't you remember?"

I thought back for a minute, to my experiences here two weeks ago. "You were captured. I remember freeing you, but that's about it." I hadn't really wanted to know what a bunch of witches and a pixie were doing locked up in one of Dante's lower levels. I'd run across them while here on other business and helped them get away, but I hadn't asked a lot of questions. "I'm a little fuzzy on details," I admitted.

"Zee mages, zey thought I was one of zee slaves, who 'ad escaped," Françoise explained. "Zey locked me up, and when Radella tried to 'elp me, zey captured her as well."

"Did you get it?"

She nodded gravely. "I was in the second group. I over'eard the spell when the others were sent. I was to go next, but zen ze news came that you were 'ere—ze other you," she explained helpfully. I nodded. "Zey closed ze portal and left us, because everyone was told to drop what zey were doing and find you."

Yeah, I bet. Tony had wanted me pretty bad. I suppose his goons thought they could finish the slave run later. I was suddenly viciously glad that they'd been denied that much, at least.

"I should never 'ave left you," Françoise said mournfully.

"I want to see the damn rune before I go anywhere else with you people," the pixie put in, crossing her tiny arms.

"Why?"

"Because you're all completely insane!" Radella snapped. Her eyes were on the vamps, who were kneeling beside the diamond pattern on the asphalt, debating whether it was worth trying to scrape anything out of the cracks, or if a new paving job would be easier.

"Because I could 'ave 'elped you," Françoise said, looking at me like she wondered if maybe I'd gotten hit in the head. Which I had, as my throbbing jaw was busy reminding me. I'd forgotten about that until just now. Oh, yeah. That suggestion was going south pretty fast.

"It wouldn't have mattered," I told her. "And you might have gotten killed."

"Better zan you!"

I shook my head, but stopped because it made it ache worse. "Since when is my life worth more than yours?"

"Since you became Pythia!"

From halfway across the lot, Mircea's head whipped around. I repressed a sigh. Damn vampire hearing.

"Yeah. That's kind of the point," I said, grabbing her hand. Françoise looked confused, but I didn't stop to explain that the Pythia is supposed to be the one protecting other people, not needing it herself. Mircea was striding toward us, looking determined, and I was not up to a verbal fencing match with him tonight. Hell, I lost those even when my brain didn't feel like it was about to throb out of my skull. "Hold on," I said, really hoping I could manage one more shift before I passed out.

Chapter 13

Sight down the barrel of the gun. Balance the butt on your other palm if you need to steady your aim. Squeeze the trigger lightly. You won't have to apply much pressure to get it to fire. I breathed slowly and watched the paper target flinch as if the bullets were cutting through flesh. Almost all of them hit outside the target range, and not a single one was inside the circle that represented the vital organs. Ironic, that.

The unused storeroom had good ventilation for an indoor locale, so Pritkin had set it up as a firing range. Daily practice was supposed to improve my aim—at least that was the theory. So far, the paper cutouts at the far end of the room hadn't had too much to worry about.

I released the empty clip and reloaded. The weapon felt the same as always in my hand; the weight, the smoky scent of the oil and powder, the almost-there smell of burnt paper, were all familiar after almost two weeks of this. When I'd picked the gun up today, that had seemed strange. Like killing a man yesterday should have changed it somehow, added weight, shown up on the sleek black surface like a mark. Something.

But it didn't.

Nine mm Beretta, clip holds fifteen rounds. Maximum effective range is fifty meters, but it's better close up. Remember to take the safety off and aim for the torso. Pritkin had been giving me pointers, determined, as he put it, to reduce my status as a giant bull's-eye in the field. And that's how I'd been thinking of the lessons: as something designed to help with defense. It had somehow never registered that defense with a gun usually meant shooting something more substantial than a paper target. That defense with a gun might mean killing.

I'd grown up around guns, had seen them so often that they were just a part of the scenery, no more remarkable than a vase or a lamp. I hadn't owned one myself, because I wasn't expected to fight. At Tony's, I'd been among the group of useful noncombatants whom other people were supposed to protect. I'd been told a hundred times that, if an attack ever came, my job was to get to one of the many bolt-holes secreted around the place and wait it out.

There had been a certain comfort in my old position that I'd never really appreciated until now. Because the simple truth was, the moment you took on a position of responsibility, there were people who would look up to you, who would expect you to shield them, who would expect you to save them. I was used to running away, was damn good at it in fact, or I wouldn't have lasted this long. I knew how to get fake IDs almost anywhere, how to change my appearance, how to blend in.

I didn't know how to keep people alive.

My clip was empty again, the little *click, click* telling me to reload. I pressed a button and missed the grab. The spent clip bumped against my shoe before spinning away on the floor. I retrieved it and manually reloaded with fifteen new bullets.

Despite the ache in my wrist, my hands were steady. I kept being surprised by that, kept expecting to fall apart. I'd washed up in front of the bathroom mirror after we got back, letting the washcloth linger on the back of my neck, cool and soothing, while I waited to dissolve. Only I hadn't yet. It was starting to really worry me.

Once when I was about six, Alphonse had come back from a job covered in blood, with a gash in his forehead that almost bisected the scalp, making him look like Frankenstein's monster before the doc stitched him up. But he'd been in a rare good mood, because the other guys, the ones he'd left lying in pieces all over a basketball court, had looked worse. They'd taken out a couple of our people in a territory dispute and, since the dead had been Alphonse's vamps, Tony had let him handle it. Alphonse had done his usual thorough job.

He'd seen me loitering around a corner, watching him with wide eyes, and had chucked me on the chin in passing. It had left a red mark on my skin, which Eugenie had scrubbed off later while inadvertently teaching me my first swear word. When I was older, I'd realized that he'd been making a point, coming back covered in blood to show that the insult had been properly avenged, but all I'd thought at the time was that it was strange to see him so relaxed. If it hadn't been for the gore, he could have been anybody returning from a good night's work.

It hadn't bothered him either.

I aimed at the target again, which was still looking pretty pristine despite the fact that the air was getting acrid. I thought of Mircea's face, his eyes reflecting fire, his body outlined in jumping, deadly flames. I wanted to touch him so badly that I could feel his fingers on my wrist, like a phantom ache. This was how reaching for something with a missing hand must feel, restless and empty and wrong. And I'd almost been left with it forever, thanks to a guy who thought that trying to electrocute someone was an acceptable way of saying hello.

The air rang with gunshots and the sound of ripping paper until the clicking noise came again. I reloaded, my eyes smarting from the smoke, wishing life was that easy. Just fill up what was empty, replace what was lost. But it wasn't. Some things couldn't be replaced. So you had to make sure you didn't lose them to begin with.

It was all the way past crazy and out the other side that I was starting to agree with Alphonse.

That afternoon, Françoise and I made our way to the imposing marble and glass edifice in the main arcade where Augustine had set up shop. My run-in with the dark mages had made one thing very clear: if Mircea hadn't been there, I'd have lasted all of about thirty seconds. If I had any hope of actually getting my hands on the Codex, I had to be better prepared. I just hoped Augustine could do what I had in mind.

Françoise had paused in front of the two large plate-glass windows that displayed selections from the ready-to-wear line. She eyed a slim flute of a dress with golden bubbles rising upwards from the hem, like champagne, but passed on without comment. Inside, a large chandelier took up most of the ceiling, its crystals formed by icicles charmed not to melt despite the candles scattered among its many tiers. Françoise immediately began browsing, although what she planned to use for money I had no idea. I'd offered to take her shopping, since she'd ended up here sans family, friends and wardrobe. But my bank account didn't run so much to pricey boutiques.

I decided to explain things if and when she found something, and walked past the staff into the small workroom in back. Nobody tried to stop me. I was back in Elvira mode, wearing a black wig and an official-looking name badge. I'd discovered that it avoided a lot of questions if I looked like an employee, although it wasn't doing my arches any good.

The workroom was so crowded with racks of garments and bolts of fabric that I couldn't even see Augustine, but I heard someone muttering in a far corner. It turned out to be the great man himself, wrestling with a piece of golden fur that appeared to be trying to eat him. He threw it off and slapped a chair down on it, then started digging in the pile of papers on a nearby desk and muttering more.

I approached with caution, because the fabric was bucking and making a valiant attempt to throw off the chair. "Uh, hello?"

"It's no use complaining," he told me quickly. "There was no show, so nobody gets paid. Including me."

"I'm not here about that."

The fur gave a heave and almost dumped him onto the floor. He pretended not to notice, but he surreptitiously slid the edge of the heavy desk over to join the chair. "Then I'm at your disposal."

"I'm thinking about a dress. Something French."

"You can't mean that complete *hack* Edouard," he said, sounding appalled. "Darling, please. I can design you something better with my eyes closed. Hell, I could design you something better *dead*!"

"I don't mean I want a French designer," I tried to explain. "Just something that looks—"

"Forget Paris. Paris is done," he told me airily. "Now, at what occasion are you planning to showcase my work?"

"I need an outfit that would fit into the late eighteenth century."

"Oh, a *costume* party. I don't do costumes." Considering that Augustine's personal style was a cross between Galliano and Liberace, I thought that was debatable. At the moment he was wearing a saffron yellow tunic with puffy sleeves over a pair of purple harem pants. A gold sash tied around his waist pirate style held not a saber but a pair of scissors, a measuring tape and a tomato-shaped pincushion.

"I don't think you understand," I told him patiently. "It's kind of important."

"Ah, you want to dress to impress," Augustine said archly. "Well, in *that* case, you've come to the right place." He pulled me over to a dressmaker's form in one of the few open spaces in the room. With a mumbled word, it took on a very familiar, very detailed shape. I had a sudden urge to throw a towel over it. "Any special orders I need to know about?" he demanded. "Some of those can affect the design."

"No. I just—"

"Because I don't want you coming to me at the last minute saying you need a charm to make you dance better or hold your liquor or be a scintillating conversationalist and just forgot to *mention* it—"

"You can do that with a dress?"

"Darling, I can do *anything* with a dress. Anything legal, that is. So don't go asking for a love potion or some nonsense, because I'm not about to lose my license."

"What else can you do?" My mind was racing with the possibilities.

"What do you want?" A bolt of blank white fabric began draping itself around the form.

"Can you make me invisible?"

Augustine sighed and flipped the edge of my wig with a finger. "A bad outfit and worse hair can do that."

I narrowed my eyes at him. "Then what about spell-proofing? Can you make it so if someone slings something nasty at me it bounces off?"

"Jealous rival?" he asked sympathetically.

"Something like that."

"How powerful is the little cat?"

"Does it matter?"

"Of course it does! I have to know how strong to make the counterspell," he said impatiently. "If it's something petty, like making you smell like a garbage truck—"

"No. I need to stop a major assault, like a dark mage could cast."

Augustine blinked at me owlishly. "Darling, *what* kind of party are you attending?"

"That's the problem. I don't know."

"Well, maybe you should think about skipping it. Who needs that kind of stress? Take the night off, do your nails."

"It's sort of mandatory."

"Hmm. This isn't really my line," he said doubtfully. "The war mages use charmed capes sometimes, to reinforce their shields, but I don't think fashion is their main priority."

Françoise poked her head in. She appeared to be wearing a small animal over the top half of her body, one with a lot of brown quills extending outward in all directions. "I 'ave found somezeeng," she told me.

Augustine stiffened. "Where did you get that? It's a prototype."

"What is it?" I asked, eyeing it warily.

"A jacket, of course," he told me. "Porcupine. Wonderful for getting rid of unwanted attention. Unfortunately, that one tends to launch quills without warning at anyone who upsets the wearer, so I don't think—"

"I'll take eet." Françoise piled an armload of other items onto the table. "And zese."

"What is all this?" I asked. Behind her were a couple of walking mountains of clothes, which I assumed to be the shop assistants, although no heads were actually visible.

"Pour les enfants," Françoise said, holding up a tiny T-shirt with WORLD'S GREATEST KID written on it in what looked like crayon.

I frowned at it and Augustine snatched it out of her hand, looking aggrieved. "An image of the child wearing it will appear under the title," he told me loftily.

"There's a place at the mall that can do that."

"And it makes the wearer have a sudden, uncontrollable fondness for vegetables."

I sighed. "We'll take it." He snapped his fingers at his over-burdened assistants, who began running around, adding things up. "About my dress," I said, now that he was in a better mood. "I thought creative geniuses like you appreciated a challenge."

He patted my cheek, which was a bit much considering that he didn't look a lot older than me. "We do, love, we do. But there's also the little matter of payment. This isn't ready-to-wear we're talking about. And for what you're asking—"

"Send the bill to Lord Mircea," Françoise said, playing with a scarf that, oddly enough, was just lying there being scarflike.

I started slightly. "What? No!"

Her pretty forehead wrinkled slightly. *"Pourquoi pas?"*

"I don't . . . that isn't . . . it wouldn't be appropriate," I said, very aware of Augustine listening avidly.

"Mais, you are his *petite amie, non?"*

"Non! I mean no, no I'm not." The frown widened, then Françoise shrugged in a way that suggested she knew denial when she saw it. "Send the bill to Casanova," I told Augustine. If he complained, I'd tell him to take it out of my overdue paycheck.

"Casanova," Augustine repeated, with an evil glint in his eye. "You know he actually expects *me* to pay for the damage to the conference room? He presented me with a ridiculous bill just this morning."

"Then present him one right back. A big one." I eyed Françoise's pile of assorted oddities. "And tack those on."

Augustine's smile took on an almost Cheshire cat quality. "Cinderella, I do believe you're going to the ball."

That evening, after I finished another shift in Hell, Françoise and I slipped out of Dante's in a shiny black Jeep.

While I waited for Alphonse and my backup to arrive, I had a few errands to do, and she had volunteered to help. Neither of us had a car, but I'd managed to find us a ride.

The tag on the front of the Jeep read 4U2DZYR. It belonged to Randy, one of the boys who worked in Casanova's version of a spa. He would have been a perfect California beach bum, complete with deep tan, sun-bleached hair and toothy white smile, except that his voice still had a Midwest twang. He was possessed by an incubus, of course, but so far he'd been on his best behavior.

"You're serious?" Randy asked me for the third time, as we pulled into the giant Wal-Mart parking lot. "You want to shop *here*?"

"Yes, I want to shop here!" I said, exasperated. There'd been a time when Wal-Mart had been pretty upscale for me, in comparison to the 25-cent bin at Goodwill or the Salvation Army. But I got the impression that there weren't a lot of Randy's clients who felt the same way. He'd had to ask one of the waitresses for directions.

He pulled into the closest available parking space, tires squealing, and stopped on a dime. He looked at me seriously over the tops of his Ray-Bans. "As long as you make sure Lord Mircea knows that I had nothing to do with this. I'm only following orders. If the boss's lady wants to go slumming—"

"You sound like I'm going to a strip club or something!" I said irritably, getting out. "And I'm not the boss's lady!"

"Oookay." Randy pried Françoise, who had the backseat in a death grip, off the upholstery. I'd forgotten to ask if she'd actually been in a car before, and judging by the wide eyes and dead white complexion, I was betting the answer was no.

"I nevair want to do zat again."

"I'm not that bad a driver," Randy said, offended.

"Yes, you are," she said fervently.

"Well the wheels have stopped rolling, sweet thing," he told her, getting an arm around her waist. He deposited her on the concrete. "You know, I've done some of my best work in backseats." This was accompanied by a huge *how-could-*

anyone-not-think-I'm-cute? grin. Which is probably the only thing that saved him.

I hauled the extensive shopping list out of my purse and waved it at them before Randy said anything else. "Can we get going? Because we don't have all day."

Eight kids plus a baby, I had discovered, need a lot of things, especially when their entire existing wardrobe was literally the clothes on their backs. And except for a few T-shirts for the tourists, Augustine's establishment didn't specialize in children's anything. He preferred his customers to be adult and very well-heeled. Hence the list.

An hour later, I was leaning against a shelf stacked with Fruit of the Loom T-shirts while Françoise terrorized various underpaid store employees. She had commandeered no fewer than four, whom she had racing back and forth, trying to find all the needed sizes. She looked a little out of place, as she was wearing one of Augustine's sophisticated creations: a long, basic black dress with a chic jacket covered in a newspaper print. I hoped no one noticed that all the headlines were today's.

Randy was standing in front of a mirrored column, admiring the flex of his bicep. "What do you think?" The muscle shirt he'd poured himself into was bright blue and perfectly matched his eyes. He knew damn well what I thought, what half the women in the store did. Either that, or we just happened to go shopping the same day every young mother in the state needed to restock her son's closet.

"I thought you didn't shop at places like this."

"A T-shirt's a T-shirt." He shrugged, causing a ripple of muscle that prompted a squeak from a nearby customer. "So, listen. You got a lot of kids."

"Yeah. So?"

For a minute, he just stood there, looking at me awkwardly, like a big kid himself. A big kid with a lot of muscles and a see-through mesh tee. "So you're putting them up in the casino, right? In a couple free rooms?"

"How do you know that?" The kitchen staff hadn't had space in the minuscule quarters that Casanova had allotted them for another nine people, so I'd had to get creative. It helped that I worked the front desk occasionally.

"Everybody knows. The staff have been working to keep the boss from finding out. But he does check the books sometimes, you know?"

"What's your point, Randy?"

"I just wanted to say that, if you need, well, any money or anything . . ." He trailed off, while I looked at him incredulously. I had no idea what his incubus was teaching him. Apparently, they hadn't gotten to the part where women were supposed to pay *him*.

"We'll be fine." If Casanova gave me any grief about the rooms, I'd have Billy rig every damn roulette game in the house. Come to think of it, he was pretty good with craps, too.

"You sure? 'Cause, I mean, I kind of get paid a lot. It wouldn't be, like, hurting me any, you know?"

Françoise was giving him the kind of look I expected to see incubi giving her. She saw me notice and gave a shrug that could have meant anything from "I was just looking" to "I haven't had sex in four hundred years, so sue me." I decided I didn't want to know.

"Thanks. I'll be in Shoes," I said, snagging the lightest of the remaining carts.

Sixteen feet—I wasn't counting the baby because so far she hadn't proven able to keep up even with socks—need a lot of shoes. I stood up from fishing around on the bottom row, trying to find a pair of Converse look-alikes in Jesse's size, and hit my head on somebody's elbow. Somebody who looked like he'd escaped from Caesars Palace and forgotten to take off the costume.

"Why are you here?" The voice echoed loudly in the large space.

I looked around frantically, but nobody seemed to be paying the ten-foot golden god in the shoe department any attention. "I could ask you the same question!" I whispered.

"I came to remind you that time grows short. Your vampire will die if the spell is not lifted."

"I'm aware of that!" I snapped.

"Then I ask again, why are you here? Have you made any progress?"

"Yes, sort of. I mean, I know where the Codex is."

"Then why have you not retrieved it?"

"It isn't that easy! And why do you care? What is Mircea to you?"

"Nothing. But your performance has not been as . . . focused . . . as I had hoped. This is an important test of your abilities, Herophile. And thus far you have let yourself be distracted by unnecessary tasks. These children are not your mission. The Codex is."

"Uh-huh." For someone who didn't care about the Codex, he sure brought it up a lot. "Well, maybe I could do a better job if I had some help! How about sticking around for a while? And while you're here we can get in a few of those lessons I keep hearing about."

"I cannot enter this realm, Herophile. This body is a projection; only you can see it. And I cannot maintain it for long."

"Then how about telling me a little more about the Codex?" Why, for example, Pritkin was willing to kill to keep it safe.

"You know all you need. Find it and complete your mission. And do it soon. There are those who would oppose you."

"I kind of noticed."

"What has happened?" he asked sharply.

"You're a god. Don't you know?"

His eyes narrowed dangerously. "Do not forget yourself, Herophile."

"My name is Cassandra."

"A poor name for the Pythia. Your namesake opposed my will and lived to regret it. Do not make the same mistake."

It was more than a little surreal, even for me, to be discussing a myth with a legend in the middle of the Wal-Mart shoe department. Especially with a clerk giving me the hairy eyeball from the next aisle over. He didn't say anything, though. Maybe a lot of his customers talked to the shoes before buying them.

"Maybe so, but it's still my name and I'm doing the best I can. Threats aren't going to speed up the process."

"Find something that will," he told me flatly, and vanished.

I sighed and fought the urge to bang my head against the metal rack and just not stop. The clerk was peering at me around the size twelves with an expression that said he was thinking about calling for security. I decided not to risk it.

I held up the red Converse wannabes. "You have these in a nine?"

Chapter 14

I slipped inside Pritkin's room the next morning, on a mission to find that rune I'd promised Radella, and stopped dead. I'd expected it to be a quick search; for some reason, I'd assumed he would keep his belongings in military precision. Only this wasn't it.

The bed was still unmade from whenever he'd slept in it last, and clothes were strewn on the floor like a hurricane had just blown through. And he'd been right—it did, indeed, have an odor. But I was less inclined to blame its onetime residents for that than the vile-smelling potions that lined a shelf on one wall.

The rickety-looking contraption was directly above the bed, something that would have worried me, since most of the substances he carried around were lethal. Still, I supposed he hadn't had a lot of choice. The opposite wall was taken up with a closet, the one facing into the club by a door and the one looking out over one side of the casino by a huge stained-glass window.

The windows were Dante's trademark, and I guess the designers had situated this one behind the dressing rooms because its Gothic splendor didn't go too well with the bar's tiki theme. But the result of such a huge window in such a small space was a room completely bathed in jewel tones: ruby, sapphire, emerald and pearl. They stained the comforter in watery, diffuse shades and splashed the floor with pools of light. I'd have found it pretty hard to get any sleep myself, but at least the subject suited him: a group of soldiers waving antique weaponry.

I reluctantly went to work, and was soon wondering more about what I didn't find than what I did. Along with some wadded-up T-shirts and enough firepower to conquer a small country, I found several pairs of jeans, a new pair of tennis shoes, a few basic toiletries and some socks still in their packages. All of said purchases bought in haste by a guy who wasn't dressing to impress. He was just replacing necessities that, presumably, couldn't be reached because he didn't dare to return to his apartment. With the Circle after him for a couple dozen reasons, most having to do with helping me, I didn't blame him there. But it still didn't explain where the wardrobe for his alter ego was stashed.

I finally picked up a small wooden case on the nightstand. I'd deliberately left it for last, hoping that I'd find the rune tucked into a sock and not need to pry into something that practically screamed personal. If I hadn't needed the damn thing so badly, I'd have been out of there like a shot. As it was, I reluctantly opened the lid.

There was no rune in sight, just a few yellowing letters and a badly faded photograph. The woman it depicted was wearing a dark hat and a high-necked dress that made her face stand out like a pale thumbprint. It was pretty indistinct, but she looked young, with regular features and light-colored eyes. She was pretty, I decided—or would have been if she'd been smiling.

I turned the box over, but if there were any hidden compartments, I couldn't find them. It was just a plain pine rectangle, without even a lining that anything could have been hidden under. I flipped the photo over. It had a studio's name on the back: J. Johnstone, Birmingham.

Pritkin had mentioned once that he'd lived in Victorian England, which made him a hell of a lot older than his thirty-something appearance, but what with the fighting and the running and the almost dying, I'd never gotten around to asking him about it. And he'd never mentioned any family. I didn't know if the picture might be his mother, his sister or even a daughter. I realized with surprise that although I could have written a book about the mage, I didn't know much about the man at all.

Billy drifted through the door, interrupting my thoughts. "Did you get it?" I asked eagerly. He spread empty hands and I sighed. I put the letters back unread—a quick feel had been enough to show that the rune hadn't been tucked into one—and centered the box carefully back on its square of dust-free wood. "What now?"

Billy gave me a look. "You know what now. You searched this room; I ransacked the den downstairs. And he wouldn't stash something that valuable just anywhere. He's got it on him."

It was worst-case scenario, so of course that had to be it. "How are your pickpocket skills?"

"Depends on whether he's paying attention. I lifted a rune for you once before, but only because you two were so busy yelling at each other that he didn't notice. You'll need to cause a distraction."

Great. Normally, picking a fight with the ever prickly mage wouldn't have been a problem, but now . . . "I don't think so," I said fervently.

"Then you may want to get gone, 'cause I passed him on my way here."

I stared at Billy blankly for a second, then what he'd said registered and I lunged for the door. It was exactly the wrong thing to do, especially when I could have shifted, but I panicked. The knob turned under my hand and, before I could breathe, I was back on the bed, a hard chest pinning me down and a knife at my throat.

I blinked nervously up at the mage, his face splashed with color from the rainbow spilling over the bed. Blue light limned his pale hair and caught on his cheekbones, making him look oddly alien for a moment. "What do you think you're doing?" he demanded.

The cold edge of the blade had dented my skin, disturbingly close to the jugular. I swallowed. "Trying not to move?"

Pritkin pulled away, scowling, the knife disappearing almost magically. "You should have given me some warning if you planned to come 'round. What if I had rigged a snare?"

I didn't answer, being too busy trying to figure out why, yet again, he looked so different. He shrugged out of the old brown leather coat, revealing a sun-faded green T-shirt and a pair of jeans. The jeans were pale blue, worn thin and smooth as silk, and loose enough to barely cling to the muscular swell of his hips. They were, in other words, the exact opposite of tight and black. His hair had also lost the spiky trendiness from the lobby. It appeared freshly washed, with bangs that needed a trim flopping into his eyes. The rest of him should have followed it into the shower: there were dark smudges all over his arms, popping the veins into relief, and one along his cheekbone.

"What have you been doing?" I asked, sitting up.

"Researching."

"In a coal mine?"

"Obscure magical texts are seldom found on hygienic computer files. Now, would you like to explain why you're here?"

I looked away before answering, having a hard time separating the regular, everyday Pritkin with the ill-fitting coat and the stupid haircut from the man who had kissed me. "I thought you'd be pleased to see me, after that scene in the lobby."

"What are you talking about?"

I didn't reply, having just registered a fact that felt important. As usual, Pritkin's T-shirt was crisscrossed with belts, sheaths and holsters. The guy was a walking arsenal, with almost every kind of portable weapon known to man. Except for one.

"You don't carry a sword," I said, something clicking in my brain.

Pritkin turned from hanging his coat in the closet, and Billy flowed over to begin ransacking it. I just hoped he did it quietly. "I don't need one, remember?"

I stared at him for a second, then leapt off the bed and grabbed him. I spun him around, trying to pull his shirt up at the same time. "What the—"

"Hold still," I said, struggling to get the buckles and straps undone, half of which seemed to have been designed simply to drive me nuts. Most of my adrenaline surges lately had resulted from life-or-death situations; it was a little disorienting to feel the same response to something that might actually be positive. But my heart had sped up until I could feel it in my throat and my hands were suddenly too clumsy to do the job. "Take your shirt off," I ordered, trying to keep my voice steady.

He turned, a half-quizzical, half-angry expression on his face. But to my surprise he didn't argue, stripping to the waist quickly and efficiently. I turned him back around and saw what I'd expected: a spill of bright color, gold and silver and rich blue-black, running from his shoulder down the length of one side.

My fingertips traced the slightly raised edges of the design, down warm skin and hard muscle, until stopped by the waistband of his jeans. I'd been a fool not to think of it before, especially as I'd watched part of it being carved into his skin. Pritkin didn't need to carry a sword anymore. He already had one, in the shape of a magical tattoo that manifested as a weapon whenever he chose.

"Thinking of getting another tat?" he asked, his voice oddly tight.

I didn't answer. His arm was braced against the wall, making the muscles stand out, and his back was tense. There was something mesmerizing about all that caged power so ruthlessly leashed, all that coiled strength so docile under my hands.

I watched two of my fingers dip below the loose, frayed waistband, still following the edge of the blade. The silky denim was warm from his body, and it gave way easily, baring a slight dimple just below the small of his back. I guess I knew why there hadn't been any underwear with his purchases, I thought hazily, as my fingers abandoned the sword to trace the tiny depression.

Pritkin suddenly spun and caught my wrist. "Careful," he said roughly. "Or have you forgotten what that *geis* of yours can do?"

And that was another mystery. There had been no warning rush of power in the lobby and there was none now, although there certainly should have been. Pritkin released me and I sat back down, feeling too warm and slightly disoriented. I couldn't seem to stop staring at his chest. The hair grew thick and dark gold over his biceps, but thinned to a dusky trail running down his stomach before disappearing below the jeans. It looked soft against all those hard muscles, and way too inviting.

I swallowed. "We have a problem."

Pritkin snorted. "Only one? That would be a change."

I flopped backwards, exhausted from the implications. Pritkin hadn't been Saleh's killer, hadn't been the man in the lobby, wasn't—probably—a traitor. I had my strongest ally back, but I also had a mysterious doppelgänger with murder and seduction in mind. And he seemed to have a definite knack for both.

I could see colors through my eyelids, vermilion, azure and jade, the window's hues filtered through flesh. They were suddenly blocked by a dark shape. I opened my eyes to find Pritkin glaring at me from far too close for comfort. "You are going to tell me exactly what is going on," he said grimly. "Right now."

And just like that, all the feelings from the lobby came back with a rush. *Don't even think about it*, I told myself sternly as my hand reached up to cup his face. My fingers ignored me, dragging across soft skin and crisp stubble, turning his head to the perfect angle for a kiss. Maybe this was what schizophrenia was like, I thought, my body screaming "forward" while my brain ordered it to stay still. My brain lost.

Before I made the conscious decision, I felt my lips brush his. Although I suspected he was cursing mentally, his body didn't seem to be listening to his brain any better than mine. The muscles under my hand were hard as iron, but he didn't pull away. And after a startled second, he gripped the nape of my neck and kissed me back.

I let my hands settle into his hair, which wasn't just gravity-defying but thick and sleek and soft, and wonderful to stroke through. Only I didn't get much of a chance, because

Pritkin kissed like he did everything else, straightforward, accepting no prisoners and with an intensity that left me breathless. It was hot and hard and desperate, like he was starving for it, and I opened my mouth and took it, because, *God*.

"You bastard," I gasped, when we finally broke apart. "I knew you were cheating!" The taste of coffee had been rich and bitter in his mouth.

"Miss Palmer—"

"I'm lying in your bed. You just kissed me senseless. I think you can risk using my first name."

"I'm risking enough as it is," he muttered.

I let my fingers dig into the hard muscles of his shoulders. His skin was warm and slightly damp from the heat of the coat, and completely hypnotic. I traced the gentle ridges of scar tissue on his shoulder, the skin slick and too smooth, where something with claws had gotten a few into him. He was an enigma, John Pritkin: a mad scientist with gun calluses and old scars and even more secrets than me.

My hands followed the swell of muscle down his arms, stroking across hard biceps, gliding lower to caress the silken skin at the inner bend of his elbow. I couldn't count the number of times I'd felt a crackle of energy when we got close, but apparently touching with *intent* made it just that much more—

"Cassie."

"Well, you went and did it now," I said dreamily. "Guess I'll have to start calling you John."

"This isn't a good idea." His voice was strained, but he didn't pull away. I took that for permission and slipped my arms between his, running my hands down the powerful back, feeling the flesh give and spring back, warm and resilient. *Stop it*, I told my hands sternly. They ignored me in favor of exploring the sleek, fascinating curve of his spine. They found the loose waistband, the warm skin, the taut muscle and the same dimple that had fascinated me earlier. I had to stroke, just a little, and Pritkin's eyes suddenly went dark jade.

"I never asked if you have an evil twin," I said vaguely. "Do you?"

He blinked. "Why?"

I tried to tell him, but I seemed to be having trouble getting enough oxygen. It was as if part of him rode the air around us, like I took him inside me with every breath. I buried my face in the curls on his chest, feeling them against my cheek, thick and warm, like his arousal pressed against my thigh.

His hands hit the bed forcefully and his face filled my vision, its expression desperate rather than angry. "Listen to me! There's something wrong. What did you mean about the lobby?" His voice poured over me, the words indistinct and meaningless. I raked my nails down his chest to the tender skin of his stomach, and a shivery below-the-skin rush of power followed every movement.

It was with a feeling of distant shock that I felt him wrench away, the colder air of the room swirling between us where there had been only moist warmth before. At the same moment, the light from the window suddenly intensified, like a floodlight had gone on behind it. It drowned the room in a color so rich, so loud, that it was almost sound.

The crimsons in the stained glass glowed until they seemed to break off, floating away from the rest of the design in a firework display of red and gold. They coalesced over the bed in a sparkling cloud of light that had a strangely familiar shape. I'd seen something like it once before, but that one had been a pale reflection of this shimmering golden haze.

"All that power, and in such a pretty package. It really is irresistible." The voice seemed to come from the air itself, whispering along my skin like a breeze.

Pritkin's head snapped up, pure rage distorting his features. "I knew it!"

"What is it?" Pritkin and the voice both ignored me. Or maybe I didn't say it aloud; I wasn't sure anymore. Everything looked the way it does after a faint: all odd angles and meaningless patterns, and blood was rushing in my ears like an incoming tide.

"You will not have her!" Pritkin snarled.

Soft laughter echoed through the room. "Who said anything about me?"

The glowing veil drifted down onto the mage, making him look as if his skin had been drenched in glitter. He screamed, there was no other word for it, and it was like a dam had burst. What had been a musky fog was now a torrential rain, and I bathed in it, in him. The room suddenly felt like the tropics in July, with a steamy, heavy heat that seemed to soak into my very pores.

His lips were on mine, his hands cradling my head so he could kiss all the breath out of my body, and he was pushing me down against the bed. And then his lips were everywhere—my collarbone, the side of my neck, the crease between my breasts, my jaw—and it hit me that he wasn't just choosing spots at random. These were places he'd *thought* about, and that was almost enough to send me over the edge.

But then he paused, a fine shudder rippling through him, vibrating down his body into mine. It caused me to arch upward and he gave a stifled scream, flinching as if my touch was actually painful. "Don't," he forced out through clenched teeth. "Don't move."

I realized with a sort of horror that he was trying to stop, that he was going to be *noble*. A crashing tide of angry despair overwhelmed me as soon as my body understood that it was going to be denied yet again, with every emotion I'd ever felt toward Pritkin surging violently through me. "No!"

I grabbed his shoulders and rolled him over, head swimming, heart racing. An alarm was blaring somewhere in my mind, but I ignored it. I buried my face against the hard muscles of his stomach. He smelled so *good*—salt and sweat and the sweet musk of skin, and I had to know if he tasted as good as he smelled. There was suddenly nothing real to me but need and the hands on my body, the body under my hands.

My tongue dragged a slow arc across him, just below his navel. His pulse was quick and frantic against my lips, the echo of it under my fingers as they moved to the fastening of his jeans. "Cassie—" Pritkin's voice sounded oddly scraped and rough, but I ignored it, except to note with approval that he'd said my name again. Twice in one day—that was a record.

I was discovering that I really liked old jeans. Once the first button came undone, the others obligingly slid out of their holes with a single tug. "Oh, God," Pritkin whispered, sounding almost panicked for some reason. He stared at me, breath heavy, and the wild need on his face warred with something close to terror. His irises were half black, with just a tiny band of green. And he was literally clinging to the bed by his fingernails, as if it was the only thing that kept the ragged torrent of emotions coursing between us from jerking him to me like a yo-yo.

I hardly noticed when the air began to move around us, drawing in toward an unseen center, catching up the clothes scattered on the floor and swirling them about. A ragged-edged cry that sounded like an incantation tore from Pritkin's throat. And a glimmer of red appeared in the shadows, like the wet flicker of the northern lights, lapping at the outlines of a man. I blinked, and the figure behind the glow stepped through, the red mirage parting like fog. I blinked again, harder this time, sure I was hallucinating, staring in disbelief from Pritkin's face to its mirror image.

"She has to die," the man said, almost conversationally. He noted Pritkin's expression and his answering smile was somehow both sweet and viciously cruel. "I promise it won't hurt."

"What is your interest in her?" Pritkin's tone was filled with loathing.

"She talked to Saleh." His double's eyes came to rest on me, and there was no life, no heat, nothing human in them, only cold appraisal. I couldn't believe I had ever confused the two men. "She knows."

Before I could clear my mind enough even to frame a question, Pritkin had launched himself off the bed onto the new arrival. He hit him straight in the chest, the momentum taking them both to the floor. They rolled around the limited space, their magic crackling together in spits and sputters, while I looked around for something, anything, to use as a weapon.

I had a bracelet, which had once been the property of a dark mage, that was always up for a rumble. Unfortunately, it had a mind of its own and didn't always follow my instructions. I didn't dare use it now, as it was not fond of Pritkin and there was a better-than-average chance that it would attack the wrong guy.

There was enough firepower in the closet to outfit a small army, but I couldn't reach it, and the only thing on this side of the room was the bedside lamp. It didn't look too sturdy, but I yanked it out of the wall anyway, just in time to see Pritkin immersed in a slow-curving maelstrom of blinding white. There was a loud crackle and power rent the air, as if lightning had struck inside the room. The flash turned me momentarily blind, and then something was on me.

He—it—was touching me, holding me down, but I could feel no heat from his body, and there was no scent, not the faintest whiff of aftershave or the leather of his coat. Even though I was used to such things from ghosts, there was a kind of horror to it, being held down by such a *blank*. Unthinkingly, I reached out with my senses, desperate to find something human to ground me. What I saw was alive and squirming, but not human—God, not human at all.

I could feel its need building like a thousand thunderstorms, an overpowering hunger that wanted nothing more than to melt into me and feed and feed and feed. A smothering cloud descended on my skin, and now I could feel it, sliding cold hands over my body, could taste the miasma of corruption lingering at the back of its throat when it kissed me. The cloud began to sink into my skin, rushing into my body as I breathed in its clammy breath, pushing past my defenses until it ran through my bloodstream sickeningly.

It touched me everywhere, consuming me from the inside out. And it had lied. It did hurt, with a horrible, draining sensation far worse than a vampire's bite. It felt like razored teeth were slicing into me everywhere, running like a blade between muscle and bone, turning even the air in my lungs to broken glass.

I was supposed to be protected from this kind of thing. My mother's only legacy was the pentagram-shaped tattoo on my back that was one of the Circle's strongest enchantments. She had once been heir to the Pythia position, before she ran away with my father and was disowned, and the star had been given to her as security. It packed quite a punch, but the *geis* interfered with it. Meaning that if I was going to get out of this, it would have to be on my own.

I tried to fight, but my arms and legs wouldn't move, all my strength pouring into the thing holding me so gently in its grasp. My body felt as heavy and lifeless as if the creature had already finished feeding. Only I knew it hadn't, because I could feel it gnawing through bone and into marrow, the lethargy ensuring that I couldn't even scream as it sucked my life away. My consciousness turned slippery and unresponsive, my body trying to shield me from what was happening, from what was coming—

And then it was gone, pulled off by Pritkin's arm around its throat. I stared at it, Pritkin's mirror image except that it glowed as brightly as flame, energized with stolen power. And just like that, the pieces fell into place.

"You're an incubus!" I was addressing the spirit, but it was Pritkin who answered.

"Only half," he snarled, wrenching the creature's neck savagely enough to have shattered a human's spine.

In a move too fast for me to see, the creature broke the mage's hold, spun and sent Pritkin sailing into the window. He struck it hard, knocking the colored glass panes out of place, sending them exploding outward. The creature whirled on me again, and his eyes were a flat, solid black, as if the pupils had bled out.

I threw out a hand, a scream rising in my throat, but I never uttered it. Because suddenly the attack just stopped. There was no sound, no movement. Nothing.

After a stunned second, I realized that the red spots in front of my eyes were a few shards of ruby glass, slung in my direction by the fight. They remained halfway through their arc, hovering in midair as if waiting for permission to fall. Everything else was also frozen in place, from the dark-eyed demon to Pritkin, caught halfway through the broken surface of the window, its sharp edges digging into his skin. In the entire room, I was the only thing moving.

Agnes, the former Pythia, had been able to do this, to literally stop time for short periods, but I'd never learned how. With an abrupt, white-hot spike of fear, I also realized that I didn't know how to undo it, either. I decided to worry about that later and deal with the problem I did know how to solve.

I grabbed a bottle off Pritkin's shelf, uncorked the stopper and threw the entire thing in the demon's face.

Other than turning his hair slightly pink, nothing happened. I panicked a little after that, and started throwing everything I could lay my hands on. Vials of liquid, clear and odorless as water, were followed by others containing syrupy, viscous substances with odors that made my head swim. But despite the fact that Pritkin's arsenal was especially designed for battling demons, nothing seemed to have the slightest effect.

I emptied the entire shelf, all the while unable to look away from the potion-streaked face in front of me. The sensation of being watched from behind those glittering black eyes was more than creepy. The hairs on the back of my neck rose as my own stare began to waver, and suddenly everything started up again.

Pritkin crashed the rest of the way through the window, and the demon screamed. The sound mixed with the silvery ring of broken glass and seemed truly agonized. I guess the potions had failed to take effect because of the timeout I'd taken, but they were sure doing something now. Some set his clothes and hair alight, searing the air with the smell of burning leather. He tried to put the flames out with his hands, but that only blistered his skin. And the last potion I'd thrown, dark red with a thick, peppery smell, made his face begin to run like melting wax.

After a moment, he gave up trying to save himself and instead grasped at me. I reached for my power, but it was sluggish, the cost of that momentary hiccup in time tremendous. I threw the lamp at him, but he batted it away with a roar, half rage and half pain. His hair was almost gone now, burnt down to the roots by the fire consuming him with inhuman glee. But it wouldn't be soon enough.

I raised my right arm, where two glowing, gaseous knives emerged from the bracelet I wore. There was only one Pritkin in the room now, and I didn't much care what they did to this one. That was lucky since they tore into the demon with their usual abandon.

"Cassie!" Billy was waving at me frantically over the smoking skull of my attacker. "Over here!"

Like I didn't know where the weapons were. "What do you think I'm trying to do?!" My knives were flying about, sticking into and out of their prey so wildly that I could barely see them. I didn't dare move. "Get me something!"

Nothing happened for a moment, then a clanging avalanche of weapons hit the floor. Billy had managed to knock over the closet shelf. Most stayed where they fell, but a single knife slid across the floor and bumped my foot. I grabbed it, but the demon was thrashing around at my feet, not staying still long enough for me to use it.

"Finish him!" Billy was flickering in his agitation. "Do it!"

"I'm trying!"

The demon couldn't see me, being blinded by the acid that had almost completely eaten away his face. But he could hear, and he rolled toward me, hands outstretched. His skin was a cracked mess of charred black and red, and the leather coat had melted against him in patches. I stared down at him, feeling suddenly queasy that I had done this to anything, even something as vile as him. What the hell was happening to me?

He turned what had been his face up to me, beseechingly, and I hesitated. In less time than it took to blink, he had me by the foot, the raw bones of his fingers sliding against my skin in a slick caress. Immediately, the horrible draining sensation was back, my power flooding into him from that one small touch.

Pain made the world go white for a heartbeat. Then I screamed and tried to jerk away, but it did nothing except to unbalance me. I fell on my butt and kicked out at the same time, hitting the blackened face hard enough that crumbled skin fell off in a withered cascade. Stark white bone showed through, but the demon only bared its teeth at me in a parody of a grin.

"You'll look worse in a moment," it whispered, and upped the speed of the drain.

For a second, the world went gray. "Don't even think about it!" Billy said frantically. "I got nothing left, Cass. Pass out and it's over!"

"I'm fine," I told him, biting the inside of my cheek hard enough to taste blood. My knives were continuing to stab and pull out, over and over, but it was as if the creature had stopped noticing them. "The neck," I told them, my voice barely audible even to me. "Sever it."

To my lasting shock, they not only heard but obeyed. They set to work with a will, sawing away at the tendons and flesh, until I heard them hit bone. Blood roared in my ears and my eyes were growing dark, but I wouldn't let them close. Little pinpricks of light had started exploding in front of my vision by the time the knives finally completed their task, severing the spine with an audible crack.

The room was immediately filled with a hurricane. Clothes, bedding and shards of glass went whizzing by in dangerous parabolas that had me clutching my head and trying to shrink into as small a space as possible. I could feel everything spin crazily around me while my gut clenched and tried to force itself up my throat and my whole body seized up like a giant cramp. I wanted to pass out. I wanted to know what was happening. I wanted to see Pritkin's face and I didn't want there to be blood on it.

Dimly I heard yelling from somewhere nearby, but I couldn't even work out the separate sounds. Scream after scream of tortured air passed over me, around me, but I huddled into myself and refused to look. Then, as quickly as it had started, it was gone. Utter silence descended, except for the sound of my faint, whistling breaths.

I rolled onto my back and stared at the ceiling. It was all I could do to heave the air into and out of my lungs. My hand lay open on the floor, fingers still slightly curled around the knife I'd never used. Even with solid concrete under me I felt dizzy, like I was going to fall right off the edge of the world. At least the creature's body was gone, I thought dully, right before I was violently sick.

It seemed to go on for a while, although my time sense was so screwed up by then that I really had no idea. My vision kept trying to go dark again, and cleared only spottily, black fading away until I could see the scuffed toes of Pritkin's boots and the pale skin on the inner side of his bicep as he held me. My head was pounding and my body was shaking in a way I'd have been embarrassed about if I hadn't been so busy trying not to give a repeat performance.

I got a hand on the floor, trying to get enough leverage to push myself upright, but Pritkin merely pulled me in a little closer. "Give it a moment." His voice dripped fury, but his fingers were warm and gentle against my skin. That was good, because I felt really odd, cold and light, like a frozen bubble.

Blood speckled him from where the window had torn his flesh, tracing winding trails from his forearm to his elbow, and his eyes looked like they were having as much trouble focusing as mine. I had no idea why he wasn't a smear on the parking lot, but then, it seemed I'd been underestimating him all along. I stared at him, speechless, but Billy Joe knew just what to say.

"So the Circle's best-known demon hunter is half demon himself," he commented, floating over from beside the closet. "I have to tell you, I didn't see that one coming."

I had to admit, neither had I.

Chapter 15

I spent the rest of the day in bed, hurting so much that even relaxing my muscles made them ache. It was hard to believe I could be this sore and live. I wasn't sure if it was because of the attack or the whole stopping-time thing. My predecessor had died shortly after pulling that trick for the last time, which maybe should have told me something. For whatever reason, my whole body felt like one big bruise.

My mental state wasn't much better. When I finally managed to sleep, my dreams were full of Pritkin's face, wearing a brilliant and unguarded grin, which alone was enough to weird me out, since it wasn't an expression I'd ever seen in real life. Then it began to sag, with waxlike rivulets of flesh running down his cheekbones to drip off his chin, eyes rolling in their sockets, the sunny grin fading to a skeletal grimace. I woke up in a cold sweat.

I stared at the patterns the bedside light made on my ceiling, consciously slowing my runaway heartbeat. *This isn't me*, I told myself furiously. *My breath doesn't catch unless I tell it to. I don't think about things I don't want to. And I don't scream like a little girl over a freaking nightmare.* I breathed in and out for a few minutes, nice and steady, until my breath was calm without my having to work for it.

Then the door opened and Pritkin was there, staring at me. There was a sudden rumbling, rushing noise and a soft rustle of air. I screamed like a little girl.

He leapt into the room, snatched me off the bed and threw me to the floor, covering my body with his own and tucking his head down. I waited for the sickening lethargy to settle in, for the horrible sucking sensation on my power to start, but nothing happened. After a minute, the whirring noise shut off. I started to feel my face burn, despite being pressed against the cold concrete floor.

"Not that I'm not grateful for being protected from the air conditioner," I mumbled, "but can I get up now?"

Pritkin released me, helped me back to bed, and vanished. Which was just as well. I still didn't have the faintest idea what to say to him.

I went back to sleep like a person falling off a cliff, and didn't dream. But by midnight, I'd slept as much as I was going to and had hit the point where boredom had overtaken aches and pains. I sat up, feeling thirsty, sweaty, and groggy. The mirror showed me a pale, washed-out version of myself, with an impression of the blanket's weave on the left side of my face. But after a very hot shower, food and four aspirin, I went to find some answers.

Pritkin wasn't at the scene of the crime. The glass had been swept up, though, and the opening had been covered with a sheet of heavy plastic printed to look like the once beautiful window. I assumed it was there as a placeholder, so that at least from the outside, everything looked semi-normal despite the chaos within. I could kind of relate.

I'd have liked a different perspective on things, but Billy was off duty, crashing in my necklace to soak up whatever energy it had managed to accumulate. The gold and ruby monstrosity, which was so ugly I usually wore it inside my clothes, was a talisman, storing magical energy from the natural world and feeding it to him in small doses. It was enough to allow him to remain active but was never as much as he'd have liked. I usually supplemented it from my own reserves, but at the moment I didn't have any.

I went looking for the only other person who might know anything and found him glaring at the slots on level two. I thought from Casanova's expression that someone must have just hit one of the big jackpots, but no. It was worse.

By then it was after one in the morning, but that's prime time for Dante's. So I'd thought it a little odd that fully a third of the main salon was empty, with row after row of forlorn slot machines silently begging to be petted, to be loved, and to be fed money. Then I'd rounded a corner and seen that there was, in fact, a good reason for their isolation.

Two of the three ancient demigoddesses known to myth as the Graeae were in residence. They looked harmless—short, wrinkled, and blind—except for Deino, who currently had the one eye they all shared. It must have been her lucky day, because when she grinned and gave me a little finger wave, I saw that she was also sporting their only tooth.

I'd accidentally helped to release the gals from their long imprisonment recently, which had made them my servants until they each saved my life. Considering how often I get into trouble, that hadn't taken long. Now they were free and able, as Pritkin had put it, "to terrorize mankind again" unless I could trap them.

It was something that I absolutely intended to get around to one of these days, only it had slipped farther and farther down the to-do list lately, displaced by more-pressing crises. Françoise had volunteered to take it on for me, as a way of saying thanks for getting her semi-regular employment. I'd felt a twinge of guilt from involving her in a mess that, no matter what spin I put on it, was all mine. But frankly, a powerful witch would likely have better luck dealing with the Graeae than I would.

Not that she seemed to be doing much at the moment. She was watching them narrowly, but making no obvious attempt to trap them. She caught my eye and shrugged. "Zey 'ave a bond."

"What?"

"A metaphysical bond," Casanova snapped. "It causes magic to treat them as a single entity."

I watched the gals while I absorbed that. Pemphredo was nowhere in sight, but Enyo was playing nickel blackjack and Deino was beside her, standing on a stool. She was gutting a poker machine, systematically strewing its mechanical innards all over the psychedelic carpeting. I guess she hadn't been happy with the payoff.

I decided I needed a little more information. "So?"

Casanova tapped the small black box Françoise held in one hand. It was a magical snare that, despite its size, was perfectly capable of trapping and holding the Graeae—one just like it had once imprisoned them for centuries. "The spell," Casanova repeated, less than patiently, "needed to get them in here and out of my hair?"

"Yeah."

"For some reason it sees the gruesome grandmas over there as three parts of a single whole, which maybe they are, for all I know. Unless they are all present, they simply don't register as being here at all, at least not to the spell. And they've figured out that we're trying to trap them."

"So they make sure that one's always missing." I finished for him. "But that doesn't explain why they're here in the first place. If they know we're after them—"

"They're staking me out," Casanova muttered.

"What?"

"They were meant to be warriors, and I think they find Vegas a little tame for their tastes. Something it rarely is around here anymore," he said, shooting me a dark glance. "They know that if all Hell is going to break loose anywhere, it'll be here. So they Just. Never. Leave."

"Speaking of Hell," I said, but he brushed me off.

"Don't even start. There's nothing I can do."

"He trashed your window—he practically killed Pritkin!"

"Considering that your mage has been stalking him for more than a century with the same thing in mind, I don't think he can complain too much."

"We need to talk."

"Yes, we do." Casanova was the poster boy for "Not Happy." "How about we start with the fact that this is not a refugee camp? I already have a load of illegal immigrants in the kitchens thanks to you—"

"That was *Tony's* idea, as you know perfectly—"

"—and now I discover that they've been joined by a group of scruffy, probably lice-infested—"

"Hey!"

"—brats, who are also occupying two of my suites, probably planning to steal me blind!"

"They're just kids."

"Children should be seen and not heard. If possible, not even seen," he told me, unmollified. "I don't have security enough to watch the terrible trio over there, clean up your messes and also babysit!"

"No one's asking you—"

He pointed an accusing finger at me. "I'm through with you, do you hear me? You and your weird friends, corrupting my staff, ruining my casino, attracting Lord Rosier's attention—"

"Who?"

"Orders or no orders, I have had enough!" I grabbed him when he tried to stomp off, which wouldn't have worked except that Françoise decided to pitch in. "Oh, this is nice," Casanova said furiously. "Assaulted, in my own casino! What's next? Tying me up?"

"Yeah, I'm sure you'd just hate that," I said sourly. "Stop with the theatrics. Pritkin's gone off somewhere and I need answers. Either give them to me or throw me out."

Casanova snorted. "Right. I'm going to evict the boss's girlfriend!"

"I'm not the boss's girlfriend!"

"Uh-huh. That's not the memo I got. The last thing I heard, from the man himself, was to lend you every possible assistance because you're—how did he phrase it?—oh, yes, *precious* to him." Casanova looked vaguely disgusted. "Of course, that was before you started making out with the mage in the middle of the damn lobby!"

"That wasn't him!"

"You know that, and I know that. Does Mircea? Because he *really* doesn't share well."

"I don't know anything," I told him grimly. "But I'm about to."

"Not from me," Casanova said flatly.

Françoise started chanting something and he paled. "Quit that! I haven't even gotten the bill for the last disaster yet!"

"Then talk. Who attacked me? And why?"

"I already told you! And I'd prefer not to mention his name

again; it might attract his attention." Casanova visibly shuddered. "Having his destructive spawn here is bad enough."

"Are you making this up?" The only group I could think of who didn't already want me dead were the demons, mainly because I didn't know any. At least, I hadn't before today, unless you counted incubi. And death and destruction weren't really their thing.

At least, I hadn't thought so.

"There are a few things I do not joke about, *chica*, and he is one of them."

"You're telling me that Pritkin's father is some demon?"

Casanova paled. "Not *some* demon. The ruler of our court."

"So this Rosier is what? A demon lord?"

"Don't use his name!"

Billy Joe had said it, and I'd even heard a sort of admission from Pritkin's own lips, but I still couldn't believe it. "But Pritkin hates demons, he's hunted them for years, he's fanatical about it . . ."

"You don't say."

"But if he's half demon himself, why would he—"

"I don't know. Or, rather, they have issues; everyone knows that. Your mage has the distinction of being the only mortal ever actually kicked out of Hell, but I don't have any specifics. I don't deal in High Court politics; I have my own problems, most of which lately revolve around you!"

I ignored the obvious attempt to change the subject. "I don't get it. How can Pritkin possibly be half-incubus?" I poked him on the arm. "You're incorporeal."

"I have a host—"

"Which is exactly my point. You need a host to, you know." I waved a hand at his body, which was looking elegant as usual in a tan linen suit and snappy orange silk tie. Casanova raised an eyebrow. "To feed, okay? And wouldn't that make the host the father of any children, and not you?"

Casanova sighed heavily, the weight of my stupidity clearly becoming too much for him to bear. But at least he answered. "The ruler of our court is powerful enough to assume human form at will, instead of having to find a host, and is therefore the only one of us to have progeny." He made a face. "Considering the result, I can't say I envy him that."

"You mean, Pritkin is the only one of his kind?"

"There are plenty of demon races out there and many of them are corporeal all the time," Casanova said crossly. "Half-demon children aren't exactly thick on the ground, but they do exist. And most of them aren't destructive maniacs."

"But no other incubi?"

"The experiment wasn't a roaring success," he pointed out dryly.

"Okay, but none of this explains why Ros—" Casanova flinched. "That demon attacked me. He only went after Pritkin when he tried to protect me."

"Protect you? That's like sending Pancho Villa to keep Che Guevara out of trouble!"

"Would you just—"

"I don't know." Casanova saw my expression. "It's the truth! I don't know and I don't want to know. The last thing I need is for certain people to decide that I'm interfering in their business!"

"Rosier killed Saleh," I said, trying to fit the pieces together. "And when he came after me, he said it was because I'd talked to him. But the only thing Saleh and I discussed was—"

"Don't tell me!" Casanova backed away with a panicked look, right into the line of dangerous-looking creatures who had just entered the salon. They'd been so quiet, I hadn't even heard them. I assumed Casanova would have, under other circumstances, but he wasn't at his best. That was even more true when he spun around and caught a glimpse of Alphonse's smirking face.

He literally snarled, and casino security, which had been trailing the nattily dressed group of vamps, closed in a little more. "I invited them!" I said, before things could turn ugly.

"You set me up!" Casanova shot me a purely vicious look. And, okay, yeah, maybe I should have brought this up a little sooner. But I'd been busy.

"They're here to help me with something, not to fight," I said. I caught Alphonse's eye, which was easy even with

Casanova in the way since he is almost seven feet tall. "Right?"

"Sure thing," he agreed smoothly, giving Casanova's shoulder a friendly squeeze that had the incubus wincing in pain. "Came to see the bikes over at the Mirage."

"You're in my territory!"

Alphonse grinned lazily. "There ain't no territories no more—or didn't you hear? The Senate outlawed 'em to cut down on the feuding." He chuckled, like that was the best joke he'd heard in a while.

"He likes motorcycles," I reminded Casanova quickly. "You know that!"

It was true. Besides photography, B-grade vampire movies and killing things, Alphonse liked big, loud bikes that belched black smoke and choked anyone unfortunate enough to be behind him. For a cold-blooded killer, he was remarkably well-rounded.

He was also really good at getting under Casanova's skin. Not that he had to work very hard. I got the impression that there was some lingering resentment over the fact that Alphonse had taken Casanova's place as Tony's second a few years back. I had no idea if that had been a purely business decision or was partly personal, but there was no doubt that the incubus resented it. And Alphonse showing up on his doorstep without so much as a by-your-leave wasn't helping.

"And if me and my lady want to do a little gambling, who's gonna stop us?"

The five huge security personnel took a collective step forward. I started to get between them and Alphonse's group, which consisted of him, Sal, three vamps I remembered from Tony's, and one that I didn't. I really didn't want to be responsible for a territory war. But Sal caught my wrist faster than I could blink and pulled me out of the way.

"Let 'em get it out of their systems now or it'll be a whole lot worse later," she said, as the two groups surged into each other. Alphonse picked up a standing ashtray, which was as big around as a small trash can, and swung it like a club. The black sand, which had been neatly impressed with Dante's logo, went flying everywhere before the ashtray caught

Casanova squarely in the stomach. He staggered back into Enyo, knocking her off her stool.

"You don't care if they kill each other?" I demanded, as Enyo righted herself, looked around, and tossed the gutted slot machine straight at Alphonse.

Sal pulled me back a few yards, to where a small bench sat near the ornate glass doors leading to the promenade. She lit a cigarette, her numerous rings catching the light better than the cobweb-covered chandeliers above our heads. "They gotta establish boundaries," she said, shrugging.

"This isn't why I brought you here!"

"Honey, this was gonna happen sooner or later anyway. Better it be now, when they still need each other."

Casanova took a flying leap, landed on Alphonse's back, and started choking him with the plastic cord from a comp card. "They don't look like they're pulling any punches to me."

"Relax. They can't afford to kill each other with Mircea's life on the line. It's just a pissing contest—let 'em get it over with and then we'll talk."

Apparently, Casanova had grabbed Enyo's comp card, and she wanted it back. Or at least I assume that was the reason she ripped him off Alphonse and threw him through the glass doors. Sal appropriated a tray of drinks from a server, who was scurrying to get out of the way, and regarded me narrowly, long red nails tapping slightly against her glass.

She'd gone all out dress-wise. Her silky white pants clung like they loved every inch of her, and her gold lamé top plunged here and was cropped there until it was really more of a concept than an actual shirt. Her honey blond hair was pulled back into a curly ponytail, and her makeup was flawless. She took in my rumpled T-shirt and jeans, which I'd thrown on while still bleary-eyed from sleep, and my rat's nest hair. "You gotta step it up, girl. You're with *Lord Mircea*," she informed me, in tones of awe.

I decided that attempting to explain my actual relationship with Mircea would be a mistake, since I wasn't even sure what it was. "So?"

"You represent the family. And this?" A dismissive gesture

indicated my complete lack of sartorial elegance. "Is downright embarrassing."

"I beg your pardon?"

"You can't go around looking like this," Sal said clearly, as if she thought I might be a little slow. Her boyfriend, who'd gotten up some momentum swinging from a chandelier, dropped onto one of Casanova's boys, who'd been beating the vamp whose name I didn't know to a pulp.

"I wasn't exactly expecting you tonight," I said defensively. "Not to mention that I'm in disguise."

"As what? A homeless person?"

I should have remembered: Mircea was in the minority among vamps for preferring understated attire. Most believed in the old adage that said, if you had it, flaunt it, and for all you were worth. Alphonse was an enthusiastic convert to that mind-set, so much so that he'd gotten into trouble more than once at court for being flashier than the boss. Tonight he was sporting one of the bespoke suits he had tailored in New York for three or four thousand bucks a pop and enough bling to make a rap star jealous. *Maybe I should have at least brushed my hair*, I thought belatedly.

Casanova staggered back in from the hall, grabbed a drink from the tray Sal had put on the end of the sofa, and belted it before sending the dish slicing through the air toward Alphonse's neck. Alphonse ducked at the last minute and it would have hit Deino, except she caught it like a Frisbee and sent it right back. Sal plucked it out of the air and set her now empty glass on it before putting it back on the sofa cushion.

"You're gonna need a look," she said thoughtfully.

"What?"

"A *persona*."

I blinked. It was disconcerting to hear words like "persona" come out of Sal's mouth. I'd never known her very well at Tony's—mostly, she'd been draped over Alphonse, dressed in something short, tight and revealing, doing a damn good impression of a dumb blonde. Actually, until that second, I'd thought she *was* a dumb blonde. "Take me, for instance. I'm an ex-saloon girl and a gun moll. You think anybody's gonna take me seriously if I show up in Dior?"

"Maybe Gaultier," I offered, before yanking my legs out of the way of a vampire, who slid across the carpet face-first before disappearing under the couch. When he didn't immediately crawl back out again, I peered underneath, only to have a hand wrap around my throat.

Sal ground her shiny silver heel into the side of his arm and he abruptly let go. I got a close-up view of her shoe and realized that stiletto heels were, in her case, aptly named. The thing was made of metal—alloyed steel by the look of it—and was sharp as a knife.

"You have to play to your strengths," she said, as I tried to rub my throat without being too obvious. "I'm a tough broad and everybody knows it, so I go with that. But in your case"—she gave me the once-over—"you ain't never gonna carry off tough."

"I can be tough," I said, stung.

"Right." Sal cracked her gum. "With those little stick arms. I think we're gonna go with elegant, so you'll match Mircea."

"But Mircea doesn't—"

"And don't you think that makes him stand out? He's saying, 'I'm so strong, I don't need to play dress-up for you assholes.' But even though he don't wear some weird medieval shit like some, he always looks good."

"I have more important things to worry about than—"

"There's nothing more important than your image," Sal told me flatly. "You gotta be impressive, or you're gonna be fighting all the time. If you don't look important, everybody's gonna assume you're a pushover. Then we have to defend you for the boss's sake and a lot of people end up dead. Just 'cause you couldn't be bothered to put on a little makeup."

My time at court had been about blending in, fading into the background, trying to avoid attention that usually didn't end well. Nothing in my past experience had taught me how to make an impression. "I don't usually dress up," I said lamely.

Sal gripped my arm, those bloodred talons denting but not quite piercing the skin. "Oh, we'll take care of that." And the calculating look on her face was the scariest thing I'd seen all night.

Chapter 16

"I can't breathe," I complained.

Sal shot me a look in the full-length mirror in front of us. "You don't need to breathe. You need to look good," she said, ruthlessly lacing up the back of my bodice. We were in the penthouse suite that she'd appropriated along with a bottle of champagne, half a dozen bellboys and the dress I'd ordered from Augustine. He had not been pleased to be woken up in the middle of the night or to have his workroom invaded, and had loudly declared that feats of genius take time and he wasn't finished yet, thank you. Then Sal bought two outfits outright and put in an order for an even dozen more and he shut up so fast his mouth made a popping sound.

"No, *you* don't need to breathe. I'm pretty sure it's a necessity for me."

"Did you always whine this much?"

"I don't think asking to be allowed to *breathe* constitutes—"

"Because I don't remember it." Sal paused to admire the very rude slogan that had just written itself across her chest. One of the outfits she'd gotten from Augustine was a black cat suit that displayed neon-colored graffiti on itself at random moments. Sal had discovered that she could influence the choice of words if she thought very hard, and she was having fun corrupting her outfit.

"Of course, I don't remember much about you at all," she continued. "You never had two words to say to anybody, except those imaginary friends of yours—"

"They were ghosts!"

"—always slinking around in the shadows, looking spooked if anyone so much as noticed you—"

"I wonder why?"

"—which as far as I can tell hasn't changed."

I sucked in a breath, planning to teach her suit a new word, except that she cinched in the waist at that moment and all the air was forced out of my lungs. "Keeping your head down is the very worst thing you can do! It makes you look vulnerable."

"Which is fair enough since I *am*, in fact—"

"You gonna hide all your life? You gotta show everybody that *they* need to be afraid of *you*, not the other way 'round. That thing you did with the Consul, that was good. It made 'em pull back a little, made 'em think. You haven't had any more problems with the Circle lately, right?"

"Other than the huge bounty they put on my head?"

"Huh. Maybe we need to make the point a little more obvious."

"Any more obvious and I'll be dead." Sal turned to pick up her champagne and a very rude phrase flashed across her backside. I scowled at it, but I wasn't going to lower myself to fight with a piece of fabric. "I haven't had any problems because they don't know where I am."

Sal paused to tip the last of the exhausted-looking bellhops. He'd just dumped a trunk big enough to conceal a body in the middle of the living room floor. And considering who it belonged to, it just might. "Honey, everyone knows where you are!" she said, as soon as he'd left. "I mean, come on. What do you think we're doin' out here?"

"Planning to beat up Casanova?"

"Other than that."

"I don't know. Rafe called you—"

"And we usually jump when he snaps his fingers," Sal said, rolling her eyes. "Alphonse's come to suck up to the new boss. And since he ain't around, you'll do."

"Uh-huh." Alphonse sucking up to me was about as likely as the earth suddenly deciding to change direction, just for a switch.

"You really don't get it, do you?" Sal looked genuinely puzzled. "There's a war on. Everybody's choosing sides. The smart ones are aligning themselves where the strength is. Like with Mircea. Like with you."

"What about Tony? He's your master."

"And I never fully appreciated how much I hated that little toad until he was gone."

"But if he comes back—"

"I'll kill him," Sal said, sounding as if she'd relish the opportunity.

"You can't. As your master—"

"He won't be my master by then. Mircea will."

Things suddenly made a lot more sense. "You want Mircea to break your bond."

"When this thing's over, we intend to still be standing— and on the winning side," Sal confirmed, shooting me a look out of suddenly shrewd blue eyes. "Not dead fighting for a man we both despise."

Wonderful. Yet another group who was depending on me, expecting me to somehow miraculously make everything right again. I decided that maybe I'd been better off alone; fewer people to disappoint that way, fewer things to screw up. "If I'm so powerful, why can't I keep those two downstairs from killing each other?"

Sal picked up the phone and handed it to me. "You want them to stop horsing around, tell them."

"Just like that."

"Exactly like that."

I looked at her blankly, but she just snapped her gum at me so I told the phone that I would like to speak to Casanova. It told me that he was rather busy at the moment. I said I'd really appreciate it if he could make the time. It asked if I would like to leave a message. Sal grabbed it out of my hand with a disgusted look. "Get your ass in there and tell him that the reigning Pythia wants to talk to him," she snapped.

So much for my disguise. If the Circle didn't already know where I was, they probably would soon. "Do you have any idea what you just did?" I demanded, feeling a migraine coming on.

Sal punched me on the arm. "You're Pythia. Start acting like it!"

I refrained from rubbing my now sore arm and glared. She glared right back. Casanova came on the line, sounding a little breathless. "What?"

"Are you through?" I asked him. "Because maybe I'm insane, but I could have sworn we were here because *your master* is about to go out of his mind, thereby forcing the Consul *to kill him*, and do I even need to bring up what happens to both of you in that case?"

Alphonse grabbed the phone, not that he needed it—vampire hearing was more than good enough to make any phone conversation a conference call. "What's the plan? We gonna break him out?"

"That would be good," I agreed.

"Rafe said you saw the master a couple days ago. If you got in then, why do you need us now?"

"Because the wards almost certainly recorded that little visit!" I said impatiently. "They'll be expecting me to try again. And the last time I removed someone from the Consul's control, she used a null bomb to trap me."

"I heard about that. Didn't believe it, though."

"Oh, null bombs exist," I assured him. "And the Consul's got a stash of them." I'd seen it for myself, and although I doubted that she wanted to use up any more of a very expensive, very scarce resource on me, the fact remained that I'd made her look bad. It hadn't been intentional, but vamps rarely cared about such trifles. And messing with the reputation of someone who ruled partly through the fear she was able to inspire was a very big deal.

"I meant I didn't believe you could pull it off," Alphonse clarified.

Neither had I. I decided it wouldn't be prudent to mention exactly how much luck had been involved. In a world where reputation was all-important, I didn't have much of one to trade on. Alphonse remembered me as Tony's tame little clairvoyant, something that was not going to convince him to do a damn thing. Thinking of me as someone gutsy enough or crazy enough to go up against the Consul would be a much better image.

Fortunately, both Alphonse and Casanova needed me to ensure that Mircea stayed alive and well. Until the *geis* was lifted, I could trust them. To a point. Probably.

"I think I know how we can do it," I said.

Casanova had been making spluttering sounds in the background. I thought someone had been choking him, but I guess not, because he suddenly piped up. "Okay then. You're insane. This explains a lot about you."

"Insane and the boss's girlfriend," I reminded him sweetly. It's probably just as well I don't speak Spanish.

Thankfully, by the time Sal received word back from the Consul that she would see us, it was almost dawn. That wouldn't have bothered the head of the Senate, as she'd long since ceased to be bound by the sun cycle, but Alphonse and company weren't in that league. So I had a day's reprieve before I found out if my plan was going to work. And since I'd already screwed up my sleep cycle, I decided to use it for other things.

Nick was holding the fort when I got to the research room. He had his nose buried in a huge, dusty old tome, but looked glad to take a break. "There's been no word on your friend, Tami," he told me before I could say anything. "Not that I have the same level of access anymore, as a fugitive from justice."

I squirmed slightly. "Yeah. Sorry about that." Someone should have warned him that I tend to have that effect on mages.

"It had to happen sooner or later. The system is antiquated, but the Council refuses to see that."

"And here I just thought they were a bunch of power-grubbing asshats."

"That, too," Nick said dryly, shutting the cover of his book. It had a familiar symbol embossed on it, silver scales bright against the worn green leather.

"The ouroboros," I said, and was immediately sorry when

his face lit up with the delighted air of a fanatic who has found a kindred soul.

"I didn't know you were interested in magical history, Cassie."

I hadn't been, before the Codex came along. Now I didn't have much choice. "Symbol of eternity, right?"

He nodded enthusiastically. "That's one interpretation. The snake—or dragon in some depictions—eats its own tail, thus sustaining its life and ensuring an eternal cycle of renewal." He flipped to the frontispiece, an almost translucent sheet covered with the image from the cover rendered in bright jewel tones. "This one was copied from an Egyptian amulet, dated to 1500 B.C., but it was also known to the Phoenicians and the Greeks, the Chinese and the Norse . . . really, it's the ultimate archetype. There's hardly a culture that didn't know it in some form!"

"How interesting." And it was, sort of. But I didn't have time for a magical history lesson. "Have you seen Pritkin today?"

I was too late; Nick was already buried in another book. "It's also one of the oldest protective symbols in the world, possibly *the* oldest. Not to mention the most widespread. The Aztecs believed that a giant serpent resided in the heavens as protection for Earth until the end of the age. The Egyptians had a similar myth. Both cultures thought that when the ouroboros' protection failed, the age of man would come to an end."

"Nick?" I waited until he looked up. He had a smudge of dust on his nose. "Bad-tempered blond, in need of a haircut?"

"John? Oh, he's around somewhere." Nick dismissed him with one hand, while grabbing another book with the other.

I plucked it out of his hand. "This is what you've been re-searching down here?" There seemed to be an awfully lot of books devoted to Nick's hobby and none to the *geis*.

He saw my expression and hurried to explain. "No, no. Or, rather, yes, but it does tie into our search."

"It does."

"Yes. You see these?" He pointed out a line of symbols on the frontispiece, rendered in silver gilt and curving around the outside of the snake's scales. "The Ephesia Grammata," he announced proudly, as if that explained anything.

"And that would be?"

"Sorry. The Ephesian Letters. They gave an added . . . oomph . . . to the protection. You often see them on amulets in conjunction with the ouroboros symbol. They were said to have been written by Solomon himself." He flipped to a line drawing showing the snake surrounding a guy on horseback with a long spear. "That's him, attacking evil," he added, pointing to the figure in the middle of the circle. "And there's the Ephesian letters again."

"But what *are* they?"

Nick blinked at me owlishly for a moment through his glasses. "You've never even heard of them?"

"Why would I ask you about them if I had?"

"It's just . . . they're famous. Even to norms." He looked slightly offended at my level of ignorance. I crossed my arms and stared at him. "They were said to have been inscribed on the statue of Artemis at Ephesus, the center of her cult in the ancient world," he explained. "She was closely associated with protective magic, and the words were considered some of the most potent *voces magicae* in existence."

"Magic words," I translated. "And what do they mean?"

"That's just it." Nick looked at me proudly, like I'd finally said something smart. "No one knows."

"What do you mean, no one knows? Why use words if you don't know what they mean?"

Nick shrugged. "Words have power, some more than others."

"And yet no one's ever figured them out?"

"Oh, we know what the individual *words* mean," he said, sounding vaguely patronizing. "The first one, *askion*, translates roughly as 'shadowless ones,' probably some reference to the gods. The problem is that each word is only a mnemonic aid, a memory prompt for a line of text."

"It's only one word out of a whole line? What happened to the rest?"

"That's the point. Together, the complete text forms a spell too important, too powerful, for anyone to risk writing it down in its entirety." He grinned, a flash of large white teeth in his freckled face. "Except once."

"Let me guess. The Codex contains the full spell."

"The oldest riddle in all of magic," Nick said dreamily. "The secret to ultimate power."

I was beginning to understand why the Dark Fey king wanted the Codex so badly. "Sounds like something people might have wanted to hold on to."

"It's the same old story," Nick said, his smile slipping. "A group of power-hungry leaders, probably of the Artemis cult, didn't want to risk it falling out of their hands. So they only transmitted the full spell orally. But when the temple burned to the ground in 356 B.C., they all died."

"And since no one had ever written it down—"

"No one knew what it meant."

"Well, that was stupid."

"Exactly. It is possible to be too careful. Sometimes you can lose more by being overly cautious than by taking a necessary risk."

"Like telling me where Pritkin is?" I asked idly.

"Yes, I—" Nick stopped, frowning. "You tricked me." He sounded more surprised than upset.

"Where is he?"

"You need to give him some time. He's—"

"Had as much as I have, and I was attacked, too. I need to talk to him, Nick."

"I really don't think—"

I leaned across the table, slamming a hand down on his precious pile of books. Keeping my temper these days was starting to take a lot more concentration than I could spare. "Here's the thing, Nick. Tonight I have to pay a visit to the Consul, who has a bit of a short fuse and is already less than pleased with me. So I really need to know if a ticked-off demon lord is likely to crash the party. And the only way I can get that information is to talk to your buddy."

"I understand, but you have to consider—"

"And when I need to do that is now."

His frown deepened. "Are you trying to intimidate me? Because I think you should know—"

"I thought all war mages were sworn to the Pythia's service." Not that they recognized me as holding the office legitimately, or had so far shown any loyalty whatsoever. But supposedly Nick felt otherwise. Or else I had to wonder what he was doing here.

"Well, yes, technically, but—"

"I'm Pythia," I reminded him. "And you're a war mage. I don't have to intimidate you for information you are duty bound to provide."

Nick blinked at me a couple of times, then sighed and rubbed his eyes. He looked like he was getting a headache. "He's in the training salle."

"Where you should have been half an hour ago," Pritkin said crisply, from behind me. I jumped and a hand reached out to steady me. "If you kept your appointments, you wouldn't have to browbeat information out of my colleague."

Nick looked as surprised to see Pritkin as I was despite the fact that he'd been facing the door. I had this weird picture flash across my mind of Pritkin simply materializing out of thin air, like his father, before I squashed it. He was corporeal, all right, just damn sneaky.

"She didn't browbeat me," Nick said, offended.

Pritkin shot him a look. "Of course not." He was wearing gray sweats that looked like he'd already run a marathon in them. He gave my outfit a long look, but didn't comment. "Get changed and come with me."

"Why?" I asked, my stomach already sinking. Because it was that time of morning, only being up half the night I hadn't noticed.

"We're going jogging."

"I don't run for recreation. I run when someone's after me with a weapon."

"That can be arranged," he muttered, pulling me out the door.

Chapter 17

After I changed into a pair of old sweatpants and a ratty tank top, we made six circuits of the underground hallways and then ran up and down the stairs until I couldn't see straight. Pritkin swore it was only about two miles, which he counted as a warm-up, but I was pretty sure he was lying. Either that, or I was even more out of shape than I'd thought.

We stopped in what had served as the gym for a now defunct acrobatic act before Pritkin appropriated it for training purposes. A few practice mats were still rolled against one wall, looking incongruous considering the rest of the decor. The room was pretty, more like a ballroom than a gym, probably originally designed for smaller conferences that wouldn't need the larger room downstairs. It had thick paneled walls running up to a spandreled ceiling, with huge mirrors on three sides and tall stained-glass windows on the other. The light they let into the room rippled like water, splashing a mosaic of color over the wooden floor.

I leaned casually against the door, trying not to look like it was holding me up, while Pritkin dug around in a large canvas bag. He kept one eye on me, as if he thought I was about to bolt. Which was totally unfair, as that had happened only once and he'd been pulling out the jump rope of doom at the time. Not to mention that the only way I could make a break for it at the moment was if someone carried me.

I expected some fiendish new exercise equipment, or another gun that he thought I might actually be able to aim. The guy lived in hope. So I blinked uncertainly at what emerged instead. "What is that for?"

"Guns jam and misfire with the application of the right spell," Pritkin said curtly, "and occasionally without it. They also aren't effective against every enemy. Spells, likewise, can be countered by shields, stronger spells, or by incapacitating the caster. Neither method is adequate on its own, particularly when, as in your case, the potential enemies come in so many varieties."

I narrowed my eyes. "Meaning what?"

He slapped the flat of an old-fashioned training sword against his leg. Its blade was wood, but it still made a loud *thwack*ing sound. "Meaning here we have it. Swords and sorcery."

"No, there *you* have it. I'm not a war mage." I'd agreed that I needed to get in better shape and to learn how to occasionally hit what I aimed at, but I hadn't signed up to be sorcerer's apprentice.

"No. You're not. Which is why you almost died yesterday."

"Um, no. I almost died because your father decided he didn't like me talking to Saleh. Something we should discuss sometime."

"I knew you were up to something at that flat."

"Yes, thanks. Not the point."

"What did he tell you?" Pritkin demanded, giving me a weird and very creepy sense of déjà vu.

I just stared at him until he cursed and twisted, hiking up the corner of his sweatshirt. The bright colors of the tattoo reassured me slightly, although I assumed they could be faked. "Maybe we need a code word," I said doubtfully.

Pritkin muttered one that I decided to ignore and shoved a sword at me. I immediately dropped it because, despite being wood, it was roughly half my body weight. It hit the floor pommel-first with a dull, ringing thud. "You can't be serious."

"It's the smallest I have. We'll get you something more appropriate later. And you evaded the question."

"No, I didn't. Saleh didn't say much. He was too preoccupied by the fact that your father killed him." I wondered how many more times I was going to have to bring up the family connection before Pritkin took the hint. Not that under normal circumstances it would have been any of my business, but almost getting the life sucked out of me wasn't normal. Not entirely unknown, but not normal.

"There are some creatures who cannot be killed," Pritkin said, ignoring me as usual. "You encountered one yesterday. Your instincts were good, but throwing potions at that one normally does nothing more than annoy him."

"He looked a little more than just annoyed to me."

"Because you somehow managed to hit him with perhaps two dozen spells, half of them corrosive to demonkind, all at the same time. I doubt if anyone else has managed as much." He shot me a look. "I would like to know how you did it."

"I stopped time. By accident," I said, as his eyebrows rose. "Agnes showed me once that it was possible, but she never had time to teach me how."

"Can you duplicate it?"

I shook my head. "I doubt it. Not without knowing what I did in the first place." And not without spending a day in bed, paying for it afterward.

"You were lucky, then," Pritkin said grimly. "Next time you may not be."

"What do you want me to do? Freak out?"

"No, I want you to learn what you can do to banish him or any demons who might take an interest in you!"

"And why would they do that?" I asked, suddenly wondering if freaking out didn't make sense after all.

"Why does anyone? You attract trouble like a magnet."

I scowled. "Don't even try it. This wasn't my normal bad luck calling and you know it. That demon was *your father* and you didn't even warn me about him!"

"I'm warning you now. A decapitation won't kill him, but it will force him back into the demon realm for a short time, perhaps a few days. Anything that causes catastrophic failure of the body he has assumed will do as much, but his shields can stop most attacks, including gunshots. And unlike most demons, he is not affected by direct sunlight. He has to drop his protection to feed, however, which gives you a moment of—"

I kicked my sword against the wall. "Pritkin!"

"You need to pay attention to this! I can't be everywhere, and even when I am"—he took a breath, as if the admission pained him—"there are some things from which I may not be able to protect you."

"I don't expect you to. But I do expect to be told the truth."

"We didn't come here to talk." He picked up my sword and shoved it back in my hands.

Maybe he hadn't, but it had definitely been on my agenda. I couldn't force the truth out of him, though. And in his case, I didn't think reminding him of my office was going to do much good. I raised the sword, getting two hands on the pommel and wishing for something less likely to result in back strain. It was about the only body part that didn't already ache.

"You want to fight, fine," I told him. "But if I prove I'm halfway competent at this, you have to answer my questions for a change."

Pritkin didn't even bother to respond, except by attacking. I twisted out of the way before the blow could land, a crochety voice echoing in my ear, its scathing comments familiar, almost soothing: *You don't have strength, girl, and you never will. Don't depend on it! If you don't need to block, don't. Your opponent may be stronger than you, but he can't hurt you if you're not there.* A second later, my sword was aimed at Pritkin's jugular, putting him back on point.

I found myself staring at cool green eyes that were suddenly assessing. The tension seemed to crank up a notch without him moving a muscle. I kept a proper distance back, which, since our swords were the same length, was close enough to be able to strike but far enough away to need only one large step forward to attack. He slowly circled me, footwork perfect, never crossing his feet or giving me any chance to unbalance him. I hadn't seen him fight with a sword before, but it looked like he'd also had a few lessons.

I mimicked his movements, my governess Eugenie's mantra in my ears: *speed, timing, balance. Slide your feet across the ground, don't jump about like a frightened rabbit!* I was a lousy shot and was beginning to doubt that I was ever going to get much better. But I did know the basics about swords. Eugenie and Rafe had sparred with me often enough growing up to ensure that. Eugenie had defended the lessons to Tony by claiming that they were more exercise than combat training.

She'd lied.

Watch for the shift in weight, the drop of a shoulder, the slight tensing of muscles that precipitates an attack. And above all, don't think! Don't think about your opponent, who he is or how well he fights or what you believe is going to happen. You don't know. Be confident but not overconfident. Stay open, flexible and ready to act or react.

Pritkin's blade swept down, then suddenly reversed its stroke as he stepped into a perfectly balanced thrust. On every wall, his mirrored self lunged with him—at empty air, because that feint was one of Rafe's favorite moves and I hadn't fallen for it. He recovered almost immediately, pivoting out of one pattern into another, far too fast for me to get behind him.

Hit the person, not the sword! It isn't the sword that's trying to kill you. And remember, taller opponents have a longer reach, but they often leave their legs exposed. It isn't only torsos and heads that are targets, girl! I made a slashing move on a downward arc, and got a glancing hit on Pritkin's left calf as he danced out of reach. I doubted it would even bruise, but with a real sword, it might have drawn blood.

Eugenie could have taken his leg off with it, but I didn't have her skill. Despite her best efforts, I never would. But unlike Rafe, she had never pulled her punches. We'd fought with wooden swords, too, which was how I knew they hurt like hell when they hit. And she'd had no compunction about spanking me across the shins or backside with the flat of her blade if I was giving less than my best. Over the years, along with a lot of bruises, I'd accumulated rudimentary skill that, it seemed, hadn't completely deserted me.

Remember to breathe. We may not have to, but you do, so use it. Strike on the exhale, it gives you more power. Great advice, but the trick was managing to land a blow at all, which was suddenly a lot harder. Parry, retreat, strike, lunge—I was moving on autopilot as Pritkin kicked it into high gear. I guess he'd decided playtime was over. And I hadn't even realized that was what we'd been doing.

Within a minute, the burn of tired muscles was working its way through my arms and shoulders, down to my spine. Sweat was dripping in my eyes, turning my vision hot and grainy, and an exhausted headache was building inside my skull. But Pritkin's sneaker-clad feet made hardly any sound against the polished wood floor, and he'd stopped telegraphing his movements. While the mirrors threw back images of him as an almost living extension of his weapon, his word flowing seamlessly into muscle and sweat and bone, I had to concentrate just to stay in the fight and not trip over my own feet.

There's no such thing as a fair fight! Use what you have, all you have: throw sand in their eyes, kick dirt, hit below the belt. Remember, your goal is survival, not a prize for chivalry. That last was one lesson, at least, that I'd never had to be told twice. I ignored the blade coming at me, concentrated on the space behind Pritkin, and shifted. A second later, I had the point of my sword in the small of his back.

I hesitated, foolishly assuming that would end it, but Pritkin apparently had other ideas. He whirled, his weapon catching mine and spinning it out of my hand, his sword point under my chin, all practically before I could blink. "I wondered how long it would take before you remembered you can do that."

I shifted before the look of amused superiority on his face had completely coalesced, and grabbed my sword from where it had skidded to a stop under the windows. I turned to find him almost on top of me, having crossed the room at a run, and I shifted again just before he got a hand on me. I tried something a little fancy, hoping to save the few seconds it would take me to turn around, and ended up facing him.

Unfortunately, my inner ears didn't appreciate the sudden change in direction and a wave of dizziness cost me more time than a spin would have. It also made me stumble into him as he started to turn and we tripped and went down to the floor together, trying to move our swords out of the way before we fell on them. I tried to pin him, but he rolled us over and grinned down at me, eyes bright, face flushed.

"That's thrice now, practically back to back. What's your limit again? Four?"

I shifted out from under him and heard him fall to the floor with a thump as I grabbed my sword back. Or maybe it was his; my hair was in my eyes, along with a lot of sweat, and I wasn't seeing too clearly. "It varies," I panted, denting the sweatshirt over his heart with the point. "On the motivation."

Pritkin's leg caught me behind the knee, and I stumbled, barely managing to move the sword before I impaled him with it. A hard body slammed me the rest of the way to the floor before I could recover, and warm breath was in my ear. "You're not sure?"

"Haven't had reason . . . to find out yet," I said savagely, trying to buck him off. Of course, it didn't work.

"It's a good trick," Pritkin said, not letting me up, "but of limited use if it's the only one in your arsenal. We're going to have to work on—"

I gave a final heave, and when it had no more effect than the others, shifted once more. It was perceptibly harder this time, and the dizziness on landing was a lot stronger. I'd aimed for the far side of the room, but by the time I recovered, Pritkin was almost there. "Enough, already!" he yelled. "Making yourself sick isn't going to—"

"You're just . . . a sore loser," I panted, trying to get my breath back. Shifting the first time had been like running up a couple of stairs; this one had felt more like ten flights.

"I wasn't aware that I had lost," he replied, sword point getting friendly with my ribs. But he wasn't taking me seriously, wasn't watching my body language, probably expecting me to shift again. So I didn't.

A twist and a step took me inside his reach, the pommel of my sword caught his chin and my foot hooked around his ankle. With a pull we were on the floor again, but this time I was on top, with a wooden blade against his neck. He made a choked noise of surprise, or maybe it was protest over the fact that I had pressed a little too hard. It wasn't enough to break the skin, but it left a mark, red and raw-looking. I rolled off, my heart threatening to pump out of my chest, my legs rubber.

I leaned back against a mirror, chest heaving. I would have liked to gloat, since I'd likely never have the opportunity again, but I didn't have enough air. "I win. So talk."

"What would you like to hear?" he asked, sitting beside me. His tone was even—the bastard wasn't even breathing heavily—but he dragged the sword point across the floor hard enough to scratch the wood. "That that creature forced himself on my mother, knowing she would die in childbirth like the hundreds of other women he'd assaulted? That only the small amount of Fey blood she possessed gave her the strength to survive until their child was born? That I exist solely because of his perverse curiosity to see if such a thing was even possible?"

I blinked. I'd had a mental list of arguments lined up to talk him into telling me something, all of which now had to be trashed. The one thing I hadn't expected was for him to just come out with it like that, with no embarrassment, no twitching. And therein lay the problem with every single conversation Pritkin and I had ever had.

I was used to the way vamps quarreled, in convoluted, subtle conversations, a dance of lies and hidden truths, more silent than spoken. I knew that dance, those steps. But with him, there were no convoluted discussions, implied threats or discreet bargains, just blunt statements of fact that left me oddly confused. I kept looking for the hidden meaning when there wasn't one. At least I hoped there wasn't.

"I'm beginning to understand why you hate demons," I finally said.

"I hate demons because they exist solely and utterly to plague humankind! They have no redeeming qualities—they are pests at best and scourges at worst—all of which should be hunted down and destroyed, one by one!"

"You're saying that in an entire race there isn't one good—"

"No."

I knew what it was to grow up feeling that something important was missing from life, to have no reason to mourn people I never knew, yet to feel their absence like an ever-present ache. Pritkin certainly had reason to hate Rosier, maybe even demons in general, but I thought genocide might be taking things a little far. "And you've met them all?" I asked, trying not to flinch under that burning green gaze.

"You grew up with vampires," Pritkin said savagely. "Would you care to guess where I spent my formative years?"

A little late, I remembered Casanova saying something about Pritkin being thrown out of Hell. I'd assumed he was exaggerating. Or not, I thought, as Pritkin jumped up and began pacing, his face redder than when we'd finished practice.

"You grew up with those creatures, yet you defend them! I have never understood that, how any human could align herself with the very beings who feed on her!"

"You're confusing demons and vamps again." He'd had that problem all along, and living around Casanova, the only incubus-possessed vamp, probably hadn't helped.

"Am I?" Tension radiated from his body, and his mouth tightened to its usual downturned line. "They're self-centered, morally bereft predators who feed off any humans foolish enough to give them the chance. I fail to see a great deal of difference!"

I was beginning to understand why Pritkin had never been a big fan of vamps. The way they and incubi fed might seem a little too close for comfort. Vamps took blood, while incubi fed directly on the life force itself, accessed through the emotions. But the distinction might get a little blurry for someone with his background.

"It's not that simple." I struggled to my feet, trying not to wince at the ache along my spine. I'd twisted too fast or stepped wrong, and rolling my head left, then right didn't seem to help. Pritkin noticed, but I didn't get a neck rub. Somehow, I hadn't expected one.

"Some vamps, like Tony, are monsters," I agreed, "but I strongly suspect he was that way before the change. There is no typical vampire, any more than there is a typical human."

He stepped closer, pain and anger warring on his face. "There is a typical demon! Rosier is no different from your friend downstairs, or from any of the others. Except in the amount of power he possesses, in the amount of pain he can cause."

"My father may not have been a monster, but he worked for one," I reminded him quietly. Pritkin wasn't the only one who'd had to face a few unhappy truths about his background. "I've had to come to terms with that, to accept that just because he refused to hand me over to Tony, doesn't mean he refused to do other things—"

"Your father was *human*," Pritkin hissed, the abrupt lash of his anger hitting me like a slap, backing me up a step.

"So are you!"

He laughed his short, humorless laugh, and I realized that I'd never heard him laugh for real. He had smiles of wry amusement occasionally, but that was as close as he came. And even they were mostly in the muscles around his eyes. I wanted to see him really laugh, just once. But, somehow, I didn't think today would be the day.

He moved suddenly, so that we were pressed together from thigh to hip to shoulder, but I refused to give ground again. "Am I? Have you never wondered why your *geis* reacts so much stronger to me than to anyone else, sees me as so much more of a threat?"

"It doesn't seem to feel that way lately." The goose bumps running up my arms were proof of that.

"Because *he* was here! He wanted to make a point, to have me demonstrate yet again that I'm no better than he is."

"Wait—Rosier can block the *geis*?"

"He is a demon lord. Human magic has no power over such a being."

"Could he remove it?"

Pritkin grabbed my arms, his fingers digging into my flesh until they were haloed with pale, bloodless outlines. "You will not seek out that creature!"

"I don't usually go around trying to find people who want me dead!" Enough of them found me all on their own. "But if whatever he did could be duplicated, maybe by another incubus—"

"No. No one else is that powerful." His words were suddenly calm again, but his eyes slid away from mine.

"Pritkin, if there's even a chance you could do something about the *geis*, I need to know." Before I went to MAGIC and did something really, really stupid.

"What do you think I've been doing?!"

"I know you've been looking for a solution in human magic, looking hard. But you hate demons so much, I wasn't sure if you'd considered . . . another alternative."

"There is no alternative," he said flatly. "Even Rosier could not break the *geis*, and he has no need to do so. His power can override it long enough for him to feed, long enough to drain you of your life and the power of your office—a fine meal indeed!"

"Is that what he wants? The power of my office?"

Pritkin didn't answer; I doubt he even heard me. He picked up a strand of my hair and gave it a sharp tug. "You see how strong this is, how resilient? Do you know what someone looks like after an incubus drains them entirely? Hair brittle as straw, skin thin and aged, youth gone, everything—" He turned away abruptly. "I have a long list of reasons to hate that creature," he said after a moment, with a bite in every word, "but at the very top is his failure to warn me about my nature, to take even one minute to help me avoid becoming what he was."

"You aren't a demon, Pritkin!"

"Tell that to my victim."

"I don't understand."

He whirled to face me, and I flinched just from his expression. "Then let me make certain that you do. When I returned from my sojourn in Hell, I decided to make a normal life for myself. I met a girl. In time, we were married. And on our wedding night, I drained her of life the same way that thing almost did to you."

I blinked. It occurred to me that I might know who the girl in the picture was, and why Pritkin had kept it. I should have known: it wasn't out of sentiment; he was using it to flog himself. I could have reminded him that it hadn't been his fault, that he hadn't had anyone to ask about his abilities, to warn him of the danger. I could have told him that if it had been me, I wouldn't have wanted him torturing himself over my death for more than a century. But I knew what response I'd get. The glare he was already sending me could have melted glass.

"It was an accident," I finally said. "You didn't know—"

"And I am certain that was a great comfort to her as she lay gasping her last," he said, biting off each word. I'd never heard his voice so clipped, so cold. "Betrayed by the one who should have protected her, by the one she trusted most. Seeing me in the end for what I truly am, and being horrified by it—as she should have been all along. As you would be, if you had any sense at all."

"Pritkin—"

He backed me up until I ran into the wall and there was nowhere left to go. The air around him crackled so restlessly that it was uncomfortable to look at him. "But they bred it out of you, didn't they? You don't mind the monsters feeding from you. You've convinced yourself that they're just like you, merely humans with a disease. Would you like to know how your vampires actually feel about you?"

I'd grown up around creatures who could kill me with the same effort I would need to squash a bug. I knew how they saw me, how they saw all humans. But just because you can kill something doesn't mean that you do. Not if that something is far more valuable alive. It was the tightrope I'd walked long before I ever knew I was on one. "I already know—"

His eyes went very green and flat, like when he'd been killing people who were too stupid to run away when they had the chance. "I don't think you do. Believe that they care, believe that they love, believe anything that makes it easier not to see the truth. But understand this. To them, *you are food.* Nothing else. Anytime you forget that, you become vulnerable. And if you make yourself a target often enough, they *will* destroy you. Not because they hate you, but because it's their nature. And *nothing* will ever change that."

I didn't try to tell him again that this was old news. Because he wasn't talking about vampires anymore, and we both knew it. And because he already looked like he'd lost a fistfight with himself. A pulse beat in his neck and his cheeks looked hot, but his eyes were shadowed. "Don't tell me what I am. Just learn how to defend yourself. From them, or from me!"

It wasn't until after he'd left that I realized I still didn't know why Rosier wanted me dead.

Chapter 18

"What, I can't leave you alone for *five minutes*?" Billy hissed. No matter how many times I body-swap—not that it's been all that many—I still get a weird tingle hearing my voice saying words my brain didn't think up. Maybe I'll get used to it eventually, but I doubt it.

I glanced at the darkened window and saw what I'd expected: a swarthy, saturnine type in a too loud suit, with slick black hair and a slight overbite. Not the prettiest face around, but also not one to attract anyone's attention. I'd have to remember to thank Alphonse for strong-arming his man into this.

Possession tends to weird vampires out, mainly because it's supposed to be impossible. Even low-level vamps are able to evict an unwanted guest with a little effort, and the stronger ones have shields formidable enough to ensure that nothing takes up residence in the first place. But Marcello had preferred allowing a hitchhiker aboard to suffering his master's punishment. So far, he'd behaved himself, staying quiet and not attempting to wrest back control. I wondered how long that was going to last.

Outside the limo, neon-lit streets melted by in chaotic smears, shimmers of light and color and noise. Billy and I were headed out of the city to our rendezvous with the Senate. I'd slipped away without telling Pritkin, mainly because he and the Consul hadn't exactly hit it off the first time they met and I didn't need any help making a bad impression. But also because as soon as I got my hands on Mircea, I was off to get the Codex and finish this thing. And I still wasn't convinced that Pritkin was all that interested in saving a vampire's life—especially not now.

It still felt strange not having him there, though: like an empty holster where there should be a gun. I hadn't realized how much I'd come to rely on his particular brand of insanity. It was too bad; what we were attempting tonight would have been right up his alley.

So I had about a thousand things to worry about and less help than I'd planned. Yet not only did that not keep Billy from bitching, but it didn't even slow him down. "You were out of it for almost a day," I pointed out.

"Well, forgive me for exhausting myself saving your life!" he snapped. "Not to mention that you were supposed to be sleeping! Not running around with gangsters planning a hit on the Senate!"

"We're not hitting the Senate," I told him patiently for maybe the sixth time. "We're going in, grabbing Mircea and getting out. No big deal." It was what I needed to believe, anyway.

"Right. Which is why you're too scared to stay in your own body." Billy paused, fidgeting.

"What?"

"My boobs don't fit in this dress. And no, I can't believe I just said that."

"Don't do that," I batted his hands away from a part of my anatomy they did not need to know any better. "You're supposed to look dignified."

"In these shoes? I'll be lucky if I don't break your neck."

"Women do this all the time. You have it for one night. Stop with the whining."

"Whining? You really want to go there, Cass? Because we can go there. We can *so* go there."

"I take it back," Sal told me. She and the rest of Alphonse's boys had been watching the exchange with slightly interested expressions—which, since they were vamps, meant they were pretty much fascinated. Her boyfriend and Casanova were in the other limo, presumably to demonstrate family solidarity to anyone who might have heard about the fight. "If this is what you put up with every day, you deserve to whine."

"I don't whine," I snapped.

"Gee, thanks for the input, Bonnie. Feel free to jump into a private conversation just any old time," Billy added. Immediately after meeting them, he'd started calling Sal and Alphonse "Bonnie and Clyde," and nothing seemed to be stopping him. And since he was in my body for the moment, I really wished he'd shut up so maybe Sal would stop fingering her automatic.

Billy fidgeted with my anatomy some more, but succeeded only in getting one breast stuck higher than the other. He regarded them sadly, head tilted slightly to the side. "You know, death has been a lot weirder than I thought."

I looked out the window at the sunset that was painting the desert a deep bloodred. We'd just left Vegas, so we were nowhere near MAGIC yet. But I could feel Mircea's presence growing with every mile, like a magnet drawing me closer. "Life can be pretty strange, too," I said.

The outside of MAGIC is a group of nondescript stucco buildings in the middle of a sea of not-too-interesting canyons. There's nothing to distinguish it from any other ranch except its isolation and the fact that there aren't any horses or day-trippers in sight. But its looks are the least of its protections. Area 51 has less security; of course, it also has less to hide.

We arrived just as the place was starting to liven up. Not that it was obvious from the exterior, which was mostly housing for the human staff members, but thanks to Marcello's senses, I could feel the activity happening beneath the ground. There was the hum of magical wards, the bright wells of energy that meant vampires, the totally different magical signatures that indicated mages and other, less familiar sensations that might be Weres or the occasional Fey. It felt how a seismic meter might look right before an earthquake hit: too much activity in too small a space, just waiting to explode. I tried not to think about how accurate that simile might be.

I followed everyone else in, trying to remember not to

duck through doorways. The low ceilings could accommodate my new height, but they still felt too close, too hard. Billy, wearing my skin, was escorted into an antechamber of the main senate hall along with Sal and Alphonse to cool their heels and await the Consul's pleasure. Considering how much she liked me, I assumed they'd be there a while. The other family members were ushered straight to Lord Mircea's rooms to hang out while the important types did their business.

The vamps had housed me upstairs with the other humans the one and only time I'd accepted their hospitality. Looking around, I could see why. Mircea's suite was a little too impressive, like an underground Renaissance palace, with lots of inlaid-marble floors, rich tapestries and crystal chandeliers reflected in too many mirrors. Three different hallways broke off from the foyer and an honest-to-God butler conducted us to a library where refreshments were milling around. The simple room I'd been housed in before was more welcoming, and far more Mircea, than this opulent blandness.

After a couple minutes of fighting off would-be blood donors, I started threading my way through the crowd. I'd almost made it to the hall when I stopped dead. Standing in the middle of the doorway was a vampire with big brown eyes, messy brown curls and a cheerful goateed face. Charming, if you ignored the whole cold-blooded murderer thing.

I could feel Marcello's unease mount at sight of the Consul's chief spy. I really couldn't blame him—it wasn't making me any happier. I didn't know why Marlowe was slumming with the help, especially with an important meeting about to start, but it probably wasn't a good sign. He tended to show up where the action was, but there was no way he could know anything interesting was about to happen here.

"You're not hungry?" he asked cheerfully.

"Ate before we left," I said, in Marcello's low voice. I was glad I didn't need my borrowed heart to beat, because it was suddenly in my throat. "I thought I'd pay my respects to the master."

"Lord Mircea is indisposed."

"Then I'll keep it short."

Casanova joined us, a suave figure in cool blue and white, with a bright print tie. He looked like he was heading for a posh party on a private yacht and managed to make Marlowe's dark, Elizabethan-era attire look like it came from a bad stage production. "I'd like to see him, too," he commented, "to thank him for my new position."

"I thought it was merely an interim appointment."

Casanova smiled slightly. "That's why I'd like to see him."

Several other vamps made tentative movements towards us, as if they were thinking of joining the party. Most didn't get a chance to see Mircea very often, and with Tony under a cloud, they probably planned to do a little groveling. *And blame everything on the fat man before the big boss gets any ideas*, Marcello added in my head.

Stop that, I thought back.

"How brave of you," Marlowe said genially. "He's not in the best of moods, these days. Most people have been keeping a somewhat . . . safer . . . distance." The newcomers scattered so fast I almost didn't see them leave.

"Just you two, then?" It was still very friendly. I felt cold sweat breaking out all over my borrowed body.

"We'll convey everyone's best wishes," Casanova said, apparently unfazed. Marlowe glanced at me. I didn't say anything, but I didn't leave, either.

He shrugged. "If you insist."

We followed him down a long hall to a large bedroom/sitting room combo. I could tell by the fist-sized hole in the door that it was Mircea's. It looked like things hadn't improved since my last visit.

Unlike the muted colors that predominated in the public rooms, it was awash in color, something I'd failed to notice on my previous visit because the lights had been off. They still were, but Marcello's eyesight was a lot better than mine, and easily picked out the bright turquoises, reds and greens of traditional Romanian folk art in niches and painted on a huge carved wardrobe. The pieces should have looked gaudy and cheap next to the rich but understated brown and cream decor, but they didn't.

Other than the colorful art, the first thing I noticed was the bed. The broken post was still listing to the left, and the covers were still rumpled but no one was in them. A quick glance confirmed that Mircea wasn't lurking in any of the room's dark corners, either. But someone else was.

"Tami!" It was out before I could stop it. Tami looked confused, Casanova gave me an "I can't take you anywhere" expression and Marlowe grinned.

"Thank you. I was wondering how to tell which of you it was," he told me pleasantly.

I was too busy goggling at Tami to pay him much attention. She looked older than I remembered, more so than should have been true for seven years, and she was too thin. Even more of a worry were her clothes—a rumpled tan suit with torn pantyhose—which would have told me something was wrong even if her expression hadn't already said that she was on her last nerve. Tami had always taken pride in her appearance, never flashy but always neat and clean. The fact that it looked like she was still wearing the clothes they'd nabbed her in really bothered me. But she was alive.

Casanova sidled up, probably wanting to be in position so I could shift us out. That had been the plan, in case anything went wrong. Too bad it wouldn't work now.

"Don't bother," I said, to get him to stop elbowing me in the ribs. "She's a null."

"What?" Casanova frowned at Tami and she frowned back, fear starting to replace the confusion on her face.

"It's okay," I told her quickly, hoping I wasn't lying. It didn't seem to reassure her much, probably because she didn't know who the hell I was.

"In what definition of the term is this okay?" Casanova demanded.

I shot him a look, but he had a point. Since my power follows my spirit, not my body, it had seemed simple enough to slip in to see Mircea in disguise and shift him out. Even if the Senate had rigged a null bomb to prevent that, it wouldn't be triggered by Marcello. I should have remembered: nothing was ever simple where the Senate was concerned.

"It was a good plan," Marlowe said, almost as if he'd been

reading my mind. He tried to look sympathetic, but that grin kept popping back out.

"Except for the part about it being a complete failure?" Casanova inquired.

"How did you get Tami?" I asked Marlowe.

"We heard that the mages had a null in their holding cells and asked to borrow her for a time," he told me readily. "We thought it would be cheaper than using up a bomb every time you visit."

And damn it, I should have thought of that. Parking a null beside Mircea's bed was the perfect solution. Unlike a bomb, Tami was "on" all the time. And the fact that a live null's power was effective only over a very limited area wouldn't matter if she was sitting right next to him. She was just as secure this way as in one of the Circle's cells, and her presence ensured that, if I showed up again, I'd be trapped until the vamps could nab me.

Like right now, for instance.

"I didn't know until we started chatting that the two of you were acquainted," Marlowe added.

I said one of Pritkin's bad words. No wonder Marlowe looked so damn happy. The Circle had handed him a major lever to use on me without even realizing it.

I decided to just skip the part where we did the threats and the bargaining and the arriving at the obvious conclusion thing. "If she's a loaner, the Circle is going to want her back," I pointed out.

If possible, Marlowe looked even more pleased. That damn grin was going to crack his face pretty soon. "We'll think of something," he assured me. "Shall we?"

I sighed. It was a good thing that I'd dressed Billy up for the occasion, because it looked like we were going to see the Consul after all. "Yeah. Let's get it over with."

Tami stopped dead when we entered the Senate hall and just stared. There was plenty to look at, from the huge red sandstone cavern to the knife-edged chandeliers to the colorful banners that hung behind the ornate seats that clustered around the huge mahogany slab of a meeting table. But I didn't need to wonder what had caused her mouth to drop open like that. It was hard to concentrate on anything else when the Consul was in the room.

I thought at first that, just for a change, she had decided to wear something that wasn't still alive. But then the gold and black snakeskin print on her caftan undulated, sending a tide of glimmering scales rolling up and down her body. And a huge snake's head rose behind her face like a hood, with gleaming black eyes that watched me malevolently. I realized with a start that she'd skinned what looked like the grand-daddy of all cobras, but somehow kept it alive. Augustine, I decided faintly, would have had fits.

Billy moved to meet me, and I was relieved to see that at least he'd solved the breast issue. Augustine's creation fit me like a glove down to the waist, where it billowed out in a bell skirt with a slight train. I wasn't into antique fashion, but I'd seen enough period movies to argue with him about authenticity: it didn't look like something Marie Antoinette would have worn to me. He'd only sniffed and informed me that (a) styles had quickly changed after the queen's head went for a meander without her body, (b) we were talking about magical fashion here, not human and (c) I was an idiot. It was kind of obvious why Augustine wasn't exactly a household name. You had to really want the clothes to put up with the guy.

But damn, he could sew. Or conjure or whatever. I hadn't really appreciated his skill back at Dante's, what with the near asphyxiation that went with it, but despite the fact that I was never going to outshine the Consul, I thought I looked pretty good.

The basis of the dress was deep midnight blue silk, but it was hard to focus on that because of what was happening on top. Or, rather, what appeared to be happening *inside* the dress, because the more you looked at it, the harder it was to remember that this was fabric and not a night sky, and that those were jewels and not an unimaginable swoop of stars. Somehow, Augustine had created a rotating band of dia-monds that looked an awful lot like the Milky Way.

When Billy got up close, Marlowe flinched and stepped

back. It took me a moment to realize why: stars are essentially millions of tiny suns. That probably explained the faint, disco-ball effect that the dress seemed to be throwing on the cavern floor, shedding a puddle of tiny prisms all around the hem.

"Cassie?" Tami was looking at Billy in disbelief, and I decided that switching back would make more sense than trying to explain at this point. Possession was not a skill I'd had when she knew me.

I slipped back inside my own skin and Marcello sighed in relief. Apparently, he hadn't enjoyed the cohabitation any more than I had. "About time," Billy muttered as he headed straight for my necklace. The tone clearly said that I'd be hearing about this later.

"It's okay, Tami," I told her, ignoring both of them. "I know you didn't do anything wrong. This is just a mix-up."

Marlowe laughed. "Mix-up? I don't think so." He'd apparently recovered from the singeing, although I noticed that he stayed a little farther back than before. There were tiny burn marks on his hose, the size of pinpricks, that I could swear hadn't been there earlier. "She's guilty as hell."

Tami had recovered enough from the initial shock to send him a pretty good glare. It looked real familiar, maybe because I'd been on the receiving end of a carbon copy very recently. "Jesse! He's your son, isn't he?" I would have gotten it before, only she hadn't had a kid of her own when I knew her. Or, at least, she hadn't mentioned one.

Tami's head jerked back to me. "Where is he? Is he all right? Are the others—"

"They're fine. They showed up a few days ago. I have them somewhere safe."

"Oh." She visibly sagged, and for a moment I thought she was going to end up on the floor. But she recovered in time to give me a hug that forced whatever air Augustine's contraption had left me out of my lungs. "Thank you, Cassie!"

"It's no big deal," I gasped. "You did the same thing for me once, if I remember. Although next time it would be kind of nice to get, oh, a phone call? You knew where I was."

"But not what you'd say. And it's easier to ask forgiveness than permission."

"You know me better than that!" I couldn't believe she'd actually thought I'd say no.

"I used to know you better than that," she corrected. "But times change. You got out of that life. Made a new start. And besides, paranoia is a *damned useful quality*." We said the last together, laughing in spite of everything, because it had been the Misfit mantra that Tami had drilled into our heads practically every day.

Tami quickly sobered, however. "I was so worried, Cassie . . . the war mages wouldn't tell me anything, and I didn't know . . . Jesse's smart, but so many things could have gone wrong and I—"

"Nothing went wrong." I grinned ruefully. "Except that he wouldn't tell me anything, either. Not that it surprises me now. He's his mamma's boy. Only I didn't know you had a son."

"I didn't plan to get pregnant. When I found out, I hid it, and when Jesse was born . . . I had a talk with his father and he agreed to take him. His wife couldn't have kids, and he somehow persuaded her to swear the baby was hers. We thought that, as long as Jesse took after him and didn't show any signs of, of anything, he could get an apprenticeship one day, have a normal life. But when he was eleven—" she swallowed. "There started to be all these fires."

It took a second before it hit me. "He's a fire starter? Wow, that's really . . . rare." I caught myself, but it didn't fool Tami.

"And really bad," she said, her mouth twisting. "It put him straight on the Circle's shit list, and they locked him up. His father spent two years petitioning to get him out, hired good lawyers, did all the right things. But they finally had to tell him it was hopeless. Something else, something minor, yeah, maybe they could have helped. But not for Jesse." Her eyebrows drew together. "And I wasn't going to put up with that shit!"

"You got him out."

Her chin jerked up. "Hell, yeah, I got him out. They always treat us nulls like we're useless, but when I walk up to a ward, it damn well goes down! But he'd been in there two years! He told me all kinds of things, how they live—like they're in prison—how nobody ever touches them—like they're contagious—and the rumors."

"What rumors?"

"You haven't heard? The Circle is talking about starting mandatory operations, as soon as the kids are old enough."

I frowned. "For what?"

"To make sure they can't reproduce, can't pollute the precious gene pool, even if they somehow get loose!"

"It's a charge the Circle denies," Marlowe put in mildly.

Tami whirled on him in a fury. "The goddamned Circle wouldn't know the truth if it bit them on the ass!"

Only Tami wouldn't think twice about telling off a master vampire in front of half the Senate, I thought, as Marlowe backed up a step. He raised his hands, mouth quirking in a smile he mostly managed to conceal. "I never said I believed them."

"But why are you here?" I asked. "I mean, I know you broke the law, but it wasn't anything that serious." Locking up a den mother in the most secure prison they possessed seemed a little overkill, even for the Circle.

Marlowe arched an eyebrow at me. "Blowing up half a dozen of the Circle's educational facilities isn't that severe? Oh, but I forgot to whom I was speaking."

I frowned at him, and then the rest of what he'd said registered. I transferred my frown to Tami. "Wait a minute! You're the Vixen Vigilante, aren't you?"

She scowled, running a hand over her creased skirt. "Do I look like a vixen to you?"

Considering what she'd been through, I thought she looked pretty good. But that didn't mean I agreed with what she was doing. "What on earth were you thinking?"

"I was thinking I needed to get my son away from those SOBs! But after I broke Jesse out, he begged me to go back in for some friends of his. And then they had friends and then the friends had friends . . . And sometimes wards weren't the only obstacles, especially once they figured out I could get past them. They started rigging booby traps, so I started carrying explosives and . . . it snowballed."

"Oh." I blinked, finding it hard to reconcile the crazed vigilante with the woman I'd known. Of course, she was probably having a similar problem with me.

"But the Circle set a trap and I fell into it, and now they want me to give up the names of everyone who's been helping me find homes for the kids. And I won't." She glared some more at Marlowe. "I don't care what you do to me. You damn vampires can drain me dry and I won't tell you a goddamned—"

"That's not why you're here," I told her, jumping in. A show of spirit was one thing; insulting the Senate was something else. I'd already done enough of that for both of us. "I want to see Mircea," I told Marlowe, pulling Tami behind me.

"He's indisposed."

"You already said that. I still want to see him."

Marlowe's expression blanked with that creepy speed the vamps sometimes showed. "No," he told me seriously. "I don't think you do."

"Where is he?" Alphonse demanded. He and Sal had been prudently keeping to the background, but they came forward now. One of the Senate guards moved to intercept, but Marlowe made a gesture and he let them pass.

"He had to be moved to a more secure area." Marlowe shot me a look. "I have need of every operative right now; I do not have the men to keep Lord Mircea safely confined."

"Confined?" The word didn't make sense in context with Mircea. He was a first-level master. They went wherever they damn well pleased. "What are you talking about?"

"He attempted to leave, I assume to find you. But he was not in full control of his faculties. We did not know what he might do if he escaped into the human population in such a state." Marlowe grimaced. "He was . . . displeased . . . to have his wishes denied. I have six men in critical condition who can attest to that fact."

I swallowed and tried for a neutral expression. I doubt I made it. When Mircea had been thinking clearly, he had ordered me away. If he was trying to track me down now, it meant that things had deteriorated—even faster than I'd expected.

"Where. Is. He?" Alphonse repeated, although it sounded more like "Don't make me eat your face."

Sal grabbed his arm while Marlowe just looked irritated. Clearly, he didn't think much of Alphonse's intelligence. It was a point of view I was coming to share. Challenging any Senate member wasn't bright, but antagonizing the chief spy was suicidal, especially for someone who was barely a third-level master.

When Marlowe ignored him, Alphonse let out what could only be called a growl. "Control your servant," Marlowe said, "or I will."

It took me a moment to realize that he was addressing me. It didn't make sense. Alphonse was not my servant. Alphonse was . . . oh, shit. "You're treating me as Mircea's second, aren't you?" It came out okay, even though my lips had gone numb.

"He named you as such while he was still . . . capable," Marlowe admitted.

Okay, this was bad. Really, really bad. It explained a lot of things, including why the Consul had yet to order me dragged off to a cell somewhere, but that was about the only positive aspect.

Technically, Mircea could appoint anyone he chose as his second, the person who spoke for the family in the event that the master was unable to do so for a time. It was the position Alphonse had held under Tony. But why on earth had Mircea chosen me? He had an entire staff at his home in Washington State, not to mention a vast family of adherents, any one of which would have made more sense as temporary guardian. I couldn't defend the family, which was a second's primary job. I had trouble just keeping myself alive! What the hell had he been thinking?

I licked my lips. It was a telling gesture that would have won me a smack upside the head from Eugenie, but they were suddenly so dry I couldn't speak otherwise. But nothing seemed to be coming out of my mouth anyway.

"Well, of course he did," Sal said. I felt an iron grip descend on my shoulder. It said, *don't you dare pass out and disgrace us all.* I straightened my spine slightly, and the pressure eased enough that I might get away with only a slight bruise. "The master and the Pythia have formed an alliance."

Marlowe's expression made it clear what he thought about that, but then the Consul spoke up and nobody else's opinion mattered. "Then you may speak for him," she told me.

I moved a little closer, but stopped before the reflection cast by my dress hit the table. I doubted the little points of light it was giving off would be more than a flea bite to her, but I didn't need any help pissing her off. I was probably going to manage that all by myself.

I looked up into that beautiful bronze face. "Why has Lord Mircea been imprisoned?"

"As you were told, for his protection. He was becoming difficult to control without inflicting damage. The snare also obviates the need for constant supervision."

"The snare? You mean you put him in—"

"We had no choice," Marlowe said quickly. "Nothing else could hold him."

Alphonse cursed and I bit my lip before I said something I probably wouldn't live long enough to regret. But despite my best efforts, I felt my blood pressure skyrocket. She was talking about the type of magical cage Françoise had tried to use on the Graeae. It was meant for dangerous criminals, which meant the designer hadn't worried about providing a lot of comfort—or about ensuring unconsciousness. The Consul's offhand comment meant that Mircea was all alone in a blank world going slowly out of his mind, with no comfort of any kind—no voice to talk to, no hand to touch. Nothing. I couldn't think of a worse fate.

"Are you going to accept that *shit*?" Alphonse hissed in my ear. His fist was clenched and he looked like a man who dearly wanted to run amok. "Because I—"

I stomped on his foot, hard, and amazingly, he shut up. "No." I looked at the Consul again. "Mircea must be set free. Immediately."

She inclined her head slightly. "You agree to complete the *geis*?"

"I didn't say that."

"Then he remains where he is," she said flatly. "We cannot cure him. In confinement, he cannot injure himself or others."

"He *is* being injured! The *geis* is driving him mad!"

"A fact you could prevent, if you chose." A flash of anger rippled across that usually impassive face. "If he had not named you head of house, I would order you locked in a room with him and we would have done with this!"

"If Mircea wanted that, he wouldn't have named me his second," I pointed out, thinking frantically. And just like that, I realized why he'd sent me away, why he had taken the only step possible to ensure that the Consul could not force us together. "He's afraid, isn't he?"

"What?" Alphonse was obviously lost, but Sal looked thoughtful. I was starting to wonder who really ran that partnership.

"You're Pythia now," she said slowly, working it out. "And the *geis* responds to power." Her eyes suddenly got wide. "Oh, shit."

That settled it. I was never going to assume Sal was slow on the uptake again. She'd gotten it a lot faster than I had.

For Alphonse's sake, I spelled it out. "When Mircea placed the *geis* on me, he was the most powerful of the parties involved, so it was under his control. It was supposed to be lifted before I became Pythia, but that didn't happen. And now Mircea is afraid that my power will override his. That, if we complete the *geis*, I won't be his servant—he'll be mine."

Alphonse looked like someone who had just had a load of bricks dumped on him. I left him to process things while I turned back to the Consul. "Tony had a portal," I told her abruptly. "He used it for his smuggling operation. You can use it to send Mircea into Faerie, where the effects of the *geis* will be lessened. He should be in control of himself there."

"The Fey will not allow it." The beautiful mask was back

in place, and so perfect that I almost thought I'd imagined the other.

"The dark will. Their king and I have an understanding. And one of his servants is available to escort Mircea to the palace, so he will not be harmed on the way. All we need is a power source to open the portal." I gave Billy a meta-physical poke. I doubted that asking him to babysit a bad-tempered pixie was going to go over well, but I didn't have a choice. I didn't trust Radella. "Make sure she doesn't try to double-cross Françoise," I told him.

"And how am I supposed to do that?"

"She can hear you," I reminded him. For some reason, she'd never had a problem with that, even in our world. "Tell her the deal is off if she tries anything."

Billy streamed halfway out of the necklace to grin at me. "This has potential."

"And don't antagonize her!"

"Of course not." He put on his wounded face.

"That will not solve the issue at hand," the Consul in-sisted, ignoring my one-sided conversation. The snake's hood behind her flexed, a long, slow ripple that cascaded down into the gleaming caftan. I didn't know if that meant anything, so I ignored it.

"I've been working on a permanent solution." I had hoped to avoid bringing this up, considering how she was almost certain to respond, but I was out of other options. "There is a counterspell."

"There is not. Our experts all agree."

"Then your experts are wrong. The counterspell is con-tained in the Codex Merlini."

Marlowe was looking at me with dawning understanding. He'd been there when the Dark Fey king had given me the commission to find the damn thing, when I'd discovered it contained a way out of the *geis*. "You found it," he said softly.

I shook my head. "Not yet. But I know how to get it."

"You will tell me," the Consul said. It was not a question. "I will send for it, and if you speak the truth, I will order Lord Mircea released. You will remain here until it is brought to me."

"You don't understand," I said, trying to keep my temper. "It isn't some*where*, it's some*when*. I'm the only one who can get it. I've been working on it for almost two weeks now!"

The Consul just looked at me. For a moment, I was afraid she'd gone into one of her famous time-outs, which could last anywhere from a few minutes to a few days, but then she blinked. "Why should I believe that you wish to help one of us?"

"One of you?" I threw out my hands in exasperation. "Except for the blood-drinking thing, I practically *am* one of you!"

Her face broke into the first smile I'd ever seen from her. After one look at it, I hoped it would also be the last. "If that were true, you would be long dead for your defiance."

Okay. Death threats aside, we were making progress. "If I wished Mircea harm, why am I here?" I asked. "What punishment could I give him that would be worse than what he's already undergoing? If I wanted him to suffer, I'd just stay away. That's how you know I want to help."

"And what do you wish in return?"

Finally, we came to it. "I want Tami freed and the charges against her dropped."

"Cassie!" I heard Tami's excited whisper behind me, felt her eyes boring a hole in the back of my neck, but I swallowed the words I knew she hoped to hear.

She wanted me to demand that something be done about those damn schools the mages were running, but I knew better. The Consul might be able to pull a few strings over a single prisoner, but changing an entire area of Circle policy would be overreaching. She didn't have that kind of authority, and asking for something I knew she couldn't provide would only make me look like I didn't really want to help Mircea. I'd already asked for more than I thought I could get—stipulating that the charges be dropped instead of simply that Tami be freed. I wasn't going to do any better. Not tonight.

"In return, I will retrieve the counterspell and free Lord Mircea from the *geis*," I said instead.

The Consul didn't blink this time. "Done. But you will take one of us with you."

"I had planned to take Alphonse—" I began, but she cut me off.

"No. A senator."

I'd been afraid of this. Why settle for just saving Mircea when there was a chance she could get the Codex, too? Only that so wasn't happening. I hadn't gone through all this to put that kind of power into vampire hands. Fortunately, she hadn't specified which senator.

I smiled, and didn't even try to make it a nicer version than hers. "Agreed."

Chapter 19

I landed on Dante's rooftop two weeks in the past, and almost I fell off. My feet were on concrete, but the bell of my skirt swung out over thin air. I grabbed the side of a turret hard enough to scrape skin, trembling slightly with the realization that a few inches to the left and I'd have landed on nothing at all. But I hadn't, I'd made it, and after a moment, I managed to pry my hands loose from the fake rock and look around.

Everything was strangely silent this far up: the traffic noise was muffled and there were no discernible sounds of combat. Everything looked normal, too, with the lights of the Strip glittering in the distance, outshining the star-studded canopy overhead. But a sudden rush of wind from the base of a tower pushed at me, hard enough to shove me back a step, and with it came the smell of gunpowder and ozone. It looked like I'd found the right place.

Moving cautiously back to the edge of the roof, I saw the parking lot spread out below in a panorama of chaos. The blue smoke had mostly dissipated on one side to reveal burned and blasted cars, a number of obviously dead bodies, and Tomas standing in front of a crowd of curious onlookers. He was doing his Obi-Wan impression—these aren't the droids you're looking for—while a wererat dragged itself toward the back door, leaving a bloody trail on the ground.

On the other side of the lot, farther from the street, cleanup had begun. It was briefly interrupted by a vamp running across the lot, waving his arms frantically, flames streaming out from the back of his jacket. Mircea moved to intercept, while more vampires emerged from a couple of silver-gray limos parked on the far side of the casino. Mircea brought the crazed vamp under control with a word, and several others jumped him with blankets, putting out the flames. Shortly afterwards, I saw myself, Françoise and a glowing dot that I assumed was the pixie flash out.

Other than Mircea, nobody seemed to notice their departure. Most of his vamps were too absorbed in getting the fires under control—when a stray spark can be deadly, you tend to pay attention. I glanced back to the other puddle of activity and saw that everyone there also looked pretty distracted. Tomas was now talking to two cops, while Louis-Cesare propped up the younger version of me so I could argue with Pritkin. It was as good an opportunity as I was going to get.

I shifted behind Mircea. "Miss me?"

His head whipped around and his eyes widened. He glanced at the spot where the other me had just disappeared, then back again. "What is this?"

I gave him a once-over. I hadn't been able to tell from the rooftop, but he was looking a little rough. His jacket was burnt in a diamond-shaped pattern all along the back, with little tatters of black material fluttering out behind him like Halloween streamers. His hair was half out of its clasp, falling askew over a slice of cheekbone, and he had ash on his chin. At least the shirt looked okay: it was heavy Chinese silk with little toggles instead of buttons, and seemed to have been protected from electrocution by the jacket.

A tiny piece of ash stood out starkly against the cream silk. I reached to brush it off, but he jerked away. "We need to get going," I said impatiently. It was probably going to be only seconds before someone saw me who shouldn't.

I reached for him again, but suddenly he just wasn't there anymore. Damn it! I'd forgotten how quickly vampires could move.

"Who are you?" The voice came from somewhere behind me.

I spun so fast that my skirts tangled around my legs. I stumbled a little, but caught myself before I went sprawling. But my hair came loose from the chic chignon Sal had managed to concoct, straggling into my eyes. I brushed it back and fumbled around on the asphalt, looking for the bobby pins. I'd told her this wasn't going to work. Elegance and I were not on a first-name basis.

I finally managed to find a couple of pins and stood up, trying to keep hold of them and not spill my overloaded purse. Marlowe had scrounged around the Senate's treasury and come up with the big bag o' jewels that was currently trying to pull my shoulder out of joint. "Portable wealth," he'd explained, when I asked him why I was carrying around a bunch of stones that made the Hope diamond look puny. "In a revolution, people want something that can be easily transported out of the country." I could argue the ease-of-transport thing, but I wasn't about to complain. I just hoped it would be enough. Unfortunately, the rocks and my gun hadn't left room for a hairbrush.

"Do you have a comb?" We probably needed to look respectable for this. The way things stood now, I wasn't sure they'd let either of us in the door.

When Mircea didn't answer, I looked up, only to see that he was holding something, and it wasn't a comb. "What's that for?"

"For you, if you do not tell me the truth."

"I already have a gun," I told him, confused. What did he think I was going to do with that thing? It wasn't a handgun; it was an M16 assault rifle. The thing was freaking huge.

And it was pointed at me.

"Oh." I suddenly got the message. I dropped the bobby pins and held up my hands, palms out. But the gun to my chest thing didn't change. "After what you just went through, it's understandable you'd be a little spooked," I said. And, wow, didn't I wish I'd thought of that earlier. "But I really am here to help. Please, take my hand and I'll prove it."

Mircea's only answer was to move back a few steps. Probably to get a better shot. Behind him, several of his vampires looked up from fire extinguisher duty and saw us. Just great.

"You can drop the glamour," he told me grimly. "I am not deceived."

"I'm not using a—" I began, but he did his disappearing act again before I could finish. It took me a moment, but I spied him across the parking lot, over by one of the limos. And, no, letting him drive off somewhere really wasn't an option.

I shifted, but in the split second it took me to get there, he had vanished. I was about to open one of the car doors, to check inside, when I caught the reflection in the windows of two blurs moving up behind me. I shifted again before the vamps could grab me, landing back across the lot, near where I'd started. I was starting to get dizzy—not a good sign. Especially when we hadn't even gotten to the damn auction yet.

I looked around, trying to spot Mircea, and almost ran into him. We both shied back, and a quick glance showed me that he'd lost the gun. Maybe he'd remembered that he didn't really need it to kill me. Or maybe he'd decided to let me get a word in. "Listen," I said. "I just want to—"

He threw a potion in my face. My mouth had been open, and I choked on an absolutely vile-tasting mess. It was green and oily and globules of it dripped down my chin to land on Billy's necklace. Wonderful. The thing had so many nooks and crannies that I'd probably never get it clean.

When I finally blinked enough of the stuff away that I could see, I found Mircea staring at me, a half-perplexed, half-angry look on his face. "That should have stripped away the glamour," he said, as if talking to himself.

"It probably would have, if I was wearing one!" I said furiously. He disappeared again. "You better hope this doesn't stain!" I yelled at the space where he'd just been, right before an arm fastened around my throat.

"You must be powerful," he whispered, his breath warm in my ear, "for that concoction to have failed."

I shifted out of the almost choke hold and landed behind him. "Will you hold still for one minute?!"

Mircea spun in another movement too fast for my eyes to track and grabbed me around the throat, palm to bare skin. I sighed in relief. "Thank you," I said sincerely, and shifted us before anyone else noticed our game of keep-away.

A moment later, I found myself pinned against a hard, cold brick wall. My body was busy informing me that maybe I'd done a few too many jumps lately, and I'd landed in a puddle and gotten icy slush in my shoe. Not to mention Mircea's grip on my neck, which was a little too tight for comfort.

"Where are we? And who are you?" I couldn't see him very well, but he sounded pissed.

"*When* are we," I corrected. A thin, whirling snow was falling, catching on my goopy eyelashes. I couldn't see much of anything with his body in the way, but the night was cold and damp, not hot and arid, and there were cobblestones under our feet, not asphalt. And judging from the dizziness I was experiencing, we'd jumped at least a few centuries. "And you know who I am."

"You are not my Cassandra." The tone was flat, hard. Not one I'd ever heard from him, at least not directed at me.

"Then who am I?" I really wished the road would stay still for a minute, long enough for me to get my breath back, to *think*.

"You are a mage, hiding under a glamour, which if you do not drop"—his hand tightened fractionally—"I will drop it for you."

I swallowed, and felt it against his palm. I wondered how much longer I'd be able to do that, how much tighter that grip had to get before I couldn't swallow, couldn't breathe. It didn't feel like it had far to go, but I couldn't think of a damn thing to say to stop this. The one thing that had never occurred to me was that Mircea would mistake me for one of the people we'd been fighting. Because I knew him, instinctively, unmistakably, I'd just assumed he'd feel the same way.

Obviously I'd been wrong.

I could feel his fingers on my throat, flexing against the muscle there, and I knew I had to say something, do something, *now*. But I couldn't shift again, not this soon, not with panic and exhaustion eating at my consciousness. And I was sure I'd black out before I could remember something that might convince him to wait a minute before he killed me—

Mircea's hand abruptly fell away and I gasped, little black dots dancing in front of my eyes as my lungs fought with my throat to get enough air into my starved system. I felt his hand grip my chin, knew when he brushed my hair away from my face, but it seemed pretty trivial next to not asphyxiating. Light fingertips trailed over a couple of faint ridges on my throat, stilling directly over bright, sensitive skin.

"Where did you get this?" His voice was faint, but I wasn't sure if that was him or me. My ears were still ringing, whether from the shift or the half-choking thing I wasn't sure. It took me a couple of seconds even to understand what he was talking about. And then I realized why he'd released me, why I probably wasn't going to die tonight—at least not by his hand. I sagged against the cold brick, so relieved I would have laughed, only it would have hurt my throat too much.

"Where?" His voice was stronger now, more insistent; maybe he'd had a chance to recover from the shock. I glared at him, a hand on my abused neck. He could give me the same opportunity.

"Where do you think?" I snapped.

Bite marks were like fingerprints; no two alike. I'd been wearing the mark of his teeth in my flesh for days, like a brand. It was probably the main reason Alphonse and Sal and even the Consul, in her own way, had been so cooperative. And if they'd recognized it, Mircea certainly had.

"It is my mark, yet I did not give it to you."

"Didn't give it to me *yet*," I corrected. There was no way to hide the fact that I was from his future. His Cassie couldn't shift people through space, much less time. So I'd already given that much away. The trick was not to give anything else.

"Why didn't you tell me? I might have injured you!"

"Might have?"

His touch was back in an instant. Strong fingers wound into my hair, rubbed at the back of my neck, trailed carefully over the healing wound until I couldn't feel it anymore. Not the pain, at least, but the two little bumps remained. They weren't hard, but they were obvious, at least to me. I guess they must have been to him, too, because he bent his head and kissed them, carefully, lightly, lips soft and warm against the tiny scars.

It wasn't a particularly sensual touch, but my body reacted

immediately, with a rush of wild adrenaline. For a minute, my fingers clenched in his coat, not caring about the cold or that he smelled like smoke or that I had green goop trickling down my neck.

"They're still there," I said shakily, as he slowly stroked the length of my throat.

"They will always be there," he murmured. "You are mine. They announce the fact to all who see you."

"It's a little more common to get a ring," I said breathlessly. "Not to mention being consulted first!"

"I am a gentleman, *dulceață*," he said reprovingly. "I would never enter a lady's house—or head or body—unless she invited me."

"But I didn't—" I began, and stopped. I hadn't explicitly given permission at the time, but I hadn't exactly thrown him out of bed, either. And when I had finally managed to put up a struggle, Mircea had let go. Even as far gone as he'd been, he'd let go.

"As I thought," he murmured, and kissed me. And it was still as warm, as wet, as necessary as water. I found myself returning the kiss with an enthusiasm that I vaguely thought might not be all that ladylike, but he didn't seem to mind. He kissed me until I was dizzy with it, heat spreading through me like I'd drunk something rare and strange and addictive. So addictive that it took me a moment to remember that feeding the *geis* was not the plan here.

I tore away, chest heaving, cold air prickling along my bare arms. I hunched my shoulders against the chill and gulped down a noise that absolutely was not even a little bit like a moan. "Would you please not do that?" I whispered. It was hard enough to think as it was, without him sending my hormone levels to join my blood pressure.

"Why?" He looked genuinely puzzled.

"Because we're not . . . we don't . . . It's complicated, all right?"

Mircea was able to convey more by a small facial movement than I'd gotten from some entire conversations. At the moment, he had sarcastic *eyebrows*. "*Dulceață*, the only time I have ever left such a mark was to punish or to claim."

"Maybe I—"

"And when it is punishment, I do not feed from the neck."

I swallowed and shut up. I wasn't going to win this way. If I kept on talking, it wouldn't be long before he'd have the whole story out of me. And maybe that wouldn't matter but maybe it would. Because there weren't too many people who could contemplate the kind of torture he faced and not be tempted to try to avert it. He wouldn't succeed, but he would almost certainly alter time in the attempt.

I glanced around, but there was no one in view. I could see because of the light emanating from a couple of stuttering lanterns on either side of a nearby doorway. It was attached to a house that stood shoulder to shoulder with those on either side, a long row of four-story medieval dwellings listing together like old drunks. None of the others had lanterns, or shadows moving against the curtains at their windows. That, plus the fact that my power tends to take me where I need to be, meant that this was probably the place.

"There's a party in there tonight," I explained, trying for calm when my every nerve said *now* and *hurry* and *it's in there*. The idea that the Codex might be only a dozen yards away was enough to make my thoughts a little tangled even without Mircea's help. "A couple of dark mages are about to auction off a book of spells. We have to get in there and buy it or steal it or get it before anyone else does or—"

Mircea suddenly jerked me against him and pushed us both back against the wall. "Not the *time*—" I began, then the air crackled and tore, like all the lightning in Europe had decided to descend on us at once. There was a rush of wind and the world tilted horribly. A second ear-numbing crack and a flash of impossible purple light later, and an ornate barge sat in the middle of the narrow street, so large that its hull almost brushed the buildings on either side.

I stared at it, afterimages from the sudden storm dancing around the reality of a huge ship just blatantly blocking the road like that. I had only time to think, *yeah, this probably is the place*, before Mircea was dragging me into the shadows of an almost nonexistent alley between two inebriated buildings. His gaze was furiously intent. "Where are we?"

"Paris, 1793," I managed to gasp, not sure he'd be able to hear me. I'd had to lip-read to understand him, because of the symphony of mostly percussion instruments that had taken up residence in my ear canals. "At least, I hope so."

Mircea was silent for a moment, that lightning-fast brain doing some catch-up. "Why?" he finally asked.

"I told you. We're going to a party."

From over his shoulder, I watched a ramp extend outward from the barge until it touched the icy street. It was red, like the hull, where a rich crimson formed the background for great coils of gold and blue and green that my recovering eyes finally identified as an elongated dragon. Its carved snout formed the prow of the boat, with its front claws each holding a glowing golden ball, positioned almost like headlights. Its long, snakelike body ran down the side to end in a barbed tail near the prow. There were no oars or sails or other evidence of propulsion systems, not that much of anything would explain how it had gotten landlocked between buildings with no water in sight.

Four large men in gold armor came down the ramp. Their suits were covered all over in little scales, mimicking the ones on the dragon. They took up places on either side of the ramp, two by two, holding up long spears like an honor guard. Then, from the dragon's belly, floated a tiny chair holding an even tinier woman. Her impossibly small feet were wrapped in satin lotus shoes, and I didn't have to ask why the levitating chair, because no way could those minuscule things have held even her weight.

At first glance, she looked helpless, like an overdressed doll that had to be moved around by her attendants. The image contrasted starkly with the power that radiated from her like a small supernova, flooding the street with an invisible but almost suffocating force. The guards were for show; this beauty didn't need any defenders.

"Who is that?" I managed to croak.

"Ming-de, Empress of the Chinese Court—roughly the same as our Consul," Mircea whispered, his breath frosting the air in front of my face.

I watched the jeweled dragons on Ming-de's dress coil and

twist and writhe in ways that I initially thought were due to the flickering lantern light. But no, a small gold one scurried along the hem of her gown, bright as fire against the crimson silk, and I realized they had minds of their own. "But how did she get here?"

"Ley-line travel," Mircea said, as the whole party proceeded indoors in a stately procession.

"What?"

There was another flash, of green this time, and a crash loud enough to make me jump. I blinked, and when I looked again, a large gray elephant complete with gold howdah was standing behind Ming-de's barge. The elephant didn't appear to have as much room as it would like, and it let out a thundering trumpet of protest. A guard's head poked up from the back of the barge and shouted something, then the huge ship lurched forward a scant few feet until it hit a lamppost and had to stop. It was starting to look like a party where the hosts hadn't thought enough about parking.

After a moment, the elephant knelt and an Indian couple got out. They were wearing gorgeous outfits of peacock blues and greens, although nothing seemed to be moving. Between them they had on as many jewels as I had in my little bag, and the sapphire on the guy's turban alone was as big as my fist. But they didn't have to denude themselves for the auction; when they headed for the door, a small flying carpet bobbed along in the air behind them, carrying a chest. I felt my stomach fall. If these were examples of the bidders I was up against, I was in trouble.

"Okay. What is going on?" I demanded.

"Maharaja Parindra of the Indian Durbar. Like our Senate," Mircea explained. "I believe the woman is Gazala, his second."

"But how did they *get* here?"

"They came through the ley lines."

"You said that before. Not helping."

Mircea quirked an eyebrow at me. "You have never surfed a ley line?"

"I don't even know what that means."

"Really? Remind me to take you sometime. I think you will find it . . . exhilarating."

I stared at him and tried really hard to remember what, exactly, we were talking about. His mouth pursed into an odd almost-smile, his earlier intensity forgotten or, more likely, masked. "I will be happy to elucidate later. But for now, I would appreciate a more coherent explanation of our presence here."

"We're going to bid on a spell book. You just saw our competition."

Mircea gave me a skeptical look. "I know Ming-de well, but only because I was once the Senate's liaison to her court. And I have met Parindra but once, because both have a reputation for rarely traveling beyond their own lands. If they wanted such an item, they would send a servant."

"Well, obviously they didn't," I said, rummaging around in the remains of Mircea's jacket until I found a handkerchief. I wiped away as much as I could of whatever he'd thrown at me; luckily it had mostly dried and a lot of it dusted off. "At least it doesn't smell," I said sadly.

Mircea took the handkerchief and set to work on a green smear on my neck. His knuckles barely brushed me, and even then it was through the satiny weave of the linen. It was an odd sensation, close enough to not quite touch, warm enough to not quite feel, the sleeve of his jacket whispering along my bare arm. "Why did you come back for me?" he murmured, stroking lightly, pressing just hard enough for me to feel the embroidered initials on the cloth. "Do I not exist in your time?"

Define "exist," I thought, as the small square worked its way downward, the banded ends just tickling the top of my breasts. "The Consul wouldn't let me come alone," I breathed.

When I'd talked to Billy about taking Mircea along, he'd still been relatively lucid—as much as the *geis* allowed anyone to be. But if the Consul had been desperate enough to order him confined, then he was too far gone to help me. And I really needed competent help.

If Mircea died, I had no doubt that the Consul would blame it on me. And, unlike the Circle, who seemed to have too many problems to concentrate all their energy on hunting me down, she struck me as the single-minded type. If she wanted me dead, I had the definite impression that I would get dead. Really fast.

"You could have chosen another senator," Mircea pointed out.

I couldn't come up with a convincing lie with goose bumps trailing over my skin, following his caress with slavish devotion. "The other you was busy," I said, snatching the damn handkerchief away before I went out of my mind. This wasn't going anywhere and I wasn't a masochist.

"For something that important, I would have thought I could have made the time," Mircea said lightly.

And yes, I was busted, because no way would he have sent anyone else to take care of something that concerned him so personally. But I still wasn't telling him anything. "You're just going to have to trust me," I said.

"Even though you will not do me the same honor?"

I took a deep breath and concentrated on not banging my head into the wall. "There's not a lot more I can tell you. I've probably said too much already. All you need to know is that we have to get that book or we're both in a lot of trouble."

Mircea took a moment to process this. I was certain he wasn't going to let it go, wasn't going to just take my word for it. But then he held out his arm. "May I assume that this counts as a first date?"

"Oh, we're way past that," I said, before I thought.

He smiled slowly. "Good to know."

Chapter 20

The guy who answered the door was in his early forties, with thinning hair under the wig that sat askew on his head, and many teeth already rotted away. He didn't look like somebody who should have been able to defeat a legendary wizard, but maybe he was just the butler. We followed him through a narrow hall and up a staircase to a library. It contained an ornately carved marble fireplace, bookcases lining two walls, mother-of-pearl detailing on dark wood moldings and about three dozen guests.

All of whom paused to look at us as the butler or whoever he was made introductions. I hadn't heard Mircea give his name, but the man knew it anyway, although I was just "and guest." I needn't have worried about our appearance: Mircea managed to make losing the coat seem like a fashion statement. I saw several other male guests surreptitiously shuck theirs after a moment, not wanting to miss out on a new trend. But one remained unmoved, muffled head to toe in a thick black cape that swept the ground and didn't leave so much as a nose visible. That was okay with me, because the people I could see were disturbing enough.

A woman appeared in front of us carrying a basket of knitted blue, white and red rosettes. I chose not to poke a hole in Augustine's creation, and carried mine, but I didn't like it. It felt funny; I couldn't figure out what material had been used.

"Human hair, probably from the guillotined," Mircea murmured. I quickly slid it onto a nearby table.

A moment later, a pretty, dark-eyed French girl sashayed

up with a tray of wineglasses. She gave Mircea one and then just stood there, apparently waiting for him to finish it so she could give him another. It looked like the rest of the room was out of luck. But he didn't drink, I noticed; he just held the delicate stem casually in one hand, the bloodred contents glimmering in the low light.

I took one off her tray and downed most of it in a gulp. It was good, and the head-clearing fumes were better. Mircea watched me with a smile and switched our glasses, giving me his full one.

"You don't like wine?" I asked, sipping at my new drink with a little more decorum.

"Under certain circumstances."

"Such as?"

"Remind me to show you sometime," he murmured as our group was joined by a stunningly beautiful woman.

She was Japanese, or at least she looked Asian and had origami hummingbirds buzzing about, holding up her hand-painted train. And she was only the first of many. Despite the fact that we found a dark corner beside the fireplace to wait for the main event, a steady stream of people made their way over to speak to us. Or, more accurately, to speak to Mircea, since most of them barely gave me a glance. I couldn't help but notice that a disproportionate number of them seemed to be attractive and female.

I don't know why this surprised me. It had been the same way at court, when Mircea came for an extended visit to Tony. I'd overheard the staff complaining that they'd never had so many guests; even vamps who loathed Tony had shown up to pay their respects. Because Mircea wasn't just a Senate member, he was a Basarab, which pretty much put him in the movie star category as far as vampires were concerned.

Or maybe rock star, I thought, restraining myself from forcibly removing the hand that the current groupie, a statuesque auburn-haired witch, had placed on his arm. He moved back on the pretense of setting his empty glass on the mantel, and his admirer moved with him. His mouth curved into a rueful smile that, for a moment, I wanted to taste so badly that I couldn't even think.

I didn't blame the groupies. Much. Mircea was perfectly capable of using his looks and reputation to his advantage—it was practically a job requirement. But the hell of it was that most of the time he *wasn't* doing it on purpose. He simply enjoyed his surroundings, wherever he was and whatever he was doing, with an unconscious sensuality that was just as much a part of him as his hair color.

Even with the extra power my office lent me, the *geis* was strengthening. Just standing beside him was enough to get my heart racing, my pulse pounding. And my body was getting noticeably slower at obeying my brain's commands to look away, to not touch, to not notice every little thing about him. Like the way his hair still held the faint memory of the cold wind outside. Like the warmth of his skin when he touched the notch in my upper lip with a fingertip.

"A spec of potion," he murmured, his finger trailing over my lips.

Of course, sometimes he *was* doing it on purpose.

I looked up to meet eyes that were quiet and intense and focused. Under that gaze, it was easy to believe that I was the only person in the room who held any value for him, the only one on earth who mattered. But I'd seen that look before, and not just directed at me. Shy people became talkative, aggressive people became amenable and plain people blossomed, trying to live up to the regard they saw in his eyes. Or thought they saw.

I held his gaze for a drawn-taut moment before I blinked and looked away, angry that he was trying this on me, confused that he was doing it *now*, and I met the eyes of a dark-haired female vampire. Her garnet dress clung to some dangerous curves, and her silver mantilla framed a face so beautiful that for a moment I could only stare. She presented a hand, but I ignored it; it was too high to shake, so I assumed it wasn't aimed at me.

Mircea dutifully kissed it and said something to her in Spanish, but her eyes remained on me. This went on for an uncomfortably long time, but she didn't say anything, so I didn't either. After a while, she decided to look at him instead. They had a brief conversation that I couldn't follow, but then, I didn't really need to. She was pretty good at conveying information silently. She stared into his face, batting her eyelashes, trailing her finger around the low neckline of her dress, running her hands up and down the sides of her body, and speaking in husky tones. Every look, every movement, said she wanted him, with perfect frankness and no shame at all. I looked away before I was tempted to do something really stupid.

Eventually she moved away, but not before shooting another strange look in my direction. "Old friend?" I asked, trying to make it light.

"Acquaintance," he murmured. His eyes were on a couple of new arrivals—both male vampires. They bowed in his direction and he nodded back, but his pose stiffened slightly. For the usually tightly controlled Mircea, it was the equivalent of someone else throwing a fit. Things suddenly began to make sense.

More than two hundred years of living adds a lot of strength, even to a first-level master. And vamps can sense changes in another's power level as easily as a human might notice a new hairstyle. Any vampire who got too close was likely to realize that something about Mircea was seriously off. He had used me to distract the woman, but I doubted the same trick would work on the men.

"You seemed really friendly for acquaintances," I commented, not bothering to keep the bite out of my tone. I resented being part of his ploy, even if I agreed with the reason for it.

"The contessa and I served on the European Senate together for some time. She was surprised to see me," Mircea said, as we watched the two vampires take their tricolor decoration with identical bland expressions. They started to circulate, but not in our direction. "I am supposed to be in New York at the moment, scouting out the possibility of beginning a new senate there."

"Great." That was all I needed, for the Mircea of this time to get back only to have Contessa Whoever quiz him about his Paris vacation.

"Do not concern yourself. She died in a duel before I returned. We spoke mostly about you, in any case."

"Me? Why?"

"She wanted to know why you wear my mark. I refused it to her some time ago and she expressed herself . . . surprised . . . that I had favored you."

"You refused *her*?" I imagine she was pretty surprised. I was looking fairly decent, having wiped most of the potion off and finger-combed my flyaway hair, but I wasn't in the contessa's league. I hadn't needed her expression to tell me that I never would be.

"She wanted into my bed less for pleasure than for the political advantage it would gain her," Mircea said mildly.

"You're not serious." What, was the woman stoned?

"There have been many through the years who have shared her view. When you have wealth or power, there are always those who will find such things more attractive than you."

"Then they're idiots." It was out before I could stop it.

Mircea suddenly laughed, his eyes alight. "You didn't ask me what answer I gave her, *dulceață*."

I was probably going to regret this, but I had to know. "What?"

He leaned over and captured my hand, holding it dramatically to his chest. "That you have bewitched me."

"You didn't really tell her that."

He pressed a swift kiss on the pulse point of my wrist. "In those very words." I snatched my hand back, glaring. All I needed was another enemy to have to watch for tonight.

"She called you prince, didn't she?" I asked, deciding on a change of topic. I don't speak Spanish, but the term is the same in Italian. "I thought you were a count."

"There were no counts in Wallachia when I was young," Mircea said, letting me get away with it. "The term was *voivode*. The English sometimes translated it as 'count palatine'; others preferred 'governor' or, occasionally, 'prince.' We ruled a small country." He shrugged.

"Why don't you use it anymore?"

"The idea of a Romanian count was popularized a bit too

much once Stoker's book came out. It would have been imprudent thereafter."

We were interrupted by the arrival of yet another gorgeous groupie. Apparently, all the homely girls had decided to take the night off. I stared into the distance and tried to think about more important things while she giggled and flirted. It didn't help much. I wasn't stupid, despite public opinion. I'd known all along that I couldn't have this. But making goo-goo eyes at him with me *standing right there* was not only tacky, it was insulting, and I'd had about enough. I slid my arm through his, sending the hussy my best glare. The galaxy rotating around my feet suddenly expanded, broadening its width by maybe a foot, enough that the hem of her dress caught fire. She was a witch, not a vampire, so she put out the small flames with a murmured word. But she didn't stick around afterwards.

I glanced at Mircea, belatedly realizing that I might have set him alight, too. But no pinprick-sized holes appeared in his black trousers and I didn't see any small wisps of smoke. Which didn't make sense, come to think of it. "Why aren't you on fire?"

He raised an eyebrow. "Did you wish me to be?"

"No, but . . . the dress had, uh, a slight effect on Marlowe." And it hadn't even been that bright then.

The eyebrow climbed a little higher. "You set Senator Marlowe on fire?"

"Well, not intentionally." Mircea just looked at me. "We were in the Senate chamber and he got a little too—"

"In the Senate chamber?"

I frowned at him. His face seemed to be twitching for some reason. "Yes, he'd dragged me to see the Consul—"

"You set him on fire in the Senate chamber in front of the Consul."

"It was only a little fire," I said, then stopped because he'd broken into laughter, his whole face crinkling up with it, all bright teeth and curving, irresistible mouth. "He put it out," I said defensively. He just kept laughing.

"*Dulceață*," he finally gasped, "as much as I would give to have seen that, it would be as well if you did not repeat the performance this evening."

"I'm not—"

"I only mention it because I believe Ming-de wishes an audience."

"What?"

He inclined his head slightly at the opposite side of the room, where the Chinese version of a consul was flanked by her four bodyguards. "It would be prudent to refrain from setting the Chinese Empress ablaze."

"She looks busy," I said weakly. It was true—she had already gathered a large court of admirers—but I'd also had enough formidable females for one evening. Mircea didn't bother replying, just used our linked arms to pull me through the room.

We stopped in front of the dais on which Ming-de had parked her thronelike chair. It had dragons, too, writhing around the back of the seat, but at least they weren't moving. Unlike the fans that had taken up residence on either side of her head, fluttering and waving in the air like two overactive butterflies. No one was holding them, the guards' hands being preoccupied with the spears that, since they were vampires, I assumed were mostly ceremonial. Especially as the fans were razor-edged, and could probably go from circulating air to cleaving flesh at a moment's notice.

I'd been so preoccupied with the spectacle that was Ming-de that I hadn't immediately noticed that she was talking until Mircea nudged me with his foot. I looked away from the dancing fans to liquid black eyes set in a tiny oval face. Ming-de looked all of about twenty and yes, she was startlingly pretty. I sighed. Of course she'd wanted to see Mircea.

Only she wasn't looking at him. I wondered if maybe I should get a sign VICTIM OF ROGUE SPELL, NOT A THREAT before anyone started planning to remove the competition. Ming-de held out a hand with ridiculously long, bright red nails. I was so focused on them—the thumbnail alone had to be six inches long and was curled outward, like a spring—that it took me a few seconds to notice that she was poking something at me.

It was a staff with an ugly brown knot on the end. I shied

back before it could cut out my heart or something. But it followed me until I managed to focus, despite having it almost shoved up my nose. The knot resolved itself into a shrunken head wearing a tiny blue captain's hat on its thin hair.

"Her Imperial Majesty, the Empress Ming-de, Holy Highness of the Present and Future Time, Lady of Ten Thousand Years, would like to ask you a question," it said in a bored monotone that managed to convey absolute disgust with me, its mistress, and the world in general.

I blinked. "You're not Chinese." The British accent sort of gave it away, that and the fact that the remaining strands of hair were red.

The head gave a long-suffering sigh. "I wouldn't be much bloody use as an interpreter if I were, now would I? And how did you know?"

"Well, I just—"

"It's the hat, isn't it? She makes me wear it so people will ask."

"Ask what?"

"D'you see? It always works. It's part of my punishment, to have to tell the story of my tragic life and painful death to every Tom, Dick and Harry before they'll *answer a simple question.*"

"Okay. Sorry. What's the question?"

It eyed me suspiciously. "You don't want to hear about my tragic life and painful death?"

"Not really."

It suddenly looked offended. "And why not? My death isn't interesting enough for you? What would it take, eh? Perhaps if Robespierre was hanging here, damn him, you'd care to have a listen, hmm?"

"I don't—"

"But a simple East India Company captain who made the mistake of firing on the wrong ship, oh, no, not enough to trouble yourself about?"

"Look!" I said, glaring. "I'm not having a great night here. Tell me, don't tell me—I don't care!"

"Well, there's no cause to yell," it said huffily. "The mistress simply wants to know the name of your seamstress."

"What?"

"The mage who enchanted your gown," it explained, in a tone that made it clear that the biggest trial in the afterlife was dealing with people like me.

"He isn't . . . available right now." Which was true enough, since he hadn't been born yet.

"Trying to keep the secret all to yourself, eh? Mistress won't like that," it said gleefully.

Mircea and Ming-de had been chatting while I talked with the help. I hadn't even tried to follow their conversation, which was in Mandarin, but I did recognize the phrase "Codex Merlini." And even if not, Mircea's suddenly tightened grip would have gotten my attention.

"We're here for the *Codex*?" he whispered.

I looked at him, wondering what all the fuss was about. "Yes. I told you—"

"You said a spell book!" Mircea started bowing and murmuring a rapid stream of Chinese and pulling me away from Ming-de.

"That's what it is!"

"*Dulceață*, describing the Codex Merlini as a spell book is roughly the same as calling the *Titanic* a boat!"

I didn't get what was going on, but I couldn't help but notice that we were heading straight for the door. "Wait! Where are we going?"

"Away from here."

I pulled backwards—why, I don't know since it did exactly no good at all. "But the bidding is about to start!"

"That's what I'm afraid of," he muttered, just as all the lights went out.

The room hadn't had much light before, only a few random candles, but now it was pitch-dark. I felt an arm slip around my waist and yelped, before recognizing the thrill of the *geis*. People were murmuring and milling around on all sides as Mircea made a beeline through the crowd, practically carrying me.

I didn't understand what was wrong with him; no one seemed happy about the sudden blackout, but nothing threatening appeared to be taking place, either. By the time we reached the stairwell, my eyes had adjusted enough to see by the light my gown threw off. The room was all starlight and shadow and appeared just as before. Until a bunch of dark shapes crashed in through the windows.

Mircea pulled me into his arms and all but flew to the foyer, where we met another half dozen dark shapes coming up. My eyes couldn't focus on them, but I didn't think that had anything to do with the lack of light. And then we were back upstairs, in about the same time it would have taken me to shift. Mircea paused at the library landing to avoid the mage who stumbled backwards out the door, Ming-de's flying fans buzzing around his head like angry wasps. One of them hit a candle sconce in passing and sliced it clean in two.

I glanced in the library door and saw nothing but a firestorm of spells, crashes and yells, all of it too bright to let my eyes pick out any details. Then Mircea grabbed a mage who was blocking the stairwell going up, and threw him downstairs. He hit the group of dark shapes who were all trying to fit up the narrow stairway at the same time, and most of them tumbled backwards. The fans followed like they were on a mission.

By the time I blinked, we were on the next level, where a mage was facing off with the contessa. Her pretty mantilla had expanded into a glittering net that wrapped around him like a spider's web. Right before we took the last flight of stairs, she jerked him to her, fangs already bared and glistening.

Someone grabbed my foot as we reached the attic level, but Mircea made a backwards kick and I heard the sound of whoever it was tumbling down the stairs. He wrenched open the door to what looked like a servant's bedroom, got a window open and had us out onto the slick, icy sill before I could protest. Then he paused, staring down at the main entrance below, where several dozen dark figures were heading in the front door. *They must have run out of windows to break*, I thought blankly.

"Can you do what you did at the casino?" Mircea asked,

his voice a lot calmer than it had any right to be under the circumstances.

"What? No, not yet." The dizziness and nausea of that many shifts in close succession had mostly passed, but I still felt wiped out. I doubted I could have shifted myself, much less two of us.

Mircea didn't ask any questions, just moved me into a fireman's carry over his right shoulder. Which left me able to see the cloaked figure who burst into the room behind us. It was the hooded party guest. Still didn't want to see what was under there, I decided.

"I am going to have to jump, *dulceaţă*," Mircea said, giving the newcomer an uninterested glance.

"Jump? What?" I was sure I'd heard wrong.

The cloak sent a spell hurtling down the stairwell, then barred the door by shoving a heavy wardrobe against it. "If you're going to jump, do it, or get out of the way!" it snarled.

And that's when I began to wonder when I'd gotten tipped down the rabbit hole. *Stress*, I thought vaguely. *That has to be it.* "I am waiting for the rest of the mages to enter in order to plant the bomb," Mircea replied tersely.

"What bomb?" The cloaked figure and I said it at the same time.

"The one the war mages of the Paris coven are setting to destroy this house and, they hope, the Codex along with it."

No wonder he'd freaked out down there, or what passed for it for him. He must have heard about this evening somewhere. And if it was interesting enough for people to tell stories about, I really didn't want to hang around. But I couldn't leave. Not when we were so damn close!

"Why destroy it?" I asked. "Don't they want it for themselves?"

"Yes, which is why they're currently searching. But if they don't find it, they will destroy this house and everything in it, rather than let it fall into the hands of the dark."

"The Codex isn't here," the cloak said, muscling its way out the window. Now there were three of us perched on the icy roof. "The coven is going to kill dozens of people needlessly!"

"I doubt that," Mircea said, nodding to where a fight had started in front of the house between the mages and the party guests, most of whom seemed to have gotten out of the death trap of a library just fine.

I flinched back as Parindra zipped past, so fast that the breeze ruffled my hair; it looked like he'd found another use for his carpet. He tossed something onto the crowd of mages below that exploded in a yellow haze that ate through their shields like acid and set a lot of them ablaze. It also caused the back of the barge to catch fire, which spooked the elephant.

The beast let out an unhappy bellow and went on a rampage, picking up a mage with its trunk and tossing him against a nearby house, which he hit with a sickening crunch. The attack scattered the rest of the mages, who went running in all directions to avoid being crushed by the elephant or by the heavy howdah, which had slipped halfway off its back and was getting slung around like a jewel-encrusted battering ram.

"That should do it," Mircea said.

"Wait. What are you talking about? Do what?" I asked, and felt his muscles tense beneath me. The commotion had left the area directly below us momentarily free of mages, I realized, and Mircea intended to take advantage of it. "Oh, no. No, no. See, I'm starting to develop a problem with heights and—"

"Hold on," he said, and we were airborne.

I didn't even have time to scream. I felt a rush of cold wind, a brief weightless feeling, and then we smashed into the deck of the ship. Mircea took the brunt of the fall, but it tore me out of his arms and sent me careening into the cloak, which had apparently jumped right along with us. It didn't feel like a vamp under there—no faint tingle was running up my spine—but how the hell had a human managed that jump and lived?

I didn't have time to find out, because a spell hit the barge, making it shudder and buck beneath us, sending both of us reeling into the railing, right beside where a mage was trying to climb on board. A guy dressed like Ming-de's attendants ran over and started stabbing at him with a spear, but the mage had managed to retain his shields, and all it did was piss him off. He came over the side, and he and the guard went down in a tangle of limbs, before rolling straight into me and the cloak. I got a foot to the stomach, which knocked the wind out of me, but the cloak fared worse, its head slamming hard into the heavy wooden railing of the barge.

Mircea had gotten back to his feet and staggered over to the rail. He barely pulled back before a spell sizzled past, exploding against the stone facade of the house behind us. It was hardly the only one. Spells were being flung around everywhere, making the dark sky look almost as light as day, if daylight came in every color of the rainbow.

"I will never get you through this alive, not without a shield," he said grimly. "And I am too drained at present to provide one. I will have to improvise." He had a brief conversation with the remaining Chinese vamp. "Zihao will protect you. Do not leave the ship," he added, right before jumping over the side.

"Mircea!" I peered over the edge of the barge, but the whole street was a working anthill of activity, and I couldn't see him. I did see someone else, though.

The contessa had apparently finished her meal and come for dessert, and I didn't have to ask who she'd slated to fill that role. Damn it! I knew something like this was going to happen.

She vaulted up on deck and said something in Spanish, which I didn't understand, and smiled viciously, which I did. I tried to get to my feet, but the train Augustine had added to the dress got in the way, wrapping around my ankles like a rope. She started laughing while I tugged at the silky material, which just plain refused to rip or to let go. Then she leaned over and freed my feet with a flick of her wrist.

"If you want heem, fight for heem, but on your feet, witch," she told me, as Zihao managed to find something else to do at the far end of the ship. Apparently defending my life did not include getting disemboweled by a jealous Senate member. I honestly couldn't blame him there.

I scrambled up and smiled tentatively. "That was very, uh, decent, of you," I said hopefully. Maybe we could work this out.

That glittering silver net rose up behind her head like a

frame for her beautiful face. "Not really." She smiled. "I prefer to dine standing."

Or maybe not.

The lacy trap launched itself at me, like it had the mage who I was certain hadn't made it out of the house. But it stopped halfway between us, caught in a field of stars that had suddenly swirled up all around me, like a galaxy in miniature. For a few seconds, the mantilla hung in the air, immovable object meeting irresistible force. Then everything exploded outward like a star going nova.

I flung an arm over my eyes to shut out the glare, and when I looked again, the contessa was just standing there, as if nothing had happened. I didn't think that was the case, though. Because I could see pieces of the battle behind her, through the hundreds of little holes the starlight had carved right through her body. And then she fell, toppling off the side of the barge into the road below.

I stood there, staring down at her crumpled body, shocked and more than a little freaked. I was alive, but possibly not for long. Because a master vampire wouldn't be killed by something like that. Hurt, maddened, enraged, yes; killed, no. She could get up any second and, as soon as she did, I was toast. I really needed to get off this barge.

Zihao came by while I was trying to see an opening somewhere, anywhere, in the melee. He'd lost the spear, but had improvised a new weapon out of a large oar, which he started to ram through the cape's head. "Wait!" I sank to my knees, which were pretty wobbly anyway, and spread out my hands. The stars had gone back to their usual places and they didn't appear to be rotating anymore. But the guard paused anyway.

He said something that, once again, I didn't understand. I was starting to envy Ming-de her translation device, however temperamental. He finally seemed to realize that we had a failure to communicate. He jerked a thumb between the cloak and me, as if to ask if we were together, and I nodded vigorously. It wasn't true, but whoever was under there wasn't with the other side, either, and I'd seen enough blood for one evening.

That seemed to satisfy the guard, who ambled off to attack

someone else. I turned my attention to the cloak, and wondered if I'd wasted my time defending a corpse. Because the man underneath lay motionless, one pale arm outflung, the hood still obscuring his face. He didn't even look like he was breathing, although there was so much loose material that it was hard to tell. But the arm was warm and it looked human enough, so I tugged back the hood to check for injuries.

And stopped dead.

I could hear the madness going on all around me, the elephant rampaging, glass breaking, people swearing. But none of it seemed as real as the face in the middle of all that black, cast in a myriad of colors by flying spells. A very familiar face.

No. I must have been hit in the head and had just failed to notice, because I had to be hallucinating. I blinked hard a couple of times, but it didn't help: the face stubbornly stayed the same. I pressed the heels of my hands against my eyes and sat like that for a minute, not hyperventilating because that would be weak and I couldn't afford that, but maybe breathing a little hard. By the time I let my hands fall to my lap again, I'd managed to get a grip. A bit of a grip. Sort of.

I stared down at the face and, okay, maybe started hyperventilating just a little as my brain tried to twist around the crazy, stupid, completely impossible thing my eyes insisted on showing me. But they were wrong—they had to be—because that couldn't be Pritkin. I'd left him at Dante's, under the happy belief that I was turning in early. And unless he'd found a time machine somewhere, he was still there. But it wasn't Rosier, either. Because although I knew for a fact that the demon lord could bleed, I doubted he'd have been knocked unconscious by a minor head wound.

He did look a little different, I thought numbly, with longish red-gold hair falling in his eyes, brushing his shoulders. He looked younger, his face a bit thinner, making his nose look even larger than usual and throwing his cheekbones into stark relief. His lips, always thin anyway, were a fine slash across his jaw.

But I guess he'd have needed some kind of disguise. Couldn't just look the same, lifetime after lifetime; someone was bound to notice. Maybe that's why he knew so little about vampires. Wouldn't be smart to hang around with creatures as old as you, who might remember a face from a few hundred years ago, no matter what disguise it wore. And Pritkin had never been stupid.

No. Not Pritkin, I corrected myself. I heard the voice of a cranky djinn in my head, telling me that the author of the Codex had been half incubus. And Casanova had said that in all history there had been only one of those.

I stared at the face under the ridiculous pageboy—God, he'd never had a decent haircut, had he?—and didn't believe it. But the fact remained, I only knew of one half-incubus, British mage with a serious hard-on for the Codex who was around in 1793. And Pritkin wasn't his name.

Damn it! I'd even said it once myself—he just didn't look like a John. But, suddenly, he did look an awful lot like a Merlin.

Chapter 21

The eyelids fluttered and the next moment I was speared by a familiar green gaze. I did my best to look concerned and nonthreatening—which wasn't hard when I was almost sitting on my gun and I was a slower draw than Pritkin anyway. I hadn't had time to check for weapons, but with him that was kind of superfluous. He was always armed to the teeth.

The green eyes flickered over me in the same objective threat assessment that I remembered from every time we'd encountered an enemy. It had been a while since I was on the receiving end, but I remembered it vividly. Despite the cold, I was sweating in less than ten seconds.

Pritkin uncoiled himself, eyes tracking my every breath as he slowly sat up, dizzy but hiding it well enough that if I hadn't known him, I would've missed it. "And to think, I believed the vampire to be the greater threat," he said, glancing quickly over the rail and back again.

"I'm not a threat," I told him, still feeling numb. Other than the hair, he looked . . . the same. Just the same. I kept expecting him to demand coffee and tell me off for something.

"You wear well the mask of the distressed innocent," he said, watching me with ice-water eyes as he got to his feet. "But unlike the vampire, I will not underestimate you."

"I mean, I'm no threat to you," I clarified. "We're on the same side."

"A paltry subterfuge," he sneered. "I know what you seek, whom you serve. It is because of fools like you that we are all tottering on the brink of destruction!"

He took a step back until his thigh hit the railing, then swung a leg over. I had no idea where he thought he was going in all that, but knowing him, he'd risk it. And I couldn't allow that. If anyone here was likely to know where the Codex was, it was the man who wrote it.

"Please!" I said desperately. "I don't serve anyone! We can work together, help each other—"

"If you are not in service to that revengeful soul, then you have been deluded by those who have entered into his destructive projects. If the latter, know this: I know not what lies you have been told, but we have no safety but in resistance, no hope of securing our rights and lives but in opposing the power which has unquestionably the design to invade and subvert us!"

I was still trying to decode that when I saw a nightmare rise from the ground behind him. The contessa's body looked oddly like Swiss cheese, with bloody holes in the remains of her black gown, but strands of red flesh and purple veins had already started to weave between the gaps, filling them in. And I knew the score as well as anyone: if a vampire can move, she is deadly, and this one was back on her feet. One of the holes had taken out an eye, leaving a burnt crater in what had been a beautiful face, but the other focused on me malevolently.

I was so dead.

My dress remained motionless—still pretty, but useless as far as defense went. I started fumbling in my bag, scattering jewels across the burning deck while trying to find the gun that probably wouldn't help me anyway. Then I heard a strange whooshing sound and looked up to see a column of flame where the contessa had been and an empty potion vial in Pritkin's hand.

She screamed and ran into the crowd, straight into the path of the elephant. It trumpeted its fear at the sight of a stream of fire headed right for it, and I guess its instinct was to try to put it out, because one of those massive feet came down with the force of a steam-driven pylon, right on top of her. And then another one for good measure. And then I looked away because it was either that or be really ill.

"You did me a service," Pritkin was saying. "That was the return. Do not presume on my goodwill again." He climbed onto the railing, still watching me out of the corner of his eye, and when Parindra made another flying swoop, he caught hold of the edge of the carpet and was gone.

"Pritkin!" I shouted the wrong name, but it didn't matter; by the time the words were out of my mouth, he was already out of earshot. He was not, however, out of trouble.

It took Parindra all of a second to notice that he'd picked up a hitchhiker. He kicked out with his foot, but Pritkin grimly held on, which seemed to annoy the Indian Consul. He took the rug straight up, five or six stories above the tops of the houses, before trying again. This time, he succeeded, dislodging Pritkin with a kick that looked vicious even from this far away, and that sent him flying off into the night.

I stared, my heart in my throat, knowing that even a mage couldn't survive a fall from that height. But before the scream working its way up my throat could get out, a filmy mass formed above his head, glowing pale blue against the black sky, like a neon jellyfish. The bottom of it flowed over Pritkin's hands and arms, the rest ballooning up overhead, slowing his rate of descent to a crawl.

I'd known shields could do a lot of things, but a parachute was a new one. It was working, though, and unless there was a breeze I couldn't feel, he was in at least some control of the thing. And he wasn't trying to get back into the house; he was navigating a course in the other direction.

"Human magic never ceases to amaze," Mircea said from behind me.

I whirled. "We have to get him!"

"Ming-de has agreed to take us with her when she makes her exit, which will be very soon. I do not know how she will react to having an unknown mage on board."

"Not help him—*get* him! He has the Codex!"

Mircea's gaze sharpened. "You're certain? You saw it?"

"I didn't need to," I said viciously. "He's trying to leave. And there's no way he'd do that unless he already has what he wants." Somewhere, under that monster of a cape, he had it on him. And now he was getting away with it.

Mircea was looking at me oddly. "You know this mage?" I did a double take, then remembered that Mircea hadn't seen Pritkin without the hood up on the cape. That was good as far as the integrity of the timeline went, but it meant that he didn't know the conniving, devious, dangerous son of a bitch we were up against.

Before I could answer, there was a flash of red light and a crack that was audible even over the sounds of battle. And between one blink and the next, Pritkin simply vanished. "What the . . . He's gone!"

"Stay here." Mircea jumped over the railing, wading through the carnage to where Ming-de had just emerged from the house. Her thronelike chair was back in hover mode, gliding serenely through the chaos, her fans cutting a broad swath in front of her while her guards hacked and slashed at everything on either side. But the fans apparently recognized Mircea, because they let him through to talk with their mistress.

In a moment, he was back, using a knife he took off a passing mage to pry at one of the orbs in the dragon's claws. "What are you doing?"

"I promised to take you through the ley lines. It seems I will keep that promise sooner than I had thought." With a flick of the wrist, the orb came loose in his hand. Ming-de floated gently up the ramp, which pulled in after her. The whole ship began to shake, and slowly rose off the ground, like the hot-air balloon it wasn't.

"Wait!" I raised my voice to be heard over the sound of a couple dozen spells hitting the barge all at once; it looked like the mages weren't too pleased at Ming-de's early exit. "I don't understand!"

"I will explain later. But if you wish to catch the mage, we must move quickly."

"But ley lines are massive energy sources!" The way the pixie had described them, they were a cross between a volcanic eruption and a nuclear reactor. "We can't go in there!"

"I assure you, we can," Mircea said, putting an arm around my waist as the shuddering barge cleared the rooftops.

"That wasn't what I meant," I said shrilly, as he jumped up

onto the narrow railing around the barge, balancing us there with a complete lack of appreciation for little things like rickety construction, pissed-off war mages and, oh, gravity.

"Hold on."

I shook my head violently. "No, see, every time you say something like that, we end up doing something really—" Mircea crouched slightly and his muscles tensed. "Listen to me!" I shrieked. "We *can't*—"

And then we did. Mircea jumped into what for a second was only thin air, then we were swept sideways into a rushing maelstrom of light and color, like being in the middle of bloodred rapids all pelting madly for a waterfall the size of Niagara. Flashes of blinding light exploded all around us, while molten channels of pure energy raced alongside and arced overhead. There was so much for my mind to take in that it was a moment before I realized we weren't frying.

"We do not have shields like the mages," Mircea said, looking euphoric, "but entering a ley line, even merely skimming the top, without them is madness. The energy forces would consume us in an instant."

"Then why aren't they?"

He pointed out a faint golden bubble of energy glowing softly all around us. Next to the pulsing swirl of the ley line, it was almost invisible. "The stronger mages can use the lines for rapid transport over short distances with merely their personal shields. Longer journeys require something more substantial."

I stared around, amazed, as the energy stream rocketed us forward. "How did you even know this was here? There was nothing visible."

"Not with the eyes, perhaps. But you could sense it, too, if you knew what to look for." I was impressed for a moment, until Mircea suddenly grinned. "Or you can do what most of us do, and carry a map."

"But you don't have a map."

"I lived in Paris for many years; I long ago memorized the lines' locations," he admitted. "I used them all the time."

"You carried around something like that?" I gestured at the orb in his hands. The thing was as big as a soccer ball.

"There are pocket-sized shields, although they don't give such a smooth ride." A particularly large eddy in the electric current sent us spinning off to the left for a moment.

"Smooth?" I asked, clutching his arm to keep from falling.

"Oh, yes." Mircea caressed the little sphere lovingly while somehow bringing us back into the center of the stream, where it was slightly calmer. "I will hate to have to return this." He grinned at me again, obviously exulting in the wild ride. "It's more than a shield. It can also help you find the lines, by glowing brighter when one is near, and can open a fissure if placed directly in its path."

"But how are we supposed to find the mage in all this?"

Mircea pointed to a whirlpool of light up ahead. "Someone exited the line there, not long ago. I did not notice any other ley-line activity before his, did you?"

"I don't know." Between the spells and the duel and the whole thing with Pritkin, half a dozen could have been activated at once and I probably wouldn't have noticed.

"We will have to risk it," Mircea said. "Hold on."

"You know, I am *really* starting to hate that—"

And then we were falling, careening for the side of the line through a maelstrom of light and sound. For a moment I thought something had gone terribly wrong. But with a sudden absence of color and a resounding boom, like a peal of thunder, we were once more standing on solid ground.

"The Latin Quarter," I heard Mircea say, while my eyes fought to adjust. The shifting, brilliant colors of the line left pulsing shadows on my vision, like fireworks against the deep black of the sky. "This area is a warren of small streets even in our time. This will not be as simple as I'd hoped."

I finally managed to focus on the only remaining source of light, the orb in his hands. It was glowing softly, although if it was still putting a shield around us, I couldn't see it. Of course, I couldn't see much of anything else, either. Beyond the small puddle of light, all I could make out were buildings rearing darkly on every side, reaching for the great span of the galaxy overhead.

"How can you tell where we are?" Even with vampiric sight, this was dark.

"That particular line runs through central Paris and the Ile de la Cité. And I can smell the Seine."

Good for him. I could smell mostly layers of garbage that lay rotting in the gutters despite the cold weather. My shoe squelched in something slimy that stuck to my sole and sent up the vinegar reek of decaying fruit. Horse manure and the sharp scent of human urine were everywhere, as if the streets had been drenched with them. Somehow, the swashbuckling movies never mention that sort of thing.

"This way." Mircea took my arm, which was a good thing because the cobblestones were uneven and what parts weren't covered by a thin layer of ice were slimy.

The dark, winding street was too quiet, and so narrow that I constantly felt like someone was about to lean out from the shadows and grab me. Considering Pritkin's preference for offense over defense, there was at least a chance that someone would. But we came to the end with no problems, and discovered a slightly brighter scene lit by a sliver of moon: the Seine, with the soaring towers of Notre Dame beyond it. The light snow of earlier in the evening had melted on the cobblestones, turning them into an icy mirror that reflected the huge cathedral perfectly. Unfortunately, they did not also reflect Pritkin.

Mircea's head lifted, as if scenting the air. All I could smell was rotting fish and evidence that maybe clean-water laws hadn't come into effect yet, but Mircea must have been able to filter those out. He started for the gaping mouth of another street, but before we could get there, a nearby hay-filled cart burst into flames. It sat beside the road, burning merrily for a moment, then hurtled straight at us.

Mircea pushed me out of the way, but lost valuable seconds in the process and ended up not quite clearing all of the flying bits of hay. I'd seen him handle fire before with aplomb, but there must have been something different about this one—maybe some potion residue still clinging to it— because it didn't go out. Instead, it caught on the heavy fabric of his shirt and started to spread.

He tore off the shirt and flung it into the river, where it hissed and went out, but by then the fire had spread to his hair. Before I could reach him to try batting it out with my hands, he was suddenly gone, and I heard a splash. I whirled around to see ripples spreading over the water.

A moment later, his head broke the surface. The fire was out, but I didn't have time to breathe a sigh of relief before a knife slid against my throat. I froze.

"I do believe I mentioned that it would be unwise to follow me," Pritkin said.

"It would be equally unwise to injure her," Mircea said. I didn't see him move, but Pritkin tensed.

"Stay where you are, vampire!" I felt the knife blade dent my skin, and a tiny trickle of warmth ran down my neck. Mircea halted, dripping, only a couple of yards away.

"You wish a very painful death, mage," he said, and despite being covered in river slime that was slowly oozing down his chest, he made it sound believable. The orb had fallen from his hand when he went in the water, rolled against a too-tall cobblestone and stopped. As far as I could see by its low light, other than a few nasty-looking burns on his chest, he appeared to be okay. That did not make me any less furious with Pritkin.

I struggled, too mad to care that this wasn't the same man who had held a knife to my throat once before. That Pritkin had had no reason to hurt me; this one, on the other hand, rightfully assumed that I wanted to steal from him. "Are you crazy? You could have killed him!"

"And may yet. I have given you fair warning; if you refuse to heed, I must and will have recourse to other means."

"Like killing two people over a stupid spell? For God's sake—"

"And which deity would you be invoking?" Pritkin asked, as the knife blade bit a little deeper. I was starting to feel blood pooling in the hollow of my throat. Even more worrying were Mircea's eyes, which had flooded amber and were currently brighter than our substitute for a lantern. He was pissed. And that was so not good.

Mircea rarely lost his temper, but when he did, it was

scary. I'd already seen it twice and really didn't want another demonstration. Especially since Pritkin couldn't die tonight. Neither of these men knew it, but one day, they would work together to make some pretty impressive history. Some of which would be mine. I needed the Codex, but my life depended on having them both alive when the dust cleared.

"Listen to me," I said, my voice low and urgent. "We'll leave you alone. You can have the damn book. All we need is one spell. Give it to us and we'll go."

"One spell," Pritkin mused, while starting to move us backwards. I couldn't imagine what he was doing; with Mircea's speed, a few extra yards were meaningless. "And I wonder which that would be?"

I would have told him, but he'd increased the pressure enough that I was afraid the next thing I said would be the last thing. "Release her, mage, and I will consider allowing you to survive your punishment," Mircea said, very softly.

"And if you refrain from dogging my heels, I will consider letting her go, once my work is done," Pritkin replied. He sounded calm, but the heartbeat in the chest behind me was a little too loud for that. Mircea started to say something else, but Pritkin didn't give him the chance. He reached up with his hand as if grabbing something in the air, and the night ripped open like a wound, all pulsing red against the dark. Mircea jumped, but too late; the ley line snatched us off our feet and we were gone.

The tumbling torrent spewed us out on what felt like a dirt road a moment later, but before I could even start to focus on the surroundings, we'd caught another line, this one blue, and vanished again. I lost track of how many we crisscrossed after that, the colors all running together—blue, white, purple, back to blue, and then red again. It was a much more turbulent ride than with the empress's shield, and most of the time I barely had a chance to take a few stumbling steps before we were off again.

My eyes didn't have time to adjust, but my other senses picked up on random clues at each stop: the pungent smell of rotting seaweed and the call of seagulls; the scent of manure and the bleat of sheep; the heat of some enclosed space and the stench of spilled wine. We'd just arrived at the last one, with afterimages still dancing in front of my eyes, when there was another crack and a brilliant flash of red and Mircea stepped out of nothing.

Pritkin swore and a fireball appeared in the air in front of us. I yelled, Mircea dodged and the fireball exploded— against the orb, which had been its target all along. For some reason, I expected the gold ball to shatter like glass, but it was made of sterner stuff. When the flames cleared, it looked exactly the same. Pritkin had used the moment of the explosion to tear open another ley line, this one yellow. It pulsed like a small sun right above our heads, and I could feel the pull of it, even as Mircea grabbed for us.

He got a hand on Pritkin, but the heavy folds of the cape made it hard to tell where the mage's body was, and instead of an arm, he wrapped a fist around a handful of black cloth. The cape tore away as Pritkin made a flying lunge for the orb, scooping it up right as we were sucked into a golden void.

After a brief, tumultuous ride, a slap of wind hit my face and we dropped onto a surface that oozed wetly around my shoes. I leaned against something that felt like stone, my eyes refusing to focus on anything except leaping shadows, my lungs threatening to rebel against the sharpness of the night air. It was like jumping in the deep end of the pool when it's not quite warm enough to swim, and the shock is all you can feel until you break the surface, gasping.

When I could focus again, all I saw in place of that jumping stream of vivid color was a world of black, stretching out around me in every direction like Pritkin's missing cloak. But I could hear him gasping somewhere nearby, sounding about as frazzled as I felt. And I remembered Mircea saying that extended travel isn't recommended without some kind of advanced shield. Maybe that's why we'd stopped; maybe all the jumping around before he stole the orb had exhausted Pritkin. Too bad I was in no shape to capitalize on it.

I hung on to the frigid rock until it slowly came into focus. It was part of a stone and wood fence bordering an empty field, with nothing to see in the distance but charcoal smudges that might have been trees. Gray streamers of mist curled up from the wet ground, twisting around our ankles clammily, as Pritkin fumbled in his clothes for something. At his feet, the orb shone dimly through a veil of caked-on grime, having been treated to a mud bath when we landed.

It looked like I was on my own.

I sized this new Pritkin up as my heartbeat cautiously returned to normal. There were no fashionable knee pants, embroidered waistcoats or powdered wigs in evidence. He was dressed simply in a white shirt with long, full sleeves that, despite the weather, had been rolled up to show muscled forearms, and slim gray trousers that wouldn't have looked that out of place two hundred years later. Of course, they were crisscrossed with a load of armaments, differing from his usual stash only in the lack of automated weapons.

The only jarring note was the sweep of gold-red hair. For some reason, I couldn't seem to stop staring at it. I kept wanting to think of him as the man I knew, the one I occasionally called friend, but the hair wouldn't let me. I glared at it resentfully, trying to come to grips with the rapid way my world had shifted. I'd already mourned our friendship, already dealt with his betrayal. Only to have to reevaluate him all over again, to start to trust—just to find out that I'd been right the first time.

It didn't matter if Pritkin had the Codex now or not. He'd written the damn thing. He'd known the spell to lift the *geis* all along, and just hadn't given it to me. And there was no way to excuse that. He didn't need to blow his cover. He could have pretended to find it in one of those old tomes; he could have pretended to rediscover it; he could have done a lot of things rather than stand by and watch Mircea die. But he'd said it himself: vampires were little better than demons in his book.

And the only good demon was a dead one.

I tamped down a surge of pure rage. I couldn't afford to explode now. If I didn't get that spell, Pritkin won and Mircea died. And neither of those was acceptable.

I was still glaring at him when he suddenly grabbed me by both arms. "The map! What did you do with it?"

"What map?"

He gave me a hard shake, which didn't help me think any better, if that was the intention. "The map to the location of the Codex!"

"I thought we were bidding on the Codex itself. Are you telling me they didn't have it?"

"They did not wish to bring it to the auction, in case someone tried to make off with it," he said, looking me over as though he thought I might have shoved the map down my cleavage. As if there was room for a napkin down there. "If you do not wish to suffer the indignity of a reveal spell, I suggest you give it to me now."

"I don't have it! And what indignity?"

Pritkin passed a hand over me, not touching, just hovering a few inches from the now inert silk. The dress glowed again briefly, but apparently it was out of gas because nothing happened. Nothing except that it suddenly became transparent— along with everything else I was wearing.

"What the hell?!" I jumped behind the fence post, which along with the poor light, was enough to act as pretty good cover. It didn't make me feel much better. "What kind of a lunatic are you?"

Pritkin didn't answer, although his jaw clenched a little more tightly. "Give me my property and I will reverse the spell."

"I told you already! I don't have it!"

With another brief hand wave and a muttered word, the fence post went transparent, too. I shrieked and went running down a line of wooden rails to the next stone post, Pritkin mirroring my actions on the other side. We stopped, facing each other, with the post between us. "Don't you dare!" I said, when he raised a hand.

"Then give me what I want!"

"Go to Hell!"

"I just came back," he snarled, and the post disappeared. Before I could run again, he jumped over the fence and a strong hand latched onto the back of my neck. I struggled, but I couldn't move, and I finally stopped.

I felt him drop his hand and step back. He must have

knocked the mud off the orb, because its light suddenly danced on the glasslike rocks in front of me. The transparent stone and the orb light startled a small creature that had made a burrow under the post, sending it scurrying away into the dark.

I could feel Pritkin's gaze, ruthless and uncompromising and focused as it ran over the back of my body, like a phantom touch. I wanted to shift again so badly I could taste it, but even if it had been possible, where would I go? I needed the Codex, and Pritkin had it. At least he'd better have it, or I was going to kill him. Slowly.

"Turn around," he said after a moment.

I hugged the invisible fencepost, telling myself I was being stupid. *Get it over with, and maybe he'll listen to you. Just do it and don't think about it*—great advice, except that it was Pritkin and, despite everything, that made it different. Weirdly enough, I thought a stranger's eyes would have bothered me less.

"I don't have the map," I repeated, trying not to notice that it was really cold and that my body was reacting predictably.

"I regret that I cannot take your word for that," he said stiffly, and it almost sounded sincere. It also sounded implacable. When I still didn't move, I felt him come up behind me. "I find this distasteful. Do not make it more so by forcing me to search you physically." His tone left me in no doubt at all that he'd do it.

I took a deep breath. "I'll make you a deal. I'll show you mine if you show me yours."

"What?" He sounded confused. I guess they didn't have that saying in English yet.

"Do the reveal thing on yourself and I'll turn around."

"I'm not hiding anything!"

"Neither am I! And fair is fair. Or are you just looking for an excuse to do that search?"

Pritkin muttered something that sounded fairly vicious. "My clothes are warded! Even if I wished to accede to your demand, it would not work on them."

"Then strip."

"I beg your pardon?" He sounded almost polite suddenly, as if he believed he couldn't possibly have heard right.

"Take them off."

"And let you curse me without protection?" I couldn't see his face, but I could hear the sneer in his voice.

"You'll still have your shields," I pointed out. "And if you're so worried that I might overpower you, keep your weapons on." There was silence for a long moment. "If you're any kind of gentleman, you'll do it," I added, getting desperate.

I held my breath, sure that it wouldn't work, that he couldn't possibly fall for that old line. But I guess it wasn't so old in the 1790s, because the next moment I heard more muffled swearing and the soft sounds of clothes being pulled off. "Very well," a pissed-off voice said after a few seconds. "*Now* will you turn around?"

"How do I know you really did it?"

"Are you questioning my honor?" He sounded incredulous.

"Let's just say I'm not feeling especially trusting. Make the post opaque again, and come around front. If you haven't lied to me, I'll step out from behind it and we'll get this over with."

Pritkin didn't bother to swear this time. The rocks suddenly went opaque and he stomped around in front of the post. He was carrying a gun in one hand and still wearing a knife in a sheath strapped to one calf, but he hadn't bothered with the rest. I guess that was meant to make a point about how unlikely my beating him in a fight would be.

"Now keep your part of the bargain," he said through gritted teeth. Or maybe he'd clamped them to keep them from chattering. He did look cold, I thought with no sympathy whatsoever.

I sized him up as green eyes glared at me past a curtain of red-gold hair. He made no attempt to cover himself. How noble. Then I got a good look at him, and my eyes widened. Despite the temperature, he didn't really have any reason for modesty.

"As soon as you turn around," I finally managed to say. He started to argue, but I raised an eyebrow. "It's only fair."

Pritkin threw up his hands, but he did turn around, flashing those fascinating dimples. This time I didn't pause to admire the view. As soon as his back was turned, I grabbed his clothes and the orb, tore open a ley line and disappeared.

Chapter 22

It hadn't been difficult to snag the line with the orb's help, especially when I already knew where it was. Getting anywhere, I soon discovered, was a little harder. With Mircea, I'd thought of the lines as rivers of power, but this one was more like the rapids, with bumps and currents and eddies battering me every which way.

The bubble of protection provided by the orb kept the energy stream from frying me, but that was about it; there was no steering wheel, no seat belts and, worse, no brakes. I was slammed against first one side and then the other, before the thing flipped totally upside down, dropping me the length of my body before I was caught by the bottom of the sphere. It was the carnival ride from Hell, and I didn't know how to get off.

I gathered my stolen booty into a wad and hastily tied my skirts around it to keep it from getting slung all over the place. Then I set about trying to figure out how this thing worked. Through trial and error, I found that I could maneuver the small circle of protection by pressing on one side or the other of the orb, although it was nowhere near as easy as Mircea had made it look. A small rotation could cause me to go careening off in that direction for what felt like a mile. I quickly learned to scale back my movements, caressing the orb with tiny motions of my thumbs.

It was about as easy as trying to guide a plastic beach ball through the incoming tide using chopsticks, but slowly I got a little better. I managed to position myself close to the side of the line, which is where people seemed to enter and leave. The current was rockier there, not as stable as in the middle of the stream, and I got buffeted about even more as I tried to bump the bubble back into my world.

The ley line seemed to have a kind of skin stretching over it formed of extra-thick bands of power that made leaving even trickier than I'd expected. Every time I pushed at the line, it pushed back, forcing me to have to spend time maneuvering back into position again. But finally I managed to rock just the right way and half of the bubble cleared the energy field.

Which is when things went from bad to really, really bad.

The orb kept my feet and legs in place, suspended in the bucking, whirling energy stream, but I guess it didn't operate beyond the confines of the lines, because the part of me that was outside was totally exposed to the elements. I found myself hanging upside down, my hair blowing in a fast breeze, as I tore over the darkened city. My eyes were flooded with tears from the slap of frigid air, but if I squinted, I could see the Seine glittering far, far below, twining through Paris like a silver snake. I'd forgotten: ley lines didn't always follow the ground.

I couldn't scream, there was too much air in my face, and I could barely see. The pouch I'd made of my skirts ensured that they weren't in my face, but it kept bumping into me, hard enough to hurt. Damn it, what had he been carrying, anyway?

Even worse, although whatever gravity field the line exerted was keeping me from plunging to my death, it wouldn't hold once the orb slipped completely free. It didn't feel like that would be long in coming, because more of my body was coming into view all the time and I didn't know how to stop it.

I also didn't know how to use my rudimentary shields as a parachute, even if they were strong enough to bear my weight, which I doubted. War mages apparently learned all kinds of uses for their personal protection, but as I'd once reminded Pitkin, I wasn't one. I watched the pulsing river of power all around me and wondered if I'd just completely screwed myself. Then the ley line took a sudden plunge, like an invisible roller coaster, and headed straight for the ground.

I did scream then, although the sound tore out of my throat and away before I could hear it. My ears were filled with rushing wind and vertigo, as the line twisted and turned and suddenly headed back up again. For the next few minutes, it climbed and dove, spun and plunged, until I was so dizzy, I didn't even know which way was up anymore.

Dangling by only one leg, my body almost free of the small protection the orb afforded, I saw a huge, dark shape rushing toward me. I could see the line up ahead, and it was climbing again, high, so high, over the city that, if I fell, there would be nothing to catch me. Whatever the shape was, I had to grab it.

I pulled and yanked, freeing myself by inches as the dark blob grew bigger. It was a building of some kind, but I couldn't make out details. My hair was in my eyes, obscuring what little vision the wind and panic-induced tears had left me. I put a hand out blindly, and out of nowhere, a horned creature with a bored expression jumped in front of me.

My foot slid free of the line, and all my weight was suddenly hanging from my arms, arms that had grabbed the monster in a death grip and weren't letting go. My feet swung out over nothing, before slamming with the force of inertia into the side of something hard. The impact caused a shudder to rack my body, and for a moment my grip loosened. But the creature never moved, never so much as twitched, and carefully, I renewed my grip.

After a few seconds gasping for breath, I peered through a curtain of tangled hair to see a leering, doglike face sticking out its tongue at me. I blinked at it, but its expression didn't change. After another few seconds, my brain caught up and informed me that whatever my hands were clutching, it wasn't alive.

I was suspended from a stone gargoyle that looked out over what would probably have been a panoramic view of Paris had it been daytime. Below, tiny lights occasionally lit up bits of the world between the shadows, and a sliver of moon danced on the Seine. I was on top of Notre Dame. Somehow I'd come full circle.

My arms were tired, my shoulders ached and it was a very long way down. With a lot of muffled swearing, I hauled my body over the side of the parapet and dropped onto the floor. My knees gave way and I abruptly sat down, clinging gratefully to the heavenly feel of a non-moving surface. The stone floor was cold and wet with half-melted snow, but for a second I seriously thought about kissing it.

The stars seemed to be spinning around above me, so I sat there, panting, until they stopped. The orb had landed a few yards away, and I watched it pulsing its strange light against the high stone wall of the parapet. At least Pritkin couldn't follow me, I realized, and the idea cheered me up immensely.

I started searching the area for Pritkin's clothing, which had scattered everywhere when I landed and the knot in my skirts came loose. I collected it into a small bundle in front of me and set about carefully examining each piece. I'd gotten away with a pair of woolen trousers, a white linen shirt with drawstring ties at neck and wrists, a potion-studded belt, a pair of sturdy leather boots and some warm woolen socks.

I regarded the latter with a twinge of guilt. I hadn't expected him to be so literal, to even remove his footwear. Apparently, he'd believed that a bargain was a bargain, and I hadn't made any exceptions to my demand. Or maybe he'd felt bad about subjecting me to that. Maybe he'd thought he deserved a few cold toes, at least . . . Okay, no. Probably not. But still, the socks made me feel a little bad.

Not bad enough to keep me from putting them on, though. The boots were too large, but I pulled them on as well, lacing them as tight as I could. I'd lost my shoes somewhere over Paris, and I wasn't going to search for Mircea barefoot.

I looked through everything twice, then went back through it one more time, checking every seam for hidden compartments. I even held the little potion bottles up to the light, just in case he'd somehow stuffed a slip of paper into one of them, but no dice. The map wasn't there.

Of course not, I thought furiously. I'd hoped that he'd been so ready to assume I'd stolen it that he hadn't checked thoroughly before accusing me. But it looked like he'd been telling the truth. He really had lost it. And that meant it could be anywhere: still on the barge, trodden underfoot in the battle, or dropped as he dangled from his shields ten stories above the city. I would never find it.

I got up on tiptoe and leaned over the parapet, to see if anything might have fallen below. For the most part, the sky was brighter than the city, with buildings casting black shadows that wiped out everything in their path, like big slices of the world were just gone. But the famous rose window glowed as brightly as a searchlight against the black sky, illuminating the cobblestone expanse in front of the main doors of the cathedral. Nothing was there.

I was still standing there, trying to think what to do, when a brilliant yellow flash lit the night sky. I looked up to see half of an enraged, naked war mage leaning out of a ley line, his hair whipping across his livid face as he shot straight at me. I yelped and stumbled back, cursing myself. It looked like Pritkin wasn't as exhausted as I'd thought. And with his shields intact, he didn't need clothes or toys to access the ley lines. I scooped up his weapons in my transparent skirts and ran for it.

He landed right behind me, his eyes wild, his hair smoking from the energy that had leaked through his overtaxed shields. For the first time he looked like his father's son. I looked around frantically and spied a single wooden door inside the bell tower. Mercifully, it wasn't locked.

I saw Pritkin for a split second as I spun around to close it, silhouetted against the dim gray arches leading out to the parapet. He was almost to the door already, just a few steps behind me, as if he hadn't even broken his stride in leaving the line behind. I didn't try reasoning with him; his expression told me how well that was likely to go over. I slammed the door in his face, threw the bolt and fled.

The winding, claustrophobic staircase was so narrow that my dress brushed it on either side, and it was completely black except for the orb's dim glow and occasional tiny elongated windows that showed slivers of the slightly less black outside. I could see maybe two steps in front of me as I wound my way downwards, trying to hurry without slipping on stones that were already slick with hundreds of years of wear.

I heard a crash behind me, and burning bits of wood cascaded down the steps along with a lot of sparks. It looked like Pritkin had used a fireball spell on the door. Luckily, the curves of the staircase shielded me from most of it, while he had to traverse a minefield of fiery splinters in bare feet. Unluckily for me, he seemed to manage it just fine.

He grabbed me when I was barely halfway down the stairs, and the impact made me lose my footing. We tumbled, half falling, half rolling down the narrow, twisting spiral. I'd been holding the contents of his potion belt in the folds of my dress, and as I fell, little vials were slung everywhere. Some tumbled along with us, while others exploded against the walls, flooding the stairwell with a pungent stench that immediately brought tears to my eyes. Something must have splashed on Pritkin, because he cursed and let go.

I heard him falling, but I couldn't help him. I lost my grip on the orb, which went bouncing down the stairs, disappearing around a turn and leaving the stairwell in complete darkness. The only reason I didn't follow it was because I'd gotten my fingernails into one of the narrow windows, the only possible traction. The stench from the potions was unbelievable, but the cold night air from the window allowed me to breathe. I clung there, straining to hear over my own gasps, but there was no sound other than the wind outside.

"Are you hurt?" I finally yelled, but only echoes answered. I didn't hear so much as a groan from below. The stairwell was suddenly eerily quiet.

I bit my lip, but there wasn't really anything to think about. Even if I hadn't been worried about Pritkin, there was no other way out. There was only one staircase from the bell tower and I was on it. And ley-line travel was impossible, even if I was willing to risk that again, with the orb at the bottom of the staircase.

After another deep breath, I took the plunge, through a miasma of fumes and shattered vials that crunched under my boots. At the bottom of the stairs, the orb had halted at a

wooden door, presumably leading outside. Next to its small
puddle of light, Pritkin lay on his side in a crumpled heap,
not moving. I forgot about caution and ran down the last few
steps, kneeling in the small area before the door, desperately
feeling for a pulse under the skin of his neck.

He was warm, which I took as a good sign, but for a long
moment I couldn't feel anything else. Heavy strands of hair
had wrapped around his neck, and I tugged them loose before
trying again. I almost sobbed with relief when I finally found
it, a tiny pulse that beat strong and sure under my fingertips.
But a sticky wetness dripped off his jaw onto my hand, and
after a little exploration, I found a nasty-looking cut on his
scalp and another on his upper arm.

I propped open the door to let some of the vapors out, and
turned back to find Pritkin on his feet. "It's only fair," he said
nastily, before grabbing me by the shoulders and slamming
me back against the unforgiving stone of the wall.

"Let go of me!" I twisted and fought, but he held me there
while his eyes did a visual strip search by the faint light of
the orb.

"Give it to me!"

"I don't have it!"

"No more lies!" Pritkin hissed.

"I never found it!" I yelled, pushing at him but getting
nowhere. "Now let me go or I swear—" He shut me up by
kissing me, hard and angry, so angry that I didn't know
what to do except let him, silenced by him swallowing all
my air. It was oddly like he was yelling at me in a new way,
since all the old ones hadn't worked. I felt the scrape of
stubble and the indent of his fingers through the silk, pressing me closer, then he tore away, those icy eyes vibrantly
green.

"Tell me!"

Startled out of fighting for a moment, I stared up at him,
panting. There was drying blood tightening the skin on his
forehead and a blooming bruise on his chin, but his eyes were
glittering brighter than I'd ever seen them. A sweet, heavy
warmth started to spread through me, and despite the cold
I could feel sweat springing to the surface of my skin.

Suddenly the idea of Pritkin as half incubus seemed plausible for the first time.

The suggestion surged through my veins, almost like a drug. "I was looking for it when you attacked me," I said, not fighting it. I was telling the truth, and I needed to save my strength to escape. "I thought you had it on you, but it wasn't in your clothes."

"I said no more lies!" Pritkin kissed me again, hard, taking my lower lip in his teeth, biting. His lips were cold and a little chapped from the winter wind, but his kiss was deep, hot and hungry. My heart sped up, flight reflexes kicking in, but I wasn't pushing him away. Suddenly my hands were clutching his shoulders, my nails clawing at the bunched muscles they found there, and I was kissing him back, brutally.

I wrapped my right leg around his, feeling him hard against my silk-clad thigh, while he tore at the lacings on my back. I wasn't wearing much underneath the dress—the tight fit had made a bra unnecessary—which became obvious when he pushed the dress down to my waist. The feel of the freezing air on my skin slammed me back into my body, as he ran his hands over me. The only minor satisfaction was that he didn't look much better than I did. His skin was shiny with sweat, and it was running out of his hair and down the back of his neck. And despite everything, I wanted to bury my face in that limp hair, to lick that glistening skin, to bite that flexing shoulder.

"Where is it?" He grasped me by the shoulders, shaking me roughly. The motion caused the dress to slide even farther, the silky lining slipping over my skin with a soft hiss until it crumpled around my feet, the transparent fabric looking like a heap of plastic wrap. I was left standing there in the freezing cold, wearing only panties and thigh-highs and Pritkin's oversized boots.

Rage and hurt thickened my throat for a moment, so that all I could do was look at him, eyes burning, as he continued his search. He didn't strip me, but his hands ran over every inch, stopping only at the tops of my stolen footwear. "You don't have it on you!" He glared up at me accusingly, his hands still on my calves.

"As I told you!" It took everything I had not to kick him in the face.

"You had time to hide it!"

He started on the laces to his boots, while I furiously tried to think. I didn't think another denial was likely to do me any good, not when he wasn't even listening to me. "It drains your power, doesn't it?" I said instead. "Seducing someone who resists you?"

In a flash, he had my wrists pinned against the rock, his hips pressed up against me, between my legs. "Not when they're practically starved for it," he said softly. "It must be unsatisfying, lying with a corpse, night after night. I can feel the frustration in you, the desperation, the *need*."

I stared up into green eyes that glittered so brightly they might have been on fire. And for an odd, out-of-body moment, I really wanted to claw them out. "At least I know what Mircea is!" I spat. "Can your lovers say the same?"

Shock lit those eyes for an instant, before it was masked behind the certainty that I was bluffing. "And what am I?"

He'd had to guess about my weak spot, sensing the buildup of emotion from weeks of battling the *geis* but not knowing the real cause. But I didn't have to speculate about his.

"I knew as soon as I saw you," I said flatly, hating myself even as I uttered the words. It's never easier to twist the knife than with someone who once trusted you enough to bare his secrets. But I didn't have a choice. If he tried another suggestion, I honestly didn't know if I had the strength left to fight it. "You're half incubus."

A look flashed across Pritkin's face for an instant, like he'd been slapped, hard, and was trying to hide how much it hurt. "How did you know?"

I ignored the question. I had to do this while I actually had his attention, or there was no telling where this would end. "If I'm lying, why did I take your things?" I demanded, my heart hammering. "I could have been long gone before you showed up, if I hadn't taken the time to search your belongings. Why do that if I already had the map? Now let go!"

For a second, something like doubt flickered behind his eyes. Then his chin jerked out in familiar stubbornness. "I will let you go when you return my property."

"I can't return what I never had," I snapped, throwing everything I had into wrenching out of his grip. He didn't come after me and I snatched up my dress, before remembering that it was useless for concealment. I put it on anyway—the stairs were damn cold. "If you wouldn't mind," I said through gritted teeth.

His gaze moved down my body again and my skin tightened from just the pressure of his eyes. Then he blinked and looked away. With a quick gesture from him, my dress suddenly became a lot more opaque. I didn't thank him for it.

I headed for the door, only to have it slam in my face. "We are not finished here," Pritkin barked.

I whirled, so angry I couldn't even see, and tripped on the too long skirt. He helped me up and without a word turned me around and did up the lacings. His fingers were cool against my overheated skin, and swiftly competent. The only reason I let him touch me was the certainty that if I returned to Mircea like this, he'd kill Pritkin.

Not that that didn't have a certain appeal.

"Let go of me," I said icily as soon as he'd finished. I felt betrayed and absolutely livid, but my body wasn't smart enough to know it. It had liked the feel of his hands, wanted more of it, wanted it now. It was almost like there were two of me, one who heartily approved of the mage and one who would have dearly loved to see him dead.

Then something occurred to me that I should have noticed before. "The *geis*. It didn't flare."

"You said it yourself," Pritkin said tightly. "I am half incubus. I can break through *geasa* during feeding."

I stared at him, speechless, as a myriad of pieces clicked into place. Rosier could overcome the *geis*, so of course his son should have been able to do so. But he hadn't, at least not in our time. He'd preferred to suffer excruciating pain, on more than one occasion, rather than . . . what? Risk getting too close to me? Be tempted to repeat what had happened with his wife? A wife this Pritkin hadn't had yet, I realized. No wonder he wasn't so worried about using his abilities, wasn't so careful to avoid touching anyone.

A memory of how much touching had just been going on flashed across my mind and I felt a wave of heat rise in my cheeks. God, I *hated* him. But I hated the *geis* just a little bit more.

"I want the *geis* removed," I said abruptly. "That's why I need the Codex. Can you do it?"

He looked at me incredulously. "You expect me to believe that you have gone to such lengths for no more than that?"

"Why do you want it, if not for a spell?" I countered.

"To destroy it! It is the only way to be certain that it never falls into the hands of people such as yourself!"

"Give me the spell to reverse the *geis*, and you can do anything with the Codex you damn well please! I won't care."

There was dead silence for a minute, while he stared at me with a half-bewildered, half-angry expression. For the first time he looked like my Pritkin, the brash, sardonic, brutally honest man I knew. "Why did you not merely say so?" he finally demanded.

"I just did! Now, are you going to give it to me or not?"

Pritkin passed a hand over me, and I could feel my aura crackle. "You carry two *geasa*, not one," he informed me after a moment. "And they are oddly intertwined. I have not seen this configuration before. How did it occur?"

"It's a long story." And not one I could tell him anyway. "Can you lift it?"

"Perhaps. If you return my map."

"How many times do I have to say this? I. Don't. Have. It."

"If you didn't take it, then where—" his eyes widened. "My cloak!"

It took me a second, but I got it. A wide grin broke over my face that I didn't even try to make less than vicious. "That would be the one you were wearing when you stole the map, wouldn't it? The one Mircea grabbed before we left?"

Pritkin snarled and I grinned wider. He said a few words,

none in a language I knew. Probably some ancient British version of "screw you."

"Are you going to give me the counterspell or not?" I demanded.

"Persuade the vampire to give me the map, and I will give you the spell," he finally said, although it sounded like it choked him.

I sagged back against the wall, suddenly exhausted. "Done."

We retraced our steps, but the cellar was empty and the raucous tavern on top of it was filled with people who were not Mircea. "Would he go after the Codex on his own?" Pritkin demanded.

"I don't think so." Mircea was after me, not the Codex. "But he'll know that you'll discover it missing pretty soon. He'll expect you to come after him. And he'll expect a fight. So he wouldn't have stayed here—it's too public."

"Where would he go?" Pritkin demanded.

I opened my mouth to point out that mind reading wasn't one of my skills, but abruptly shut it again. *The rose window*, I thought, seeing it lit up in my memory like a huge Christmas ornament. It was the middle of the night, and the streets around the cathedral had been deserted. Where better to hold a showdown?

I said as much and Pritkin made a noise that in anyone else would have signaled an incipient heart attack. But he pulled me back into the cellar and ripped a ley line open almost savagely, like tearing the air. A moment later, after another wild ride between worlds, we were pushing open the main doors of the old church.

On either side of us were long stained-glass windows, glowing faintly with the reflected light of a few dozen candles. Not surprisingly, they looked a lot more authentic than the ones in the casino, with the glass rolling in subtle lines toward the bottom of the panes, thicker there than at the top, brittle with age even two hundred years ago. More candles lit a sweeping line of similar masterpieces leading toward the darkened front of the church. Where Mircea stood, washing up at a holy water font.

"That is not possible," Pritkin said, staring at him in disbelief. He couldn't have sounded more shocked if Mircea had been sipping blood from a communion chalice.

Mircea must have heard us come in, but he continued what he was doing. He stood with his back to us, the candlelight on his bare skin causing his muscles to fall into sharp relief. He'd washed the river gunk out of his hair and now he threw it back, the water droplets shimmering in the light. The scene looked for all the world like a really good romance novel cover.

I sighed and Pritkin turned his glare on me. "He's a vampire!" he said, as if I hadn't noticed.

"Yeah. And?"

"I believe the mage is surprised that I do not burst into flames from the holy water," Mircea said, toweling off with what looked suspiciously like an altar cloth. I was a little surprised myself, considering that he's Catholic. But then I got a better look at it and realized that it, like the cathedral, had seen better days.

Boxes, barrels and casks were piled here and there, clogging all but the main aisle, which was marred by a lot of muddy footprints. Outside, I hadn't been able to avoid noticing that the probably saintly but definitely creepy statues around the entrance had been vandalized. It didn't look like the revolution cared for religion all that much.

"But, of course!" Pritkin sneered. "The water is not sacred at the moment! The Jacobins made certain of that!"

"They vandalized the cathedral before turning it into a 'Temple to Reason,'" Mircea agreed, probably for my benefit. "Which, considering their excesses, does seem somewhat ironic."

"They defiled it," Pritkin snapped. "Naturally it now embraces something equally foul!"

"But," Mircea continued, "as we are not of their ilk, let us make good on the name. I have found that most men can be reasonable, given the right incentive." He held something up in two fingers of one hand, while continuing to towel his hair with the other.

"That is mine!" Pritkin took a step forward before he caught himself.

"And you have something that belongs to me. I suggest a trade," Mircea said, turning around at last.

I saw it when he recognized Pritkin; it was nothing overt, but for an instant his body stiffened and his eyes slid to me. I shook my head briefly, but stopped when Pritkin glanced between the two of us. "What subterfuge is this?" he demanded. "Do you take me for a fool?"

"No, not a fool," Mircea said, with the air of a man who didn't know quite what to make of him. I wondered how long it would take him to put it together. Magical humans could live as long as two hundred years, so there might be a few still around who were alive at the time of the French Revolution. But they wouldn't look thirty-five.

"This is how we shall proceed," Pritkin said crisply. "You will take the map outside and leave it beside the ley line. I will pick it up and open a fissure. As soon as I have verified that it is authentic, I will give you the spell."

"He already knows the spell I need," I explained.

Mircea switched his incredulous look from the mage to me. "And you trust him to give it to you?"

"I am not the one whose honor is in question!" Pritkin said, furious.

"You kidnapped and tried to kill her!"

"I kidnapped her so I wouldn't *have* to kill her!"

"Mage, by all that is holy, I swear—"

"Holy?" Pritkin's sneer was the same as always. "You dare to even use such a term, you—"

"Shut up!" I yelled, and it echoed oddly off the sides of the cathedral, like a ghostly loudspeaker. I could *not* take one more minute of this. "We don't have a choice," I told Mircea more calmly.

"He has already proven himself treacherous! Trusting him again—"

"I'm not asking you to trust him. I'm asking you to trust me. Please."

Mircea didn't answer, but he crossed the space and grabbed Pritkin's arm, so fast that I didn't even see him move. "If you harm her, you will never see the map again," he said softly. "You will not live long enough to see anything again."

Pritkin tried to shrug him off, but found that he couldn't. "If you speak the truth, I have no need to harm her!" he said viciously. "Now release me!"

Mircea reluctantly complied, after a squeeze that made Pritkin set his jaw in pain, and we all trooped back outside. Pritkin stubbornly didn't rub his arm, although it had probably lost circulation, and he took care to keep us both clearly in view. Mircea put the map in the center of the cobblestone pavement and moved back half a dozen yards, which in vampire terms meant he may as well not have bothered to move at all. He could cross that much space in a heartbeat.

I looked pointedly at Pritkin. He waved a hand at me and uttered a few guttural syllables. Nothing happened. He frowned and did it again. "I didn't feel anything," I said, except my blood pressure starting to rise.

"It was not successful."

"You said you could lift it!"

Mircea's lip curled. "You can never trust a mage."

Pritkin glared at him briefly, but it wasn't even close to his best attempt. He looked preoccupied, a finger tapping against his lips. "Tell me, was a method of egress attached to the spells when they were placed, in the event that something went wrong?"

"Yes, but that's already been tried," I said, exasperated.

"What was it?"

I glared, but I had no choice but to answer. I didn't know what information he needed to make the spell work. "Sex with the originator or someone of his choosing. But nothing happened."

It wasn't as crazy as it sounds. The ritual to complete the power transfer from the old Pythia to me had required that I lose my virginity. It was a fairly standard clause in the ancient world, where sex played a part in everything from healing spells to worship. But it had given Mircea an idea. He had made sex the condition for the release of the *geis* as well.

It must have seemed foolproof: the *geis* would protect me until the ritual, whereupon it would be broken by the same act that made me Pythia, thereby ensuring that Mircea didn't end up bound to my power. It would have worked, too, except that the spell had been doubled before the transfer was complete. Tomas had afterwards served as Mircea's stand-in for the ritual, and I became Pythia right on schedule—but with the *geis* still alive and kicking.

"You are sure?" Pritkin insisted. "Because if the *geis* expands beyond its original parameters it becomes, in effect, a new spell. And in that case, the counterspell will not prove efficacious. That is the reason additional precautions are usually taken."

"The *geis*?" Mircea's gaze sharpened.

"Don't ask," I snapped, still glaring at Pritkin. "And yes, I'm sure!"

"Then there is nothing to be done," Pritkin said with a slight shrug.

"Don't lie to me. I need the real counterspell!"

"You already have it."

"I don't believe you!" I grabbed his shirt, not caring about the possible consequences. I felt like screaming in frustration. "Give it to me! I have to lift this thing. You don't understand!"

"I have done all I can! Now give me my property!"

"I'd sooner see it destroyed than give it to you!" I told him, so angry I could barely see. I should have known. Every time I trusted that man, *every single time*, I ended up like this, teary-eyed and fuming. There is a saying: insanity is doing the same thing over and over and expecting different results. Or maybe that was stupidity.

Pritkin swore. "Is outraged modesty worth so high a price?"

I smiled at him fiercely. "I guess I'm just vindictive like that."

"Give it to me and we part, if not friends, at least not enemies," he warned. "And believe me when I say, madam—you do not want me for an enemy."

"Maybe I didn't make myself clear," I said grimly, kicking

the map back toward Mircea. "No *geis*, no map. Either lift this thing or you'll never see the Codex again. I swear it!"

Pritkin didn't reply, except by doing the last thing I'd expected. He threw off my hold as if it wasn't there and jumped straight at Mircea. I was knocked to the side, and by the time I sat up they'd already taken the fight halfway across the cobblestone expanse, back toward the cathedral.

Mircea might have been drained from the attack at the casino, but a master vampire is still a master vampire, something Pritkin was learning the hard way. The fight was over so quickly, it was almost a non-event. A vicious jab from Mircea's elbow sent the mage staggering back into the huge old cathedral doors, which he hit with a sickening thud. Pritkin must have been pretty drained, too, because his shields didn't manifest to cushion the impact.

He ricocheted off the doors and sprawled limply on the steps, in a pose that called to mind a cast-aside doll. Mircea nonetheless started toward him as I scrambled to my feet. "Mircea! Don't kill him!"

He looked up and hesitated slightly, then gave a small nod. He'd seen Pritkin in our time; he knew he wasn't supposed to die tonight. I ran forward, worried that it was already too late, that the cracking noise I'd heard had been Pritkin's skull. But when I knelt beside him, I couldn't find any major injuries. I checked his pulse, then pulled up an eyelid. He might have been faking it on the stairwell; I wasn't sure. But he'd been out cold on the barge, and if this wasn't the real deal, he was a damn fine actor.

"He's unconscious," Mircea confirmed. He could sense things like blood pressure, and he would know if the mage was faking.

Mircea carried Pritkin inside the cathedral and we covered him with his cape. The place was deserted and it was still hours before dawn. He would be undisturbed until he came around. But it was too quiet and the place had a weird air about it, not like a church where people regularly congregate but like one of those deserted crypts at Pere Lachaise, beautiful but forgotten. I didn't like leaving him there.

Mircea caught my arm, pulling me away from the mage. "He will live," he assured me. "But when he awakens—"

He had a point. Pritkin wasn't the type to give up, even with a possible concussion. And the last thing we needed was for Mircea to have to inflict even more damage. "Where to next?" I asked wearily. I was cold and hungry and now that the adrenaline rush was wearing off, my eyes kept wanting to close. I was really not looking forward to an exhausting search.

"We both need to rest before we go on your treasure hunt," Mircea said, echoing my thoughts. He frowned for a moment, and then his face cleared. "I know just the place."

Chapter 23

A short ley-line trip later and we stood before a thick oak plank with a brass doorknocker in the shape of a dragon consuming its own tail. I blinked at it blearily. Was the thing following me? Mircea let it thud against the door a few times, but no one answered.

"Most of my servants are at my country estate," he told me, knocking again, louder this time. "But there should be a caretaker here. He doesn't like to travel."

I stared at the house, which looked completely deserted, and wondered if he was sure about that. With the master away, maybe the caretaker had left for parts where there weren't daily decapitations. "I don't think anyone's home," I ventured, peering in the window. I couldn't tell much about the inside since there were sheets thrown over all the furniture, but it felt as empty as the cathedral.

Mircea only smiled. "He's a little slow."

"So when you said you lived in Paris—"

"I meant here." Mircea paused to pound on the door, actually shaking the heavy wood. "Before I joined the North American Senate, I belonged to the European one. And it has been based in Paris since the early Middle Ages."

He started to knock again, but the door was wrenched open by a tiny old man with a large nose and watery blue eyes. He peered at us myopically from under an oversized wig, while spewing a string of angry French. He punctuated whatever he was saying with wild waves of his cane, but

without its support he lost his balance and would have toppled down the stairs if Mircea hadn't caught him.

"Demmed young ruffians!" he raged, in between attempts
to bite Mircea's wrist. But despite being a vampire, he seemed
to have only one fang, and it never managed to connect with
anything.

"Horatiu! It's me!" Mircea's voice echoed up and down the
street as he practically screamed in the old man's ear.

"Eh?" the vamp squinted, but apparently it didn't help his
eyesight.

Mircea sighed. "I gave you a cord for your spectacles," he
said, rummaging around in the old man's coat. "Why aren't
you wearing them?"

"'m a vampire. Don't need spectacles!" Mircea was informed, as the man slapped at his hands. Mircea ignored him
and finally came up with a pair of pince-nez. He settled them
on the vamp's long nose and smiled at him encouragingly.
"It's me," he repeated.

"I know that!" the old man said tetchily. "Might have sent
word you was coming. Got nothing prepared," he bitched, but
he did let us in the door.

We walked at a snail's pace through a hall and up a large
staircase. Horatiu was carrying a candle that wavered and
flickered, casting leaping shadows on the walls, and it gave
me my first clear look at Mircea. Despite the earlier libations,
he was still missing half his outfit, had dirt and dust all over
the part remaining, and a strand of something suspiciously
like seaweed was clinging tenaciously to his hair. Seeing him
like that was probably a once-in-a-lifetime experience. I'd
treasure it.

"You're going to need to change before you see the other
me again," I said, trying not to laugh. "Something that looks
as much like your old outfit as possible."

Mircea shot me a look that said he'd noticed my amusement. "I have several black suits."

"But the shirt—"

"I also have quite a few of those."

"Really. It didn't look off-the-rack to me."

"It wasn't. Ming-de sends me one every year, on my birthday."

"How kind of her. Any particular reason?"

Mircea blinked lazily. "I don't suppose you would like to tell me what the mage meant by 'outraged modesty'?"

I licked my lips, feeling a residual tingle on my tongue that tasted suspiciously like a certain psycho war mage. "Not really."

"Then I think I, too, will keep my secrets, *dulceață*."

"Yeah, but you have more than me," I muttered.

He quirked an eyebrow. "I am beginning to wonder."

We ended up in Mircea's rooms, which were composed of a small dressing room and a larger bedroom. The painted wardrobe I'd seen at MAGIC had pride of place, beside a silk tapestry showing a green dragon eating its own tail. I stared at it in exhaustion. It was starting to get creepy. "The ouroboros."

"The symbol of the Sárkány Lovagrend," Mircea corrected me, his eyes on Horatiu.

"What?"

"The Order of the Dragon," he translated, moving closer to his servant. The old man was doing something near the fireplace that faced the large bed. It took me a moment to figure out what, because the paper spill he was holding was pressed to a soot-covered brick several feet to the left of the grate instead of to one of the dusty logs. "It was a society set up in Hungary by King Sigismund. My father became a member and . . . Let me do that," Mircea offered, his eyes on the rapidly burning paper.

Horatiu smacked him on the shoulder. "Didn't I teach you anything about respecting your station?" he demanded. "Always running about, playing with the servants' children, thinking that cheeky grin of yours was going to let you get away with all sorts of irresponsible behavior."

"So nothing's changed," I murmured.

Mircea sent me a wounded look while wrestling the old man for the spill. "What a nice blaze," he said loudly, managing to get the paper away from Horatiu just before it set his hand on fire.

Horatiu regarded the cold interior of the fireplace proudly. "Yes it is, isn't it?"

After a few moments, Mircea managed to coax the logs to life. "I don't suppose there's anything to eat?" he asked. He didn't look hopeful, but my stomach grumbled expectantly anyway.

"Eat?" Horatiu peered at me blankly. Apparently he'd assumed that Mircea had brought takeout.

"She is my guest!" Mircea said emphatically.

Horatiu muttered something that sounded disappointed. "Well, I suppose I could go out and try to find someone," he said doubtfully. "But with all the troubles nowadays, the streets are often deserted after dark."

"I meant for her."

"Eh?"

"Is there any food suitable for a human?" Mircea asked patiently.

"Well, if you'd sent word," Horatiu said huffily. "I can't be expected to know you'll be bringing home one of them, can I? Not to mention that the shops are mostly empty in any case, what with everything going to the army!"

"A 'no' would have sufficed," Mircea said. His glance at me was rueful. "My apologies. My hospitality is usually somewhat more . . . hospitable."

"Not a problem." I sat on the plush rug in front of the hearth and stretched my hands out to the fire. For the first time that night, I was almost warm and I didn't have to worry about someone sneaking up on me.

"The cellars are intact, I believe?" Mircea inquired.

"Yes, yes. Plenty of wine." Horatiu just stood there. So did Mircea. "Do you want me to go get some?" the old man finally asked.

"That would be nice," Mircea said politely. Horatiu tottered off, still muttering to himself, just loudly enough to be understood. Mircea sighed and started searching a squat cabinet in a corner.

"It is an ouroboros, though, right? The order's symbol?" My eyes had wandered back to the tapestry. The dragon's scales were green, and its eyes, picked out in gold thread, seemed to move in the low light of the fire.

"Yes, I suppose," Mircea said absently. "It is an ancient protection symbol, of a girdle of power encasing something precious. And that's what they were trying to do—guard Europe from Turkish invasion. Why?"

"I keep seeing it lately, everywhere I go. It's starting to weird me out."

Mircea laughed. "The ouroboros is the mages' emblem. It is ubiquitous in our world."

"But they just use a plain silver circle," I protested. I'd always thought it showed a real lack of imagination. The oldest magical organization on earth, and that was the best they could do?

"The older version of their symbol was an ouroboros. It was stylized over time into something easier to reproduce. They say they chose it because it is the alchemical symbol for purity, and silver stands for wisdom." Mircea's tone left no doubt as to what he thought of that claim.

"Protection, purity and wisdom." A lot of things came to mind when I thought of the Circle. Those three weren't on the list.

Mircea held out a dusty bottle. "Burgundy," he said triumphantly.

"But you just sent Horatiu for wine."

"Yes, a fact he'll remember for perhaps five minutes." He filled a couple of glasses that looked reasonably clean and passed me one.

"Thanks." I took a sip. It was good. "What happened to him?"

"Horatiu?" I nodded. "I am afraid I did."

"What? But isn't changing someone that old considered kind of . . . inadvisable?"

"Very much." Mircea ignored his wine in favor of rummaging around in the wardrobe. He soon produced a paper-wrapped package that smelled like sandalwood. "Yes, I thought I would have another." He lifted up a corner of the paper. "And it's in white."

I narrowed my eyes at it. Ming-de's little gift, I assumed. "You look better in color," I snapped.

He sent me a sultry look over his shoulder. "Really? Most women think I look better in nothing at all."

I backpedaled fast. "So why did you change him, then?"

Mircea shrugged. "He was my childhood tutor. I visited him on his deathbed, to find his skin as pallid as the sheets but his mind as sharp as ever. He knew he was dying, and he was highly incensed about it. He lay there, his body failing, and demanded that I *do* something, in the same voice he'd used to terrorize me as a child—"

"And you caved?"

"I agreed to his proposition," Mircea said with dignity.

"You caved."

He sighed and pulled on the shirt. "I'm afraid so."

"But why is he like that? If you turned him, shouldn't he have vampiric sight?" Not to mention hearing, sense of balance and the ability to cross a room faster than a meandering caterpillar.

"Normally, yes. But Horatiu was dying when he went through the transformation; had I hesitated at all, he would have been gone. And changing someone in such extremely poor health is, as you said, inadvisable."

"Then why do it?" An eternity like that wouldn't have struck me as a great gift.

Mircea poked at the fire, not that it needed it. The room was already warming up nicely. "Because I did not know what I was doing," he admitted, having tortured the logs to his satisfaction. "You forget, I was not chosen for this life; I received it because of an old woman's hatred for my family. I was cursed."

"What does that have to do with Horatiu?"

"Everything. I had no one to advise me, *dulceață*. No one to give me any knowledge of my new state. Perhaps in another time it would have been different. Today, the Senate itself oversees such masterless vampires as are created, few though they are. But then . . . nothing was so simple then. I didn't know this would be his fate."

"I never thought about what it must have been like for you," I said slowly, "to suddenly wake up changed."

He smiled grimly. "It did not happen as quickly as that. It was a week before the transformation was complete, and even then . . . Such things were fables, stories told to frighten children! How could such a thing have happened? To me, a good Catholic?"

"But vampirism is a metaphysical disease. It doesn't have anything to do with—"

"But I didn't know that, Cassie. I didn't know anything. I could enter a church, pray the rosary, do things I had always been told were impossible for the damned. And yet the sunlight I'd walked in all my life suddenly burned me, the food of my youth no longer nourished me, and even my body was changing in ways that, at the time, appalled me. I did not wish to see more than everyone else, to hear things better left unknown, to toss and turn in my bed, feeling every heartbeat within a mile calling out to me . . ."

"You accepted it in time, though."

"I don't know that that is quite the word I would use," Mircea said dryly. He unself-consciously stripped off the bedraggled trousers, laying them on the bed, where he tackled them with a brush. "I was in denial, refusing to admit, even to myself, what was happening."

"When did that change?"

"When the nobles caught up with me. Ours was an elected monarchy—anyone with the correct bloodline was a candidate—and they had decided to support a rival branch of the family. And in those days, the common way of changing power was to kill the ones who currently had it."

I'd heard the story of his change long ago, but he'd made it sound like a grand adventure. It wasn't sounding so much like that now. I was beginning to suspect that the version I'd received as a child had been a highly selective account.

"They killed Father first. He'd sent me on an ill-fated crusade against the Turks, and despite the fact that the troops I led had acquitted themselves well, we lost the war. I was . . . less than popular . . . thereafter, with nobles who had not bestirred themselves to help in the fight. Making me watch his death was intended as retribution."

He paused to tackle a particularly tough stain, then continued. "They scalped him, a trick we'd learned from the Turks. It involved peeling away the skin of the face while the victims still lived, torturing them and making them unrecognizable at the same time. When they finished, they blinded me with hot pokers so his mutilated body would be the last thing I ever saw. Then they buried me alive."

"Oh, my God."

"I lay there, hearing the clods of earth falling onto my coffin, and assumed it was the end," he said, sitting on the edge of the bed to pull his trousers back on. "I waited for my air to run out, for death, for judgment, for something . . . but hours passed and nothing happened. Nothing except that my eyes mended, allowing me to see despite there being no light. I finally had to face the fact that something a little . . . strange . . . was going on."

"What did you do?"

Mircea shrugged. "I dug my way out. It had rained overnight, making the ground soft. Otherwise I might not have managed it. Afterwards, I lay on the wet earth, gulping in air that I clearly no longer needed, and wondered what to do. I was a monster; I'd finally accepted that. But I was a damn weak one. I hadn't had any nourishment since the change and my body had had to repair considerable damage from the fight and the torture that followed it. I knew I was in no fit state to face them again."

"How did you survive?" I asked urgently. I really wanted to know. Our situations weren't identical, but there were enough similarities for me to hope for a nugget of wisdom. Mircea hadn't known how to be a vampire any more than I knew how to be the Pythia. Yet he'd managed.

His eyes narrowed slightly at my tone, and I cringed inwardly. I was tired and not guarding my voice as well as I should. I'd probably just told him a lot more than I'd intended.

"By luck and some timely help," he said after a pause. "My clothes, other than the filthy ones I had on, money and possessions were in Tirgoviste—where many of those who had just tried to kill me resided. I had to risk going back there, and as luck would have it, I was seen by one of my attackers. He didn't realize how weak I was and did not dare to take me on himself. But he ran to summon the others."

"But if they'd just buried you, why did they believe him?" Most people would ask anyone who came bearing tales of the walking dead if maybe he'd been drinking a little too much.

Before answering, Mircea came to join me. Since I was still sitting by the hearth, far too near the fire's random sparks for a vampire's liking, the move worried me. So did the casual smile on his face. "Spoken like a true modern woman," he said lightly. "But at that time, many people accepted the old legends about *nosferatu* as fact. And they knew how to deal with any of us who dared to show our face."

He sat down and relaxed, digging his bare toes into the deep, rich carpeting, and his eyes fixed on the hem of my gown. I looked down only to realize that the dirty ends of Pritkin's boots were peeking out from under the silk. I'd forgotten I was wearing them, just like he'd forgotten to search them. I felt myself blushing at the memory of exactly why we'd been so distracted.

I tried to tuck my feet back under the material, but it didn't do any good. Mircea knelt in front of me and pulled my foot into his hands, staring at the dirty, clunky boot incredulously. "Where did you get this?"

"Um." It was about a size ten, and obviously a man's. Mircea scraped at a bit of mud coating the heel and a knife popped out. It fell to the floor, making a small ringing sound, and we both stared at it for a beat.

"You're wearing the mage's *shoes*?"

"Technically, they're boots."

Mircea's eyes narrowed. "Yes, I can see that. Why are you wearing them?"

"My feet were cold."

"And he made a gentlemanly gesture?" His tone dripped sarcasm.

"Not exactly."

"You stole his shoes." Mircea sounded like he didn't quite believe it.

"Boots. And I didn't exactly . . . I mean, he wasn't using them at the time."

"And why not?"

"Um."

Mircea pulled the other offending boot off and tossed the pair of them to the other side of the room. They landed with a crash against the heavy wood paneling, sending a shower of caked dirt scattering across the floor. Which left him staring at Pritkin's socks.

They were woven from a coarse gray wool that in no way matched my dress and, like the boots, were oversized. Mircea didn't comment this time, just yanked them off and threw them after the shoes. "My feet are going to get cold," I protested.

"I will find you something more appropriate," he informed me tightly, pulling my feet into his lap.

He hadn't yet buttoned the shirt, and when he moved, the firelight did amazing things to the muscles on his chest. He started rubbing my arches, just too hard to tickle, and it felt so good I had to look away. It was a mistake, letting him know he was getting to me, but it was either that or get up and move—an even bigger red flag.

"How did you get out of there?" I asked, changing the subject.

"Out of where?"

"The town."

"With Horatiu's help," he said, rubbing my instep with hot, firm strokes. He had incredible hands—long, slim and skilled—and the warmth of his touch through the filter of my silk stocking was more than a little disconcerting.

"I take it he was younger then?"

"By quite a few years. The family's hold on the throne had never been completely secure, and we had been trained from childhood to be ready to flee at a moment's notice. Horatiu retrieved my emergency funds, some clothes and a horse, and hid me until nightfall. I was getting ready to go when he rode up, insisting on coming with me as far as the border. I tried to dissuade him, but he was as hardheaded as ever. And fortunately so. I wouldn't have made it alone, not in those first few months. Even with his help, there were some very close calls."

I caught his hand, needing to break contact in order to think. "Is there anything you'd do differently?"

Mircea let his hand lie still in mine, although the other kept hold of my leg, those long fingers curled around my ankle. "At the time, I believed that I was doing the only thing I could. I was leaving until they stopped searching for me, until I grew strong enough to defend myself and the political winds changed once again. But I departed too quickly, with too much left undone. Some of my mistakes I rectified later, but others . . . could not be redeemed."

That might have been true, but it wasn't what I needed to hear. "If you were going to give the old you some advice, what would it be?"

Mircea was silent for a long moment. "That when you become something more, you must often give up something to claim it."

"That doesn't sound very helpful!"

"Perhaps not, but there are no hard and fast rules in survival. I did what we all do when faced with something we believe beyond our abilities."

"And what's that?"

"The best I could."

"And when that wasn't good enough?" I whispered, finally admitting what I'd been trying not to think about. That I wasn't good enough. That the former Pythia had said it herself, in what I was beginning to think had been a prophecy: that I'd be either the best of us or the very worst. I had no idea what that first part meant, but I could really see the latter as a possibility.

"I found help."

"Such as?"

"The family," he said simply. "They stood behind me. Gave me something to fight for besides my own survival. Helped me believe that we would triumph, even when I sometimes doubted it myself."

"The family," I repeated dully. The very thing I didn't have.

"Not the one of my birth. It was shattered, first by Father's death and later by Vlad's betrayal. But in time, I built a new one. I had Horatiu, then Radu and, eventually, others."

Great advice—for another vampire. But I couldn't just go out and make a family for myself. And every one I'd ever had had disappeared through murder or betrayal or bad luck.

"Well, some of us don't have a family to fall back on," I said bitterly.

"You have a family, *dulceață,*" he told me, pulling me close. He moved slowly, giving me time to protest, to move away. When I didn't, one hand circled my waist, the other cupping the back of my neck, his touch careful but sure. "You've always had one."

"The family is loyal to you, not to me."

"But as I am loyal to you, it amounts to the same thing."

"Are you?" I searched his face. It was beautiful, flames dancing in those dark eyes, shining on his hair. And as usual it told me exactly nothing. "I'm a seer, not a telepath, Mircea. I'm not even as good as a vamp at telling when someone is lying."

"What do you feel?" He was breathing softly through his mouth and I felt it on my lips, warm and heavy. For a second, the memory of his mouth was so vivid I wasn't sure we weren't kissing right now. It was all too easy to imagine loving Mircea. It was even easier to imagine the problems it could cause.

"The last things I can trust are my feelings!" I told him unsteadily. "Especially for you!"

"Ah, *dulceață,*" he murmured. "You will learn as I did: family are the only ones you *can* trust."

He took my face in his hands and smiled against my lips, and when I felt it, I couldn't help smiling, too. I could feel his chuckle where my hand rested against his chest, and the thud of his heart picking up speed. I clung to him, my hands finding warm skin under his shirt, spreading across his back.

When he finally kissed me, it was nothing like Pritkin's touch. Mircea was certain, but unhurried. Instead of bruising strength and dominance, he used a gentle, sure pressure that caught at my senses just as thoroughly. His hand stroked over my cheek as his tongue teased mine, warm and silky, transforming sweetness languorously into heat. The only word for the way Mircea kissed was "lush."

"Your skin is cold," he murmured, settling me against him. His body heat was at my back while the fire warmed me from the front. My dress had ridden up, above my knees, and the dry heat of the flames felt good on my legs.

I knew I couldn't let this continue, but I was exhausted and my defenses were low. And that familiar voice was back, the one that told me I could put a stop to this, in one more minute. Nothing would happen in just a minute, I'd be so careful . . . One of Mircea's hands stayed on my waist, while another found its way underneath my skirts, skimming up my left calf before sliding around to the back of my thigh. He began stroking lightly, rubbing small circles through the silk stocking. Suddenly my pulse was pounding, my vision going blurry, my skin warming all over.

"We can't," I told him unsteadily, trying to remember why that was important.

His fingers had found the band at the top of my thigh-high. They tightened, flexing and unflexing, scraping blunt fingernails over the lace. When they dipped under the top, I couldn't help but shiver. "Oh, I am fairly certain we can," he said.

I met his eyes, brimming with heat and humor, and felt something inside expanding, decompressing. It was as if it had been there all along but there hadn't been room for it until now. I was suddenly afraid that we could, too.

Chapter 24

I realized that the dress was being undone, but then nails scratched lightly down the length of my back and I forgot why that was a problem. The double heat from Mircea's body and the fire had caused sweat to pool between my shoulder blades, hovering on the verge of trickling down my spine. As each ribbon pulled loose, his tongue was there, licking up the salt drops, tracing patterns on my skin. His lips brushed lightly over me, closing briefly on the individual knobs along my spine, sucking gently.

"You don't understand. The *geis*—" I stopped because a particularly hard shiver had caught me. I had the definite sensation of being on a train with no brakes heading straight off a cliff. Mircea chuckled, which wasn't anything like reassuring, and it was also a little alarming how fast the clothing was coming off. But then he was murmuring low, musical Romanian against my shoulder, and I understood every word down to my bones.

I felt the silk slip and start to fall as the material pulled apart. He laid me on the rug and bent over my right leg, touching his lips to the inside of my thigh. My shiver turned into goose bumps when his tongue met skin through the silk, and his teeth closed around the lace top of my stocking.

"Mircea, listen to me," I said quickly, to cover the stab of arousal caused by watching him pull my stocking down with his teeth. "The *geis* went wrong. It isn't the original spell anymore, it—"

"Is delightful," he said, having tugged the stocking completely off.

"Now, maybe. But it gets stronger!"

Mircea had curled his hand around my other thigh, his thumb resting on the lace edge of my remaining stocking. He started absently moving it a little bit up and down until he hit a particularly sensitive spot and paused. He stroked lightly, as if he somehow knew exactly what his touch was doing to me, while I tried to remember how to breathe.

"I look forward to it," he whispered, before pulling me into a kiss as slow and luxurious as cold honey.

Things became a little hazy for a few moments after that. I remember him stripping me slowly, his expression hungry and intent and strangely tender. I remember swift fingers slowing to stroke over bare skin while he watched me with suddenly dark eyes. I remember being stretched out on the blanket with big, careful hands, and touched everywhere, while the fire muttered smokily to itself and the snow fell harder outside.

"Mircea—" I stopped because a finger painted my lips with wine, silencing me before he kissed it away. More wine followed, running down my torso in dark red rivulets. I inhaled a deep, stuttering breath as he started licking a trail downward.

He brushed over a nipple, sucking gently as I shivered, tracing patterns on my skin with his tongue. Every touch of his lips, every breath, caused pleasure to run like wildfire along my nerves. *I guess I finally know how he takes his wine*, I thought hazily, before he suddenly thrust into my navel and I lost all thought.

Wine dribbled down my stomach, over my hips, down my thighs. He looked up, eyes gleaming with more than just candlelight, as he stroked over the center of me. My whole body tightened with longing for what I'd never gotten to have, what I'd never stopped wanting. I shuddered and pushed back against the fingertips when they passed over me again, and the hand withdrew.

I stared down the length of my body at him, aching, uncomprehending, until one finger returned, coated with wine, and slowly pressed inside. Tension leapt in my muscles at the intrusion, even though I'd wanted it, but the instinctive tightening of my body couldn't stop the slow, deliberate penetration. Then it withdrew and a warm tongue replaced it, chasing the wine, tasting it, tasting me, as his thumbs traced restless little circles on my hips.

I was the one to break eye contact first, molten heat flooding out reason, my head dropping back to the rug even as I arched upward. His tongue talked softly to me, some unknown language of the body. But it seemed that part of me understood, part of me was pretty close to fluent, because ripple after ripple of pleasure spilled through me. He teased me by flicking his tongue just a little too slowly until I whimpered helplessly.

The darkened windows reflected the impossible sight of that proud head bowed over me, that clever tongue pleasuring me. I closed my eyes and breathed through it, desperately; almost too much sensation. He had begun with a gentle touch, but it quickly grew more assured, more demanding, until his hands tightened on my hips, jerking me nearer in an almost greedy way. And I guess my body must have been talking to him, too, because somehow he knew the pace I wanted, knew exactly the touch I craved. Pleasure slid up and down my spine like hot wax until it gave up and melted entirely.

Without being asked, I shifted my legs farther apart for his touch. And the *geis* instantly rewarded me: the feeling I had whenever I resisted, like my chest had been caught in a vise, suddenly eased. I took what felt like my first full breath in days.

And it terrified me.

I'd been a fool to think I could control this, crazy to let it go this far. If I became Mircea's servant things would be bad, but if he became mine, they might be even worse. I didn't think the Consul would be too pleased about having one of her senators under anyone's control, especially mine. I didn't even have to guess what her response would be: if I didn't stop this, I was either a slave or dead.

My body was no longer taking orders from my brain—I literally wasn't in control anymore—but I could still talk.

"Mircea, listen to me. We have to—" I stopped suddenly, unable to finish; I was too busy swallowing the groan that wanted to slip free of my throat.

He heard the small noise I couldn't quite suppress, and it crinkled the corners of his eyes. "I was beginning to worry," he said lightly. "Most women are not still coherent at this point."

I kissed him to wipe the smirk off his face, jerking him up to me by the two halves of his shirt. He drove the kiss deep as I shoved the silk off his shoulders and worked it down his arms. A toggle went skittering across the floor, but the heavy material wouldn't rip—it caught on his wrists. I pulled back, glaring at it, and tugged harder, until it finally came off. Mircea let me, his eyes glinting, a smile playing over his lips. I ignored it this time.

"I'm glad you're braver than your counterpart," I said, as he laid me back on the rug. I still had one stocking on, I noticed. It looked a little strange, as it was all I was wearing.

"What counterpart?" Mircea murmured, kissing his way downward again.

"The one from my time."

"And why is that?" he asked, his breath ghosting over me.

I tilted my head back, already so close—"He was afraid to touch me."

Mircea rested his chin on my stomach and looked at me with hot, golden eyes. One hand curved around my hip possessively. "I doubt that. As a famous Frenchman once said, the best way of enlarging and multiplying one's desires is to try to limit them."

"Even if they make me your master?" I gasped.

For a long moment, nothing happened. Then Mircea abruptly moved over me, his arms braced on either side of my body, his face staring directly into mine. His pupils were still dilated, and his skin was flushed. But unlike me, he was in command of himself. "What do you mean?" he demanded.

"The *geis* responds to power." His hair whispered across my breasts, a petal-soft sensation that was suddenly almost unbearable. I whimpered, and had to struggle not to reach for him. "And now that I'm Pythia . . ."

His eyes widened. Pain and surprise clashed on his face with something darker, more basic. "There is a chance that your power is the greater."

I just nodded, barely able to manage that. My skin felt like it was on fire, my pulse was pounding and my willpower was gone. I slid my thigh between his legs and put my arm around his back and just held on. I bit my lip to stifle the sounds that wanted to come up my throat, the demands I wanted to make.

I shuddered and made a helpless noise as his arms went around me, cradling me against him. He kissed me, murmuring, "It's all right, it will be all right," against my hair, and I sobbed wordlessly back, struggling weakly, trying to tell him that it wasn't, it wasn't all right.

Mircea started stroking in long, soothing paths from the base of my skull to the small of my back, over and over, murmuring soft nonsense things. Suddenly all the fight went out of me and every muscle went liquid, a low roaring in my ears. He'd hit me with a suggestion, I realized. Normally, it would have infuriated me to not even be asked, but at the moment I was absurdly grateful for it. The warmth and certainty of safety lulled me, pulling me under so gradually, I didn't even realize when I relaxed into sleep.

I awoke when the door slammed open and Horatiu tottered in. It wasn't much later, judging by the lack of light outside. I was sweating, and the blanket someone had placed over me had tangled around my body, plastering itself to my limbs. The fire was going strong and the room was too hot.

"Where is the master?" Horatiu asked, his voice quavering.

I sat up, holding my head. It hurt, and I felt dry-mouthed and groggy. The usual telltale signs of a powerful suggestion having worn off. Mircea must have had to use the big guns to overcome the *geis*, and the result was worse than a hangover. I got up and staggered to the window, throwing it open and gulping in a few lungfuls of cold, crisp air.

"The master?" Horatiu repeated.

I blinked at him over my shoulder. He had a bottle of wine perched precariously on a tarnished silver platter and his hands were shaking, making it tremble badly enough that I

was afraid it would fall. "I don't know," I said, moving to
help, and a second later he had me around my already abused
throat.

I didn't need to watch the age spots fading, the shape of the
hands gripping me reforming, to know who had me. "How
did you find us?" I demanded, not bothering to struggle.

"You were kind enough to mention the vampire's name in
my hearing," Pritkin sneered. "And it seems he is well known
in Paris. Discovering where 'Lord Mircea' has his residence
wasn't difficult!"

"Tell me you didn't hurt the old man," I said, wondering
what he'd done with the real Horatiu. Hoping a slip of my
tongue hadn't just ended a centuries-old life.

Pritkin's bark of a laugh echoed harshly in my ears. "I
found him asleep, with the tray beside him. I left him so. My
quarrel is not with him."

"No. Your quarrel is with me, and my patience is not
endless," Mircea hissed. He'd appeared in the doorway, a
tray similar to Horatiu's in his hands. It was loaded with
food—a round loaf of bread, butter, jam—that he'd somehow rounded up.

"Then let me try it no further!" Pritkin said, pulling a dark
sphere out from under his cloak. "Give me my property or we
all die. Right here. Right now."

"The map will do you no good dead!"

"Nor will it you!" Pritkin snapped.

"I said we were reasonable men. It appears I overrated one
of us," Mircea replied. His hands flexed slightly and his lips
drew back from his teeth. I swear I could almost see his fangs
lengthening. I felt like screaming at both of them that we
couldn't afford a fight when it could end with one or all of us
dead. But it wouldn't have done any good. So I went with
something that would.

While Pritkin stood glaring at Mircea, I shifted behind him
and grabbed the small sphere from his hand. I threw it out the
window even as he turned, shock on his face, and Mircea
grabbed us both and jerked us out of the room. The door shut
just as an explosion rocked the front of the house. The whole
thing had taken less than ten seconds.

"Are you quite mad?" Mircea asked me conversationally. "That was a dislocator."

I didn't have time to respond, because Pritkin let out a roar of pure rage and threw himself at Mircea.

They crashed backwards, through the railing and down the stairs, hitting the bottom and then rolling straight into a large mirror. It shuddered, but didn't break, at least not until Mircea grabbed Pritkin by the collar and threw him into it. The fracturing glass made a sound like crinkling tinfoil, cracking in jagged streaks of broken lightning that radiated out from his shoulders like wings. Then the mirror came crashing down, scattering glass everywhere, and Pritkin grabbed up a large shard and made a swipe straight at Mircea's neck.

I didn't see what happened then, because they carried the fight into the next room, out of sight. I jerked up the blanket I still wore and ran to the bottom of the stairs, but had to slow down to pick my way through the shards of mirror. And, right at the bottom of the steps, my bare foot encountered something that wasn't wood or glass—a folded scrap of paper.

It was a single heavy sheet containing a mass of scribbled instructions. A mass of very familiar scribbled instructions. I stared at it in disbelief; I guess I knew who'd been running the auction now.

My head whipped up at the sound of an explosion, and I ran into the reception room to find a section of the floorboards charred black and smoking. But a broken vial lay nearby, so it had been a potion, not a spell. It looked like both men were too drained to try anything fancier than old-fashioned hand-to-hand, which meant that I had a few extra seconds before someone ended up dead.

A candelabra had been knocked to one side in the impact, and most of the candles had sizzled out against the floor, but one continued burning. I held it to a corner of the map and yelled, "Take off the *geis* or I torch it!"

The fight froze. Mircea looked up with a hand locked around Pritkin's neck, while the mage halted the knife that had been heading for Mircea's chest. "I already did!" Pritkin spat, face livid even in the almost nonexistent light. "There is *no* chance, none at all, that the counterspell would not have been sufficient, were you not opposing it!"

"I didn't do anything!"

"You lie! What was your plan? For your vampire to find the Codex while you distracted me?" I stared at him, speechless. I hadn't been the one doing the distracting! "Your intent all along was to find the Codex at any cost!"

I felt my chest heave with something similar to the expression on Pritkin's face. "Well, if not, it pretty much is now," I said furiously.

"It won't do you any good!" He watched with a panicked expression as a tiny flame started eating away at the corner of the map. "It doesn't contain a starting point—that was to be given verbally to the winner of the sale."

"Then I'll look up the auctioneer. I'm sure he can be reasonable."

"Perhaps he would be, if he lived!"

Mircea opened his hand and got to his feet. "We appear to be at an impasse," he told Pritkin. "You have the starting point, but not the map. We have the map, but not the starting point. We can achieve our goal only by cooperation." It was a good speech, but he followed it with a smile that made the mage drop a hand to his belt, which contained its usual row of deadly little vials.

I ignored them and watched the flame grow, consuming the artwork that someone had painstakingly painted at the bottom of the page. Considering how sloppy the rest of the map was, it stood out. Particularly because it hadn't been included on the version I would one day be given by a kindly-looking old man in a pretty French garden. It was a perfectly rendered, golden ouroboros, its tiny scales glinting in the candlelight.

"What are you doing?" Pritkin demanded, as the hungry flames leapt higher. "If you burn it, you will never find it. Even if the vampire made a copy, it won't contain the starting point! And I won't help you!"

"I guess I'll have to take my chances," I said, watching the bright yellow flame leap higher.

"You cannot be serious!" Pritkin made a move toward me,

but Mircea knocked him back with a casual blow that staggered him. The mage struggled to his feet, staring at me with anger and confusion on his face.

"I don't think I've ever been more serious in my life," I said honestly.

He helplessly watched the paper turn brown and crisp up, and I saw it the moment realization hit his eyes. If no one found the Codex, it would slowly unwrite itself, tucked away in whatever burrow the mages had found for it. And if anyone ever did come across it, it would be useless to them—as much so as if he had retrieved and destroyed it himself.

The three of us watched the paper burn to a cinder. Pritkin looked at me, an unreadable expression on his face, as he carefully ground it to powder under his heel. Then he simply turned around and left. A moment later, a flash of blue lit the front of the house like a strobe light, and he was gone.

"I did not make a copy," Mircea told me quietly. "I can attempt to reproduce it from memory if you like, but it was quite complex."

"No." I stared down at the map, my head reeling. "It really wasn't."

"Do you know, *dulceaţă*, most of my dates have involved rather less dirt."

"Don't complain. You should see this place in two hundred years," I said, thrusting the relit candelabra at him.

Mircea gingerly took the rack of candles while I got his knife under the gold ouroboros set into the line of skulls. It came out easily; the plaster had barely had time to set. Behind it was a small leather tube embedded in solid rock. With a little work, I got an edge up, and a second later it slid out into my hands. I stared at the limestone-dusted cylinder and could have cried.

Whatever starting point the auctioneer—Manassier's grandfather, I assumed—had told Pritkin had been a fake. And the copies of the map that were floating around, say with his grandson, were useless to anyone who might stumble across them. Unless you knew the secret, they would just send would-be treasure hunters on a wild-goose chase. Like one of them would me, two hundred years from now.

No wonder Manassier hadn't minded giving me the map; he'd known it was useless. The real clue had been the drawing at the bottom of the page, a drawing the copies hadn't had. A drawing the Pritkin of this era had never had time to notice.

I fumbled getting the tube open, my hands numb with equal parts cold and excitement. I finally took the candles back from Mircea and let him do it. A sheaf of parchment emerged a moment later, golden with age but still perfectly legible. "I don't believe it," I whispered. All that time, it had been right here. I'd even touched the tiny symbol marking the spot. Touched it, and then run right on by. "I can't believe it's over."

"It isn't," Mircea said, scanning a page. He flipped through several others, and his frown grew deeper. "Unless you perhaps read Welsh?"

"Welsh?" I snatched the sheaf from him and a brittle edge flaked off and fell to the ground. The thing was practically disintegrating just from being held. I was more careful after that, but it was easy to see that Mircea was right: the pages were all covered in the same sort of gibberish Pritkin used for taking his notes. I couldn't read a word of it. "Damn it!"

"It is not one of my languages," Mircea said before I could ask. "However, there are mages in this period who would be able to translate it, and possibly cast the spell for you."

I watched as a small curl at the end of a letter slowly disappeared. It had been attached to the final word on the last page—a word that was already unwriting itself. *Relax*, I told myself sternly. *What are the odds that it's part of the spell I need?* I sighed. With my luck, they were actually pretty good.

"We have to hurry," I said, carefully rolling the brittle pages back together.

"That would not be wise. Engaging the help of mages is always dangerous. I will have to do some checking, to be certain that we contact someone who will not immediately betray us."

"You're telling me they're all as crazy as Pritkin?"

"If they recognized what they were handling, probably," he said dryly.

I handed the pages back to Mircea and replaced the golden marker in the damp plaster. There was no need to worry about taking the Codex with us; the ouroboros had been undisturbed when Pritkin and I first passed it. All those rumors had been lies: no one else had ever found it.

"I think I know someone who might be able to help, but I have to go back to my time to talk to him." I just hoped I had the strength to get us back. I grabbed Mircea's hand—there was one way to find out. "Hold on," I told him, and shifted.

Chapter 25

Dante's was as quiet as it ever got when I returned to my time after dropping Mircea at his. So nobody saw me collapse against a wall. Goddamn, I really needed to stop shifting for a while. It felt like my head was about to explode. The throbbing affected even my vision: for a few moments, the whole corridor looked like the inside of a heart—red and pulsating.

But I'd ended up where I needed to be, in the hallway leading to the research room. And Nick was there, his nose stuck in a book as usual, looking as scholarly as I really hoped he was. "Cassie!" He stood up abruptly, looking alarmed, and it occurred to me that maybe I should have gone for a quick shower first. But that could wait; the Codex couldn't.

Limestone dust sifted out of my hair onto the table as I spread out the parchment sheets, pushing books off everywhere in the process. "Can you read this?" I demanded, ignoring Nick's squawks. "It's important!"

He settled down after a moment, scholarly curiosity taking over, and quickly scanned a few lines. "Welsh," he mused, "an especially antiquated, if not to say *peculiar*, variety."

"But can you read it?"

"Oh, yes, I think so. In time. It isn't one of my chief languages, you know, but I have had some—"

"I need it now, Nick." I gestured at the scattered sheets. "Somewhere in there is the spell to lift the *geis*, and it would be extra nice to get it before Mircea goes completely around the bend." Or before it managed to disappear.

Nick suddenly stilled, not moving, not even breathing, and for a second it was creepily like what a vamp could do. "This"—he stopped and swallowed—"this is the Codex, isn't it? You found it."

"Yeah, only it doesn't do me much good since I can't read it." He just sat there, so I nudged him with a toe. "Now, Nick."

"Right, right." He came back to life with a vengeance, sifting through the pages rapidly, looking for the right spell. "This may take a while," he muttered. "There are hundreds of spells here and I don't see an index . . . oh, wait."

"You found one?"

"Better." His bangs flopped in his eyes and he pushed them impatiently back. "I may have found the spell."

"You're serious?" I stared at him, scarcely daring to hope. The damn *geis* had thwarted me at every turn for weeks; it was almost impossible to believe that I might be free of it in a few minutes.

"This may take some time, Cassie. You can, uh, go get changed if you want."

Yes, I definitely needed to freshen up. My hands were covered in small bruises, my nails were cracked and there was dirt pressed into the grooves of my palms. My hair was a frazzled mess and I was covered in dust from the brief spelunking trip. But Nick was just going to have to deal with me in all my witchy glory, because no way was the Codex leaving my sight. No freaking way.

He got a good look at my expression and gave up, going back to translating duty. I sat down opposite him and peered into the ubiquitous little china pot. But only a vague floral scent remained. I put a call in to the kitchens for some coffee, figuring both of us could use it, and concentrated on not falling asleep until it got there.

"How much do you know about the Circle, Cassie?" Nick asked suddenly.

I yawned. "Other than that they want to kill me? Not a lot."

"Yes, I am aware that you have had your differences in the past."

"And present. Is there a point, Nick?" I wanted translation, not conversation.

"Well, yes, actually. It's just that, I thought you should know—you're not alone. There are many of us who have been growing dissatisfied with the Circle for some time. Only we don't all agree about the remedy. Some of us see the whole system as the problem, not simply the group in power at the moment. We view the war as a chance to change old ideas, to remake it, in fact, into something closer to the type of government the vampires have. Then there wouldn't be little groups of megalomaniacs making crucial mistakes for everyone."

Actually I thought that pretty much summed up the Senate. "You mean, with one person in charge?"

"Not necessarily. Just a more centralized authority, with better oversight of everyone's activities and more checks and balances on their behavior."

"There aren't a lot of checks and balances on the Senate," I pointed out. "None, in fact."

"Yet it works! Instead of elections turning into popularity contests, you have the best people appointed for each position by a concerned, capable leader."

"I don't think I'd describe the Consul quite that way," I said dryly. "She got her position by being the strongest and the craftiest, full stop."

"But she rules well. People respect her."

"People *fear* her!"

"All strong leaders are feared by the ignorant," Nick commented, patently not listening to a word I said. "We could learn a great deal from the vampires, if prejudice did not stand in the way."

I laughed; I just couldn't help it. The mages seemed to have a seriously warped view of the vamps. Pritkin saw them as evil incarnate, while Nick was determined to set them on a pedestal. He didn't look too pleased at my amusement, though, so I tried to explain while he looked up a particularly obscure word.

"The vamp system works because of the bonds that force subordinate vampires to do the will of their masters and require masters to answer for the infractions of their followers. The mages don't have that kind of setup. And you can't expect people to—"

"Perhaps if we did, we could coordinate our efforts and stamp out the dark once and for all!" he interrupted. "As it is, they stay one step ahead of us merely by crossing into another coven's territory, and by the time we get through all the debates and favors and bribes and finally get the needed permission to go after them, they're gone again!"

He was looking pretty annoyed, with flushed cheeks under all those freckles. I'd have changed the subject, but something was bugging me. "I thought the Circle was the central authority. Isn't it in charge of the whole magical community?"

"No," he snapped. "That's the problem. What we have now is sort of an umbrella organization. Not every coven worldwide belongs to it—we're especially spotty in Asia—and even those who are members joined at different times and with different agreements."

"I didn't know that." The vamps always talked about the Circle like it was synonymous with mages in general. Of course, in this country it might be. I'd never thought about it being different anywhere else.

"It's a total hodgepodge!" Nick said heatedly. "Some covens don't allow searches of their territory at all and others only after receiving definite proof that questionable activity is going on. And, of course, sometimes we don't have proof, just a gut feeling or a tip from someone they don't recognize as a legitimate source. And explaining that our sources wouldn't know the dark well enough to have information if they *were* legit gets us nowhere nine times out of ten. It would be so much easier if we all answered to one authority."

"A dictatorship, in other words." Pritkin had come into the room without my hearing him. I jumped, trying to stand up and whirl around at the same time, and almost ended up on the floor. He caught me, and I tore away as soon as I could find my feet, panting a little, glaring a lot. "I see you made it back safely."

"It doesn't have to be anything of the kind," Nick argued,

apparently not realizing that no one was listening to him any-more.

Pritkin looked like he'd just come from a bath; his hair—short and pale blond again—was plastered down in wet strands that disturbed me for some reason I couldn't quite define. Maybe because it drew attention to his face, like the older, longer version had. Maybe because it made me remember the last time I'd seen it wet, slick with sweat and glistening.

God, I *hated* him!

"You!" I couldn't even talk, I had so many things I wanted to say. "You knew!" It was the only thing I could get out, the only words that didn't threaten to choke me.

"No, I didn't. At the time, I merely thought you were a competent witch who was attempting to rob me."

"Don't lie! You saw me shift!"

"I thought you'd clouded my mind, you or the vampire. My defenses were down, my shields almost exhausted. It seemed a reasonable conclusion."

"And when we met again? You didn't recognize me?"

"After so long, no. Not immediately. I had wondered a few times, but I didn't know. Not until I saw the dress." He looked over the tattered remains. "It was memorable."

"More than me, it would seem," I said tightly.

"Nick, if you could give us a moment?"

"But I'm right in the middle of . . ." He saw the looks we turned on him and gulped. "Or—or I could go see what's keeping that coffee," he squeaked, and headed out the door. He tried to take the page he was working on with him, but I held out a hand and he reluctantly handed it over.

"You found it, then." Pritkin's voice held no emotion what-soever. He'd learned a lot in two hundred years.

"And I'm keeping it."

"I'm afraid I can't allow that, Cassie."

I laughed, and even to me, it sounded bitter. "Oh, it's Cassie, now, is it? So, let me make sure I have it straight. It's Ms. Palmer when you're pretending to be loyal, and Cassie when you're stabbing me in the back. Good to know."

Pritkin flinched slightly, but he never dropped his gaze. "You don't understand what's at stake."

"And that would be why, I wonder? *Because nobody ever tells me anything?*" That last was pretty much a scream, but I didn't care. I'd known that seeing him again would be hard, I just hadn't known how hard. I'd been right before. Burying emotions was a hell of a lot better than experiencing them, especially when they felt like this.

"I will tell you what you want to know, if you will promise to hear me out before shifting. If you thought you were a target before, it is nothing to what you will be with that thing in your possession. It *must* be destroyed!"

I couldn't have shifted to save my life; I was having a hard time even standing up. But Pritkin didn't know that. It gave me an advantage, a lever to finally pry some answers out of him. But for the life of me, I couldn't work up much enthusiasm about it.

"I've spent my whole life playing games," I told him quietly. "It's the vamp's favorite pastime. A whisper here, a wink there, a clue that may or may not go anywhere and may or may not have been dropped on purpose. I'm tired of games. I just want someone to tell me the truth. Haven't I earned that much yet?"

Pritkin closed his eyes briefly, and swallowed, a brief bob of his Adam's apple up and down. I searched his still-youthful face, trying to peer behind the mask. To see a thousand years of experience. But there was nothing.

I'd grown up around creatures who never showed their age, at least not physically. But you could always tell the older ones, and not just by the aura of power they gave off. There was a gravity to them, like air took on extra weight when they entered a room. As if everything about them was somehow *more*: deeper, brighter, richer.

He opened his eyes, but I didn't look away. I scrutinized him, trying to keep the Consul in mind, the way she felt, the way she drew all eyes without seemingly doing a thing. I watched a faint blush spread across his cheekbones as I continued to inspect him, and mentally shook my head. No. No way was he that old.

Which left the sojourn in Hell. He'd said that much of his younger years had been spent there, but also that he'd just got back in 1793. Which was crazy. If he'd disappeared from history because he had, in fact, disappeared from earth, then he'd left in the early Middle Ages. And if he'd only just returned . . . a thousand years on earth would scar a person; what would a millennium in the demon realms do?

How would it be, I wondered, to be snatched into a world you knew nothing about, where your only use was as a trophy? Some kind of freakish experiment for your father to show off? And what had Pritkin done to get thrown out anyway? How exactly did someone get tossed out of Hell?

"Rosier tried to kill you so that you couldn't do what you have just done—retrieve the Codex and with it a spell known as the Ephesian Letters," he finally said.

Maybe it was because I was tired, or under the strain of being near Pritkin and not being able to touch him, to hit him, to run my hands through his hair and make it stand *up*, damn it, but I was having a hard time following. "What?"

"They were words carved into the ancient Temple of Artemis at Ephesus—"

"Nick told me what the Ephesian Letters are," I said impatiently. "Why does anyone care about an old spell?"

"Because of what it can do. What, in fact, it *did* do, thousands of years ago." Pritkin sat on the edge of the table. "What it will continue to do, if no one ever casts the counterspell that I foolishly wrote down. Merlin the wise, indeed."

"Then I was right. You *are* Merlin." I found it hard to take in, despite all the evidence. Pritkin was just . . . Pritkin. Not some legend out of another time.

"Myrddin, in fact, not that I used the name for long. A French poet thought it sounded obscene and changed it. Fair enough; he changed everything else."

"Then the stories aren't true? There was no Camelot, or Lancelot or Arthur—"

"Oh, there was an Arthur, after a fashion. And I can see his face, if he read half the things written about him! That rumor about his sister alone—he'd have cut out someone's heart for that one." He thought for a moment. "Or she would. Frightening woman."

"So you're what, like a thousand years old?" I still didn't believe it.

"Not . . . precisely. I was born in the sixth century, but did not manage to live even one normal life span before Rosier came to claim me. And time in the demon realms runs differently from here, much like in Faerie. Only more so. I was there, as far as I can tell, barely a human decade. But when I returned"—he shook his head, and there was still wonder on his face—"the world had changed."

"When I met you in Paris, you told me that you'd only just come back. Was that when you returned?"

"More or less. I had been back a few years by then, enough to learn my way around to some degree, but not enough to keep from being pickpocketed by a spell that hadn't even been invented in my day but was old hat in the eighteenth century."

"By Manassier's grandfather."

"Yes. He and an associate were living in that nebulous world betwixt and between. The Circle had rejected them for unbecoming conduct—and, I suspect, gross incompetence—but they didn't have any skills wanted by the dark. They made a precarious living relieving naive country bumpkins of their worldly possessions and, whenever possible, draining them of their magic. They couldn't get past my shields to make the latter possible, but they did manage to make off with the Codex."

"And that mysterious spell you were going to tell me about."

Pritkin propped his head on one hand, a tired gesture I could never remember seeing before. "I have made many mistakes in life, but the worst of all had to be writing down that blasted spell."

"But Nick said it was never written down. That it was lost after the temple burned and the priests all died."

"One survived and, in extreme old age, left exactly one copy. I don't know whether he was senile, or merely unwilling to let his most precious secret die with him. Perhaps he'd forgotten what it does; maybe he never knew. I only know that I found his scribbled ramblings in an old temple in Angelsey. How they got there." He shrugged. "Possibly a Roman legionary picked them up as a curiosity in the East before being reassigned. I never knew."

"How did you find it?"

"Because I was searching for it. Not that spell specifically but anything old that might have survived. I didn't have high hopes—the place had been burnt by the Romans during their Druid-killing sprees, and what was left was plundered by the Saxons a few centuries later. But no one had thought an old scroll to be of much use, especially one in a language none of them could read, and it somehow survived. Languages have always been a specialty of mine. And I pounced on it."

"For what?"

"For curiosity partly. For the rest . . . I was so proud of myself, thought I'd found my life's work, before I understood how long that life might be. It seemed an utter good—cataloging and preserving the old knowledge at a time in which the whole world seemed to be coming down around our ears. I had no way of knowing that what I recorded might well bring that to pass much more efficiently than the damn Saxons ever could!"

"But what does it do?" I thought I was going to go crazy if he didn't just tell me.

"The Ephesian Letters is a spell and a counterspell in one, depending on voice, inflection and which way it is read. One way closes a door; the other opens it."

"What door?"

"The door between worlds. Rosier fears that if the spell is found, someone might reverse it, opening a gateway to rivals his kind have not had to face in—" He had been sorting through the pile of pages at his elbow and had picked one out of the group. It must have been the translation Nick was working on, unless ancient Ephesian priests used lined notebook paper. His breath caught. "What is this?"

I glanced at it. "Nick was translating the counterspell for me, for the *geis*."

"This isn't the counterspell," Pritkin said, his face draining of color as I watched. I glanced down at the paper, but it didn't make much sense.

ASKION: Shadowless ones. *Where gods once ruled,*
KATASKION: Shadowy. *Humans now do.*
LIX: Earth. *Earth is blocked*
TETRAX: Time. *To Time's Guardian.*
DAMNAMENEUS: Sun overpowered. *With this, the sun is overpowered.*
AISION: True Voice. *And the oracle speaks with a true voice.*

Pritkin grabbed me by the arms. "Take us back, quickly!"

"Back where?"

"To the moment Nick got up to leave! I have to catch him!"

"Why, what did he—"

"There's no time to explain. Just do it!"

I pushed a limp strand of hair out of my eyes and tried to focus. God, I was so tired. "I can't shift right now. Maybe tomorrow—"

Pritkin swore. "If I don't find him, there won't *be* a tomorrow!" And he was gone. I didn't even see him leave, just the door slamming shut behind him.

Chapter 26

And then the lights went out. I sat there in the dark and seriously thought about putting my head down and going to sleep. It was nice and quiet down here, and maybe no one would find me until morning.

If there was a morning.

I groaned and got up. As I'd always suspected, being in charge sucked. Especially when no one even realized you were.

I felt around until I was sure I had the entire Codex, rolled it all, including the translation of the spell I *didn't* need, into a tube and wrapped a rubber band around it. Then I shoved the whole thing down my bodice. Mircea hadn't laced it as tightly as Sal, but it still fit snugly, and with the tube down there taking up what little room there was, breathing once more became an issue. But at least no one was budging that thing. Now if I didn't pass out from lack of air, everything would be fine.

I eased out into the corridor and tried to remember how far it was to the fire stairs. But it's not the sort of thing you really notice when the lights are on. I'd covered what I thought was about the right distance when someone grabbed me.

I screamed and somebody yelled and then I was slammed up against the wall. It hurt and I was already in a foul mood. I didn't hold back at all when I kneed whoever-it-was in the groin.

"You'd better hope that doesn't scar!" Casanova hissed.

"You're a vampire. You'll heal. What are you doing here?"

"It's *my* casino!" he said, a little shrilly. "I have every right to be here. It's you and your hoodlum friends who need to go, before you cause any more trouble!"

"Avoiding trouble is not a big motivator for me these days. Not dying is a big motivator for me; not watching Mircea go insane is a big motivator for me. Speaking of which—"

"The Senate isn't here, but I just received word that they're on their way. And I haven't been confirmed in this job yet, you know! How do you think it's going to look when the Consul shows up and the whole damn place is dark?"

"Why is *she* coming here?" That was all I needed.

"How the hell should I know? Do I look like someone who is regularly consulted on Senate matters? I try to stay as far away from those crazy bastards as possible." He paused. "Lord Mircea excepting, of course."

"Of course. Why is it dark in here?"

"Because one of those freeloaders you dumped on me has caused a blackout!"

"You can't be sure it's the kids," I said, feeling guilty.

"Oh, no? Well, the power company says we have power. They all but called me an idiot when I called them just now! Yet, no lights. And, if I may point out, no slot machines, no table games, no anything. I'm losing a fortune here!"

"It's been all of ten minutes. Relax. I'll take care of it."

"You're damn right you will. Right now!"

"Stop yelling. I have a bigger problem. Have you seen Nick?"

"Yes, how do you think I found you? He said—"

I grabbed Casanova by what felt like his lapels and shook him. "Where is he?"

He pried my hands off with a curse. "Again, how the hell should I know? And this is imported Italian silk, all right?"

"Where did you see him?"

"In the lobby. I ran into him right after the lights went out. He was trying to find a way out of here and I was trying to find you. We traded information."

"You helped him leave?" I grabbed Casanova again, despite his curse.

"I pointed him in the right direction; I didn't personally escort him out. And what difference does it make?"

"You have to stop him!"

"I'll make you a deal. Get those urchins of yours to undo whatever they did wrong *this* time and I'll have the mage detained. I've got a near panic going on in the lobby!"

"Fine." I doubted the low-level vamps Casanova employed would have much luck stopping a war mage, but maybe they could slow him down long enough for Pritkin to locate him.

Casanova called security on his cell phone while we navigated the dark stairs. It turned out that he hadn't been exaggerating the situation in the lobby. A few security people had flashlights that they were waving around like strobes over the frightened crowd, while others yelled contradictory instructions through bullhorns. A bunch of gamers were playing guitars and singing in the corner, in the faint glow of the lighters they held over their heads. I thought I recognized the tune, but the words seemed to be something about the nazgul. And the pterodactyl things were watching it all out of bright, hungry eyes.

I scanned the room for Nick, but it was really difficult to make out faces. Casanova started toward the security team, most of whom were over by the moat. Boats poled along by Charons in black robes and death masks usually ferried people back and forth between the entrance and the lobby, but they were beached due to the lack of light, and the drawbridge that served as an alternate entrance appeared to be stuck in the open position.

A couple of impatient types had decided to try wading the moat and found it deeper than they'd expected. The security detail was fishing them out, while preventing anyone else from following. And another guard was forcibly restraining someone who already had one foot in the water.

Someone who looked an awful lot like Nick.

"There!" I pointed, but Casanova was ahead of me. A gesture sent two of his vampire guards to help the beleaguered human, but Nick somehow dodged them, making for the backstage areas and, presumably, the employee exits.

"Tell security to close off the exits," I told Casanova.

"Which ones?"

"All of them!" I wasn't taking a chance on Nick doubling back, something that would be all too easy in this crowd.

Casanova got busy on the phone as I tried to keep track of Nick in the squirming, flickering mass of humanity. For five long minutes I lost sight of him; then one of the pterodactyl things screeched and I looked skyward. I grabbed Casanova's arm and pointed. "Look!"

Several security men's flashlights followed my gesture. The twin beams illuminated the figure of a man, who looked like he was somehow walking on thin air. Casanova blinked. "What's that crazy bastard think he's doing?"

"What is he standing on?" I hadn't thought the mages numbered levitation in their repertoire.

"The catwalks. They're painted the same color as the ceiling so nobody notices them. We use them for making repairs." Casanova grabbed a flashlight from the nearest guard and shone it between a maze of glittering rock formations. I still couldn't see what he was talking about, but Nick was obviously standing on something.

"Why is he up there?"

"He's probably trying to make it out onto the roof, assuming he doesn't break his fool neck first." Casanova cursed. "My insurance premiums are going to skyrocket if he falls."

"Why would he?"

"Because the catwalks also serve as support for the larger stalactites, with the rocks protruding right down through the middle of them!"

Nick had stopped in front of a rock that looked too wide to reach around, and I was sure he wouldn't make it. But I should have known better. Nick might look harmless, but he was a war mage. Luckily, so was Pritkin, and he'd seen him, too. The flashlights illuminated a bright blond head scrambling to catch up, but Nick had a good lead. He thrust a dagger into the side of the fake rock, making an extra foothold for himself, and used it to hop around the obstacle.

"Can he really get to the roof?" I demanded, clutching Casanova's arm tight enough to make the beam wiggle. I knew he couldn't reach the level with the turrets, where I'd been two weeks ago, but the lower one over the entrance would be even better from his perspective. It was tantalizingly close to the ground.

"If he gets all the way across, yes. There's an access hatch onto the roof for repairing the main sign." Casanova glanced at me. "How badly do you want him down?"

"Bad. Why?"

"Because some of my guards are armed."

"You can't start shooting in a roomful of people!"

"We can pass it off as part of the show," he said, gesturing around. Most of the trapped tourists had decided that this must be unscheduled entertainment and had paused their complaints long enough to crane their necks upwards, straining to see through the gloom.

"Will you pass it off if someone dies? Bullets ricochet!"

"My boys are good shots."

"And he's a mage. None will get through his shields. Can you get someone outside, to intercept him?"

Before Casanova could answer, Nick spotted his pursuer and threw a spell, just as Pritkin was edging around the fat stalactite. It hit the mass of fake rock dead on, causing it to crack down the middle and sending a rain of plaster into the watching crowd. That was followed by a shower of sparks as Pritkin and Nick simultaneously threw spells at each other. The audience cheered, but it was the final straw for the pterodactyl things, who launched themselves into the air and went screeching toward the fight.

"Casanova!"

"I can't call them off—don't even ask."

"What do you mean? Are you in charge around here or aren't you?!"

One of the creatures targeted Pritkin, clawing and pecking at his shields. The other creature went after Nick, but he fired a spell at it that singed one of its batlike wings, sending it wheeling away over the crowd. It was soon back for more, but in the meantime he'd made it to the next stalactite.

"Not when it comes to security," Casanova said rapidly.

"The wards are designed to act independently. There's nothing I can do as long as those two keep tossing magic around!"

I bit my lip and watched the creature attacking Pritkin make a vicious jab with its beak. It penetrated halfway into his shields, then stopped as its head became stuck. It began thrashing around, forcing him to drop to his knees and clutch the beam to keep from being pulled off by its attempt to free itself. Meanwhile, Nick was getting much too close to the exit.

Pritkin managed to focus despite the beating he was taking from the giant wings, and threw a spell at Nick, collapsing the section of catwalk he was standing on. It fell into the moat with a splash and a sizzle, sending up a cloud of steam in its wake and barely missing a Charon that had been a little late docking his boat. I looked up in time to see that Nick had somehow snagged the next section. He pulled himself onto it while fending off his creature with a few more spells, heedless of the crowd watching raptly below.

Pritkin was handicapped by trying not to hit the crowd, but Nick felt no such compunction. Sooner or later, he was going to miss and send a deadly spell into the mass of tourists. I couldn't do anything for Pritkin; I wasn't a mage. But I could possibly get the lights back on and help security clear the area.

"Let's go." I tugged on Casanova. "The kids are probably in the kitchens."

He grabbed me by the arm and we muscled our way to the stairs, since the elevators weren't working. At the bottom we paused by a stained-glass window where a little weak light from outside was leaking in. It didn't help visibility much; I was mostly looking at a long black tunnel where I should have been able to see bright medieval banners overhead, a line of armor going down either side and the room-service kitchens off to the left.

I'd started toward the kitchen door anyway when, out of the darkness, there was a low, slow hiss, like scales sliding against the floor. I froze. I didn't know what it was, but that sort of sound is never good. It coiled along my nerves, making the hairs stand up on my arms.

"I've seen this movie," Casanova said tightly. "Everyone dies in the end."

"Shut up!"

"You don't understand—I know that slither!"

A black mist began sending dark fingers running across the stone of the floor. And everywhere they touched, what little light there was went out. "What is it?"

I could hear him swallow. "The darkness isn't caused by the absence of light, but by the presence of something else. Something that, believe me, you don't want to see."

Yeah, except that dying in the dark didn't sound all that appealing, either. I grabbed him before he could get away, crushing that expensive sleeve ruthlessly. "What. Is. It?"

"I told you—"

"Casanova! There is a very good chance there are *children* down here. What the hell is out there?"

He didn't answer, just shone the flashlight at the ceiling. The walls in this section were dark wood, but the ceiling was painted white, picked out along the edges in gold scrollwork. The thing was hard to see, as it was also bloodless white. It was clinging to the ceiling upside down, head cocked to one side, watching. It was like a parody of a child, small and half formed, glistening wetly across all its surfaces. It looked blind, with no glimmer of eyes under the skin stretched tight across its sockets, but its head turned toward me unerringly.

"Cassie." It spoke in Pritkin's voice. It sounded sympathetic. "If you don't run, I'll kill you quickly, and I'll leave the kids alone."

I swallowed the noise that wanted to crawl out of my throat and made a quick weapons assessment. Mine consisted wholly of a couple of misbehaving knives, since I'd lost my purse somewhere along the line. Not good. But there was a whole line of weapons in the hands of the suits of armor lining the corridor. They looked as lifeless and empty as museum pieces, but were actually part of the security system.

"Casanova," I said very carefully. "Order the guards to attack it."

"I can't." He shook his head frantically, looking more panicked than I'd ever seen him.

"What do you mean, you can't? If you let me die, Mircea will kill you."

"And if you aid her, I will," the thing on the ceiling said, as if it was part of the conversation. "It is difficult, serving two masters, isn't it? I warned you it would become awkward one day."

"Two?" I finally got it. "That's Rosier, isn't it?" Casanova nodded dumbly. "You're not supposed to be back yet," I told the demon accusingly. Hadn't Pritkin said it would take at least a couple of days for him to recover? It hadn't been that long, had it? With all the time-hopping, I wasn't sure, but I didn't think so.

The thing tilted its head the other way—why, I don't know. It didn't have any eyes so it couldn't have been to see any better. "Well, I'm not at my best," it finally said.

I looked over at the twitching Casanova, who was going to collapse at any moment. "Go," I told him. "Help Pritkin. Do not let Nick get out of here and do not let him talk to anyone. I'll deal with this."

"You'll deal with this?" Casanova stared at me with no expression, like he just couldn't find one that fit.

"Yeah." I looked up again. It was gruesome, but it was small. I decided I could take it. "I already killed you once."

"Ah, yes, so you did. But then, that would be why I brought friends," it said mildly. Casanova fled.

"Friends?"

"Servants of a colleague who owes me a favor. My boys are good for many things, but killing is not really their forte. Now, usually I would make this relatively quick," it continued. "But after the other day, I am afraid I will have to break my habit. A little matter of prestige. You know how it is."

"Sure." Out of the corner of my eye, I saw something small and glowy emerge from the stairs.

"Now hold still, because this is going to hurt like a bitch."

"Right back at you," the pixie said, and threw her tiny sword like an arrow. It hit the thing square in the not-eyes, provoking a shriek of mingled pain and rage.

I twisted my neck around and saw Françoise running down the stairs toward me, looking more than a little frazzled. Her dress was torn in three different places, one of which was oozing a widening stain, and her eyes were huge. Radella, darting around in the air in front of me, looked okay, however. Human weapons might not be able to hurt a demon, but it looked like the Fey had more luck.

I turned around to face Rosier, feeling somewhat calmer. Only to see pieces of the darkness peeling away from the floor, from the corners and from the walls, all along the corridor. I still couldn't focus on any of them, but I got the feeling that Casanova had probably been right: I didn't want to.

"Uh-oh," the pixie said unhelpfully.

"What's going on?" I asked, and Françoise broke into a rapid stream of French that I didn't have the time or the ability to translate. "Radella!"

"We've been trying to get to the children." She gestured toward the end of the hall. "That thing has half of them trapped in the kitchen."

"Are they all right?"

"For now. The staff is protecting them, but they won't hold. Not if those things attack."

"But Fey magic works on demons!"

Radella zoomed in front of my face, her own furious. "Yes, and if I had warriors to work with instead of cooks, it might even be enough! As it is—"

"What are you saying? You can't break through?"

"We stormed the back door. I managed to get past their forces, but the witch almost got herself killed. And I can't do much alone."

Billy Joe floated down through the ceiling. "We got another problem," he said quickly, not even pausing to chew me out for leaving him with this mess. "Our buddy over there sent some of his boys upstairs. They're there now, with the kids. And I have no power against demons, Cass."

He, Françoise and Radella were all looking at me, and after a stunned second I realized that they were waiting for instructions. Like I was supposed to know how to get us out of this. *And Agnes would have*, I thought grimly. *Maybe even Myra would have had a few ideas.* But I had nothing.

"I have a proposition for you, pixie," Rosier gasped. I

looked up to see that he had worked Radella's sword loose. What was left of it dropped to the ground with a clatter. It wasn't much more than a hilt—the rest appeared to have been eaten away, like with acid. "Leave now and I will waive retribution for your misguided actions."

"I may have a better offer," I said quickly.

Radella looked from the remains of her sword to me. "It better be a good one, human!"

"How would you like to have the rune? Not just to cast, but permanently? It only takes a month to recharge after each use, so you could have as many children as you want. Your friends could even . . ."

I trailed off because she had gone motionless, as if all the bones had suddenly liquefied inside her skin. She looked for a minute like she'd had the air knocked out of her, but then she licked her lips, slow and precise, and looked at me with a drowning expression in those huge lavender eyes. "What do you want?" It came out as a whisper.

"Find a way to get the kids out and it's yours."

"Are you deaf? I already told you, there is no way!"

"Can the demons follow you into Faerie?"

"What? No! Or if they did, they wouldn't last long," she said with an evil smile. "But how does that—"

"Go back into the kitchen and summon the portal. Take the kids into Faerie, then return with them once it's safe."

"And how do I do that? Even assuming I could break through the lines again, I'd need a death to power the portal. And your ghost told me—"

"You'll have it."

"What?"

"No way, Cass. Stop right there." For once Billy sounded deadly serious. Which meant he was quicker on the uptake than Radella.

"There will be a death," I told her. One way or the other. "Does it matter which of us it is, me or that thing?"

The pixie was silent for a moment. "No. The spell won't care."

Françoise had been looking back and forth between the

two of us, trying to keep up with the conversation. "What? What is this? What is 'appening?"

"In a minute. Radella, did you see a little girl in the kitchen—blond, brown eyes, about five?"

"There were several younger children. I didn't—"

"Clutching a bear? She never goes anywhere without it."

"No."

I nodded. It was the first good news I'd heard. "Billy, I need you to find a way out of the casino for the kids upstairs. One of them, a little girl, is clairvoyant. She should be able to hear you. Get the kids out into the open. Into direct sunlight." Pritkin had said that worked on most demons. I only hoped these were among that number.

"Right. I'll go play with the kiddies while you sacrifice yourself. Not happening."

"I don't have time to argue!" I said, tugging off his necklace and putting it into Françoise's hands. "Give this to the little clairvoyant. I think her name is Jeannie," I told her. She took it, but looked very confused; I wasn't sure how much of this she was able to understand.

"What do you think you're doing?" Billy demanded.

"If I don't make it, she'll look after you."

"That's not the point!" he said, more angry than I'd ever seen him.

"Billy will find you a way out," I told Françoise. "Look for three old crones—they will probably be in the lobby." Casanova had said the Graeae were drawn to trouble. I just hoped they hadn't decided to take the day off. "They'll help you get to the kids."

"A ghost, three old women and a witch who has already fought us and lost," Rosier mused. "Personally, I would reconsider, pixie."

I didn't even bother to look at Radella. I knew how she'd choose; the expression on her face had been eloquent. Besides, Françoise had me in a hug that was threatening to choke me. "No! I weel not leave you again!"

"I am Pythia!" I said, detaching her arms with a less-than-dignified struggle. "And you will do as I say."

"Yes, do as she says, witch. You're no match for us," Rosier added helpfully.

Françoise turned on him, eyes furious, and uttered a single, harsh word. It wasn't the liquid syllables of French, or any other language I knew. It was low and guttural, and the power behind it made my skin crawl. Something flew straight at Rosier, something I couldn't see too well in the low light, but he turned it back with a tiny, casual gesture. The spell slammed into the stained-glass window above my head, sending a shower of brightly colored shards raining down all around me.

I grabbed Françoise by the arms before she could try again, shaking her as hard as I could. "He's right! You can't help me. But you can help them! Now get out of here. Go!" I gave her a shove toward the stairs.

She looked from me to the demon and back again, confusion and pain on her face. I don't know what she would have decided if Rosier hadn't flicked a finger, sending several dark shapes peeling away from the main mass. They didn't bother with the stairs, but shot straight up through the ceiling. Straight toward the rest of the children.

I was going to point out that Rosier must be more worried about her power than he let on, to send reinforcements. But I didn't get the chance. Françoise turned and ran.

Billy didn't budge. "Billy!"

"I—this—you can't seriously expect me to—"

"You can bring the cavalry back here once the kids are safe."

"You'll be dead by then!"

Rosier laughed. Apparently demons could hear ghosts, too.

"And how do you expect to prevent that if you stay?" I demanded. "Go where you can do some good!"

"Don't ask me to do this."

"Billy, please," I stopped, not knowing how to convince him. If he refused to help, it decreased Françoise's chances by a hell of a lot. The longer the kids stayed in the dark, the longer Rosier's servants had to find a way to destroy them. And Misfits or not, they were only children.

"The Cassie and Billy show, remember?" he said, suddenly tentative. "Where you go, I go."

"Except that doesn't work anymore." And God, didn't I miss the days when it did. "Please, Billy. Do this one thing for me."

His shoulders sagged and his face crumpled. "It better not be the last thing, is all," he said, quietly furious. "Because if you end up dead, I'm going to make your afterlife hell!"

Radella fluttered in front of my face the second he disappeared. "If you die, how do I get the rune?" she demanded.

"Pritkin. He'll give it to you, assuming you get the kids back safely. You can do that, right?"

"Yes."

"And take the kitchen staff with you." Miranda had said they'd defend a crèche with their lives. I wasn't real keen on having her prove it.

"But . . . they're Fey. Dark Fey," Radella said, as if maybe I hadn't noticed.

"What difference does that make? Just take them with you!" I didn't know that the demons would attack them once the kids were gone. But I didn't know that they wouldn't, either. Rosier certainly seemed to have the concept of revenge down cold.

Radella was silent for a moment. Then I heard a softly spoken, lyrical sentence, almost like bells ringing. "What was that?"

"Nothing." She sounded embarrassed. "Just . . . good luck, Cassie."

I felt the rush of air as she flew past me, and Rosier smiled his ghastly smile. "A Fey blessing. So rare. And so useless, outside Faerie." The black cloud had finished assembling minutes before and hung in the air behind Rosier, awaiting his pleasure. "I told you I'd trade you the lives of the children for your sacrifice. You should have made the deal. Now you die, and so do they."

I was going to tell him that I preferred to trust my allies over his word. But I didn't get the chance. The hideous, squirming mass suddenly froze, like soldiers coming to attention. Then it dove, straight at me.

Chapter 27

I screamed, too exhausted to even pretend I wasn't terrified.
The damn knights remained inert, incapable of detecting the
creatures who were about to kill me. But a plume of fire, the
strength of maybe a couple dozen flamethrowers, shot out of
the other end of the corridor.

Maybe Casanova had installed some new security measure; I didn't know. But whatever it was, it was effective. The
cloud screamed with the sound of a hundred voices, and
writhed madly in the air, a twisting, burning black mass that
reminded me of the maggots working on Saleh's headless
body.

The glare of the flames glinting off the armor shed more
light on the scene, although I might have been happier in the
dark. Rosier dropped from the ceiling to land in the middle of
the corridor with a faint plopping sound. Then something
jumped me from behind, sinking what felt like a rack of small
knives into my back.

I shrieked and staggered back, hitting the wall and driving
the claws in that much farther. I lurched back into the room
and let my gaseous knives loose, but they took one look at the
larger fight going on a few yards away and deserted me. I
looked around frantically, but although there were about a
hundred weapons of various kinds in the knights' hands I
didn't see any that would help dislodge something that high
on my back that I couldn't even see.

Another of the things latched on to my left arm, piercing deep enough to hit bone, while another attached itself

to my right thigh. I went down to my knees, blinded by
pain and shock, only to realize that the things weren't continuing the attack. Instead, they forced me onto my back,
pinning me down, waiting. I raised my head a little to look
between my feet, and saw why.

Rosier was crawling my way, dragging himself forward
with those spindly arms, his rudimentary legs trailing behind.
His face turned unerringly toward me, despite the empty eye
sockets, and over the screeching of the burning demons I
could hear the soft sound of scales whispering over the floor.
He looked harmless, a vague, unfinished creature with a
toothless mouth and small, barely formed claws. But I so
didn't want him touching me.

He flowed bonelessly over my feet and onto my legs, long,
too flexible fingers curling around my calves, my knees, my
thighs as he pulled himself along the length of my body. And
already I could feel a faint echo of that horrible, draining sensation. He was beginning to feed.

Despite my every muscle singing with tension, I couldn't
even turn over to try to dislodge him. My arms were pinned
by the weight of his servants and my strength was steadily
flowing out, what little remained of it. Curled on the floor at
my sides, my hands lay still and useless.

He settled heavily onto my stomach, his little claws ripping at the seams of my skirt, pulling it apart to expose the unprotected flesh of my belly. That obscene mouth opened and
I could see right inside it, right into the corpse-like hue of his
gullet. He licked a clammy line across my skin. "You taste
sweet."

"Get off," I said thickly.

He couldn't have grinned. But he gave that impression
anyway as he pinned me with that blind gaze. "Oh, I intend
to."

I felt a claw bite into my side, sinking deep. And without
words, without him opening that obscene mouth again, I
knew what he planned to do. He was going to slit me like he
had the skirt, opening me up so he could feed on something
more substantial than mere power. He planned to eat me alive.

A feeling—not quite pain, more like raw nerve endings firing on automatic—crackled upward from my stomach to my mouth. I swallowed it down, refusing to scream again. But my eyes rolled up into my head as I felt that claw start to move through my flesh.

He withdrew it for a moment, to lick daintily at his red-stained skin, letting me watch as drops of my blood ran down his arm. One fell off his elbow onto my lower stomach, and he paused to lick it up, his tongue slick and cold against my skin. Then he inserted the claw again, and ripped me open a little wider.

He was deliberately going slowly, splitting flesh and skin a centimeter at a time, pausing every few seconds to lick the jagged edges of the wound, sending violent, sickened shudders through me. He wanted me to know that this was going to be a very long process. And I suddenly understood: he'd wanted the others to go after the kids so he could afford to take his time.

And he would have, except for the crazed djinn with the machete. "Saleh!" I was so happy to see him I cried.

"Hey, sweetheart." He did a double take. "You look rough." The machete swung, slicing off a rudimentary arm and knocking Rosier into the side wall, where he landed with a sickening crunch.

"It's been one of those days," I gasped, trying to strain my neck to see how much damage Rosier had done. It felt like a lot. It felt like too much.

"Tell me about it," Saleh said. "You wouldn't believe the trouble I had tracking this guy down." He made another swing but missed. "Stand still, damn you!" he ordered, slashing at the demon. But the creature moved unbelievably fast, even without those skeletal legs, and dodged enough blows to keep himself in one piece.

Saleh might have found his prey, but it looked like he lacked the power to take his revenge. Even though Rosier didn't seem nearly as interested in preserving his life as he did in ending mine. And Billy was right: there was no way the cavalry was going to get here in time.

Saleh did manage to hack the thing off my left arm in passing, although I would have preferred him to free the right, given the choice. But I wasn't about to argue. I got a grip on one of the nearby window shards, one that looked a lot like a claw itself, red and glittering, tapering from a wedge base to a needle-fine spike. Pritkin had said that Rosier had to lower his defenses to feed. It looked like I was going to get a chance to test the theory.

Rosier jumped for me, a misshapen white blur against the dark, landing with enough force to knock the wind out of me. I couldn't breathe, couldn't see, but I could feel. Before the lethargy started again, before he could render me completely helpless, I reached out for the slick surface of his skin and drove the shard as deep as I could into his side.

He screamed, but there was little blood, little bodily fluid of any kind. And the spongy flesh closed up around the wound almost immediately. So I plunged the shard in again and this time I left it, while feeling around for others. Some were too blunt to use, but here was a nice blue one with a jagged edge; there a deep green with a fissure making it into a double blade; and over there, almost at the end of my reach, was a pearly white, so cracked and splintered along the edge that it was almost serrated—and cut about as well, too.

One of the black things was trying to grab my free arm, while its master screamed and thrashed about and tried to eject multiple knives all at once. "You will pay for that," he told me, blood dripping from his mouth onto my stomach, mingling with my own.

"Maybe, but not today," I gasped, as Saleh rose up behind him. I didn't even have time to flinch before the wide blade took off Rosier's head.

Blood spurted out then, a river of it, as if something much larger than the tiny body slumped across me had been killed. I lay in a pool of it as the whirlwind started up again, its sound almost immediately overshadowed by the familiar scream of air that signaled a ley-line fissure. Or, in this case, a portal.

"You better run," Saleh told me, as the stream of fire holding off the demon cloud halted abruptly. But I couldn't run, could barely crawl, and there was no time in any case. The cloud dove for me, a screaming mass of hysterical hate, only to be hit by a hail of bullets from the stairwell as a dozen vamps flowed into the room.

"Is this a private party?" Alphonse asked, crushing the black thing hanging off my thigh under a heavy motorcycle boot. "Or can anyone join?"

Sal pried the creature off my back and stomped heavily on its center. It screeched and writhed and melted away, leaving only what looked like a scorch mark on the stones below.

"You do know how to throw a party," she said as she pulled the last creature from my right arm and slung it against the wall. She looked me over. "But you were right. Elegance isn't your thing."

I lay back against the fake stone of the floor, listening as the demons and vamps fought it out all around us. It didn't sound like the demons liked automatic gunfire any more than they did fire. I watched the last of them being pounded into nothingness by Alphonse's size twelve boots while Sal examined my various wounds. What was left of Rosier's body was nearby, a wasted scrap of bloody white flesh. I thought seriously about throwing up, but decided it was too much trouble.

Sal checked out my thigh and shoulders and pronounced them only flesh wounds. The stomach was worse, wide enough to need stitches, but I borrowed her belt and bunched enough of the skirt under it to serve as a makeshift bandage and to keep me decent, all at the same time. *Multitasking, that's how you get things done*, I thought, and burst into giggles.

"None of that," Sal said reprovingly. "Have hysterics later. The Consul's on her way and she's gonna want to know—did you get it?"

"Hell, yes, I got it. And if she's coming, maybe she can get off her ass and help with some of the dirty work for a change!"

All the blood drained from Sal's face, and her eyes fixed on a point just over my left shoulder. "And with what 'dirty work' precisely do you require aid?" a husky voice asked from behind me.

God knows what I would have said, but before I could even turn around, Jesse ran out of the dark and jumped in front of me. "I got it!" he yelled, and sent a plume of flame straight at the Consul.

She met it with the blinding wall of sand, dry as a desert, hot as hell, that I had once seen eat a couple of vampires alive. Only she wasn't throwing it outward at us, I realized after a moment, when my flesh stayed on my bones; she was using it as a shield. I got Jesse around the middle and screamed in his ear. "Cut it out! She's a friend!"

The fire abruptly vanished, and he stood there looking a little sheepish. "Uh. Sorry?"

"Not strong at all?" I asked.

He shrugged. "Well, maybe a little strong." I guess now I knew who had taken on a cluster of angry demons.

"Why weren't you with the others?" I demanded.

"I was on my way down here when two of those things attacked me. I fried 'em," he told me happily.

"Then you could have gotten into the kitchen! You could have gone with Radella and the others!"

"And leave you like this?" He sounded insulted.

The Consul dropped the sandstorm and Jesse did a double take, then just stared, trying to prove that "eyes as big as saucers" wasn't an exaggeration. I guess he hadn't gotten a good look at her before. She arched one eyebrow in a way that reminded me eerily of Mircea. "Friend?"

I smiled weakly. "Well, you know. Not an enemy."

"That remains to be seen," she said, holding out a jeweled hand.

I blinked at it for a moment until I realized what she wanted. She expected me to hand over the Codex. And I'd already admitted that I had it. I figured I had maybe a minute to fork it over before she had me strip-searched.

"Uh," I said wittily. My brain was exhausted, my body was in serious pain, and I had nothing left. I couldn't let her take it, not when Pritkin had been willing to go to such lengths to see it destroyed. I still didn't understand exactly what it did, but I knew enough to think that maybe he'd had a point. Because no way was the *geis* the only reason she wanted it. Ming-de and Parindra hadn't had a sick vampire, and they'd seemed pretty keen.

The Consul didn't say anything, but she didn't lower her arm, either. "Give me the Codex, Cassandra."

"That wasn't the deal," I reminded her. "I agreed to save Mircea. That was all."

"We will attend to our own." She pulled someone forward who had been standing behind her. Tami. "Give me the book and I will give you your friend."

"You'll give her to me anyway. As soon as Mircea is healed, she is free. You've sworn it."

Those sloe eyes narrowed. "But he isn't healed. Not yet."

It took me a second, but I got it. "And you have him." I had the counterspell, but I couldn't heal Mircea if I didn't know where he was. And that left Tami under the Consul's manicured thumb until she chose to release her. Or until she gave her back to the Circle.

"So you've decided what? That you want the Codex more than you want to save Mircea?"

"Once I have the Codex, our mages can cast the spell."

How inconveniently true. "And if I refuse to give it to you?"

The Consul's grip on Tami's arm tightened slightly. "I do not think you will refuse."

"And I think she will," a ringing voice said behind me. The corridor was suddenly flooded with a blinding golden light. "Well done, Herophile. You have fulfilled your quest!"

I didn't need to turn around to know who was standing there. The Consul's expression, one of mild surprise, was enough. For her, that was practically a goggle.

I shifted my eyes, while moving Jesse and me back a few feet, toward the shattered window. "What do I get, a gold star?"

The ten-foot golden god in the too short tunic laughed, and it echoed off the walls. "Give me the Codex and you may have anything you like. It's our world now, Herophile!"

Behind him, I could see a whole row of dark-coated figures, and the rotting fruit smell that accompanied them told me what they were. Dark mages. I guess they were there for bad little Pythias who didn't do what they were told.

"Because I already have a gold circle," I continued. "The

Codex was hidden behind one. I should have thought of you when I saw it."

"Gold is the alchemical sign for the sun, yes," he said, still approving.

"I did wonder. Because the Circle's symbol is silver."

"Like the moon. Artemis' emblem, that damn traitor," he said casually.

The Consul's beautiful face found an expression, and it wasn't one I liked. "You're working with our enemies," she hissed, and Tami gave a sudden cry as her arm was squeezed tight.

"She gave her priests the spell, didn't she?" I continued, ignoring it. The Consul hadn't gotten to be two thousand years old by being stupid. If I gave her enough, she'd figure it out for herself.

"She was always ridiculously sentimental," he agreed. "She thought we were being too hard on mankind, that your people were in danger of disappearing altogether."

"Were we?"

"Don't be ridiculous," he said carelessly. "You breed like rabbits."

"Lucky us." My tired brain was having trouble piecing things together. Since he was in a good mood, I decided to let him help. "So the ouroboros is the spell to block your kind from our world."

He laughed. He was happy, even jocular. Of course he was. I hadn't told him no, yet. "It was the symbol for Solomon's protection spell, the one that trapped me here, the one I undid when I defeated that bitch at Delphi. The Pythoness, they called her—the last of a line of powerful witches who maintained the spell he had cast. I killed one of them and made her home my chief temple and her daughters my servants: Phemonoe and Herophile. I even kept the name: 'pythia' means python, you know."

No, I hadn't. But I was learning all kinds of things lately. "With her death, the original spell lapsed, because there was no one to maintain it," I reasoned. "And the paths between worlds were opened again. Until Artemis decided to give the spell back to mankind." He nodded. "But her priests are dead. Who maintained it after the destruction of her temple?"

"The Silver Circle, of course." He looked surprised that I hadn't known that. "But they forgot. I had given the Pythias part of my power. And when my people were barred—"

"The power remained."

"And allowed me to communicate, albeit with great difficulty, with my priestesses," he acknowledged. "But the damn Circle corrupted them, turned them against me, blocked the only link I still had with this world. I couldn't get anywhere with any of them!"

"Until I came along." I was suddenly feeling really queasy.

"Yes. I thought I had a good candidate in Myra, but she fizzled out." He dismissed the former heir with a wave. "She was more interested consolidating her own position than in following my lead. I was quite pleased when you disposed of her."

"I didn't."

He shrugged. "You helped. Thus winning you many friends, young Herophile. Artemis never bothered to consider that the spell barring us from earth would close those worlds linked with yours as well. Faerie, for example, which depended on our magic and has been in decline since we left. They will be glad to see our return."

"That would explain why some of the Fey are so eager to get their hands on the Codex," I said.

He beamed approval. "They understand that the old ways were best, for your people as well as for us. Think of all we have to teach you."

"Yeah, you keep promising to tell me what's going on."

"As I have done. Give me the Codex, Herophile, and take your rightful place as the chief of my servants."

"You keep calling me that, when I've already told you." I took a deep breath and moved a little closer to the Consul. "My name is Cassandra."

Apollo's face immediately changed. "Yes," he hissed, "the name your mother gave you. Do you know why, little seer?"

"No."

"Because she had a vision. Saw that her daughter would be

the one to free me. Saw that, if you became Pythia, the spell would be unraveled and I and my kind would return. She knew your destiny, but she couldn't bring herself to kill you—her only real chance. Instead, she ran, and named you after another rebellious servant of mine, in an act of defiance. It was a decision that cost her her life." He held out a hand. "Don't make the same mistake. Give me what is mine!"

I glanced at the Consul. She didn't nod or blink or anything so obvious, but something shifted behind her eyes. I really hoped I was reading her right, because if not, I was toast.

I pulled the Codex out of my bodice, and Apollo's eyes immediately focused on it. One last gamble; one last chance. Because I didn't need it, after all; I knew the author. And he really, really owed me one. "Jesse," I said briefly, "do your thing."

"What?" His eyes had hardly left his mother the whole time. I didn't know how much he had understood, but I didn't need him to understand. I just needed him to do what he did best.

"Fry it," I said.

"You cannot circumvent fate, Herophile!" Apollo snarled. "The Circle is weakening, fracturing from within. And when it falls, the spell falls with it! Don't choose the losing side!"

"I'm not." I tossed the Codex into the air. Time seemed to slow down as it flipped once, twice—then a plume of fire thicker than my leg caught it before it even approached the top of its arc. When the flames cleared, there wasn't enough left to make ashes. "And my name is Cassandra."

"You might have done well to remember your namesake's fate, *Cassandra*," he spit, as two dark mages started toward me.

And the vampires just stood there. I desperately tried to shift out with Jesse, but I was too tired, and nothing happened. At least, nothing normal.

A bubble formed out of nothing and bobbed around just out of reach, heavy and strangely thick, distorting the room in its reflective surface. And then there was another one, smaller than the first, and for a moment the two were bouncing around like helium balloons, colliding and rising and drifting with no particular direction. Until the larger one drifted against the taller mage.

Instead of bouncing off, it clung to his outstretched arm, flowing over the leather of his coat like molasses. And despite my panic, I couldn't seem to look away. Because the sleeve under the bubble was changing.

The leather grew dark and hard and started to crack, and the mage began to scream as the sleeve dusted away like the cover on one of Pritkin's old books. It flaked and crumbled until I could see the arm underneath. Only it wasn't an arm anymore, I realized, as the mage tore away from me. He left behind the tattered remains of the sleeve and the hand clutching my wrist, which was now nothing more than a collection of bones under brown, papery skin.

I flinched and the bones collapsed, hitting the ground with a dry rattle. I looked up to see the mage staring at me, a look of horror on his face as it aged decades in a few short seconds. I gasped, realization slamming into me even before a clear, almost transparent substance peeled away from him. It reformed itself into a bubble that floated off a few feet before popping out of existence. What was left of his body collapsed like a deflated balloon.

I stared at him, remembering the dead mages in the fight with Mircea two weeks ago. I thought they'd been hit by friendly fire, by a spell gone awry. Looked like it hadn't been so friendly after all.

"I see you have had lessons from someone." Apollo was seething. "The traitor Agnes must have had more time with you than I thought. No matter—you cannot defeat them all." And the entire line of mages surged toward me.

I watched them come out of blurry, exhausted eyes. What had that been, anyway, some way of speeding up time within a small area? I didn't know, but one thing was sure: I couldn't do it again. If I hadn't been holding on to Jesse, I'd have been on the floor already.

But the mages didn't reach me this time. The ones on the front row, six in all, were met by a stinging desert storm that blew up out of nowhere and concentrated only on their bodies. They were shrouded in whirling, dancing sand for maybe twenty seconds, and when it dissipated, the only things left to fall to the floor were bones and metal weapons. The rest of the mages were met by angry vampires, half of them Senate members, and the fight was on.

I clutched Jesse and stared at the Consul. "You took your time!"

"If we are to be allies, I had to be certain that you are strong enough to be an asset," she replied serenely. "I assume you have the spell to break the *geis* memorized?"

"I know who does," I replied.

"And that would be?"

"The mage Pritkin. I . . . told it to him."

She raised an eyebrow, but didn't call me on the obvious lie. "You had best hurry, then. He was battling another mage in the lobby earlier. I do not think he was winning."

I started for the stairs but was called back by Jesse's cry. "What about Mom?"

I looked at the Consul. "If we're to be allies, I'd think you could trust me."

She looked at me for a long minute, then released her hold on Tami. "Do not disappoint me, *Pythia*."

The tone was menacing, but it was the first time she'd ever used my title. On balance, I decided it was a positive step. I picked up my skirts and ran.

Chapter 28

I woke up in an unfamiliar bed in a posh room painted a soft, muted blue. The curtains were tightly drawn, so I assumed it was daylight outside because a vampire sat beside my bed. "You ran into the wall," Sal said, looking up from buffing her nails. "It was real embarrassing."

I sat up and immediately regretted it. Everything hurt. "I did not."

"Yeah, you really did. Bam! Out like a light. Not that you weren't pretty close already."

I felt my head and, sure enough, there was a big, fat bruise. "I feel like shit."

"You look worse. On the plus side, we won the battle. And what you did with those two mages was pretty cool."

"So, you're saying what? I'm breaking even?"

"Just about." She laid something hard and cold on my chest. "A little girl dropped this off for you. Said to tell you that your necklace is haunted."

I wrapped my fist around the familiar weight and felt the brief energy sizzle that told me Billy was in residence, soaking up energy. "I know," I said tearfully. "The kids are all right, then?"

"I guess." She grimaced. "There seem to be a lot of them around."

"And Françoise and Radella and—"

"What do I look like? The six o'clock news? Ask the mage if you want to know."

"Pritkin! How is—"

"He's fine. After you took a nosedive, the Consul sent Marlowe after him. Turns out, he didn't need the help. He'd already killed the guy."

I swallowed and lay back. Nick. She meant Nick. And Pritkin had had to kill him because I'd been stupid enough to hand Nick the answer to all his dreams. Or at least, he'd probably thought so. I remembered his face when he'd told me that the Codex was the key to ultimate power. Too bad he hadn't understood—the power didn't go to us.

"I need to see him," I told Sal.

"Good." She got up and stretched, and her cat suit told me that I was a pain in the ass in big purple letters. "Because he's really starting to get on my nerves."

"He's here?"

Sal rolled her eyes. "Oh, yeah. And I don't know how you put up with him."

"He kinda grows on you."

"Uh-huh." She didn't look convinced. "Oh, and one other thing." She tapped a black box beside the bed with a long fingernail. "The Consul left this for you. And she's getting snippy."

I almost asked what it was, before I remembered: Mircea. Sal was right. I wasn't done yet. We might have won the battle, but my personal war remained to be fought.

I nodded and Sal left, or tried to. She'd barely opened the door when Pritkin barged past her. He didn't look like he'd bathed or changed, but his hair was once again an independent entity. "They said you destroyed it!"

"I'm fine," I said, checking under the covers to see that I actually had clothes on. I did, although it was a T-shirt and sweatpants, not the ruined evening dress. I sat up again. "Thanks for asking."

Pritkin waved it away. "I spoke with the doctor who attended you earlier. I knew you were well. Did you destroy it?"

"Yes."

"All of it?"

I sighed. "No, I left out the important bits. Yes, all of it! There wasn't so much as a cinder left after Jesse torched it. Relax. It's over."

"It will never be over. Another Pythia could go back, find it again—"

I burst out laughing, but quit because it hurt. "Yeah, because it was so damn easy."

"It could happen," he said stubbornly.

"And all I can say is, good luck to her. She'll need it." I looked at him more seriously. "I'd like to ask a question—and get an honest answer. For a change."

"You want to know why I kept you in the dark."

"That would be the one. Why not just tell me what was going on?"

He looked at me in disbelief. "What reason did I have to assume that you would choose the Circle's side over Apollo's? He could give you everything: security, the knowledge you need about your power, wealth . . . whereas the Circle—"

"Has been trying its best to kill me." I took a moment to absorb that. I didn't like to admit it, but I kind of saw his point. With so much at stake, even if he'd wanted to tell me, he couldn't have risked it. I wasn't sure I'd have risked it.

"They were afraid of what an untrained Pythia might do," he continued, "given what Myra already had done. She was brought up knowing how dangerous that creature was, being warned against him, yet she still fell in line with his plans. As many others have done."

"It does explain a lot," I agreed. "I've been wondering why Tony, who pretty much defines 'paranoid,' would join a risky rebellion. But I guess he didn't think it would be much of a risk with a god on his side."

"Which was what the Circle assumed you would think. And once their attempts to remove you failed, they were even more certain that you would side against them as soon as you realized that you had such an ally." He looked at me curiously. "In truth, I am not entirely sure why you did not."

I shot him a look. "I've read the old legends, part of them anyway. Enough to guess what things would be like with his group here again."

"Is that all?" Pritkin looked skeptical. "Because you would have been his favorite, a pampered pet, a—"

"Slave," I finished flatly. "I would have been his slave." I'd already had one master, and that had been more than enough. "I said that no one would ever control me again like Tony did. I meant it."

Pritkin's jaw tightened. "That kind of power would be very attractive to many. Regardless of the price they had to pay for it."

"I'm sorry about Nick," I said, knowing what he had to be thinking.

He didn't flinch, but his eyes were shadowed. "It was necessary," he said tersely. "He'd seen the spell; he could have told others."

"He *would* have told others. He spent half an hour telling me all about what's wrong with the Circle, how it's a big bureaucratic mess that just needs a firm hand to straighten out. His hand, I assume."

"He was feeling you out, trying to discover if you would support his position."

"Yeah. He didn't seem too happy when I laughed at him."

Pritkin regarded me for a long moment. "You are an unusual person . . . Lady Cassandra."

I blinked, sure for a moment that I'd heard wrong. "What did you call me?"

"You have chosen a new reign title, I believe."

"Yeah. But since when do you use it?"

"Since you've earned it."

"Along with a lot of enemies." My list of problems now included a pissed-off demon lord, the Dark Fey king—who was still waiting impatiently for the Codex—and an angry god. To keep the last of those from turning mankind back into his playthings, I had to protect the Silver Circle from annihilation, even though they were facing a war with his allies and still wanted me dead themselves. And, oh, yeah, I was in the last place I'd wanted to be, allied with the Senate in the thick of the fight.

"A hazard of office." Pritkin shrugged. "There were many who did not care for Lady Phemonoe."

Yeah, like the ones who had killed her. "She once told me that I'd be the very best of us, or the very worst," I admitted.

"I didn't know what that meant for a long time. I think I do now. Either my reign will see the office finally under the control of the Pythia, instead of the Circle or some ancient being, or it will see me, and everyone else, become slaves to that creature."

"That won't happen."

I almost pointed out that it very nearly *had* happened, but I didn't feel like getting into a fight. "Which kind of brings us to something else I wanted to ask you," I said instead. "The Circle maintains the ouroboros spell now, right?"

"Yes. Power is drawn from the Circle collectively, as no one mage could possibly sustain such a thing alone."

That was what I'd been afraid of. "Okay, so exactly how many 'blows' can the Circle take before they can't keep up the spell anymore?"

"I don't know."

"Guess."

"I can't. All I can tell you is that when the spell was laid, the Circle was considerably smaller than it is now. Presumably we have some leeway before a crisis point is reached. But as the war heats up, there will be casualties. And every loss will become progressively more dangerous."

"Because it could be the one that lets the old gods return."

"They're not gods! They're strong, but primarily because their magic is so different from ours that it is difficult to counter. And there is certainly nothing godlike about their attitudes! Petty, arrogant, cruel beings without a shred of—"

"My point," I said, raising my voice, "is that if the Circle weakens too far, the spell snaps. So how do we keep that from happening? It's a little hard to save the lives of a bunch of people who are still trying to kill me!"

Pritkin ran a hand through his hair agitatedly. "I am well aware of that! We will have to manage some kind of rapprochement. If we continue to fight amongst ourselves, our enemies will have a definite advantage."

"And even if we win the war, if the Circle is weakened enough that the spell shatters—"

"Then we've lost anyway." Pritkin finished for me grimly.

"How would you suggest we begin? The Circle hates me."

"I don't know. With its current leadership . . . I don't know," he repeated. "It will not be easy. But above all else, you have to show them that you are not a puppet of the vampires. That isn't the case, I know," he said, forestalling my protest, "but that is how it appears. You live here, surrounded by them; you wear Mircea's mark; you are bound to him by the *geis*—"

"About that last one—I assume you are going to help me break it?"

There was a commotion outside, then the door burst open and Casanova ran in. He batted away Sal's hands. "Let go of me, woman!"

"What else have I been doing?" Pritkin asked incredulously. "What more would you have me do?"

Casanova looked at me. "Feeling better, are we?" It didn't sound concerned. It sounded pissed.

"Not particularly, no." I looked at Pritkin. "Cast the spell, of course."

"Good," Casanova snapped. "Because, thanks to you, neither am I!"

"What spell?" Pritkin asked, looking confused.

"The one to remove the *geis*!" I said impatiently. "I had to destroy the Codex, remember? I don't have it. But you do, so it doesn't matter."

"Are you paying attention?" Casanova demanded.

"Maybe when you stop insulting me, I'll think about it," I told him.

"Because Françoise won't do anything about those women, and the pixie won't do anything for anyone until she gets some rune she keeps raving about, and somebody has to!"

"What women?"

"We already tried that," Pritkin said, starting to look worried.

"The Graeae!" Casanova said, throwing up his hands. "They helped Françoise get the kids out—I personally think they just like killing demons, or anything else that stands still long enough—and now she won't even attempt to trap them.

And they're currently all three downstairs! Together! If you hurry—"

"Tried what?" I asked Pritkin.

"The counterspell. I cast it for you in France. Twice."

I stared at him, Casanova momentarily forgotten. "That was a fake. It didn't work."

"It didn't work," he agreed, "but it wasn't a fake."

"What are you saying?"

"I'm saying that *all three of them* are *together* right now!" Casanova raged. "Who knows when we'll get this opportunity again? Get up, get down there and talk some sense into that witch!"

I stared at Pritkin. "It has to work. We've already tried everything else!"

He just shook his head. "I cast it on you not only in France, but here in our time as well. It failed. That is why I have been searching for an alternative."

"Well?" Casanova demanded.

"And?" I asked Pritkin frantically.

"Nothing. I do not understand why the *geis* is behaving this way. It shouldn't still be there—it can't still be there. And yet it is."

"Are you even listening to me?" Casanova all but screamed.

"Yes!" I snapped. "The Graeae are downstairs, all together, and you want me to trap them before—" I stopped, staring at him.

"Yes. So let's go." He hauled me to my feet.

"My thoughts exactly," I said, grabbing Mircea's trap and Pritkin's hand.

"Where are we going?" Pritkin asked, looking confused.

"To end this!"

We reappeared in Mircea's suite at MAGIC. It was two weeks in the past, just after I'd dropped him off following our time in Paris. I'd concentrated on him instead of a place when I shifted, because I hadn't known for certain where he'd be. But I hadn't counted on catching him coming out of the shower.

"*Dulceață.* Always a pleasure," he said, unselfconsciously toweling himself off. He glanced at Pritkin. "Why?" he asked, obviously pained.

"He isn't here to fight. We need to cast a spell on you," I said quickly, and then realized that maybe I should have worked up to it a little more.

Under a lot of wet brown strands, an eyebrow raised in a sardonic arch. "You do not know magic, Cassie. Therefore I assume that what you meant to say is that *he* needs to cast a spell."

Wow. Less than thirty seconds and we were already to the "Cassie" stage. I wondered how long it would be before we hit Cassandra. Before I could say anything, four large vampires rushed into the room, guns drawn and scowls on their faces. They stopped inside the bathroom door, and stood there, looking blankly from Mircea to Pritkin to me.

Pritkin drew a gun, but Mircea didn't react, except to drape a towel around his waist. "Yes?" he asked politely.

"The wards," one of the vamps said, a little awkwardly. He was taller and more muscle-bound than the others, but judging by the energy he gave off, also probably the youngest. "They indicated an intruder." He scowled, his eyes on the gun in Pritkin's hand.

"They were mistaken," Mircea said smoothly, as if we weren't standing right there.

Three of the vamps immediately bowed. "Our apologies, my lord," one of them murmured formally. "I will have the wards checked before any erroneous reports are filed. Although it could take an hour or so."

"See that it does."

"Yes, sir."

Three of the vamps started for the door, but the bigger one hesitated. "My lord, with respect, the Consul said most definitely that any unregistered persons should be detained and reported as possible—"

"But there are no such persons here," Mircea repeated.

"My lord!" He swept an arm to indicate the scowling war mage and beat-up clairvoyant currently crowding Mircea's bathroom. "They are standing right—"

"Do you see anyone?" Mircea asked one of the other guards.

"No sir!" he replied, looking right at me.

"They must have done something to fool your minds! There are two mages *right*—"

Mircea made a small gesture, and the vamp suddenly stopped talking. His eyes darted around my general direction, but could no longer seem to find me. "But—but there *were* people here!" Mircea raised an eyebrow and the vamp's companions dragged him from the room.

I stared worriedly at the door. "Will they be back?"

"No. But they will have to report this, in an hour or so. I take it your business will need no more time than that? Because if so, I shall need to make further arrangements."

"I'm not really sure how long it will take," I said awkwardly. That depended on just how difficult he was about to be, among other things. "It's, uh, kind of complicated."

Suddenly he laughed and gestured for me to precede him into the bedroom. "With you, when is it ever anything else?"

Like the bathroom, the outer areas of the suite were lit with candles, not electricity. I remembered why: this was the night the war began, at least officially—the night MAGIC was attacked. The big wards were up, and they don't mesh well with electricity. The dim light didn't prevent me from seeing Mircea's inquiring look, however.

I sighed and glanced at Pritkin, who had settled himself into the chair Tami would later occupy. He shrugged unhelpfully. We'd been over this already—there was no way Mircea was going to agree without some kind of explanation. But I didn't have to like it.

"It's a long story," I said quickly, before I lost my nerve, "but basically, there was this accident with the timeline and the *geis* was doubled. And then it started growing or morphing or something, and I was going out of my mind until I inherited the Pythia's power. It gave me a reprieve, but you ended up half crazy and, well, in here." I held out the black box. "The Consul ordered you locked up so you wouldn't, um, run amok or . . . or anything."

"Basically?" Mircea repeated dryly.

"Well, yeah, pretty much. But I think I know why the counterspell won't work. Because the *geis* was put on two of you—one in the current timeline and one in the past. But since only one of you is present whenever we try the spell, it doesn't think you're all there. So to speak."

"I beg your pardon?"

"It's like with the Graeae," I explained impatiently. "I accidentally set them loose and we've been trying to trap them again ever since. Only it seems they register as one person for the sake of any magic used on them, and if one of the three is missing, the spell won't work. So they just make sure that they are never all together anymore. Then we can cast the spell all day and nothing will happen."

"Let me see if I understand," Mircea said, pulling on another of Ming-de's little gifts. "You believe the *geis* views the two of me on whom it was placed as one person."

"Because you are."

"But because I hold the spell in two separate timelines, if it encounters only one of me, it does not view me as a complete person, and therefore will not work?"

"Exactly. We all have to be present at the same time—two of you and one of me, because I had it placed on me only once, but you had it done twice. Once by the mage who initiated the spell and once by me. At least, I hope I have that figured right, because if we need another me this is really going to get complicated."

"Going to?" Pritkin muttered.

"That would be why, in Paris, your dress did not harm me," Mircea mused, ignoring him. "Because, linked as we were by the *geis*, it saw us as one. And, of course, it would not harm its owner."

"Well, two-thirds of its owner, but yeah, that's it."

"I am in there, am I?" Mircea slipped onyx cuff links into the French cuffs on his shirt and eyed the box skeptically.

"We can let you out," I said dubiously, "but I don't think . . . that is, I'm not sure how you'll react. Marlowe said he couldn't control you, there at the end . . ."

"Can we get on with this?" Pritkin demanded.

Mircea ignored him, but he gave me back a frown. "Has it

not occurred to you that the mage has deceived you? Perhaps
in an attempt to get into this very room, past security, to as-
sassinate me in a vulnerable position?"

"Do mages frequently do that?" I asked, surprised.

"A few dark ones have tried. After what happened to the
last one, I have had a reprieve for some years." He glanced at
Pritkin. "But perhaps the lesson has been forgotten, and must
be taught again."

Pritkin leapt up from his chair. "If I intended to harm you,
I have had more than enough time already!"

Mircea bared his teeth in an expression that in no way re-
sembled a smile. "Feel free to try."

I refrained from throwing something, but it was close. I'd
known bringing Pritkin was a bad idea, but after the debacle
with Nick, I hadn't dared to trust anyone else. Not to mention
that he was the only one who knew the spell. It had to be him,
and it had to be now.

"I honestly don't know how much time you have left," I
told Mircea quietly. "If we do nothing, the spell will run its
course and you'll die anyway."

"The spell was never designed to kill," he reproved. "Not
in its wildest permutation."

"No, but it can drive someone mad! And then the Consul
will do the killing for you."

Mircea paused, his eyes sliding to the snare. He regarded
it for a long moment, expressionless. I guess it would be a little weird—okay, a *lot* weird—to imagine yourself trapped in
there when you were standing right beside it. "The Senate has
many experts at its disposal. Surely they can find a solution."

"That's already been tried. Do you think the Consul would
have had you imprisoned if there was an alternative?"

"But would not this counterspell remove the *geis* from me,
as well as from your Mircea? And thereby change time?"

"No, we don't think so." It was one of the things I'd asked
Pritkin before we left. "It's being cast on the three of us, to
break the bond we all share. But it can't affect anyone who
isn't here, which includes the Cassie of this time. So your link
with her should remain and, uh, run its course."

"Leading to a great deal of trouble."

"I'm afraid so. But there's no other choice—not if you want the present timeline to continue."

"The one in which you are Pythia." I didn't answer, but I didn't have to. Mircea had known since the battle at Dante's that his crazy gamble had paid off. He looked thoughtful for a moment, but then his eyes slid to Pritkin and his expression hardened. "I know you think you are acting for the best, *dulceață*, but you do not know what our enemies are—"

Pritkin swore and, before I could stop him, said something in a low, guttural language that sounded awfully familiar. Before I could blink, before he even finished speaking, Mircea had pressed him against the wall, a fist in his shirt and murder in his eyes. "Mircea, no!" I grabbed his free arm. "I thought we were going to wait until he agreed!" I said to Pritkin, furious.

"He would never have agreed," he spat, "and it doesn't matter anyway."

"Doesn't matter? He could kill you!" Laying a spell on a master vamp without his permission was considered so stupid that there wasn't even a law against it. There didn't need to be—most who tried it didn't survive long enough for a trial.

"You don't understand. The *geis*—"

"What about it?"

Pritkin looked like he'd swallowed a handful of nails. "Can't you feel it? The spell didn't work. The *geis* is still there!"

Chapter 29

"That's impossible! You said—"

"I said your theory seemed plausible *if* the spell had not morphed into something new. Obviously it has. In the hundred years since you placed it on the vampire, it has had more than enough time to grow, to change, to become a new spell. As a result, the counterspell won't work. Because the spell it was designed to offset no longer exists!"

"You're telling me we went through all that for nothing? That we'll just die anyway?"

"Not for nothing. In the process, we discovered—" He glanced at Mircea and hesitated. "Much of interest."

And, yeah, that might be true, but knowing what was really behind the war wouldn't do me much good if I wasn't alive to fight it. "That doesn't help!"

"I told you all along that I doubted the counterspell would work," he informed me, in the tone that made me want to hit him even more than usual.

I was about to return a scathing reply, when I suddenly remembered. He had said that, but he'd said something else, too. Something that I'd forgotten because I'd been so fixated on the Codex. There was another way to break the *geis*, one that Mircea had woven into the spell himself.

My heart sped up as I ran the idea over in my head. All three components of the *geis* were here now: me and both Mirceas. The counterspell didn't work, but that was because the original spell had changed form, not because my theory had been wrong. But Pritkin had said that the fail-safe was part of the *geis* and that it would morph along with it. So the fail-safe should still work.

"There might be an alternative," I said slowly.

"What alternative?" Pritkin asked, his eyes narrowing.

I looked at Mircea. "Do you remember, when you had the original spell cast, you had the mage put an escape clause in place?"

"A fail-safe, yes. I was advised to do so by everyone with whom I spoke. It is a common precaution, as the *duthracht geis* is famous for—" Mircea stopped, understanding flooding his eyes, followed immediately by a stubborn glint. "*Dulceață*—" he began warningly.

"It didn't work with Tomas," I said, speaking quickly before he made up his mind, "because he was a substitute, but for only one of you. And just like with the counterspell, the fail-safe will only work if there's two of you, uh, participating."

"Cassie—"

"You must be out of your mind!" Pritkin broke in. "If it doesn't succeed, you could end up tied to him forever!"

"That won't happen."

"You don't know that! There is no telling what might occur with a spell left to its own devices for that long!" Mircea hadn't spoken, hadn't moved. But suddenly the security detail was back. "I suppose it only requires the right master for you to knuckle under—is that it?" Pritkin sneered as they started manhandling him from the room. "You were brought up as a vampire's little lapdog—I should have thought you'd prefer not to die one as well!"

The door slammed shut, although I could still hear him ranting as they towed him down the hall. "You can't hurt him. He has to go back with me."

"Their orders are merely to detain him," Mircea said, looking at me narrowly. "I thought you would prefer to discuss this in private."

"Yes. Well." I stopped and mentally pushed Pritkin's accusations away. I had to concentrate if I was going to get this right. If I was going to make Mircea *understand*. "If I've figured this right, and I'm pretty sure I have because we've tried everything else, then . . . it has to be all of us. The fail-safe was never an independent entity but was tied to the *geis* itself. So when the *geis* changed, the fail-safe changed right along with it. That's why built-in safety measures are used with the *duthracht*. Because even if it does go haywire, they will still counter it."

"What has to be all of us?"

I narrowed my eyes. Mircea knew more about magic than I did, so he'd followed me perfectly well. He just wanted to make me spell it out.

I paused, sure for a moment that I couldn't get the words out, that they wouldn't fit past my throat. "The sex thing," I finally blurted. "It needs to be all of us." Which was absolutely the most shocking thing anybody had ever said for the long moment before Mircea smiled.

"You know, *dulceață*, when I told you that I enjoy a wide range of experiences, I did not expect you to take me quite so literally." He started buttoning up the shirt. I assumed by the fact that he was getting dressed that I must not have been as clear as I'd thought.

"What are you doing?" I demanded. "I told you, we have to have sex now!"

"No, I believe the term you used for a threesome was 'the thing.'" Mircea slipped on his suit coat. "I admit to having few reservations about personal relations, but one rule I do try to maintain." He leaned over and kissed me lightly on the cheek. "If the lady cannot bear to say it," he whispered, "we don't do it."

I pushed him back and glared at him, hands on hips, immediately pissed. "No one made you put the *geis* on me," I told him, pushing a finger into that completely clothed chest. The soft, luxurious weave of Chinese silk met my hand, something that didn't make me any happier. "No one told you to make sex the condition to break it! I've been through hell to figure a way out of this and now that I have, you're playing hard to get?!"

His amusement, if anything, seemed to ratchet up a notch. I guess Sal was right; I didn't do tough well. "You have to admit, *dulceață*, that your story does seem somewhat—"

"Strip," I ordered.

Mircea stood there by the bedpost, giving me a disbelieving lift of an eyebrow, and a look that clearly said, *You did not just order me to take off my clothes.* Except that I had, and I gave him a stubborn chin raise in response. Very slowly, he pulled off the suit coat and dropped it onto the bed. His look challenged me to take something off as well.

I tossed my head at him. Fine. After the week I'd had, that didn't seem like much of a challenge at all. I reached back and unhooked the catch at the top of my dress. Sal had refused to let me visit "the master" in my old sweats, and had cobbled together an outfit for me. One tug had the zipper down on the dress and the satin material sliding over my curves until it was no more than an icy blue puddle around my feet. I still wore a strapless satin bra and panties set, purchased to match the dress, and a corset in white.

The corset was a slightly jarring note, but I hadn't had a choice. Whoever they'd had patch me up had done a good job, and a glamour had covered most of the assorted cuts, bruises and claw marks. But the fact remained that I don't heal like a vamp. Underneath the white lace and ribbons was an ugly two-inch-long scar that we'd been afraid would bleed through onto my pretty new dress.

"You are serious." Mircea was frowning.

I spread my hands. "Yes! Yes, I'm serious! What is the problem?"

He looked torn between exasperation and disbelief. "You know the problem! You explained it to me. And I do not intend to spend the rest of my life bound to the wishes of a—" He cut off abruptly.

"Of a what?" I could feel my temper rising.

He recovered quickly. "Of a young lady who, however charming, knows so little about our world."

"I'm learning fast," I said, "and don't patronize me." I was pretty sure the word he'd almost uttered had been "child." And whatever else was true of me, that wasn't. Not since the age of fourteen, when I'd run away and learned exactly the kind of world I lived in.

"I wouldn't dream of it," he said, unruffled. "Any more than I would dream of completing such a dangerous spell."

"We're not completing it! Two of us would have done that. The fail-safe wouldn't have worked if we'd had sex in London, because all three of us weren't there. But here and now, it will override the *geis*."

"You can't be certain of that."

"Maybe not. But I *can* be certain that you'll die if the *geis* isn't broken. Would you prefer that to living under someone else's mastery?"

"I cannot say," he replied mildly. "Having never had a master. But I did die once. It wasn't so bad, as I recall."

"Mircea!"

"Cassie, would you listen to yourself? You expect me to believe that another version of me is in there"—he nodded toward the snare—"and that the three of us must copulate to break the *geis* despite the fact that one of us is very likely mad?"

"You think I'm lying to you?"

"I have already told you what I think—that you have been deceived. You must—"

"I must do nothing. I'm Pythia. Which, in case you missed it, means I outrank you."

Mircea caught my hands, which had been trying to get the loops of silk that served as buttonholes on his shirt loose from their toggles. I really wanted that damn thing off. "You are Pythia because we put you there!"

I gave a sudden push. He ended up sprawled on the bed. "*Dulceață*—"

"I have the title because I've damned well earned it! Stop assuming that I'm the same little girl you left at Tony's. I'm not."

"Mages are treacherous," he said stubbornly. "And this one has obviously—"

I stopped him by placing one foot on the edge of the bed, between his legs, while balancing on the other. I didn't spend much time in four-inch heels, and I wasn't sure how long I could stay there. "Take it off," I ordered, nudging his inner thigh with the toe of my shoe. I'd let Sal talk me into ice blue satin heels with a strap around the ankle and toes studded with crystals in a starburst pattern. I'd thought they were a little much, but for some reason she had absolutely insisted on the shoes.

"A pretty thing. Much nicer than your last footwear selection."

I gently nudged him again, and this time I didn't hit his thigh. He breathed in sharply. Mircea could pretend all he wanted, but at least one part of him wasn't completely indifferent to my proposition. "Cassandra," he began, his tone menacing, and I repressed a grin. Okay, now I knew I was getting to him.

The shoe continued its work, moving in circles that grew bigger with every sweep, grazing but never quite touching. Just a little encouragement, though it didn't feel like he needed much. "It's too risky," he told me stubbornly. "If you're wrong—"

"I'm not wrong."

"You don't know that. You admitted it yourself."

I nudged him again and his eyes dropped to half-mast. "I thought family were the only ones you can trust. So trust me, Mircea."

He didn't answer, but his hand slowly closed around my ankle, then smoothed down over my heel to the spike. He stroked his thumb over the silken material, up and down, until I started to feel a little giddy. I was beginning to understand why Sal had pushed for the shoes.

"I told you to take it off," I repeated. I could already feel my leg going wobbly. Mircea managed to get the tiny jeweled buckle around my ankle undone one-handed and slipped the pump off. Then his lips were on my foot. It wasn't something I'd expected, and it caught me off guard. The feel of his tongue dragging along my arch, was enough to make my toes curl and my breath catch.

"What about the other you?" I asked, while my brain could still form sentences.

"What about him?" he murmured, before his teeth closed over my heel. He bit down, a fairly gentle nip, but my knee buckled from the sensation. I twitched and wobbled, and had to grab the bedpost to keep my balance.

"Damn it," I muttered.

Mircea grinned at me, unrepentant, and pulled me down beside him. "The mage did not curse me earlier. Did you not wonder why?"

I stared at that beautiful face. It was close enough to kiss, but I didn't think that was what he had in mind. "He wants to help."

"Perhaps. But is it not equally possible that he has arranged a trap?"

"He has no reason to—"

"Tensions have been rising between us and the Black Circle for some time. They would love nothing better than to strike a preemptive blow. And what could be better than killing a Senate member and the new Pythia, all at once? He made sure to exit the room—"

"Because you *threw him out*!"

"—something he could have easily anticipated. Once we are alone, he would expect curiosity to compel us to open the box, and thereby spring the trap on ourselves. And once the general alarm was raised, he could slip away in the confusion."

And I thought I was paranoid. "That isn't—" I stopped, because he wasn't listening to me anymore. He looked up and, for a moment, his gaze was somewhere else.

"The mage is becoming difficult for the guards to handle. I will return shortly." He rolled off the bed and headed for the door.

"Mircea!"

He looked at me over his shoulder, his face grave. "I will not kill him, Cassie. But I will have the truth of this—of a lot of things. One way or the other."

I watched him go, wondering how things could possibly have gone so bad so fast. I'd known Mircea distrusted mages—all vamps did—but I'd foolishly assumed that a life-or-death situation would override that. And it probably would have, if he'd believed that was what we were facing. But he'd convinced himself that Pritkin was a dark mage

assassin and I was the naive dupe he'd conned into helping
him. If I needed his cooperation, I was toast.

For the fail-safe to kick in, I needed only two components:
proximity and sex. I was pretty sure I still had the former.
Mircea wouldn't want anyone interfering in family business,
so he would almost certainly question Pritkin here, in his
suite. From what I'd seen, it was pretty extensive, but not any
more so than a large house. Which meant that they were
somewhere nearby.

It was the second part of the equation that was problem-
atic. I'd assumed we all three had to be present and actively
involved to break the *geis*, but what if we didn't? I bit my
lip, furiously trying to think of anything anyone had said
that might give me a clue one way or the other, but there was
nothing. It was a fifty-fifty gamble: proximity to two
Mirceas and sex with one of them would either break the
geis or it wouldn't. And if I gambled and lost, I'd end up
completing the very bond I'd been trying to avoid.

Billy had advised me once to never gamble unless I could
afford to lose. But not gambling now would lose me Mircea.
And I didn't think I could live with that.

I stared at the innocent-looking box on the nightstand and
wondered if I was nuts. Marlowe hadn't been able to handle
him; the Consul had been spooked enough to order him
locked up; and here I was about to release him. What if he
didn't recognize me? What if I registered as no more than
food? I'd seen how fast he could feed; I'd be dead before anyone could stop him.

I can shift out if he's too much for me, I told myself, hoping it was true. Yeah, and then what? If this didn't work, I was
out of ideas. If this didn't work—I pushed the thought aside
as seriously counterproductive and gingerly picked up the
box.

Pritkin had told me something else once, too: the *geis* responded to the caster's deepest desires. And right here, right
now, there was nothing Mircea and I wanted more than to
have it gone for good. I just hoped that was going to be
enough. I placed the box in the middle of the bed and took a
deep breath.

And then I let him out.

The figure of a man suddenly appeared on the bed beside me. At first, he looked to be asleep, until I looked closer and saw his face, tucked halfway into the pillow and lined with pain. His hand clutched blindly at my shoulder, clenching as tightly as his jaw, for a long minute. And then, slowly, hesitantly, almost as if it had forgotten how, it relaxed.

This man was no threat, I realized, blinking back tears as I watched him. He barely even seemed to know where he was. I tried to comb my fingers through his hair, but they got stuck over and over in all the snarls. "Mircea?" I whispered.

His lashes were clumped together and he didn't open them at the sound of my voice. He didn't reply, either, but a tentative hand wandered up to my neck. His fingers slid along the curve of my flesh to rest above the pulse of the jugular, right over the two small scars he had made.

I gazed down at him with wet eyes and a heartbeat so rapid it felt like I was about to faint. Then he blindly grasped for me, making these choked, desperate noises in his throat that I finally realized were words. He was asking me if I was sure.

"I've never been surer about anything," I said fervently, and the decision was suddenly just that easy. I couldn't let him die. All the logical arguments in the world couldn't change that one simple fact. This whole time, I'd been battling for his life as much as for mine, and I wasn't about to lose him now.

It was easy to turn him over with my hand on his chest. It was much less easy to ignore the heat of his skin, the tight nipples riding over lean muscle or the strong thump of his heartbeat. I liked the way his breath caught, the way his stomach hollowed under his rib cage, when my thighs touched his sides.

I wasn't kidding myself—I knew how any relationship between us was going to go. Sooner or later, Mircea would do something unforgivable, probably at the Consul's behest. Or I would make a demand and he wouldn't give in. Even without the Circle's suspicion hanging over us, there was a clock ticking every second we were together, the distant sound of the oncoming train. I knew, I'd always known, that I couldn't keep this. But for this one night I could have him. And I wanted it all.

I pressed my palm against him and was rewarded with a hitching, indrawn breath. He was thick and uncut, tender at the tip, irresistible. He was darker here, rose and gold, and it was fascinating the way the flush shifted under the pressure of my slowly moving fingers. I brushed my lips over the side of him, drinking deeply of his familiar scent. It made it easy to accustom myself to the strangeness of what I was doing.

I licked, a long, slow trail from base to head, letting my tongue wander and slide and *yes*—a gasp spurred me on. I did it again, and felt him shudder above me. I didn't hesitate after that. I *needed* this—the thick glide of his flesh past my lips, salty and bitter and sweet on my tongue.

Mircea pulled me up before I was ready, pressing against me with tongue and teeth and lips shredded with bite marks from weeks of torture. He cried out when we kissed, but I don't think it was from pain. I wrapped myself in his body, all hard muscle, sweat-drenched skin and matted hair, and felt him begin to press inside. Blunt, thick strength took me, sinking deep. I shifted up, wanting even more, and in a moment he was so far inside that there was no distance left to close.

He paused for a moment, and we stared at each other, his eyes finally wide open, wild and pained and so golden that I couldn't see any brown. When he finally began to move, there were no short thrusts from his hips, but an unrelenting deluge, the muscles of his arms and the power of his thighs reducing his body to one long undulation. And suddenly, every cell was screaming to get closer, to clench tight around him on the downstroke, to live inside his taste and smell, to feel every thrust in my teeth. For a moment it was almost like being possessed, only it seemed to go both ways. Some part of me whispered through him with every thrust into my body, which in turn increased my own pleasure until I was sure I would die of it.

"Perfect," he said brokenly, before swooping in for another kiss. Mouth open, tongue plunging deep, he stroked in perfect time with his movements inside me.

And it was suddenly too hard, too fast, too *much*. My

breathing fractured into harsh, quick gasps when I could get air at all, my body spasming as my mind fought to sort it all out. But it was complete sensory overload, pinned inescapably, pummeled by every forceful movement, the pain blending with the pleasure. He pounded into me while growling into my mouth, biting my lips, saying the same thing with breath and hands and body. *Mine!* It whispered through me with every deep thrust. *Mine.* Every frantic push of his hips, every deep, wet kiss echoed with it. *Mine, mine.*

And then, whether my body could take it or not, it was suddenly even more. Between one breath and the next, we became an extension of each other's passion, somehow living inside the other's skin, more like one body than two. His pleasure felt like mine, was mine. He swallowed and I felt it in my throat; he lost himself in the motions of having me, and I felt his every stroke.

His fingertips brushed against my scars with a deep inner thrill (*mine, mine*) before dropping to my hip, caressing the soft roundness. His hand was on my breast, and I felt my own shivery skin through his fingertips, knew the sensation of my shudder passing down another's spine, felt his joy as my muscles quivered and then relaxed, surrendering completely.

Orgasm was both heavenly and painful when it finally came. It felt like we were breaking through a barrier into each other, falling deep, tearing loose from the last pretense of control. He thrust again and again—no finesse, no thought, just this, the rapture of it. Every touch burned through me, the pleasure that burst inside my veins echoed in his. I couldn't tell which one of us gave that raw, stuttering cry: *mine, mine, mine.*

Without warning, everything came apart. The sensations, color, heat, pleasure, were so intense that I worried I might never be able to put myself together again, intense enough to hurt and make me beg him to stop, beg him to never stop. It went on and on, waves of pleasure in time with Mircea's unsteady thrusts, sparked harder by the wild shocks that emanated from me, from him, from me, until I couldn't remember how to breathe anymore.

He suddenly stopped, and there was an odd look in his

eyes, surprised and a little broken, but mostly amazed. I was pretty amazed too, because I'd never made anyone look like that before. He stayed there for a long moment, staring at me, before rolling off, and pulling me back against him, his chest rising and falling harshly as he breathed.

He pulled the coverlet up over both of us, making a warm little cocoon. It was easy to just lie there, watching the nearest candle gutter and wax dribble over the holder. It finally went out, leaving the room dim, shadowed and strangely cozy. And it was while we lay there in a tangle of limbs, unsure quite where one body left off and the other began, that I felt it. Nothing dramatic, nothing extreme, just a small snap. But suddenly I was entirely back in my own skin again.

The *geis* was gone.

"*Dulceață*," Mircea breathed. And I felt it as soon as he said my name, an even, soft hum of something that recognized me and welcomed me like it had known me forever. But it wasn't a spell. It was the way I'd always felt around him, something that had been masked by the *geis* and its constant low, stirring heat, its hunger and desperation and pain. This was less overpowering but deeper, more persistent and sweet. I kissed him softly and it tasted amazing, warm and familiar and home.

"Are you all right?" I asked, but I knew the answer even before he smiled slightly and opened his eyes. Long lashes dipped over too-sharp cheekbones, but I felt the same weightless flutter in my stomach as always when that gaze met mine.

"I will be."

Compared to all my problems, saving the life of one man didn't seem like much of an accomplishment. So why was I suddenly grinning like an idiot? Maybe because, somewhere along the line, I'd learned to take my triumphs where I could get them. Tomorrow there would be trouble and danger and pain, and I didn't know if I would be smart enough or strong enough or capable enough to handle it all, especially now that I understood what I was up against. But I knew one thing: today, finally, something had gone right.

"The other you will be back soon," I said, hoping he was

lucid enough to understand. "And I told him too much. He can't be allowed to keep those memories."

"No one can erase a master's mind," he said hoarsely. "I doubt even the Consul herself could do it."

"But if you remember, you'll try to change things—"

"I did. I searched for the mage, but never found him, and returned here only to discover that you were also gone. Afterwards, I reconsidered what you had said, and tried to break the *geis* before it had a chance to be doubled, but the war intervened. And once it did, there was nothing to be done but see this through to the end."

I stared at him in disbelief. "But you didn't know what happened after you left! You didn't know we succeeded!"

"I knew you. I could not believe that you would leave without completing your mission. I had to trust that you'd found a way to break it."

"That's why you sent me away," I said, my head reeling. "Why you wouldn't let Rafe bring me to you."

"I did not want to change this future," he agreed. "When he went to you despite my orders, and you came to me . . . For a brief moment, I thought it was over. But then I remembered: I had not yet been imprisoned, your clothes were wrong, and there was no snare on the bedside table. It was too soon. It was the closest I came to breaking."

I couldn't imagine it, that solitary, agonizing wait, not even knowing for certain that we would win in the end, that it wouldn't all be for nothing. I didn't think I could have done it. I didn't understand how he had.

Before I could say anything, the door burst open and Pritkin dashed in. His coat was missing, half his potions were gone and he had a gun in each hand. I wondered how he'd managed to get the door open. He kicked it shut behind him. "Did it work?" he demanded.

"Yes, no thanks to you!"

"No thanks to me? How else would you have gotten that creature out of here?"

"You planned this?"

"Of course!"

"But . . . what if I'd listened to you? What if I hadn't dared—"

Pritkin gave me his old impatient look. "You *never* listen to me!"

"That's not the point!"

Someone put a fist through five inches of Romanian oak and almost grabbed him before he could skip away. "We can discuss this later," he said quickly. "Get us the hell out of here!"

I gazed at Mircea, still feeling stunned. "You might have hoped I'd be successful," I said, "but you couldn't have *known*—"

"I knew you," he repeated. "Therefore I knew how it ends."

I grabbed both their hands, just as the door exploded off its hinges. "How it begins!" I said, and shifted.

This October, *USA Today* bestselling author
Karen Chance
introduces a new kind of heroine: the tough and
sexy daughter of a vampire.
Read on for an exciting excerpt from

Midnight's Daughter

Available October 2008 from Onyx

My least favorite dead guy had his feet up on my desk. I hate that. His boots were probably cleaner than my blotter, but still. It showed a lack of respect.

I pushed the offending size-tens onto the floor and scowled. "Whatever it is, the answer's no."

"Okay, Dory. Your call." Kyle was looking amiable—never a good sign. "I should've known you wouldn't care what happened to Claire. After all, there's not likely to be any money in it"—he paused to glance around my rat hole of an office—"and you don't appear to be in a position to do anything gratis."

I had been on the way to my feet to haul his undead ass out the door, but at his words I slowly sat back down. Kyle was a real lowlife, even for a vamp, but once in a while he heard something useful—which explained why I hadn't yet given in to temptation and staked him. And where Claire, my roommate and best friend, was concerned, I'd take anything I could get. She'd been missing for almost a month, and I'd already gone through every lead I had. Twice. Before loser boy showed up, I'd been about to start through the file a third time in case I'd somehow missed something, even though I knew I hadn't. And every hour that passed made it less likely I'd be pleased with what I found at the end of the search.

"Talk," I said, hoping he'd make me beat it out of him. I had a lot of pent-up frustration that needed to go somewhere. But, of course, he decided to find some manners. Or what passes for them in our circle.

"Word is, she's alive. I thought she'd have been juiced and packed up for sale by now, but talk on the street is that she wasn't kidnapped at all."

By "juiced" he meant a disgusting black-arts process in which a projective null, a witch or wizard capable of blocking out magical energy for a certain radius around them, is made into a weapon known as a null bomb. Their energy is siphoned away to make a device capable of bringing all magic in an area to a standstill. How far and how long the effect extends depends on the strength of the null being sacrificed—the younger and the more powerful, the more energy they have to give. And Claire was both very young and very powerful.

Making her even more attractive was the fact that the harvesters, as the mages who specialized in the very illegal practice were known, could currently command a premium for their wares. The Vampire Senate, the self-styled guardian of all North American vampires, was currently at war with the dark mages of the Black Circle, and the price for magical weapons had gone through the roof. The idea that someone had taken Claire to make into a tool for their stupid war was the main reason I was running myself ragged trying to find her.

"The rumor is that she ran off with one of Michael's crew," Kyle was saying. He leaned in to smile in my face, showing enough fang that I knew how much he was enjoying this. He'd tried to chat me up when we'd first met, and he hadn't taken my screams of laughter well. He'd been waiting for something to throw in my face, and this was his big chance. "Seems she got knocked up."

I smiled back. "That little lie is going to cost you," I promised, slipping a hand into my desk drawer. Claire, the witch with "girl power" practically stamped on her forehead, running off with a lowlife connected with Michael's stable? Didn't think so.

Kyle held up grubby hands with telltale brown stains on them. Leftovers from whoever had been lunch, I guessed. I would have advised him that his love life might improve if he paid someone to scrape the dried blood out from under his

nails once in a while, if I hadn't thought he'd eat the mani-
curist.

"No lies, Dory. Not between you and me." He sat back and
crossed his legs, looking far too much at ease for my taste.
"And you haven't heard the best part yet. Rumor has it that the
father's not exactly human, if you know what I mean." His
grin turned feral. "Passing me up because you were afraid to
bring another half-breed into the world was a waste of time,
wasn't it? Looks like you're about to be auntie to a bouncing
baby dhampir."

I didn't have to glance in the mirror behind his head to
know that my expression hadn't changed despite the shock.
After five hundred years of practice, anyone can perfect a decent poker face. Even someone as naturally . . . expressive . . .
as I am.

"Actually, I shot you down because homicidal psychos
with dog breath don't turn me on," I said pleasantly, pulling
my hand out of the drawer and throwing an unstoppered vial
in his face. The holy water stuff is a myth, but there are other
concoctions that don't sit too well with the smarmy undead,
and that was one of them. The dragon's blood wouldn't kill
him, but he wouldn't look too good for a few days, either. Of
course, since it was Kyle, it was a good bet no one would notice the difference.

I tossed his screaming body out the window after he gave
up the rest of the few facts he knew, like the name of a bar
where I might locate a few of Michael's thugs. He bounced
off the sidewalk three stories below and slammed into a
parked car, denting the metal with his forehead before crawling off down the street. Too bad it wasn't daylight.

If Claire had been harvested, she was almost surely dead
by now. But there was a slim chance that Kyle the perpetually
smarmy had actually heard something useful. And any lead,
however slim, was better than what I had.

I paused only long enough to grimace at my reflection,
which looked almost as bad as I felt. I needed makeup to conceal the dark circles that were almost as black as my eye
color, and washing my greasy brown hair for the first time in
a week wouldn't hurt either. No chance of doing the femme

fatale thing tonight, but that was okay by me. I get cranky without a full eight hours a night of beauty sleep, and since I'd had maybe that much total in the past week, I was feeling surly. I picked up a length of lead pipe and added it to the collection under my coat. There were plenty of other ways to get information.

An hour later, I was sitting on a pile of corpses, frowning. The bar where I'd found two of Michael's stable feasting on a half-dead teenager was now a wreck of shattered tables and broken glass. I shifted to avoid the pool of multicolored blood seeping from the bodies under me, and stared into the darkness outside. Kyle, it seemed, had not been lying about everything. As one of the boys had helpfully explained after I introduced his head to the bar top a few dozen times, Michael did have Claire. And if he hadn't lied about that, there was the teeniest chance he hadn't lied at all. But I'd still have to see it to believe it.

I tossed a handkerchief at the dazed boy leaning on the body of one of his recent attackers. He looked at it blankly. "For your neck," I explained. Vampires didn't have to bite to feed—in fact, it was against the rules since it left hard-to-explain corpses behind if they got carried away. But no one had been paying much attention to the law lately. Usually that was the way I liked it, but it did leave me with a dilemma now.

Normally the mages would be willing to help a witch in a jam, especially a powerful null like Claire. If nothing else, she was a useful tool they didn't want to lose to the magical black market. The Silver Circle, the so-called white-magic users, would have doubtless sent some of their thugs after Michael in more normal times, but I doubted they could spare any at the moment. There was a war on, and they were allied with the Senate against an array of forces that were scary enough to make anyone blanch. Not to mention that they hated my guts. If I wanted Claire back, I was going to have to manage it myself.

"What . . ." The boy stopped, swallowed, and tried again. "What were those . . . things?"

I got up, moved around the bar and reached for the top

shelf. What the hell, I was going to torch the place anyway. "You want a drink?"

He tried to get to his feet, but was too weak and collapsed again. "No," he said dully. "Just tell me."

I threw back a double of Tanqueray and slid the rest of the bottle into one of the deep pockets in my black denim coat. I ignored his question and walked back around the bar. My sense of smell can usually tell a human from anything else from across a room, but the state of the bar was interfering. Dust and smoke hung in the air, and rivers of blood and bile, and whatever fluid several of the odder demon races used as fuel, ran underfoot. I was pretty sure I knew what I was dealing with, but wanted to be certain.

I kicked the head of a Varos demon out of the way and crouched in front of the boy, sniffing cautiously. A gout of blood—green, so not his—had splattered in the direct center of his chest. It stank to high heaven and explained my confusion. I took the unused handkerchief from him and wiped it off. Even after all he'd been through, he didn't look afraid. Being five foot two and dimpled has long been one of my chief assets.

"You were here for a while, right?" I asked. It was a stupid question—he had six sets of bite marks on his skinny, nude body, and none of them looked to be the same size. Vamps have to know each other pretty well to do group feedings, since it's considered an intimate act, so he'd probably been lying around as the free bar snack for a few hours at least. But I wanted to start slow to give him a chance to gather whatever was left of his wits, since there was a chance he'd heard something useful. The two vamps I'd found had told me that there had been a third, who left a half hour or so before I arrived, and that he was one of Michael's lower-level masters. That didn't mean he knew any more than they did, but he could hardly know less.

"I don't get it," the boy told me shakily. "You killed them. You killed all of them. Why couldn't I do that?"

"Because you aren't dhampir." The voice that answered for me was pitched low, from near the shattered door, but it carried. I knew that voice in a thousand moods and tones, from the whip-crack of anger to the caress of pride, although the latter had never been directed at me. I tensed but didn't bother to look up. Wonderful. Just what I needed to make my day complete.

The boy was staring at the newcomer with relief. *Sure*, I thought sourly. *I do the work, but you save the worshipful looks for the handsome devil with the charming smile. Just don't forget that he could rip your throat out with a single gnash of those pearly white teeth. For all the charisma and expensive tailoring, he's a predator.*

One even more dangerous than I am.

I busied myself pouring some of the expensive alcohol in my pocket over the clean portion of the handkerchief and pressed it ruthlessly to the worst of the boy's wounds. He screamed, but neither of us paid any attention. We were used to it.

"He'll need medical attention," the voice said as the dark-haired vamp who owned it crossed the room carefully to avoid messing up his two-thousand-dollar suit and Ferragamo loafers. He smelled of good brandy, nicotine and fresh pine. I've never really gotten that last one, but it's always there. Maybe it's some terribly costly cologne, mixed at an Italian perfumer's shop for his exclusive use, or possibly it's just my imagination. A memory of home, maybe.

"I'm sure the Senate can arrange something, considering that they went out of their way only last month to proclaim that this sort of thing doesn't happen anymore." I sloshed a bit more Tanqueray onto the bite marks at the boy's neck and chest, before moving on to the ugly tear in his thigh. He fainted a few seconds later, which left us with—on my part at least—an uncomfortable silence. I broke it first, more interested in getting this over with than winning some kind of power play. "What do you want?"

"To talk to you," he said calmly. "I need your help."

I did look up at that. In five hundred years, I had never heard those words pass his lips. Hadn't ever thought to, either. "Come again?"

"I will be happy to repeat myself, Dorina, but I believe you heard me the first time. We need to talk, and the young man needs attention. We can obtain both at—"

"I'm not going there."

"At my apartment, I was about to say. I am well aware of your sentiments towards the Senate."

I refrained from glaring, but doubted that my vaunted poker face was good enough to fool him. It never had been before. Besides, he could hear my heart rate speed up with the extra adrenaline of anger, and probably detect the telltale flush my pale skin couldn't hide. I told myself I didn't care. It had been twelve years since I saw him last, and that had ended with my threatening to kill him—for something like the thousandth time—and storming out. He always got to me. Always. Even when he wasn't trying. I didn't think this was likely to be any different.

He reached out to take the unconscious boy in his arms, assuming with that unchanging conceit of his that I'd agree to whatever plan he made. I didn't object, since taking the kid to a local hospital would entail explaining who or what had done this to him, something that would challenge even my ability to stretch the truth. And running to the Senate's local branch was definitely out, considering what had happened the last time I'd dropped by. Insurance had probably covered the damage, of course, and the place had needed remodeling, but I doubted they saw it that way. I could take the kid back to my house, but although I could deal with his physical injuries, I couldn't erase all this from his memory. But the overgroomed bastard at my side could manage it with little more than a thought.

"I didn't know you had a place in New York," I said, and that worried me. There was no reason for him to be here, much less with what was probably an outrageously expensive Central Park–view apartment. Vamps tend to be territorial by nature and usually stick close to home. Of course, the Senate outlawed the old boundaries some time ago to cut down on feuds, so technically he could go wherever he wanted, but as far as I knew he had no business or personal interests in New York. Except maybe me.

"It's a recent acquisition."

I narrowed my eyes and followed him out the door. That could mean a lot of things, from his getting a lark to spend some of the millions he'd accumulated through the centuries to his dueling another master and acquiring their possessions. I really hoped it was one of those and not some plot to keep up with me. I was well aware that I was dealing with a Senate member, one of the most powerful and dangerous vamps on the planet. I'd been underestimated too many times myself to ever do it to anyone else, no matter how human he looked. Especially not this one.

"Well, I hope it has a shower," I said, pouring the rest of the booze over a nearby pile of highly flammable vamp bodies and tossing on a match. "I need a bath."

The apartment was posh, Fifth Avenue, and did indeed have a park view. I was relieved to see that it was also furnished in the designer bland beiges and creams meant to be acceptable to virtually any taste—other than mine. That meant he hadn't been here long enough to impose his personal style, so maybe he hadn't been spying on me. I didn't waste breath sighing in relief, but focused on the only other occupant of the room. I hadn't been dragged off to the Senate's local base of operations, but unless I was mistaken, at least one of its members was sitting on a pale camel-colored sofa, waiting for us.

The strange vamp flowed to his feet when we came in, his eyes sweeping over the boy before coming to rest on me. I braced for the usual reaction, but didn't get it. That told me either he'd been warned ahead of time or he was even better than I was at the whole poker-face thing. Not surprising—since they don't have to breathe or have a heartbeat unless they choose, most vamps don't have a lot of tells. Especially not the old ones, and I was guessing from the sense of power this one wore like a cloak that he was a lot older than his thirtysomething face appeared.

I examined him with interest, since I'd never seen him before. That was unusual, if he was as old as I thought. The newbies come and go, most of them dead before they manage to outlive a normal human—so much for immortality—but I try to keep up with the major players in the vamp world. There aren't that many first-level masters out there, but this one was not in my extensive mental filing cabinet. I quickly added a new file.

He was dressed in an understated outfit my host might have worn if he'd decided it was casual day, an ensemble designed to enhance what nature had bestowed with a liberal hand. The off-white sweater was tight enough to show off a nice upper body, and the tan suede pants hugged muscular thighs. A spill of rich auburn hair was trying to escape from a gold clip at his nape. It looked like the kind of hair women on shampoo commercials have—luxurious, overabundant and shiny. It should have looked effeminate on a man, as should the long-lashed blue-gray eyes, but the broad shoulders and strong, arrogant jaw were all male. I frowned at him. Vamps had plenty of advantages already; they didn't need good looks, too. I catalogued his scent—a combination of whisky, fine leather and, oddly, butterscotch—for future reference, and returned my attention to his companion.

"There is a shower in the bath down the hall, or you may use the one in my room if you like," I was told. "It's through the bedroom at the end of the corridor."

My host placed the boy on the sofa, heedless of the expensive upholstery, and whoever the auburn-haired vamp was, he moved without a word to help. He didn't even bother to keep an eye on me as he did so, which I found vaguely insulting. I'd killed his kind for half a millennium and I didn't even rate a blink? He must figure the odds were in his favor. Considering that I was in a room with two first-level masters, he was probably right.

I went down a hall that smelled faintly of some generic air freshener. They probably advertised it as "lilac-scented," but it reminded me more of vats of chemicals than wide open fields and flowers. There is a downside to supersharp senses, as there is with so much else about me.

Of course, there is an upside, too. I cocked an ear, but there was nothing much to hear. A girl was on the phone next door, complaining to a girlfriend about some guy, and someone down a floor was either talking to their cat or having a psychotic episode, but both voices were clearer than the soft noises coming from the living room. The vamps were presumably cleaning the wounds better than I'd been able to do at the bar, and bandaging the boy up. I knew nobody was planning a snack—it would be like offering people used to Beluga caviar and Dom Perignon a sack of stale Fritos and a flat Coke. Sloppy seconds weren't likely to appeal.

I let myself into the big master bedroom and looked around. Opulent, understated, rich. What a surprise. In here the decorator had gone out on a limb and chosen a gray color palette, everything from charcoal on the bedding to ash on the walls. I frowned with distaste and craved my paints so badly, my palms itched. A good half hour of work on the bare stretch over the bed would make all the difference. I've never gotten a security deposit back yet, but, then, in my line of work, that was pretty much a given anyway. And I've never lived with flat, gray walls.

The bathroom was all blinding-white subway tiles in what I guess was supposed to be industrial chic. I took white—of course—towels out of the closet and got my filthy self into the chrome and glass shower. At least it was big.

I leaned my head against the soon-steamy wall and tried not to imagine Claire with a tiny version of myself in her arms. Dhampirs, children of human women and male vampires, were never a good thing. Luckily, we are really rare, since dead sperm don't swim too well. However, there had been a few cases in which a newly made vamp just out of the grave had been able to sire a child. The kids were usually born barking mad and lived very short, very violent lives.

Of course, not all dhampirs were the same. Just like with human children, you never knew how the genes were going to combine. I'd known a few rare ones who took after their mothers and managed to live—mostly—normal lives. But for heightened senses and strength, you might never have known what they were. But those were even rarer than the rare breed itself, and I somehow doubted Claire would get so lucky.

I knew her. Whatever the story behind her child's conception, she would love it, nurture it and defend it fiercely, at least until it grew up enough to throw her off a building in a fit of rage it wouldn't even remember. I really, really hoped Kyle had been lying. Otherwise I would be faced with killing my best friend's kid, along with any affection she'd ever had for me, or with waiting for her violent death.

It would be useless to try to talk to Claire. She'd never understand how much danger she was in, nor be willing to take the necessary steps to ensure her safety. It was that damn respect for life she was always lecturing me about, the same one that made her a strict vegetarian and forced me to have to sneak out to eat barbecue. _After all,_ I could hear her argue, _I've known you for years and you've never wanted to kill me._ She'd only be hurt and confused if I explained just how wrong she was. Whatever control I may have acquired through long centuries of practice, I'm still a monster. And like the one who sired me, I'll always love death and destruction a little bit more than I do anything, or anyone, else.

I don't know much about my mother, except that she was a young serving girl dumb enough to believe that the local lord's handsome son wasn't just having a good time with her. They'd been together for several months before he was cursed with vampirism, a state he failed to recognize immediately. Unlike the usual way of making a vamp, the curse took a while to complete the transformation. There was no big death scene and no dramatic clawing his way out of his own grave. Instead, he'd shrugged off the gypsy's mutterings as the ravings of a madwoman and gone about his usual love-'em-and-leave-'em lifestyle for a fateful few days. Fortunately I was the only one to whom he'd passed his newly acquired vampiric genes in the meantime.

Long story short, nine months later, after he'd gone off to get his undead head together, a bouncing baby me entered the world, only to find that the world wasn't happy to see me. The humans where I grew up were pretty savvy about all things vampire and figured out what I was the first time they saw my baby fangs. Mother was told to drown me in the river and save everyone a lot of trouble. I don't know to this day whether I'm happy or not that she gave me away to a passing gypsy band instead. She died in a plague some years later, so I never knew her. And my father—well, let's just say we have issues.

I don't guess that is too surprising, considering that dhampirs and vampires are mortal enemies. Some legends say that God lets dhampirs exist to keep a check on the number of vamps out there. A more scientific explanation is that the predator instinct in vamps is necessary to allow them to feed, but it plays hell with a body that has an adrenal system to overload. But I think at least part of the anger we carry is a natural reaction to being forced into a world where we have zero chance of ever belonging. Vampires hate and fear us, and usually try to kill us on sight. For a while humans think we're one of them, until one of the rages takes us and our true nature becomes all too obvious. Then we're on the run again, trying to avoid angry mobs of both species while attempting to carve a niche out of their world for ourselves.

Most of my kind burn out early, either by overtaxing their systems or—far more often—dying in a fight. I only know of one other dhampir as old as I am, a batty Indian fakir who lives in the desert of Rajasthan, as far away from human habitation as he can get. It took me more than two months to find him the only time I'd bothered, and he didn't have much useful advice to impart. He manages to keep a lid on things by meditating the centuries away, controlling his true nature by simply denying it any contact with possible prey. That really isn't my style. I prefer the traditional method of letting my second nature out occasionally to hunt, providing that it only kills the undead. Or demons, or the occasional were, or pretty much anything that isn't human. It's messy, but it works, and it even led to my current job.

I soaped up my greasy hair and wondered whether that was why I'd been tracked down. It seemed unlikely. If the Senate wanted someone dead, they sure as hell didn't need to hire me to do it. They had plenty of their own muscle and an intelligence department second to none. One cut-rate assassin they could do without.

There was also the little matter that I had a habit of refusing assignments unless I knew the circumstances involved—all of them. I had promised myself to limit my sprees to those who, as the saying goes, deserved killing. I figured that since it was my hand on the ax—or the stake or the rifle or whatever—it was up to me to be certain I didn't take out someone who had merely irritated a local loan shark. But that nosiness, as the Senate would view it, would have put me off their list of hired talent even if the accident of my birth hadn't already made me persona non grata in a big way. So my skills at the hunt were probably not what was needed here.

I couldn't for the life of me figure out what else it could be, though. Occasionally I earned a few bucks checking the supernatural underground for people with problems that the human authorities couldn't manage or even understand. But again, there was nothing I could offer that the Senate couldn't do itself and probably far better. All things considered, I was stumped. Not that it mattered anyway. As soon as I got a few answers out of Buffet Boy, I'd be off hunting Michael. Whatever the Senate wanted, it could damn well come up with some other way to get it. And as for my host, he could drop dead. Again.